PASSIONATE DESIRE

Nicole unlocked the door and opened it slightly, then turned to Mark. "Thanks again. I hope we can do this again soon," she said.

"Definitely."

She smiled shyly and said, "Good night."

Mark took her hand and moved closer to her. He tilted his head to kiss her. Nicole instantly moved to close the slight distance between them as she tilted her head up to meet his. He had waited all night to put his arms around her and hold her. He couldn't wait any longer. He enfolded her in his arms and she did the same. They kissed with an urgency that told of the longing they had for one another and the yearning they had to be together again. It was a kiss filled with passion, desire and love. As they kissed, they seemed to be trying to hold one another tighter and tighter, as if to meld their bodies together.

BOOK YOUR PLACE ON OUR WEBSITE AND MAKE THE ARABESQUE ROMANCE CONNECTION!

We've created a customized website just for our very special Arabesque readers, where you can get the inside scoop on everything that's going on with Arabesque romance novels.

When you come online, you'll have the exciting opportunity to:

- View covers of upcoming books

- Learn about our future publishing schedule (listed by publication month and author)

- Find out when your favorite authors will be visiting a city near you

- Search for and order backlist books

- Check out author bios and background information

- Send e-mail to your favorite authors

- Join us in weekly chats with authors, readers and other guests

- Get writing guidelines

- AND MUCH MORE!

Visit our website at
http://www.arabesquebooks.com

A TEST OF TIME

Cheryl Faye

ARABESQUE

BET
BOOKS

BET Publications, LLC
www.msbet.com
www.arabesquebooks.com

ARABESQUE BOOKS are published by

BET Publications, LLC
c/o BET BOOKS
One BET Plaza
1900 W Place NE
Washington, D.C. 20018-1211

First Printing: November, 1999
10 9 8 7 6 5 4 3 2 1

Printed in the United States of America

*This book is dedicated to Bernard E. Lawley, Sr.
I know our love will stand the test of time.*

I give thanks to God for all his blessings. I believe that if you do the right thing, or at least make an effort to do the right thing, good things will happen to you. With all the blessings that have been bestowed upon me, I feel that I must have been doing something right. Thank you, Lord, for watching over me.

Thank you to my family and friends (you know who you are) for your constant love and support. You are invaluable to me.

PROLOGUE

September 11

It was two thirty in the afternoon when Nicole "Nicky" Peterson entered the penthouse for the first time since leaving two weeks prior. She prayed as she put her key in the door that Mark was still at the office. It was not that she didn't want to see him; that was, of course, the reason for her being there, but she still had to gather her courage before seeing him face to face.

As she walked into the living room, she was immediately taken back to the first time she had come into this beautiful apartment. She had been as nervous then as she was now.

She was glad their housekeeper, Angie, was not in. She needed to be alone for a while.

As always, the place was immaculate. The huge, white, semi-circular leather sofa looked as though it had never been sat upon, although she and Mark had shared many hours of love-making upon its plush cushions. She glanced over at the white baby grand piano and had a flashback to their wedding day. They had been married right here.

She put her pocketbook down and walked back to the nursery. Everything was exactly as she had left it. She laid Tiandra on the changing table and proceeded to change her diaper. When she was finished, she laid her in the crib. Within minutes, Tiandra was fast asleep.

As Nicole stood by the crib watching their daughter sleep, she was at once reminded of the day Tiandra was born. Mark had been so happy at witnessing the birth of their daughter that he had been at a loss for words. He had cried and smothered her with kisses as he thanked her over and over. Her labor had been very difficult and Mark apologized for not being able to bear the pains for her.

Nicole walked back to the living room and went to the bar to fix a drink. The past two weeks had been the longest of her life. Many times she had considered coming back, but she let her older sister, Desiree, convince her that he would probably do it again.

Nicole never considered the times prior to her discovery, when she and Mark had been very happy together, happier than Nicole had imagined she could ever be. She never reflected on all that Mark had done for her or unselfishly given her.

He had given her jewelry, furs and practically unlimited access to cash, most of which sat in her bank account accruing interest. Since marrying Mark, Nicole began to experience the joy of traveling. He unleashed a desire in her to see the world when he took her to Paris for their honeymoon. Since then, they had visited Egypt, Rome, and on more than a few occasions, the Caribbean. Due to his hectic schedule and the fact that he was a workaholic, he didn't always travel with her, but he still encouraged her to do so. He told her he wanted her to see the world.

Aside from material possessions, Mark also showered her with love and affection. He devoted his free time, what little he had, to his "beautiful wife," as he always referred to her. Mark told her that before meeting her, he had never even considered marriage. He told her time and again how much he loved being married to her.

His doting on her and his adoration made Nicole feel as though she was living in a dream. To be loved by someone the way Mark loved her was a dream come true, a dream that for some people never becomes a reality.

Not once in making the decision to leave him did Nicole reflect on these points. She never considered how selfish she was being to Mark when he, in turn, had always been selfless when it came to her happiness. Instead of considering how he would feel about her leaving and taking Tiandra, who everyone knew was the love of his life, she chose to ignore that. Now she was here to tell him their marriage was over. Although she would never admit it, it was no longer simply a matter of being betrayed. It was now a matter of pride. She had come this far, there was no way she could back down now.

Chapter One

At one o'clock in the afternoon, on June Fifteenth, Lucien stepped up to the lectern microphone. "Ladies and gentlemen, please, may I have your attention." The buzzing of voices quickly died. "Thank you. My name is Lucien Rogers, as some of you know, and I'd like to thank you all for coming out to celebrate the beginning of what we all hope to be a long and prosperous relationship between the city of Ocho Rios on this beautiful island of Jamaica, which is my home, and Mr. Mark Peterson, who is my friend and the president and CEO of Peterson & Company, a real estate investment firm based in New York City." Lucien looked at Mark and smiled. "The occasion is, of course, to mark the grand opening of a new luxury resort, built here by Mr. Peterson, Paradise Cove."

Everyone applauded.

"I am very excited to be here to welcome you all because I feel somewhat responsible for this union," Lucien continued. "Mark and I met about eight years ago . . .''

* * *

Nicole Peterson reached over and took her husband's hand as she listened to their friend's kind words. She glanced down at their sleeping daughter resting against her bosom, then looked at Mark and smiled proudly. He looked into her eyes and smiled.

She vividly recalled the first time she had laid eyes on him. He was the most handsome man she had ever seen. His aura of strength and confidence were distinct and one could not help but admire him. In her eyes, he was even more handsome now. His neatly trimmed salt-and-pepper mustache complemented his sublime facial features and his beautiful brown eyes.

Her memory transported her back to the day they met two and a half years ago. It had been a very exciting time in her life. It was the beginning of a new year and she had just moved away from her parents and into her own apartment for the first time. She had just started a new job at Peterson & Company as the administrative assistant to Mark's vice president.

He had looked so sexy that morning that when he walked out of the reception area of his firm, she sat there imagining what he would look like in the nude. It was minutes later, however, that he shattered her wonderful image of him. He'd stormed back to the reception desk, yelling because key members of his staff were missing in action and she was sitting in the reception area waiting for one of them.

She remembered, with a smile now, that his first words to her were an impatient, "Who are you?" To her horror, after she told him who she was, he recruited her to be his secretary for the day. Initially, she had been positive that she would not remain at Peterson & Company long because of his disgusting attitude. By the end of the day, however, her feelings for him had once again returned to those first ones. He had taken her aside and apologized for his rude behavior, explaining that his less-than-pleasant demeanor was due to stress about a very important meeting he was having later in the day. When he apologized, he also told her that she had been the only one who had not let him down that day. Although she had been sure he would never be more to her than a mere daydream, that was when the seeds of her love for him took root.

It was at Peterson & Company's annual Fourth of July picnic later that year that she got her first inkling he was interested in her. While they were in the swimming pool that afternoon, his charm, and the fact that he was irresistible to her in his bikini swimming trunks, directly influenced her decision to get into the pool at the deep end, although she could not swim. She even allowed him to give her a piggyback ride. When she realized that they were becoming too familiar with one another, Nicole got out of the pool and returned to the picnic area, leaving him in the pool. She had been very apprehensive about seeing him at work after that, but he was very pleasant and made no reference to their shenanigans.

A month later, while she and her best friend, Yvonne Rogers, were in Ocho Rios, Jamaica, on vacation, she realized that what she was feeling for Mark was more than a crush. To her sheer delight, she found that he felt the same for her. By pure coincidence, they met one night at a restaurant on the island. Mark was there with Lucien to survey the land they were now sitting on. They all had dinner together and afterwards, Mark and Lucien took them to a night club. Yvonne and Lucien hit it off right away, and, although Nicole knew this was her chance to be with Mark the way she had always dreamed, she was reluctant to do so because of their professional relationship. Once again, however, he was able to convince her that was safe with him.

When he kissed her for the first time in the middle of a crowded dance floor, she knew there was no turning back. He confessed his love for her and she did the same, although she told him their affair would have to remain in Jamaica. Regardless of the strength of her feelings for him and her belief in his feelings for her, in her heart she didn't believe they could ever be more than the secret lovers they had been.

By October of that same year, they both realized that they could no longer deny the intensity of the feelings between them. Nicole quit her job at Peterson & Company just before Thanksgiving and Mark proposed to her on December first, her thirtieth birthday. They were married on New Year's Eve.

Now, a year and a half later, they were more in love with each other than they had ever been. She was the mother of his child and they now owned a beautiful island resort. Her life was perfect.

". . . so without further ado," Nicole heard Lucien say, "it is my great pleasure to introduce my friend, Mark Peterson."

The audience applauded thunderously.

Before Mark rose from his seat, he leaned over and kissed Nicole.

"I love you," she whispered and smiled proudly.

Mark stepped up to the lectern, and he and Lucien embraced.

Nicole was so proud as she watched him, tears sprang to her eyes. He was so handsome in the custom-tailored, beige linen suit he was wearing with an off-white cotton shirt and cream-colored silk tie with blue and red accents.

Ashlei Brown also admired Mark as he stepped up to the lectern. She was proud of him, too. Usually when she was in the presence of both Mark and Nicole, Ashlei felt pangs of jealousy, but not today. Today she felt a bond with him because of the part she had played in making his dream a reality.

Ashlei was the founder, President, and Chief Architect of the architectural firm, Brown Industries, Inc. She was the only black woman in New York City that could claim such a title, and she was very proud of that fact. She counted herself lucky to have been able to win the bid to build Paradise Cove.

Ashlei was a tall, slender, and strikingly beautiful amaretto-complexioned woman who, from their first meeting a little more than a year ago, had been determined to win the affections of Mark Peterson, in addition to the bid for building rights. To her great surprise and disappointment, when she was positive that she had him exactly where she wanted him, alone in a hotel room with his wife a thousand miles away, he quickly berated her for trying to seduce him.

Although she had been forced to cool her emotions after that, Ashlei had not given up on the idea that Mark Peterson would one day be hers.

"Thank you," Mark said to his audience when the applause died. "Thank you, very much. Lucien, you're too modest." Everyone laughed. "I'm very happy to be here today and I'm grateful to you all for being here with me to celebrate the embodiment of my dream.

"In acknowledging his part in this venture, Lucien neglected to tell you that when I informed him of my interest in building here, he was responsible for putting me on to this location, aside from assisting me in obtaining the proper licenses, et cetera, I needed to get started."

He turned to Lucien and said, "Thank you, friend, for all of your unselfish support."

Lucien smiled and nodded in acknowledgment.

"I'd also like to thank the Governor General of Ocho Rios for allowing me to build here. Thank you, sir, for your time and patience and generosity."

He continued, "Of course, in building any structure, one must, if not knowledgeable in the sciences of building, enlist the services of one who is. Although I financed this project, it could never have been completed without the skill of a gifted architect. I was fortunate enough to be introduced, at the onset of this project, to one of the most gifted architects in the field. Ashlei, stand up." Ashlei stood and smiled graciously at Mark for his acknowledgment of her. With all sincerity, Mark continued, "Thank you, Ashlei, for having the eyes to see inside my mind. What I could only visualize, you have actualized. Thank you for all the time and hard work you so unselfishly provided. As much as this is my baby, so is it yours. Without you, we'd all be sitting in a vacant lot right now. Ladies and gentlemen, Ashlei Brown, President and founder of the architectural firm, Brown Industries, Incorporated.''

Everyone applauded enthusiastically.

Ashlei was in tears. It was the most beautiful tribute she had ever received.

When the applause died, Mark continued. ''Last, but most certainly not least, I'd like to thank my beautiful wife, Nicole. Come here, baby.''

Nicole blushed and handed Tiandra to Yvonne. She got up from her seat and joined Mark at the lectern.

As she walked toward him, Mark glowed with the love he felt for her. She was as beautiful as the day she first walked into his establishment. She was just as sexy, too. The red and white dress she wore showed off her exquisite figure. There was no physical indication that she had given birth less than two months ago. He was glad she had begun to wear her hair short and natural again. While she was pregnant, she had let it grow. He had always felt she was too beautiful to hide behind makeup and lots of hair.

He put his arm around her waist and kissed her sensuously on the mouth. To the audience he said, ''This lady is my driving force. Whenever I have doubts, she tells me I can do it. She pushes me to do the best that I can do. She puts up with me when I put in long hours at the office or when I'm away from home for weeks at a time on business. She stuck with me through all the ups and downs while this project was being completed, and for the majority of the time she was home alone and carrying our infant daughter who is just six weeks old today. She has been by my side every step of the way. Without her, this day would have no significance.'' He turned to face her and so everyone could hear, said, ''Thank you, Nicole, for being who you are. I love you.'' Then he kissed her. Everyone applauded.

The pang of jealousy Ashlei felt at witnessing this was sharp.

''Okay, I know you people didn't come here to see me making out with my wife.'' Everyone laughed, except Ashlei, that is. ''We're here to cut the ribbon, opening the doors to Paradise Cove. Although I'd love to do the honors myself, I will humbly turn the scissors over to this beautiful woman by my side. Nicole, be my guest.''

As the photographers positioned themselves, Mark, now holding Tiandra, stood with Nicole, Lucien, Yvonne, Ashlei, the Governor General and his wife stood on both sides of the ribbon. Mark held the ribbon as Nicole poised herself to cut it.

''Ready?'' she asked Mark.

''Whenever you are,'' Mark said with a smile.

''Okay, here it goes,'' she said excitedly. She cut the ribbon.

The audience applauded and Nicole hugged Mark as she whispered, ''Congratulations, honey. I'm so proud of you.''

''Thank you, Nicole,'' he said. He kissed her deeply.

Everyone stepped up to offer their congratulations to Mark.

About ten minutes later, everyone poured into the lobby to partake of the festivities. Mark took Nicole's hand and pulled her into his office, closing and locking the door behind them. He immediately grabbed her around her waist and picked her up, spinning around twice before he put her back down. Before he said a word, he gave her a long, passionate kiss.

He was on top of the world. He had come a long way from the days when he had to steal food for his four brothers and two sisters because of their mother's drug habit. He had come a long way from the days when people constantly told him he would never amount to anything.

Mark knew, too, that had it not been for his high school basketball coach, James Adams, he could not be sure where he would be today. He wished Coach Adams could be with him now to see what a success he had become. He cringed when he thought of how he almost blew everything when a knee injury in college made it impossible for him to play professional basketball like he had always dreamed. Furthermore, he regretted it was not until after Coach Adams died that he had realized that, by giving up after he had been injured, he had hurt the one person who cared for him unconditionally. The coach's death opened his eyes, and he had made a promise to himself and to the spirit of Coach Adams that he would not let the time and life lessons the coach had unselfishly given him be in vain.

He had worked many twelve- to sixteen-hour days to get where he was now. He was forty-two years old and President of the most successful black-owned real estate investment firm in the city of New York. As a self-made millionaire, he had people eating out of his hands. Gone were the days when people looked at him in fear simply because he was a six foot three inch, two-hundred-pound black man. Now they looked at him with awe and treated him with respect wherever he went.

Building this resort had been a dream he was not totally sure would ever come to fruition. But here he was, standing in his office, in his hotel, on his land with the love of his life in his arms. He knew, too, that without Nicole's constant support and confidence, this might still be just a dream for him.

When their lips parted, Nicole looked up at his face. Tears of joy glistened in his eyes and his smile seemed to brighten up the room.

"We did it, baby. We really did it," he said happily.

"You did it, Mark. I'm so proud of you. So very proud."

"I can't believe it's finished."

"Believe it, baby. We're standing in it. This is a beautiful resort, Mark. It really is."

Mark put his hand up to his face to wipe his eyes.

Nicole was happy for him. She was happy for them. They had gone through some rough times at the onset of this project with Ashlei's advances and her own insecurities, but they stuck by one another and made it through.

"I couldn't have done this without you, you know that, right?" Mark said.

"I didn't do anything."

"I needed you to stand beside me, no matter what, and you did."

Nicole gazed into his eyes and reached up to caress his face. "I love you. I'll always stand beside you, through thick and thin. For better or for worse, till death do us part."

He turned his head and kissed the palm of her hand. "I love you, Nicole. This is for you. I know as long as I've got you, I can do anything."

They held each other and shared a very passionate kiss.

"I always knew our time would come, Nicole. This is it. This is our time."

They kissed once again before Mark said, "Come on, sweetheart. Let's go to our party." With that, Nicole put her arm in Mark's and they left the office to rejoin their guests.

Chapter Two

About two hours after the festivities began, Nicole told Mark that she was taking Tiandra up to their suite to feed her and let her nap. About twenty minutes after that, Mark excused himself. He went back to his office in the lobby to call his office in New York. He was quite caught up in the excitement of the day and was already a bit intoxicated.

No one noticed when Ashlei slipped out, five minutes after Mark. She saw Mark leave and had seen Nicole step out a while before. She figured initially that Mark was going to be with Nicole, but noticed when he went into his office instead. She hadn't said anything to him about the speech he made at the ribbon-cutting ceremony, but she wanted to thank him for his kind words on her behalf. She had convinced herself that there was a hidden connotation behind them.

The door to his office was cracked just enough that she could see he was on the phone. She tapped lightly, peeking in so he could see her. He motioned for her to come in and she pushed the door behind her until it was, once again, slightly ajar.

Mark was sitting on the front side of his desk and Ashlei walked to within two feet of where he sat, and waited until he was through with his call.

When he hung up the phone, his first words to her were, "Well, we did it."

She smiled and said, "Yes, we did."

"How do you feel?" he asked as he took a sip of the drink he'd brought with him.

"I feel fine," she said sweetly. "How do you feel?"

He put the glass down. "I feel great," Mark answered with a genuine smile.

"I wanted to thank you for the lovely things you said earlier. I was very flattered."

"I meant every word. I couldn't have done this without you, Ashlei." He took one of her hands in both of his and held it between them. "You've done an outstanding job and I'm very pleased at the outcome. I'm glad you won the bid."

She stepped closer to him and said, "I'm glad you gave me the opportunity."

"Your work speaks for itself. I wanted the best, and with you, the best is what I got."

"Thank you." She was actually blushing.

"Thank you, Ashlei."

She wanted to put her arms around him and kiss him so bad she could taste it, but she vividly remembered the caustic things he had said to her when she tried that once before.

"We work well together, don't we?" she said, testing the waters.

"Yes, as a matter of fact, we do."

Mark was looking directly into her eyes. She wanted to look away for fear that he would read her mind, but she didn't. She returned his stare as intently. *He wants me,* she told herself.

Suddenly, she threw all caution to the wind and stepped closer still to kiss him.

"Lucien, have you seen Nicky?"

"No, baby."

"Have you seen Mark?" Yvonne asked her husband.

"He went to his office to make a phone call. Maybe Nicky's with him," Lucien said.

"Okay. I'll be right back," Yvonne said. She brushed his lips with a gentle kiss.

When she entered the lobby, she walked straight to Mark's office. She saw the door was slightly ajar so she tapped once and went in.

"Ashlei, what are you doing?" Mark asked as he dropped her hand and immediately leaned away from her.

"Don't push me away again," she said softly. "I can see you want me."

Mark put his hands on her waist to push her away at the same instant Yvonne opened the door. She gasped and her eyes bulged at the sight in front of her.

Ashlei turned, then quickly backed away from Mark at the sight of Nicole's best friend. She lowered her head in embarrassment. Yvonne glared at her but Ashlei would not look her way again. Yvonne then turned her attention to Mark. He could tell from the look of disdain on her face that she had the wrong impression of what was going on.

"Yvonne . . ."

"Well, I guess Nicky's not in here!" she said nastily, then quickly turned and walked out.

"Yvonne, wait!" Mark called, but she didn't stop.

"Mark . . . ," Ashlei began.

He turned to Ashlei and the look on his face stilled her tongue. He knew she was probably used to having her way with the men in her life. She was, after all, a beautiful woman and a success in her own right, but they had been through this already. He had made it clear to her that he was not interested.

"You just can't take no for an answer, can you?" he said angrily.

Ashlei stood where she was, not knowing what to say.

He shook his head in disgust before he turned away from her and left the room.

Yvonne was so angry with Mark she didn't know what to do. She wanted to tell Nicole, but could not bear to see the pain she knew her revelation would cause. How could he be so bold? How dare he? With all these people here, with Nicole and Tiandra here. After everything that had happened between him and Nicole and Ashlei in the past. How dare he?

She remembered how unsure Nicole had been of herself around Ashlei when she and Mark first met her, believing that Ashlei was better than she was and that Mark wanted her because of her wealth and success. Yvonne had heard from Lucien that when Ashlei tried to seduce Mark, she had actually told Mark that Nicole was not good enough for him. From what Lucien told her, Mark told Ashlei off and threatened to take the resort project away from her because of her unwanted advances. Had that all been just a ruse?

Yvonne had always believed that Mark was the best thing that had ever happened to Nicole because he had always been so good to her. When Nicole was feeling insecure about Mark and Ashlei, Yvonne had convinced her that Mark would never cheat on her.

For her to walk in and find Ashlei standing right on top of him with his arms around her waist made her feel as though she had been duped by him, and that maybe Nicole's suspicions had been on target.

She went up to Nicole's suite and knocked on the door. Yvonne almost hoped she was not there.

"Come in," Nicole called from the other side.

Yvonne opened the door hesitantly and entered the room.

"Hi. I just came upstairs to feed Tiandra and let her nap. How's the party going?" Nicole asked cheerfully.

"All right."

Nicole immediately noticed that something was bothering her best friend. "What's the matter?"

"Nothing," Yvonne answered barely above a whisper.

Nicole was about to say something else when Mark entered the room hurriedly. He stopped dead in his tracks though when he saw Yvonne. She glared at him.

"Yvonne, you've got the wrong idea."

She turned quickly to Nicole and said, "I'll see you later," and walked out.

He didn't try to stop her.

"What's going on?" Nicole asked Mark, noticing the tension between Yvonne and Mark that had never been there before.

Although minutes earlier Mark had been feeling slightly inebriated, as he stood in front of his wife now, his head was as clear as a bell. "I was in the office downstairs on the phone when Ashlei came in to thank me for what I said earlier at the ceremony."

"That was nice what you said."

"Yeah," he sighed, "but she took it the wrong way."

"What do you mean?" Nicole asked with a frown.

"She tried to kiss me. Yvonne walked in as I was pushing her away."

"If you were pushing her away, why would Yvonne get the wrong idea?"

"I don't know, baby, but that's how it happened."

Nicole stared at him for a long moment before she spoke. Fifteen months ago, when they first met Ashlei and Mark hired her as the architect for his resort, Nicole knew, although Mark denied it, that Ashlei wanted to get her hands on him. He insisted she was overreacting to Ashlei's "friendly" nature. Nicole remembered how unsure she had been of herself due to Ashlei's wealth and success, as well as her knowledge of Ashlei's designs on him. She had been hurt when Mark continued to brush aside her feelings as being imaginative.

It was not until Ashlei had actually tried to seduce him in his hotel room on their first trip to Jamaica to visit the site that he was forced to acknowledge how on target she had been. He apologized profusely when he realized that Nicole was right, and he insisted it would never happen again because he had put her in her place, but now she was doing it again.

He stepped closer to her. "Nicole, I'm telling you the truth." He attributed her silence to disbelief.

"I thought you said it would never happen again."

"I'm sorry. I was wrong. I guess she got too comfortable."

"Do I have to talk to this witch, Mark? I'm not going to allow her to disrespect me like that." Nicole was livid.

"No, sweetheart. I'll talk to her," he said as he put his arms around her. "I'm sorry this happened again. I . . . After I told her off that time, she's been cool. I mean, we don't talk about anything but business. She really surprised me."

"Well, you'd better tell her that if she tries this crap again, I'm gonna surprise her."

"I'm really sorry, honey."

Nicole looked up into his eyes for a long moment before she shook her head and sighed. She put her arms around him and tiptoed so she could kiss him. "I love you, you know."

"I love you, too, Nicole, and I need you too much to do

anything so stupid as to hit on her, or anyone else for that matter, right here in front of all these people. I can't believe Yvonne could think that I would do something like that to you.''

''I'll talk to her,'' said Nicole.

He hugged her close as they shared an easy silence.

After a while Nicole said, ''I can understand why she would want you. After all, you are the finest man in this resort.''

Mark smiled and shook his head. ''Is Tee asleep?'' he asked, referring to their daughter by her nickname. He released Nicole and stepped over to the bassinet.

''Yes. She just went to sleep a few minutes ago.''

''Why don't you go back downstairs. I'll stay up here with her,'' Mark volunteered.

She stepped over to the bassinet with him. ''You can't do that. It's your party. They're probably wondering where you are right now.''

''Well, I'm sure they'll understand that I wanted to be with my two favorite ladies for a while,'' he said, putting his arms around her waist again.

''Well, if they don't, then tough,'' Nicole said, smiling up at him.

He kissed her lips softly and said, ''I do love you, Nicole. I need you more than I can tell you. You believe that, don't you?''

''Yes. I love you, too, Mark and I'm so proud of you.''

His pressed his lips to hers again, although, this time he pushed his tongue into her mouth and tasted the sweetness that he loved more than anything.

When their lips parted, Nicole frowned. ''I can smell that woman's perfume on you.''

''I'm sorry. I'll take a shower.''

She sucked her teeth but said, ''Don't bother. Just make sure you tell her I'm not going to stand for her mess.''

"I will." Mark wanted to kick himself for being so blind to Ashlei again.

"You'd better go on back downstairs before they send a search party after you."

"Yeah, I guess so."

"I'll be down in a little while." Then she added, "Why don't you send Angie up and she can sit with Tee until she wakes up."

"All right, sweetheart," he said, kissing her one final time before he went in search of Tiandra's nanny.

When Mark returned to the party, he noticed Ashlei standing off to the side by herself. He would deal with her later. He spotted Angie and asked her to go up and sit with Tiandra, but he was searching the crowd for Yvonne.

"Mark, where's Nicky?" his half-sister, Carol, asked as she approached him from behind.

"She's upstairs with Tiandra."

"I'm gonna go up," she said.

Mark just nodded. He was still searching the crowd for Yvonne. Suddenly, she came from behind him and started to walk past him. He grabbed her arm. "Yvonne!"

She turned an icy stare on him and said, "What do you want?"

"Yvonne, it's not what you think," he said as he pulled her aside.

"What do I think, Mark?"

"You obviously think I'm stupid enough to be fooling around with Ashlei right under Nicole's nose."

"I know what I saw."

"No, Yvonne, you don't. I told Nicole what happened and now I'm telling you." He did. "I love Nicole, Yvonne, and I would never do anything to hurt her," he explained.

She wanted to believe him. She loved him like a brother and had always thought that he was perfect for Nicole. She believed he loved Nicole but wondered if it was really so farfetched to think he would be interested in Ashlei. She looked into his eyes, satisfied that he was telling the truth, but she was angry with him, nevertheless, for allowing Ashlei to get that close. "You'd better talk to that witch 'cause if I have to, she might get hurt." She shook her head in frustration and started to walk away.

Mark grabbed her arm again and said, "Yvonne, I'll talk to her."

"Make sure you do!" She pulled her arm free and walked off.

Mark was angry, mostly at himself. *How could I have been so stupid,* he thought. He'd known that Ashlei wanted him but he honestly thought she'd gotten the message before. He should have known she would try something like that after he'd had a few drinks and was alone. She probably figured since he'd said what he had about her work, he must have had some hidden agenda. But he'd had to say what he did. She was the best at what she did. As he looked around at his resort, it was evident.

He was thankful that it was Yvonne that had walked in on them and not Nicole. If she had seen what Yvonne saw, she would have probably misunderstood what had happened, too.

Chapter Three

Two months had passed since the opening of Paradise Cove. The resort was doing a booming business. It was booked solid for eight months. Of course, Mark and Nicole were both very pleased with the resort's initial success. Despite all that, Nicole was sullen this particular morning as she watched Mark pack for another trip to Ocho Rios. She wanted him to postpone the trip until next week because she had purchased tickets to a Broadway premiere.

He had been working so hard in the months leading up to, and since the resort's actual opening, that she thought he would enjoy a night of relaxation. She had made plans for the entire evening. They would have dinner at his favorite restaurant, Maxwell's, then go on to the theater. Afterwards, depending on the mood they were in, they would either go to a night club for a couple of hours or back home to spend a quiet evening together. They had not had many quiet evenings together since Tiandra's birth, and Nicole had really been looking forward to this one.

Mark had spoiled her plans, though. Last night he announced he would be flying to Ocho Rios to monitor how things were going at the resort. Since its opening, he frequently flew back and forth between New York and Jamaica. He wanted to personally make sure everything was running smoothly. He told her that once the resort was established, he would not have to do as much traveling, but until then she would have to be patient and bear with him.

Nicole didn't really mind him traveling so often because most of his trips were for one or two days at a time. Before she had Tiandra, she did a bit of traveling herself, and she did have Angie there to help her with Tiandra, so it was not as if she was always home alone. But this particular time, his timing had been terrible. When Mark told her to go to the premiere by herself or take her mother or one of her sisters, she blew her stack.

Nicole had surprised him with her show of temper. He didn't think it warranted all the fuss she had made. Her childish behavior, in turn, made him angry and they argued about it before going to bed.

Since she was still angry this morning, he ignored her for the most part as he went about packing for his trip. He would only be gone for two days, but that didn't seem to matter to her. She didn't want him to go at all.

Nicole was nursing Tiandra, who was now three and a half months old. Her resemblance to Mark was uncanny and, needless to say, he adored her. He doted on her constantly. He was forever bringing home stuffed animals or other little toys for her. He would hold her and rock her to sleep every night if he was home, and Nicole honestly believed that Tiandra knew when he wasn't there because it took her much longer to get Tiandra to sleep if he wasn't.

By the time Mark was dressed and ready to leave for the office, Nicole had burped Tiandra and placed her back in her crib in the nursery. Mark went there to kiss her good-bye. Nicole followed him.

"Bye, beautiful. Daddy'll see you when he gets back, okay?" he cooed. "I love you, precious. You're my beautiful little girl. I'll miss you." He covered her little face with kisses.

Nicole loved to watch him with Tiandra. She had to admit, regardless of how angry she was at the time, that he was a wonderfully loving father.

When Mark was through smothering Tiandra with kisses, he gently placed her back in her crib. He walked past Nicole and back to their bedroom. She followed, not saying a word. He checked his clothes in the dresser mirror then bent down to pick up his overnight bag. He turned to Nicole and saw that she was still brooding over his trip. He shook his head sadly and quietly said, "I'll see you when I get back."

When she didn't respond, he turned and walked out.

When Mark arrived in Jamaica that evening, his mood had lightened considerably. He had forgotten about Nicole's unyielding disposition because he had business to take care of. He didn't have time to worry about something as insignificant as a Broadway premiere.

When he arrived at the resort, his manager, Noel, was in the hotel lobby waiting to greet him. "Good afternoon, Mr. Peterson."

"Good afternoon, Noel. How are you?"

"Fine, thank you. How was your flight?" Noel asked.

"It was fine, thank you. Is my suite ready?"

"Yes, sir. I'll have Tyrone take your bag right up."

"Thank you."

As Mark walked in the direction of the elevators, a familiar voice called his name. To his surprise, standing across the lobby was his old flame, Diane Carey. A smile crossed his face.

He had been seeing Diane for almost three years when he and Nicole first met. Although he had genuinely liked her, he had never been in love with her. Their relationship had been one of convenience. He "kept" her financially comfortable and she was, more than anything else, his main source of sexual gratification.

Nicole had been working for him for three months when he ended his relationship with Diane. Although at the time he had never even made so much as a gesture to Nicole to give her a hint of his feelings for her, he had known even then that she was the woman for him. He didn't feel he had any reason to continue seeing Diane when Nicole was the woman he really wanted.

As he crossed the lobby to speak to her, Mark could not help but notice how good she looked. It appeared that she was either heading to or returning from the pool as she was wearing a gold two-piece bathing suit under a sheer white cover-up. He was glad to see that she had been taking care of herself. In truth, though, he wondered who was keeping her now.

"Hello, Diane," he said with a smile.

"Hello, Diane? Is that it? No kiss? I haven't seen you in over two years. You can do better than that, can't you?" she remarked.

He chuckled as he bent to kiss her cheek. "How've you been?" he asked.

"I've been fine. How about you?"

"Pretty good. I can't complain."

"Nice place you've got here."

"Thank you. Are you staying here?"

"Of course. Where else would I stay in Jamaica? I figured I'd come down and see if it was as fabulous as I'd heard. I wish I could have been here for the grand opening. I heard you had quite a big bash to celebrate."

"Yes, it was nice. So tell me, are you disappointed?"

"No, not at all. It's wonderful. Congratulations," she said sincerely.

"Thank you."

"So, how's married life?" Diane asked, changing the subject suddenly.

"Wonderful."

"I hear you're a father now, too."

"That's right."

"A little girl, am I correct?"

"Yes."

"That's nice. What's her name?"

"Tiandra."

"That's pretty. I know you must have pictures," Diane said.

"Well, actually, I don't have any wallet-size pictures. I have an eight-by-ten that I carry when I'm on the road but it's in my bag."

"Wow, that's something."

She was thinking of how much he must have changed since she last saw him. She really could not picture Mark as a family man. He had always been the quintessential bachelor.

"I understand you married a girl that worked in your office."

"That's right. You seem to know an awful lot about what I've been doing. Have you been keeping tabs on me?" Mark asked.

"But of course," she answered with a chuckle.

Mark just shook his head. "So what else have you been up to lately, Diane?"

"I got married, too."

He was stunned. "Wow! When?"

"About a year ago. I'm a widow, though."

"Oh, I'm sorry," he said sympathetically.

"That's okay. He was killed in a car accident. He was pretty well off though and he left me a good deal of money so I can't complain."

Why did that not surprise him? Although they had been together for years, he had always known that her number one concern was the size of a man's bank account. That had not been a problem for him, though. She had never gotten more from him than he wanted her to have.

"How long were you married?" he asked out of curiosity.

"Five months."

"You don't sound too upset," Mark noticed.

She shrugged her shoulders. "What can I do? Of course, I was upset when it happened. I cared for him a great deal, but it's been seven months. Life goes on," she said nonchalantly.

"Yeah, I guess so." In truth, though, he couldn't imagine his life without Nicole.

"Are you just getting in?"

"Huh?"

"Are you just getting in? Did you just arrive today?" she asked.

"Oh, yeah. I've got a few things here that I want to look over. I try to come down at least every two weeks to keep a check on things until we get established," Mark explained.

"That's understandable. Are you still a workaholic?"

Mark laughed and said, "If you mean do I still enjoy making money, the answer is yes." He suddenly looked at his watch.

"Listen, Diane, I've got to run. I have a couple of phone calls I have to make before it gets too late."

"Okay," she said. Then, "What are you doing later this evening?"

"Nothing special, why?"

"Why don't we have dinner? How about I meet you right here at about seven thirty. Is that all right?"

"Sure, okay. Let me go on up to my suite. I'll see you later."

"Okay," Diane said as Mark began to walk away. She called to him, "Mark."

He turned. "Yeah?"

"It's good to see you," she said with a smile.

He smiled in return and said, "You, too."

Chapter Four

It was ninety degrees in New York City and Nicole refused to go out in such sweltering heat. She was more than happy to stay inside her cool, air-conditioned penthouse. She couldn't get Mark off her mind, either. He had been angry when he left that morning. It was the first time he had ever gone away without kissing her good-bye. She couldn't blame him though, because the more she thought about it, the more she realized that all the fuss she had made was senseless. She couldn't even explain why she had gotten so upset. She had behaved just like a spoiled brat. She hadn't even said good-bye when he left. *God, how stupid can I be,* she thought. Mark always bent over backwards to make her happy and now because he couldn't go to a stupid premiere, she had behaved like a monster. She had to do something to make up for her silliness.

* * *

When Mark reached his suite, his bag was already there. As he went about unpacking, he thought about Diane. She looked good and, he had to admit, it was good seeing her. She seemed to be more settled now than when they were together. He wondered, though, what she was doing for herself other than collecting her dead husband's estate.

Thinking about Diane caused an image of Nicole to flash through his mind. His heart was heavy because he left her like he had. They had never parted on such bad terms before. *Why did she get so upset when I told her I couldn't make that premiere?* He couldn't understand it. It didn't seem like such a big deal to him, but she had practically thrown a tantrum. She had never behaved that way before. She had not even said good-bye to him when he left.

He was sorry he had left without trying to make peace with her. Already, he missed her more than ever before. He was glad he would be here for only two days. He wanted nothing more than to see her so he could hold her in his arms and tell her how much he loved her.

He decided to call her. He picked up the telephone and dialed the number. He was very disappointed when he got a busy signal. He decided to call back later to kiss her good night and tell her how much he missed her.

Later that afternoon, Nicole decided that she would fly to Jamaica to apologize to Mark in person for the temper tantrum she had thrown unnecessarily. She opted not to take Tiandra with her because she wanted to be alone with him. Maybe they could stay a couple of days extra and make a mini-vacation out of it. She only prayed he would be happy to see her and that he would forgive her.

* * *

Mark met Diane at seven thirty and they walked to a nearby restaurant for dinner. As they waited for their meal, they made small talk.

"How long have you been here?" he asked. "You've got a great tan."

"Thanks. Yesterday made a week."

"How long do you plan to stay?"

"I'm not sure. I like Jamaica. This is my first time being here and I love it."

"It seems to have that effect on everyone. That's one reason I decided to build here," Mark said matter of factly.

"Your resort is beautiful. I love my suite. It's tremendous and the view is spectacular. How'd you find this spot?" she asked curiously.

"A friend of mine that lives in Montego Bay showed it to me. When I told him I wanted to build a small resort here, he said he had the perfect place for me to do it. He was right."

"Yeah, it is in a great location."

"Have you seen any other parts of Jamaica besides Ocho Rios?"

"Oh, yeah. The day after I arrived, I went up to the nude beach at Negril for a couple of days. It was beautiful there. I've got a very even tan all over," she said seductively.

Mark chuckled. "I bet."

"So how come you didn't bring your wife . . . What's her name?" she asked, although she already knew it.

"Nicole."

"Yeah. How come you didn't bring Nicole with you?"

"She doesn't always travel with me. She's at home with Tiandra. Besides, I'll be flying back the day after tomorrow, anyway."

"You're only staying for two days?"

"Uh-huh."

"Can I ask you a personal question, Mark?"

"Sure, but if it's too personal, I won't answer," he said.

"Are you really happy?"

Mark smiled at her and said, "Yes, I am."

"I just can't picture you married with children. You were always such a bachelor."

Mark laughed. "Times change, Diane. People change. Hmph, I can't picture you being married. I was quite surprised when you told me that."

"Well, I was kind of surprised when I said yes, myself."

They both laughed.

"So what are you doing now? Are you working or are you a woman of leisure?" he asked, expecting to hear the latter.

"I'm in business for myself."

"Really? What kind of business?" he was curious to know since she had no work experience and only a high school diploma when they had broken up two and a half years ago.

"I own and operate a female escort service."

Mark had a wicked grin on his face when he said, "A female escort service."

"It's legitimate," Diane said defensively.

"I didn't say anything."

"Yeah, but you had that look on your face."

"What look?" Mark asked innocently.

"You know what look. I run a legitimate escort service. I'm not a pimp," Diane said.

"I wasn't implying that you were."

They were both silent for a few minutes.

"You know," Diane started, "I wasn't surprised when I heard you'd married Nicole."

"No?"

"No. I was a little hurt, but I knew you had it bad for her."

Mark tilted his head away from her in surprise. "How could you have known that? The first time Nicole and I got together wasn't until that summer. You and I broke up in March."

"Yes, but she started working for you that January. You used to talk about her to me. You never talked about anyone from your office. I knew you liked her even then."

Mark was reflective for a moment. "Did I really do that?"

"Yes, you did. I was jealous of her because that's when we started going sour."

"But I wasn't even seeing her then. She didn't even know how I felt."

"I knew," Diane said softly. She pressed her lips together briefly before she repeated, "I knew." She took a sip of her drink before she added, "I thought you had a policy about mixing business with pleasure."

"We weren't really fooling around while she was working for me," Mark lied.

"Then how'd you end up being married?"

"Well, to be honest with you, before we got together, I knew I was going to marry her."

"Were you that much in love with her?"

"Yes, and I still am. Sometimes when I think about it, I figure it's like an obsession."

"Is that good?"

"I don't know. It feels good. I'm not sorry I married her. Never have been. She makes me very happy. I've never been happier in my life," Mark admitted.

That revelation hurt Diane more than she cared to admit, but she didn't let it show. "Don't you guys ever argue? I know you can't always be happy with her. All couples argue sometime."

"Sure, we argue. We had an argument last night. As a matter of fact, she was still angry with me when I left this morning. I don't know why, but she was," he said pensively.

Diane could see that he was bothered by Nicole's anger at him. "What happened, if I can be so nosy?" she asked cautiously.

"I don't know. It seemed so petty."

"Maybe she didn't want you to leave, or maybe she wanted to come with you," Diane suggested.

"No, it wasn't that. She could have come if she wanted to. I wouldn't have stopped her. I wish she was here now."

"You really love her that much?"

He looked Diane squarely in the eye and said, "Yes. Very much."

Because Angie was out of town that day attending a funeral, Nicole called Mark's sister Carol to ask if she would keep Tiandra while she was gone. She told Carol about their argument and that she wanted to surprise Mark and make up with him. Carol thought Nicole's idea was very romantic. She told her, "If I know Mark, and I think I know him pretty well, he'll be ecstatic about seeing you. I'm sure he's probably forgotten all about the argument, anyway."

"I certainly hope so," Nicole told her.

"Bring Tiandra over. I'll keep her. You go and get your man, honey."

Nicole called the airline and made a reservation for the earliest flight to Jamaica leaving the next morning. She took Tiandra over to Carol's house, then came back to pack a few things. She had a five forty-five a.m. flight. She called Mark's chauffeur, Bobby, and asked him to come by the house at four thirty to take her to the airport.

She laid out the clothes she would wear for her trip, then took a shower and went to bed.

Tomorrow she would be with Mark and everything would be all right once more.

As Diane and Mark were preparing to leave the restaurant after their meal together, Diane, feeling reminiscent about being with him, asked, "Mark, will you stay with me tonight?" She didn't really expect him to say yes but she figured she had nothing to lose.

Mark was not surprised by Diane's question. Before he could respond, however, Diane added, "I know how you feel about your wife and I don't want to try and change that. I'm just happy to see you and well, I thought maybe for old times sake, we could . . ."

"Diane, before you say anything else, I want you to know I'm flattered that you want me to spend the night with you. I'll admit, I'm very glad to see you and I'm thrilled that you're doing so well for yourself, but I can't stay with you. I love Nicole and I would never betray her."

Diane was touched by his words. She had always wanted him to love her that way. "I'm sorry, Mark. I shouldn't have . . ."

"You don't have to apologize."

She looked up into his eyes and saw a tenderness that she had never seen before.

"Maybe we can have breakfast tomorrow," Mark offered.

"I'd like that."

He touched her arm gently and said, "Let's head on back."

Bobby picked Nicole up at four thirty a.m. sharp and took her to the airport. They were there in less than thirty minutes. Her flight left at exactly five forty-five, right on schedule.

Later, that same morning, Diane decided to go to Mark's room. She had lain awake half the night thinking about him, remembering the good times they used to have and the sweet love they used to make. She wanted to be with him that way again, even if it was just once more.

She had not missed the way he looked at her. She knew he wanted her, too. She'd made up her mind that she was not going to give up so easily. She was sure she could convince him to spend a few hours with her. She knew what turned him on. She knew what buttons to push. Besides, she reasoned, she had nothing to lose.

Nicole arrived in Montego Bay at nine fifty-five that morning. She hired a taxi to drive her to Ocho Rios. The ride would take about forty-five minutes.

Mark was surprised when he opened the door at ten thirty-five that morning and saw Diane standing there.

"I came for breakfast. Can I come in?"

He hesitated for a moment before he stepped aside and let her enter his suite.

"I didn't wake you, did I?"

"No. I was up."

She was dressed in a sarong that tied over her breasts and stopped just above her knee.

"I was just about to step into the shower," he said. He was nude underneath the terry cloth bathrobe he wore.

"Don't let me stop you. I'll wait."

"Have a seat. I'll be a couple of minutes," he told her as he went back to his bedroom.

Diane followed him seconds later. She spied the picture on his dresser. "Is that Tiandra?"

He turned in surprise to find that she had followed him. "Yes," he answered.

She walked over to where he stood at the dresser and picked up the frame. "She's beautiful. She looks just like you."

"Thank you. She is beautiful, isn't she?" Mark said, none too modest. He took the frame from her and gazed at his daughter's image on the photo.

Diane smiled and said, "Your pride is showing in 3-D color, Mark."

He laughed.

In that instant, Diane could not fight or deny the love she still felt for him in her heart. She stepped closer to him and looked up into his eyes with love. "Make love to me, Mark," she softly pleaded.

"Diane . . ."

"Please. I just want to be with you one more time," she sighed before he could refuse her.

She tried to reach inside his robe to touch him.

He pushed her away immediately. "No, Diane! I won't do this."

Whenever Mark stayed at Paradise Cove, he always used the same suite. It remained empty unless he was there. When Nicole arrived at the hotel, she didn't stop at the desk. She went straight to his suite. She wanted to surprise him. She hoped he hadn't left for the day.

His features were hardened in a frown. "I've already told you, I won't cheat on my wife. If you're going to insist on doing this, Diane, you have to leave."

Mark heard the light knocking on the door of his suite. He turned without another word to her and left the room to answer it.

When Mark stepped from the room, Diane removed her sarong and let it fall where she stood. She was naked underneath. She refused to give up so easily.

When Mark reached the door of his suite, instead of opening it right away like he started to, he paused and asked, "Who is it?"

"Nicole."

Mark's stomach hit his feet like a lead weight, the instant he heard her name. In the few seconds before he opened the door for her, three questions ran through his brain at top speed.

*What is she doing here? Why hadn't she called me? How will
I explain Diane?* He had done nothing wrong but he knew
without a doubt that when she saw Diane she would hit the
ceiling. He knew all too well how this looked. Mark was immediately reminded of the incident with Ashlei at the opening of
the resort. What were the chances of this happening twice? He
opened the door slowly. He wondered if his shock and dismay
were as apparent as he felt they were.

Nicole had a shy smile on her face. She was so nervous
about the reaction she might get from him because of her
behavior the day before, that she didn't even notice his despair.
"Hi," she said. "I'm sorry for the way I acted yesterday. Will
you forgive me?"

Mark's heart was beating so loudly in his ears that he could
not understand why she did not hear it. "Come in, Nicole."
As she walked into the room, Mark felt himself dying slowly
but surely. She had come all this way to apologize to him.
How was he going to tell her there was another woman in his
bedroom?

"I was hoping I could catch you before you started running
around. I know you have a lot of things to do today but I
wanted to see you and try to clear the air. I couldn't sleep last
night thinking about how foolish you must think I am. Do you
think you can forgive me? I don't want you to ever leave me
again when we're angry with one another," she said softly.

"Nicole," he faltered.

"What's wrong, Mark?" Nicole asked, now noticing how
pale he was.

"Nicole."

"Mark, what's wrong? Talk to me."

His eyes were moist when he said, "I know what you're
going to think, Nicole, but I swear I would never intentionally
do anything to hurt you. I love you. Do you believe that?"

His words gave her pause, but she said, "Of course I believe it. I would never do anything to hurt you, either. I love you, too.''

Mark wanted to hold her but how could he? He felt guilty because he had allowed Diane to get close enough to touch him. How could he tell her Diane was in the other room? In horror, he suddenly realized that there was nothing to stop Diane from coming out here. *Oh God,* he prayed, *how did I get myself in this mess?*

''Mark, did you change your mind about that shower?''

Because he was standing facing the bedroom door, Mark's mouth fell open in shock and a look of horror covered his face. Nicole turned in the direction of the woman's voice. Her mouth fell open and her heart shattered. Suddenly, she felt as if she was suffocating.

When Diane came face to face with Nicole, her blood ran cold.

Nicole turned back to Mark, her eyes pleading for an explanation but she could not form the words.

''Nicole, it's not what you think,'' he quickly explained. He turned to Diane and roared, ''What do you think you're doing?''

Nicole heard his words but they sounded muffled, as though he were underwater. She felt lightheaded. *This is not happening,* she thought. *This is a dream. Yes, that's it. I'm having a bad dream. I'll wake up and be at home in my bed with none of this having ever happened.* She turned back to the pale, naked white woman standing across the room. *This has to be a dream.* The figure of the woman standing before her began to blur. Then everything went black.

Mark saw Nicole's body begin to crumble and was able to catch her before she hit the floor. ''Oh God,'' he moaned as he grabbed her and swept her into his arms. He gently laid her on the sofa. ''Get me a cold towel!''

Diane stood where she was, her hands at her mouth, her eyes wide with shock.

''Hurry up, dammit!!''

She ran into the bathroom and wet a washcloth with cold water. She immediately ran back into the living room to give it to Mark.

Kneeling beside her, he began to wipe Nicole's face with it before he placed it on her forehead. Tears streamed down his cheeks and his heart felt as if it was being wrenched from his chest.

Diane stood in the middle of the floor watching Mark as he tried to bring her to. "Get your clothes on and get out of here," he hissed.

Diane was in a daze. She did not hear him.

"GET OUT OF HERE, DIANE!!!"

She moved quickly then. She ran back to the bedroom and picked up her sarong from where she had let it fall and tied it around her body. She slipped on her shoes as fast as she could and returned to the living room to leave. "Mark," she said, anguish apparent in her voice. He looked up at her. Anger and sadness filled his eyes. "I'm so sorry."

Once Diane was gone, Mark turned his full attention to Nicole. She lay so still that for a brief moment, he thought she wasn't breathing. *God, please let her wake up,* he prayed. His heart was beating so hard it actually hurt.

He rose from the floor to sit on the couch. He lifted her head up off the couch and laid it in his lap. As he gently wiped her face with the cold cloth, he tried to think of what he would say to her when she awoke. How could he make her understand that what she had witnessed was not what she would obviously think? He knew she would not believe him when he told her nothing had happened between him and Diane. He knew she would be furious, not only because of the way she found him, but because her pride and confidence would be rebelling with the idea that her discovery had caused her to faint.

"How could I have been so stupid?" he asked himself aloud. "Why did I let her in here?" He should have guessed that the way he left Nicole yesterday morning would be a bad omen.

He should never have left without first straightening things out with her. Nothing he had to do was so important that it could not wait until they had reconciled their differences.

Nicole spoke of how she had behaved foolishly, but he had been just as much to blame if not more so. He shouldn't have let her anger upset him like it had. If he had only tried to talk to her they probably could have come to a very good compromise about the whole thing. But no, he had succumbed to his stubborn pride and walked out. He hadn't even kissed her good-bye.

Suddenly, Nicole began to stir. "Nicole?" Mark whispered. as he caressed her face.

She opened her eyes slowly, trying to focus in on her surroundings. She looked up at him, still not fully aware.

Mark had tears in his eyes as he said, "Nicole, I know what you must be thinking but I swear to you, nothing happened."

Mark's words brought her swiftly back to reality. She jumped up and away from him. Although she was still a bit shaken, she threw him a look filled with venom and said in a voice as cold as ice, "You keep your hands off of me! Don't you dare touch me!"

"Nicole, please," he pleaded. "Let me explain."

"I don't want to hear it, Mark. There's nothing you can tell me. All this time, you've been telling me nothing but lies."

"No, baby. No! This was the first time I've seen her in over two years, but nothing happened. I swear to you."

"What?! Who was that?"

"She was an . . . an old friend," he said ashamedly.

"Oh, really? Catching up on old times, huh?" she sneered.

"Baby, no. You've got it all wrong."

"I've got it all wrong? Was I imagining her standing there butt naked? I don't think so! Do you really expect me to believe nothing happened, Mark? Don't tell me any more lies!"

"I'm not lying to you, Nicole. It's the truth. Baby," Mark said as he rose from the couch and walked toward her. "Nothing happened. I know how it looks. She just came up here this morning. I was just telling her that she had to leave when you knocked on the door. Please, believe me. I love you.''

"Stop lying to me!" Nicole yelled. "You don't love anyone but yourself! All that matters to you is YOU!" She turned away from him and in exasperation said, "God, how could I be so stupid to come down here and try to make up with you?! You weren't even thinking about me. You were too busy screwing your whore! I hate you, Mark. I hate you for hurting me like this. I hate myself for believing that you could really love me. How could I be so stupid?" With that, she collapsed on the chair and cried, her whole body racked with sobs. The old insecurity she felt when they first got together reared its ugly head, clouding her thoughts.

Her cries were so agonizing that Mark felt helpless to do anything or say anything to her. He wanted to hold her, to comfort her, but she would not let him near her. "Nicole, baby, you've got to believe me." Tears fell freely from his eyes as he stood before her. He loved her more than he ever realized before. Seeing her cry because of his stupidity filled him with unbearable remorse.

Suddenly, Nicole rose from where she had been sitting and brushed past him. She started toward the door.

"Where are you going?" Mark asked as he followed her.

"Obviously, I came at a very inconvenient time for you, so I'm leaving. You can call your old friend and tell her I left," Nicole said viciously.

Mark grabbed her arm and said, "You can't go, baby. We've got to straighten this out."

"I told you not to touch me!" The look in her eyes caused him to withdraw his hand. "And while you're at it," Nicole added as she continued toward the door, "you can tell her she won't have to worry about getting busted again, because I'm not coming back."

As Nicole spoke these last words, her voice wavered as if

she was sorry she had said them, but it was too late for her to take them back.

It felt as though a razor had pierced Mark's heart when Nicole said she was not coming back. Then he thought, *she doesn't mean that.* But he asked, "What do you mean, you're not coming back?"

She was at the door now and she turned to him. Her eyes held tears that she tried to keep from falling. She tried to put up a brave front as she said, "Just what I said. You can have her and Ashlei and all the other women you want. I won't interfere. I can see it was stupid to imagine that you could be satisfied with me. No matter what you try to tell me, I'm not like you. We're from two different worlds. You'll probably be happier with someone else."

Before she could open the door, Mark was on her. He grabbed her and spun her around to face him. "What are you talking about? You can't leave. Nicole, nothing happened," he insisted, his face awash with emotion.

Nicole looked up at him. In that instant, her life with him flashed before her eyes. She, too, realized that she loved him more than she had ever loved or would ever love anyone. She worshipped him. To find him with another woman was more than she could bear. Then for him to lie and tell her nothing happened between them . . . He wasn't supposed to be like other men who cheated on their wives. He was her man and there should never have been anyone he would want more than her. He belonged to her. But not anymore. He couldn't really love her if he would spend the night with this woman. He told her he would never hurt her, that she would never have to worry about him cheating on her. They had all been lies; and he was still lying. As she thought about this, the tears that had previously stopped began to fall once more.

"Nicole," Mark said again when she didn't answer. "You can't leave, baby. I love you! Don't you know that?" He was pleading with her. She still did not speak, nor did she move.

"Nicole," he said softly as he embraced her tightly. "I need you. Baby, please, don't leave me. I know what you're thinking but I swear it's not like that. I swear, baby. Please, just let me explain." He was crying softly.

Nicole stood there, wrapped in his embrace, her hands at her sides. She, too, was crying. She wanted to believe he loved her and needed her like he said, but how could she? He had left her the day before without so much as a good-bye kiss and the next time she sees him, he's with someone else. *No,* she thought, *I have to go.* She pulled away from him and out of his embrace. She looked into his tear-filled eyes with her own and said, "Good-bye, Mark."

She turned and opened the door to leave but he stopped her. "Nicole, please."

She pulled away again and once more said, "Good-bye." She walked out the door.

"Nicole, please, don't go."

But she kept walking. She did not turn back. If she had, she ɯould have seen the agony she felt in her heart reflected on ʼk's face.

Chapter Five

He was numb. When Nicole walked out, Mark felt as though his whole world had come crashing down on him. He could understand her being upset and angry, but he couldn't fathom the idea that she would actually leave him. *Why doesn't she believe me? Why won't she listen to me,* he wondered. As he hurriedly showered and dressed, he kept replaying in his mind the words she had spoken to him. He prayed it was just her anger that caused her to say she would leave. He told himself that once her anger died down and she listened to him, she would realize that he had done no wrong except for being gullible enough to let Diane in that morning. *Did I give Diane a mixed signal when I suggested we have breakfast?*

He could see Nicole still loved him. He hoped she would see that they belonged together; that she needed him as much as he needed her. He had to go and get her. Somehow he had to make her see that what she had witnessed was classic "believe only half of what you see." He had to make sure she knew that his love for her was without end, that it had no bounds.

Before leaving the hotel, Mark stopped to see Noel to tell him their meeting would have to be postponed. Everything had been running without a hitch, so Mark figured that putting his business off for a couple of days would not cause any major problems. Uppermost in his mind was Nicole. He had to get her back.

He figured she had probably gone to Lucien and Yvonne's house. He would go there first. Maybe Yvonne could talk to her and help her see that she would be hurting all of them if she didn't give him a chance to explain. He knew she had not thought about Tiandra when she said she was leaving. He knew she would realize that if she left, she would be hurting Tiandra most of all. She knew how he loved their daughter. There was no life for him without them.

When Nicole arrived at the Montego Bay airport, the first thing she did was exchange her return ticket for one back to New York on the first flight out. It was not scheduled to leave until two o'clock that afternoon. She had about an hour and a half to wait. Nicole prayed he would not follow her. She went to the airport lounge but as she sat there, she could not stop thinking about Mark, and this caused her to cry.

"Miss, are you all right?" A man stood over her, his face filled with concern.

Nicole was embarrassed and tried to wipe the tears from her eyes. "Yes, yes," she said quickly. "I'm fine." She got up immediately and went to the ladies' room. Once there, her tears began to flow once more. As she cried, she cursed Mark for what he had done. Not only did she feel like a fool for fainting in front of his woman, but she was embarrassed because she couldn't stop crying. She looked at herself in the mirror. Her eyes were red. Her nose was red. She looked terrible. "I hate you, Mark," she cried as she looked at her reflection. "Why'd you have to do this? Why'd you have to hurt me this way?"

"Honey, you okay?" a woman standing at the sink asked.

"Yes, I'm fine, thank you." She turned her body away from the woman and continued to cry. As she did, she also cursed herself for being so weak. She wished she could just forget him, forget that she had seen the woman coming out of his bedroom, forget that she had made a fool of herself by coming here in the first place.

She thought about the tears Mark had shed. She wanted to believe he was upset about what had happened, but it was probably just his ego and not his heart that had been injured. He had been found out. That was probably his only concern. How could he really expect her to believe nothing had happened with that woman? He was in his bathrobe. He had probably just thrown it on to answer the door. He could not deceive her anymore because now her eyes were open. She was not blind to him any longer.

"Stop crying," she said to her reflection. She was able to compose herself for a moment. She wet a paper towel and wiped her face. She had to talk to Yvonne. Talking to Yvonne always made her feel better.

* * *

When Yvonne arrived at the airport, she looked around the lounge for a few minutes but she didn't see Nicole anywhere. She was worried because although Nicole would not tell her what was happening over the phone, she could tell by the way her voice trembled that something was very wrong. She had been surprised, too, when Nicole told her she was in Montego Bay. She wondered where Mark was. In fact, she had asked Nicole where he was, but she would not give her any information when they spoke. All she said was that it was imperative that she meet her at the airport right away.

Yvonne started toward the ladies' room. She was about to open the door when she heard, "Yvonne." She turned and saw Nicole standing in a corner, practically hidden from view.

"What are you doing hiding over there?" Yvonne asked as she walked over to her with a questioning smile on her face. Nicole did not answer and Yvonne saw that she had been crying. "What's wrong?"

Nicole started to speak, but before she could get a sentence out, the tears started all over again. Yvonne put her arms around her, trying to comfort her.

"Nicky, where's Mark? Did something happen to Mark? What's wrong?" Yvonne asked, now worried herself.

"Mark . . ." Nicole moaned, her crying greatly inhibiting her speech.

"What? What about Mark? Is he all right?"

Nicole was crying uncontrollably and Yvonne knew that until she could calm her down, she would not be able to learn anything. "Nicky, come on. Let's go sit down," Yvonne said, urging her forward to an empty bench in the lounge.

Once she had Nicole seated, she tried to stop her from crying so she could talk. After a few minutes, Nicole regained her composure for the most part and was able to tell Yvonne what had happened. By the time Nicole was finished, she was crying uncontrollably again.

As Yvonne sat with Nicole trying to comfort her, she thought about what her friend had just told her. How could Mark be so thoughtless? What could he have been thinking about when he took that woman to his room? Then to lie and tell Nicole that nothing happened. She was at once reminded of the time she caught him hugged up with Ashlei at the opening party for the resort. He claimed then that he was completely innocent.

Most of the time, when Nicole had a problem or something was bothering her and she came to her for advice or consolation, Yvonne would think of something to tell her to make her feel better or at least lift her spirits. But right now, she was at a complete loss for words. She did not know what to tell Nicole. In all the years they had been friends, Yvonne had never seen her so totally devastated. She knew how much she loved Mark and she also knew about her insecurity concerning Mark's wealth and her lack thereof. She could remember how intimidated Nicole had been by Mark when she first started seeing him.

Unlike Nicole, however, Yvonne still believed that Mark loved Nicole very much. She had known him for almost as long as Nicole had, and in those years she and Mark had become good friends. They often discussed Nicole and Lucien, among other things, and although Mark had never used the words, Yvonne knew he worshipped Nicole as she did him.

It had always fascinated her that they could love each other so totally, as if their sole purpose in life had been to love one another. She could understand why Nicole was so upset. She knew Nicole had never imagined that Mark would be unfaithful to her.

"Nicky." She was still crying but not as hard as before. "What are you going to do?"

Nicole looked at Yvonne then averted her eyes. "I'm leaving him."

Yvonne thought she was hearing things. "What? What did you say?"

"I'm leaving him."

She was taking this harder than Yvonne thought. "Nicky, you don't mean that."

"Yes, I do," she said, sniffling. "He doesn't care about me, so why should I stay?"

"Nicky, you can't leave him without at least talking to him. No matter how much he hurt you, you can't believe that he doesn't love you," Yvonne said, trying hard to make her see that she was acting too hastily.

"If he loved me, he wouldn't have been with that woman. They were about to get in the shower together when I got there. I interrupted them. Mark came to the door in his robe 'cause he was probably butt naked under it. She was naked," Nicole said.

"Did you ever consider that he may have been telling the truth when he said nothing happened?" Yvonne asked, although she had her doubts, too.

"I already know he thinks I'm stupid. Do you think I'm stupid, too?"

Yvonne took a deep breath. *This is going to be tough,* she thought.

"All right, so what if he was fooling around? You know he's not likely to do it again. He knows how upset this has made you."

"It's easy for you to say 'so what.' It wasn't Lucien you caught with someone else. It was Mark. You don't know how I feel because it didn't happen to you!" Nicole said.

"If I caught Lucien with someone else, I'd be angry, sure, but I wouldn't leave him because of it. He's my husband and I wouldn't give another woman the satisfaction of knowing that I would give him up that easily," Yvonne said, trying to reason with Nicole. "Besides, he's a man. All men fool around sometimes. It's their nature. Lucien's no different. They see a pretty woman and they stop thinking with the head on their shoulders and the one between their legs takes over. Think about how much you'd be giving up if you left."

"I don't care," Nicole said, pouting like a stubborn child.

"Nicky, I know you care." She knew Nicole was hurting and that she did not realize the significance of what she was contemplating.

"No, I don't," Nicole insisted halfheartedly.

Yvonne knew otherwise. "What about Tiandra?"

At the mention of her daughter, Nicole started crying all over again.

"Nicky, you can't leave him. Tiandra needs him and you do too, even if you won't admit it. You know he's not going to let you take Tiandra away from him."

"Away from him!" Nicole said angrily. "He wasn't thinking about Tiandra when he was screwing that witch! If he cared so much, he would have at least thought about her before he jumped in bed with that slut."

Yvonne knew she should have chosen her words more carefully. But regardless of what she said, she knew as well as Nicole did that Mark would never allow her to take Tiandra away from him. He loved Tiandra with as much, if not more, devotion as he loved Nicole.

"Nicky, . . ." Yvonne started, but Nicole quickly cut her off.

"Look, Yvonne, I don't want to talk about it anymore, all right?"

"Nicky, . . ."

"I said I don't want to talk about it, so just forget I said anything to you!"

Yvonne closed her mouth. She did as Nicole said and did not say another word. She wished she could make her understand that she shouldn't be so quick to give up.

"What time is it?" Nicole suddenly asked, forgetting that she was wearing a watch.

Yvonne looked at hers and said, "It's almost twenty to two."

Nicole jumped up quickly and said, "I've got to go."

"Where are you going?" Yvonne asked, walking fast to keep up with Nicole.

"Home."

"Nicky, what about Mark?" Yvonne asked as she grabbed her arm.

"What about him?" she asked, jerking her arm out of Yvonne's grip.

"You're not going to leave him, are you?" Yvonne asked, genuinely worried. She knew there were times when, if Nicole was upset, she could act very impulsively.

"I don't know. Look, I have to go. My plane's leaving at two," Nicole said coldly. She continued walking toward the gate.

Yvonne knew she couldn't stop her so she called to her, "Call me when you get home."

Nicole did not turn back. She simply waved.

As she watched Nicole walk away, a chill ran through Yvonne's body. She didn't like the feeling she was having at all.

It was almost one o'clock by the time Mark started his drive to Lucien's house. He tried not to think about Nicole leaving him. *She can't be serious,* he told himself. *She's upset and doesn't know what she was saying.* She obviously didn't know how much he needed her. Since they had been married, he had come to know a way of life he never dreamed of having. She brought so much joy to his world that for her to leave him now would be like cutting off the air to his lungs. Not only that, he could never let her take Tiandra and he knew her well enough to know that if she left, she would try to. The day Tiandra was born had been the happiest day of their lives. He still believed that. Had she forgotten how happy they had been then? It seemed so. How could she think of a life where he, she and Tiandra were not together?

When Mark arrived at the Rogers' home, Yvonne had just returned from the airport. She was about to walk in the front door when he pulled up. When she recognized him, she stopped at the door and waited for him to get out of his car.

"Yvonne, is Nicole here?" Mark asked as he took long, determined strides toward her.

She could see how worried he was. "No, Mark, she went home."

"How long ago?"

"I just came back from the airport. Her plane left at two."

"Why didn't you stop her?" Mark asked, for lack of something better to say.

"How? She called me from the airport and asked me to meet her there. She told me what happened. She's very upset. She was talking really crazy."

"What did she say?"

Yvonne didn't want to be the one to break the bad news to him so she did not answer. She looked away.

"Yvonne," Mark said, grabbing her arm. "What did she say?"

"She said she was leaving you."

Mark released her immediately. She watched as the color left his face. She felt as if she had just stabbed him in the heart.

"Mark, she's upset. She didn't know what she was saying. You know how Nicky gets. She didn't mean it," Yvonne said trying to make him believe it, although she was not sure about it herself.

Mark's eyes began to water. "She won't listen to me. What am I supposed to do?"

"Go and get her."

"She won't talk to me. She wouldn't even let me touch her."

"She's hurt and she's angry. You've got to give her time. She doesn't really want to leave you. She loves you even if she won't admit it now," Yvonne said, trying to make him see that all was not lost.

Mark sat down in one of the chairs on the porch. He felt totally lost at that moment. He appeared so dejected to Yvonne that she almost cried for him. Instead she asked, "Mark, why'd you do it?"

He looked up at Yvonne. "I didn't."

She cut her eyes at him. "Mark."

"Yvonne, nothing happened. I swear."

"She didn't spend the night with you?"

"No. She asked me if she could. I told her no."

"How'd she end up in your shower?"

Mark sighed. "She was never in my shower. I never touched her," he said agitatedly. "She came to my room this morning, not even ten minutes before Nicole got there. I was about to . . . I was getting ready to take a shower myself." Mark paused as he looked off toward the horizon. "She followed me into the bedroom and one minute we were looking at Tiandra's picture, the next minute she was propositioning me. I had just told her she would have to leave when Nicole knocked on the door."

"But you didn't make her leave."

"I went to open the door." As he thought about his situation, Mark grew more and more depressed. "I never imagined that Nicole would come down here. We had a really dumb argument before I left and she was mad at me. I didn't even kiss her good-bye." Talking about it was getting to him and although he tried otherwise, the tears just fell. "I know what it looked like, Yvonne, I mean the way she came out there. . . . but I swear I never touched her. I love Nicole. I tried to explain to her what happened but she wouldn't listen to me."

Yvonne felt very sorry for him. She believed he was telling the truth, although she could understand why Nicole didn't. She could see how sorry he was for letting the woman into his room, and it was evident that he was hurting just as much as Nicole. She wished there was something she could tell him to make him feel better. She didn't want to see them break up. They were such a beautiful couple and they were so much in love.

"Go get her, Mark. I'm sure after she's had some time to think, she'll stop and listen to what you have to say."

Mark sighed. "Yvonne, you believe me, don't you?"

"Yes."

He got up from his seat and prepared to leave. "I'm going to go home and try talking to her again. If she calls you, tell her I'm on my way and ask her to please stay until I get there. And tell her that I love her."

"I will." She reached for his hand and tried to comfort him. "Don't worry, Mark. As long as you love each other, everything will work out."

Mark put his arms around her and said, "Thank you, Yvonne."

"You're welcome."

He kissed her cheek and started toward his car. "Wish me luck," he called to her.

"Good luck," she said sincerely.

As Mark was getting into his car, Lucien drove up. He called to Mark out of his window. "Hey, guy, where you going?"

"Home. I'll talk to you later," Mark called back, never slowing his pace.

By the time Lucien got out of his car, Mark was pulling away. "Hey, sweets," Lucien said as he walked over to Yvonne and kissed her. "What's up with Mark?"

"Come inside, baby, and I'll tell you the whole story. It's a long one."

Chapter Six

By the time Nicole arrived in New York, she had made up her mind that she was leaving Mark. The hurt he caused her by his selfish act and his lying was more than she could bear. She was convinced that if he would cheat on her once, he would do it again. The idea of having to go through this again was something she knew she would never be able to handle. She also knew she would always wonder if he was still cheating. She would rather give him up than live with him and have such strong doubts about him.

From the airport, she went straight to the penthouse. When she got there, she hurriedly packed some clothes for herself and Tiandra in one of her larger suitcases. While doing this, she tried to think of what she would tell Carol when she went to get Tiandra. She didn't want to arouse her suspicion and she didn't want to hear any more talk about what a mistake she was making. Yvonne had really disappointed her. She seemed to be taking Mark's side in this and he was the one who had done wrong. That really made her angry.

Nicole looked at the clock on the nightstand. Seven o'clock. She had to go. If she knew Mark, he was most likely on his way back here right now. She didn't want to risk seeing him because she could not bear to hear any more of his lies. She left the building through the underground garage. She was glad her car was parked there because this way she didn't have to bypass the doorman. She still hadn't figured out what she would tell Carol.

* * *

Mark's flight to New York didn't leave until ten after five. While he waited, he tried to occupy his time by making calls to a few clients and calling his New York office to see what was going on there. Although he tried to concentrate on these conversations, his mind was on Nicole. *Does she really plan to leave me,* he wondered. He didn't want to believe she would, but she was more upset than he had ever seen her.

He called Bobby to give him his flight number and told him to be at the airport at eight o'clock. His plane would not land until more like eight thirty and by the time he got through customs, it would probably be closer to nine, but he didn't want to waste any time getting to Nicole. He had to stop her before she tried to walk out of his life.

Carol was shocked to see Nicole when she opened her door. "What are you doing here? I thought you were going down to see Mark."

Thinking fast, Nicole said, "Oh, I spoke to him on the phone last night. I'm going down tonight. He wanted me to bring Tiandra. He said he misses her. You know how he is."

"Don't I ever. Well, come on in. I'll get her things for you. What time is your flight?"

"Eight thirty."

"Oh my goodness, you'd better hurry up. Why'd you wait so late to come and get her?"

"I had so much running around to do today that I didn't realize how late it was. I'm glad I had already packed a bag for myself. All I had to do was pack a few things for Tee," she answered calmly. Nicole was amazed at how cool she was as she stood before her sister-in-law and lied as if nothing was wrong. But she knew she could never tell Carol what her plans were.

When Nicole left Carol's house with Tiandra, she had no idea where she would go. She couldn't go to her parents' house because she knew, without a doubt, they would never let her stay there without Mark's knowledge. Her parents never got involved in their children's marital disputes. They loved Mark like a son, and she figured they would probably defend him if she told them why she had left.

Mark had told her she would never have to worry about him being unfaithful and she had believed him. How could she ever trust him again? She then thought about when he first started working with Ashlei Brown. He was probably doing her too, although he claimed he wasn't.

Nicole thought about going to a hotel but she didn't want to stay in a hotel indefinitely. Then it came to her. She could go to her sister Desiree's house. Knowing how strained her relationship with her sister had always been, Mark would never think to look for her there.

Desiree had never liked Mark. She told Nicole in the beginning that he would get tired of her one day and dump her. She had been so angry with her then that she had stopped speaking to her for weeks. Now, it seemed that Desiree had been right all along. Nicole knew once she told Desiree what had happened, she would let her stay without telling Mark, at least until she could find a place of her own.

When Mark's plane landed in New York, Bobby was waiting for him. "You're home early, aren't you?" he asked as he held the door open for Mark to enter the limo.

"You haven't seen Nicole, have you?" Mark asked, ignoring Bobby's question.

"I took her to the airport this morning."

"Take me to the apartment," Mark ordered.

"Yes, sir."

* * *

Something was wrong. Bobby Taylor could tell without Mark having to say a word. He had worked for Mark for eight years and had become accustomed to his mood swings.

In the beginning, Bobby had considered quitting a number of times because of Mark's attitudes, but Mark paid him well and when he was in a good mood, which was most of the time, he was really a decent brother. Actually, as far as Bobby was concerned, if he had to work for someone, he figured he couldn't have anything sweeter than this gig anyway. Mark paid him a flat salary, fifteen hundred dollars every two weeks, regardless of how many or how few times a week he used him. Occasionally, if Mark was hosting a social function at his home, Bobby would have to work the party, usually tending bar, but he always got good tips at these gatherings. When he didn't have to drive Mark around, he could use the limo at his discretion as long as Mark didn't have to wait around when he needed him. There were times, for instance, when Mark would go out of town for days at a time and he would still get paid for doing damn near nothing. At Christmas, Mark always gave him generous bonuses. The year he and Nicole got married, he had given him three thousand dollars, tax-free.

He wondered what was going on. Why had Mark asked him if he had seen Nicole? As far as he knew, she was in Jamaica.

Bobby liked Nicole. He thought she was a very classy lady. He was familiar with most of the women that Mark used to run with and he never could understand what Mark saw in some of them. Granted, they were all fine on the outside, but in the times he had driven them around and listened to their conversations, they didn't seem to have much on the cap.

He envied Mark though, because of his finesse with the ladies. He never seemed to have a problem getting any woman he wanted. Mark was a good-looking man. He turned women's heads wherever he went. Bobby knew he was not what would be considered good-looking. Aside from his very dark complexion, he thought his nose was too wide and flat and his lips were too big. But he figured, if he had money like Mark did, he probably would have no trouble getting women either. Not that he really had a problem, but he wouldn't mind trading places with Mark for a day or two.

Of all the women Mark had dealt with though, the one he disliked the most had been Diane Carey. He never could figure out what Mark saw in her, and she had been around longer than any of the others. Bobby remembered the time she had come on to him. He had been tempted to jump her, too, just for the hell of it, but when he refused her, she ran and told Mark that he had hit on her. When Mark asked him about it, Bobby told him exactly what happened. He even told Mark that he considered taking her up on her offer and that if he wanted to fire him because he thought he was trying to hit on her, then go right ahead. Mark had laughed and said, ''Yeah, like I would cut loose my most dependable man for a chick like her.''

That was when Bobby decided that this money-makin' brother was all right. Although they were not friends in the true sense of the word, they had a mutual respect and that was good enough for him.

There had been a few times, though, when he and Mark had had a few drinks together and got quite toasted, like when Tiandra was born. Mark had put his ''boss'' role in his back pocket and they were just two guys hanging out. Mark had even confided in him about his personal life on a number of occasions and whether he knew it or not or even cared, Bobby had never betrayed those confidences. Mark looked out for him and he looked out for Mark.

When Bobby met Nicole for the first time, he thought she was one of the prettiest women he had ever seen with Mark. He could tell, too, that Mark was really hung up on her. She wasn't flashy like the women Mark usually dated. She was sweet and she treated him with respect. When Mark told him he was going to marry Nicole, Bobby had been almost as happy as Mark was. She was good for Mark, probably the best thing to ever happen to him.

He hoped she was all right. The way Mark looked now, Bobby noticed as he glanced at him in the rearview mirror, was as if he was very worried about her. He wanted to ask Mark what was wrong but something told him this was not the time. So he waited.

Before Bobby could even park the car in front of the apartment building, Mark was out of the car. ''Wait here,'' he called back as he hurriedly walked into the building.

When Mark stepped into the apartment, he immediately got a bad feeling in his gut. He knew before he even looked that Nicole had already been there and gone. He hurried into the bedroom and looked in their dressing room. Her biggest Louis Vuitton suitcase was gone. So was her overnight bag. He looked into a couple of her bureau drawers and noticed that all her underwear was gone. He rushed to the nursery, although he already knew what he would find there. She had removed most of Tiandra's clothes. The diaper bag was empty and all of her lotions, baby powders and shampoo were also gone.

''Damn!'' he shouted as he slammed his fist on top of the baby's dresser. As he looked around Tiandra's room, tears began to well in his eyes. *Why is she doing this? Why is she so convinced that I would or have been cheating on her? What have I done to warrant such mistrust from her?* Had he really hurt her so bad that she would run away and take his daughter from him, too? Losing one of them was bad enough, but he could not bear losing both of them.

He wanted to cry, but knew that wouldn't bring them back. He had to make Nicole see that she belonged with him. *Where could they be?* As Mark headed back downstairs, he tried to figure out where she could have gone. He knew she wouldn't go to her parents' house because she'd know that would be the first place he'd look for her. He decided to ask the doorman what time she had left.

When Mark got back into the limo, he was very pensive. The doorman told him that he had seen Nicole come in but as far as he knew, she hadn't left. That meant she was driving. She must have gone straight to the garage and never come through the lobby.

"Where to, boss?" Bobby asked, noticing the worried expression on Mark's face.

Where's Nicole, Bobby wondered.

Mark didn't answer right away. Instead he picked up the car phone and dialed his mother-in-law. Maybe she knew where Nicole was. He closed the partition between him and his driver for privacy.

"Hello," Mrs. Johnson answered.

"Hi, Mom, this is Mark. How are you?"

"Hi, Mark. I'm fine, honey, how are you?"

"Not too good right now," he admitted.

"What's wrong, baby?"

He could hear the concern in her voice. It was obvious that Nicole was not there. "Have you seen Nicole?"

"No. Is she all right?"

"I think so. We had a fight and she's very angry and upset with me, and rightfully so. But she's gone. She packed a suitcase for herself and the baby and left. I don't know where she is," Mark said as his voice cracked.

Mrs. Johnson was quiet for a moment before she asked, "Mark, what happened?"

Mark, being too embarrassed to tell Nicole's mother the truth, said, "I don't want to talk about it right now, if that's all right. I'd just like to find them. Have you heard from her?"

"I haven't talked to her in a couple of days," Mrs. Johnson told him. "Did you hit her?"

"No. Nothing like that. I would never hit her. We just . . . I really don't want to talk about it now. Do you have any idea where she might have gone? Do you think she might be at Shelly's house or Desiree's?"

"Well, I know she's not at Shelly's house; she's in Hawaii with David. And I doubt if she'd go to Desiree's. They don't get along that well, you know that," she reminded him.

"I know."

"Are you at home, Mark?"

"No, I'm in my car. I just left the apartment. Maybe she went to Carol's house. She had to have left the baby somewhere when she flew to Jamaica."

"She went to Jamaica?"

"Yes. That's where we had the fight. She flew back before I could stop her and I wasn't able to get a flight out until three hours later. I'm going to go by my sister's house to see if she's been there. I'll call you if I find out anything and please, if she comes there, try to make her stay until I get there, or if she calls, find out where she is."

"All right."

"I'll call back later."

"Okay."

When Mark hung up, he spoke through the intercom to Bobby. "Take me to my sister's house."

"Yes, sir," Bobby answered and pulled off. *Damn,* he thought, *something's very wrong.*

When Mrs. Johnson hung up the phone, she wondered what they could have fought about to make Nicole want to leave Mark. She knew her daughter well and she knew how deeply she loved her husband. This was not like her at all. She hoped Nicole was all right.

* * *

As Mark rang the bell at Carol's house, he prayed that Nicole would be there.

When Carol opened the door to him, the first thing she said was, ''Mark! What are you doing here? Nicky just left with Tiandra to go see you in Jamaica.''

''How long ago did she leave?'' he asked urgently.

''I don't know, maybe an hour and a half, two hours ago. She said she was catching an eight thirty flight,'' Carol said, looking at her watch. ''She's already gone.''

Mark appeared to visibly shrink.

''Mark, what's wrong? Nicky called me yesterday and told me you guys had a fight and that she was going to Jamaica to see you so she could apologize. Then she came back today to get Tiandra 'cause she said she'd spoken to you and that you wanted her to bring Tiandra down.''

Mark put his face in his hands and shook his head. ''That's all she told you?''

''Yeah.''

''She didn't seem upset or anything?''

''No. She seemed really excited.''

''She was in a rush,'' he said as he moved past her into the living room.

She turned to face him. ''Well, it was about seven thirty and her plane was supposed to leave at eight thirty.''

''No. She wanted to get Tiandra and leave before I could stop her.

''What?'' Carol asked, totally perplexed.

''Nicole left me, Carol.''

''Left you? What are you talking about?''

Mark took a deep breath and proceeded to tell Carol everything. When he was finished, he felt drained.

Carol didn't know what to say. She felt responsible for letting

Nicole take Tiandra. But how could she have known? Nicole seemed so excited when she said she would be seeing Mark. She was angry that Nicole had lied to her so easily. She thought they had become good friends. She could have told her about it, but Nicole just assumed that Carol would not understand.

"Where could she have gone, Mark?"

"Do you think if I knew where she was I'd be sitting here?" he asked angrily.

Carol winced when he shouted at her but she didn't say anything. He was very upset and becoming increasingly angry, she noticed. She tried to reason with him. "She's probably in a hotel right now trying to figure this whole thing out. She's hurting, Mark."

"And I'm not? She thinks I was cheating on her."

"I know, but I can understand why. . . ." Carol stopped. Then she reasoned that she would probably take the brunt of his anger now, so why not. "Look, she feels like you betrayed her. I can imagine what I would think if I was in her place. What would you think, Mark? Once she realizes that running away is not going to change what happened, she'll be back. She loves you, Mark, that much I know. When she called me yesterday, she was so sorry for getting upset with you over such a silly thing as that play. All she wanted was to see you so you could kiss and make up. Love doesn't go away overnight, Mark. She'll be back."

Mark looked at Carol. Everyone was so sure that Nicole would be back, but they didn't know her like he did. They didn't live with her. Nicole could be stubborn at times and although he knew if he had the chance, he could make her understand the truth, he didn't think she'd even give it to him. He wished he could be as confident as everyone else was that she would see she was making a mistake and come back to him, but he had a deep feeling she wouldn't.

Chapter Seven

Two weeks had passed since Nicole walked out on Mark, and she'd never even called to let him know that she and Tiandra were all right. She had called her mother once but would not tell Mrs. Johnson where she was, either. Initially, Mark had trouble believing that Mrs. Johnson did not know where she was. When he thought about it, however, he knew she would not have kept it from him because she was just as worried and angry as he was.

He'd finally told his in-laws what had happened. He was surprised to find them so understanding. They had wanted to call the police but Mark did not want his private life made public, so he hired a private detective to find them. It had taken the detective only two days to find her.

Mark had seen Desiree at her parents' house the day before he hired the guy. She had been quite talkative. He should have guessed right off that she was up to something because she rarely had more than five words to say to him at a time. Finding out that Nicole was staying at her house really infuriated him. His first impulse had been to go there and confront them both, but he decided that would not be wise. As angry as he was, he was liable to hurt one or both of them. Instead, he decided to wait and see how long Nicole would take before she called him. The only thing he regretted about that decision was that he could not see his baby. He missed Tiandra terribly. Not seeing her or being able to hold her was killing him.

He told Nicole's parents where she was, but made them promise they would not interfere or say anything to Desiree.

They, too, had been very angry, but agreed to let him handle it.

Mark left his office that afternoon at three. He was physically and mentally exhausted. He had been so busy all week he had not had much time to concentrate on Nicole. He was grateful for this because this whole charade was beginning to take its toll on him. It was even hard for him to get dressed in the morning. Every time he entered his dressing room, he had to look at her things hanging there. He missed her so much it was painful. For a while he had even considered going against his original plan and going to Desiree's house to get her.

When he told his secretary, Denise, he was going home, she asked, "Are you all right, Mark?" She was genuinely concerned because Mark never left the office before five o'clock unless it was for business.

"I'm tired, Denise. I just want to go home and relax."

"You know, I didn't want to say anything, but you do look kind of tired. Why don't you take a couple of days off?"

"I might just do that," he said as he walked out.

Denise was really surprised at that. *He must be coming down with something.*

Nicole heard the keys in the lock and immediately sat down on the sofa to steel herself against the sounding off she knew she was about to receive. When the door opened, she actually held her breath.

Mark noticed her immediately upon setting foot in the apartment. A flood of emotions threatened to overtake him but he held them in check. He stood near the door staring at her. He wanted to go to her and hold her and tell her how much he loved and missed her, but at the same time, the anger that had been burning in him threatened to explode. He took a deep breath to collect himself. "Where's Tiandra?"

"In her crib." Even from the distance they were apart she

could clearly see the anger in his eyes. She was surprised that he hadn't yelled at her. She had expected no mercy from him. His silence threw her off.

Mark strode from the foyer and went to the nursery to see Tiandra. She was asleep. As he looked down at her, tears came to his eyes. He was so happy to see her. He didn't want to wake her, but he had to hold her. He picked her up gently and she immediately began to stir. ''Shh,'' he whispered softly as he kissed her on the top of her head. ''It's all right, precious. Daddy's got his baby. Daddy's here.'' He held her gently against his chest as tears fell from his eyes. He didn't want to let her go. He sat in the rocking chair next to her crib and cooed in her ear as she slept. ''I love you, Tiandra. Daddy loves you so much. I'm so happy you're home.'' He rocked her for almost a half hour. He had almost forgotten about Nicole.

Nicole had started to follow Mark into the nursery, but decided against it. She didn't want to wake Tiandra and she figured, correctly, that Mark wanted to be alone with her, so she sat where she was and waited for him to come out.

When he finally returned to the living room, Mark stood in the entranceway and stared at Nicole once more. After a while, he walked over to the bar, never taking his eyes off of her for more than a few seconds, and poured himself a generous scotch. He threw it down in one swallow. He then poured himself another. He took a sip from this one then slammed it on the bar. He took a deep breath and started toward her, but stopped before he came within an arm's length of her. In a soft but chilling tone, he asked, ''Where have you been?''

Nicole realized immediately that she had made a mistake by coming here without calling him first. She rose from the sofa and took a step toward him. ''Mark . . . ,'' she started.

''I ASKED YOU WHERE YOU'VE BEEN.''

Nicole jumped. His thunderous voice had taken away the last bit of courage she had left. She started to cry.

"What are you crying about?"

"You don't have to yell at me!"

Mark was so angry at her that he wanted to grab her, but was afraid he'd hurt her if he touched her right now. "How dare you take Tiandra and run out on me and not tell me where you are? How dare you?"

"You hurt me!" Nicole yelled in defense. "You were laid up in your hotel with that slut! What did you expect me to do?"

"You don't disappear! You had me going crazy wondering where you were, wondering if Tiandra was all right. You had no right to do that, no matter what you *think* I did! You had no right to take her like that! I would never do that to you. Never!"

Anger and disbelief clouded Mark's usually handsome features so thoroughly, his face looked deformed.

His eyes seemed to burn holes in Nicole's skin. She quickly realized that she had to diffuse this situation before it got out of control. "Look, Mark, I didn't come here to fight with you." She walked to the bar and with her back to him said, "I just came to tell you that I've found an apartment and I'm going to be moving in next week."

It took a couple of seconds before her words sank in. Mark turned to her. Her back was still to him. "What did you say?"

Nicole took a deep breath and faced him. "I said, it's over."

Mark was confused. *She's losing her mind.* "Are you crazy?" he asked aloud.

"Look, I've never cheated on you. You seem to find it necessary to sleep around, so I'll just step back so you can have all the women you want," Nicole said.

"What are you talking about? I didn't sleep with her. I didn't even touch her. Why won't you believe me?"

"Stop lying to me!"

"I'm not lying! Nothing happened!"

"Oh, she just magically appeared in your shower, right?"

"Nicole, I know what you saw, but I swear I never touched her. I was just as surprised as you were when she came out there like that. I know she shouldn't have been there, but I promise you it'll never happen again."

Using Desiree's words, Nicole said, "If it happened once, it could happen again."

Mark could not believe his ears. "Is that what your sister told you to say?"

"What sister?" Nicole asked, startled. "What are you talking about?"

"Desiree. Is that what she told you to say?"

"Desiree has nothing to do with this."

"Oh, are you telling me that she had no input in this?"

"Why would she?" she asked, her determination quickly fading.

"That's where you've been staying, isn't it?"

Nicole was shocked to find that Mark had known where she was. But she didn't admit it, nevertheless. "I haven't seen Desiree."

"Who's lying now, Nicole?"

"I am not."

"You're lying, Nicky. I know you've been staying with Desiree. I've known for over a week."

He never called her Nicky. "If you knew, why didn't you come there?"

"Because I wanted to see how long it would take you to come to your senses and bring your ass back home."

"I'm still leaving you," Nicole said as she turned away from him.

At hearing these words, Mark paused. He took a step toward her and asked, "Why?"

"Because this should have never happened!" she yelled as she faced him again. "You put us in this position. I was so worried that you'd still be angry with me and that you wouldn't want to see me. Then to find a naked woman in your room. Do you know how that made me feel? I wanted to die. I don't ever want to feel that way again.''

''Nicole, how do you think I felt? Do you think I wanted you to see that? I tried to think of some way to get her out of there before I even opened the door for you. Baby, she hadn't even been there ten minutes.''

''How'd she get in your bedroom?''

''She followed me. I . . .''

''What happens when someone follows you into your bedroom again? Every time you go away I'm going to be wondering if you're sharing your bed and bath with someone else. This is the second time you've let some woman get close to you like that. I won't live this way, Mark. I'd rather be alone.''

''Nicole.'' He put his arms around her. She didn't return his embrace. ''It'll never happen again. I swear, it'll never happen again. I don't want to lose you. I need you, Nicole. Please, don't do this. I need you.'' She still didn't move to embrace him but he didn't let her go. ''Hold me, Nicole. Please, hold me,'' Mark pleaded as he put her arms around him. But she let them drop as if they had no life at all. ''Don't you love me, baby? Have you stopped loving me?''

She didn't move or speak. Exasperated, Mark let her go and yelled, ''Why are you doing this? Why can't you forgive me? I was never untrue to you. I love you and I don't want to live without you, Nicole. Can't you understand that?'' With tears in his eyes, he said, ''I love you.''

Finally, she spoke. ''Why did you let this happen? Why? How am I supposed to trust you after this?''

''I've never lied to you. Never. You're the only woman in my life, baby. The only ones that matter to me are you and Tiandra,'' Mark insisted.

Nicole's sadness showed in her eyes as she looked at him. She was torn between the love she felt for him and the doubt she felt in her heart because of his carelessness. "I don't want to go through this again, Mark."

"Baby, I promise, you won't have to."

"Well, I don't know if I'm ready to take that chance."

Suddenly, he felt a tightness in his chest. He ignored it for the moment. "Nicole, please just . . ." Mark began, but stopped suddenly, clenching his teeth. The pain in his chest began to magnify. He was losing his breath. He grabbed the bar to steady himself. He looked to Nicole, his eyes begging for help.

"Mark? Mark, what's wrong?" she asked as she noticed his pain-stricken face.

He could not answer. *What's happening to me?* The pain was more than he could bear.

Nicole rushed to him as he lost his grip on the bar and sank to the floor. His head slammed against the metal base of one of the bar stools and knocked him unconscious.

"MARK!!!"

She laid him flat on the floor and placed her head on his chest to listen for his heart. It didn't seem to be beating and he was not breathing. "Oh my God," she moaned.

Immediately, without taking a second to think, she began administering CPR. "Please, God, don't let him die. Please. Don't let him die," she cried as she massaged his chest.

Suddenly, Angie entered the apartment.

Nicole yelled, "Angie! Call an ambulance! Hurry! I think Mark's had a heart attack."

Without hesitating, Angie dropped the packages she was carrying and ran to the phone. When she returned to the living room, Nicole was still kneeling over Mark. "What happened?"

"I don't know," Nicole said through her tears. "We were talking then all of a sudden he stopped, like he couldn't breathe and was in a lot a pain, then he collapsed."

Paramedics arrived at the penthouse fifteen minutes after Angie's call. They immediately began working on Mark. He was still unconscious, but he was breathing freely and, despite the praise she received from them for her quick thinking in administering CPR to Mark, Nicole was a nervous wreck.

Although they worked at a furious pace to get Mark out of the apartment, to Nicole it seemed as if they were taking forever. Actually, they had responded to the call and were there and gone in about twenty-five minutes.

When they arrived at the hospital emergency room, Nicole was immediately told to sit and wait in the visitor's waiting room. Of course, she protested. ''What do you mean, 'have a seat in the waiting room'? That's my husband in there!'' Nicole yelled hysterically.

''I understand that he's your husband, Mrs. Peterson, but there's nothing you can do for him now. Whatever has to be done will be taken care of by your husband's doctors. You would only be in the way, so please, sit down,'' the nurse said emphatically and empathetically. ''You'll be the first to receive any information on your husband's condition.''

Reluctantly, Nicole proceeded to the waiting room, but she was too nervous to sit still. She then remembered that she was the only person who knew Mark was there. She had to call her mother and Carol. With the occurrence of Mark's heart attack, Nicole forgot all about their situation. Until the moment he collapsed onto the floor in front of her, Nicole never realized how empty her life would be without him. At the thought of Mark dying, she began to cry once more. ''Please,'' she prayed softly, ''let him live. I need him. I don't want to live without him.''

The only information Nicole received in the thirty minutes she had been at the hospital was that Mark would have to undergo surgery. When Mark's physician, Dr. Boswell, told her he had suffered a severe heart attack, she cried. He also told her that Mark had had a series of minor attacks prior to this. He said it was not an uncommon occurrence in men Mark's age and with his background.

Mark had also suffered a concussion when he hit his head on the bar stool, but it was not serious. Dr. Boswell told Nicole that their main concern was a blockage in one of the primary arteries of Mark's heart, a thrombosis, that caused this attack. He asked her to sign surgical consent forms. Mark needed a bypass.

She nearly fainted upon hearing this. *How can this be happening?* Mark was so strong and healthy. At forty-two years of age, he was too young to be going through this. She signed the forms, but as Dr. Boswell left the waiting room, she pleaded, "Please, don't let him die."

Dr. Boswell looked at her with sympathetic eyes and said, "We'll do everything we can, Mrs. Peterson, I promise. If everything goes as well as we expect it should, Mark's chances of a full recovery are very good. I must commend you, though, because if you had not been trained in CPR and had panicked instead of keeping your head like you did, we probably would not be having this conversation right now. If he lives, it'll be because of you."

Dr. Boswell's words, although meant to give her hope, were instead a reminder that this whole thing was her fault.

Mr. and Mrs. Johnson were the first to arrive at the hospital after Nicole's call. Carol had not been home when Nicole called, so she left a message on her answering machine. Nicole was standing near a window in the waiting room, staring into space, when her parents arrived.

"Nicky," Mrs. Johnson said as she rushed toward her.

Nicole turned at the sound of her mother's voice and ran into her arms. "Mommy, he's in the operating room. They're performing bypass surgery on him. I'm so afraid. I don't want him to die," she cried.

Both of her parents hugged her, trying to comfort her. Mr.

Johnson whispered, "He'll pull through, baby. Don't worry. We've been praying for him. He'll pull through."

"Oh, Daddy, it's all my fault. I should have never left him."

"Shh. Come on now. It's not your fault. Stop blaming yourself. You don't know this wouldn't have happened if the circumstances were any different. Just thank God you were there with him," Mr. Johnson told her.

Nicole had not seen her parents in more than two weeks. The last time she spoke to them was when she called to tell them she and Tiandra were all right and that she was leaving Mark. She didn't know they also knew she had been at Desiree's house at the time.

Mrs. Johnson had been furious when Mark told her and Bill where Nicole was. She had wanted to call Desiree and tell her to mind her own business because she knew Desiree would be only too happy to think Nicole and Mark were breaking up. But she had promised Mark she would let him handle it. She wondered if he had gone to Desiree's house or if Nicole had finally realized she was being silly and decided to go home to her husband. She was dying to ask Nicole but she knew this was the wrong time.

Two more hours passed and still no one could tell her anything about Mark's operation. Nicole was going crazy wondering what was going on. She walked over to the nurses' station to see if there was any word from the operating room, never mind that she had just asked about ten minutes prior. As she stepped up to the desk, Carol turned the corner from the elevators.

"Nicky, where's Mark?" Carol called, all formalities aside.

Nicole turned in Carol's direction. She was glad to see her. "He's still in the operating room."

"The operating room? Why? What happened?"

"He had a heart attack and his doctor said the only chance he has to live was if they did a bypass," Nicole explained nervously.

"Oh my God. How long has he been in there?"

"Over two hours."

Carol started crying. Nicole moved to comfort her. "Get your hands off of me!" Carol demanded, throwing an angry look at Nicole. "If it wasn't for you, we wouldn't be here! I kept telling him to stop worrying about you since you didn't care about him, but would he listen to me? No! Every day he told me how much he wanted to go and get you and bring you home, but that he would wait instead to see how long it took you to come back to him. He was busting his ass every night at the damn office, sometimes until midnight so he wouldn't have to go home to an empty house and face the fact that you'd walked out on him. He couldn't sleep, he couldn't eat, he couldn't do anything because he was too busy worrying about you, and for what? You didn't even care enough to call him and tell him where you were. It's your fault that Mark had this damn heart attack. Your fault!" Carol broke down and cried, exhausted by the tongue-lashing she'd given Nicole.

Nicole, shocked by Carol s outburst, also cried. Carol had voiced the thoughts Nicole had been holding inside. To hear the anger in Carol's voice and to see the hurt in her eyes made her ashamed of the way she had behaved throughout this whole ordeal. "I'm sorry, Carol. I never wanted to hurt him. I love him."

"You don't love him! You don't care anything about him! Why are you even here?"

Mr. and Mrs. Johnson, hearing the commotion and seeing Carol's anger, felt it was time to intercede. "Carol, stop it! Stop it, now!" Mr. Johnson ordered.

"Don't tell me to stop! If it wasn't for your daughter, Mark would be fine."

"Would you please stop that yelling? This is a hospital," the desk nurse reminded them.

Mrs. Johnson, meanwhile, pulled Nicole back into the waiting room to a chair and tried to quell her tears.

"Carol, that's not fair," Mr. Johnson said. "You can't blame Nicky for Mark having a heart attack."

"He was under a lot of stress. He was worried all the time about her!" Carol said as she pointed an accusing finger at Nicole. "She took Tiandra away from him. You know how he loves her. You don't think that had any effect on him? He was a nervous wreck. All because of you, Nicky!"

Nicole was beside herself with grief now. Listening to Carol's judgment of her made her want to run and hide.

Carol walked over to where Nicole sat with her mother. "And on top of that, you have the audacity to come into my house, acting like nothing happened, and take Tiandra, lying to me! Telling me you're taking her to see Mark when you knew good and damn well that you were leaving him. How could you do that? How could you look me in the face and smile and just lie like that? We were supposed to be friends."

Nicole looked up at Carol. Guilt and shame overwhelmed her. She and Carol had been friends. She loved Carol like a sister.

Mr. Johnson, not wanting to see Nicole subjected to any more pain than she was already feeling, put his foot down. "Carol, that's enough." He did not raise his voice, but his tone quieted her. She threw him a mean look and went to sit across the room by herself.

Nicole was feeling worse than ever now. Carol was right. Nicole now saw that her handling of Mark's carelessness had been as thoughtless as his actions. She had not considered anyone's feelings but her own. It was clear to her that she had hurt many people by her thoughtlessness and even though Tiandra was still too small to even understand what was happening, Nicole knew she had hurt her and Mark, the two people she loved more than any others, most of all. Now she saw that she had hurt Carol, too. Her parents were probably also ashamed of her, even though they had not said so. She remembered when she called her mother and told her she was leaving Mark.

They had a big argument about it. Her mother had even hung up on her.

Nicole was sorry she had lied to Carol. Although Carol seemed to think it had been easy for her to do, it was one of the most difficult things she had ever done. She doubted if Carol would ever speak to her again. She would not blame her if she didn't.

With tears in her eyes, Nicole looked at her parents. They both sat quietly beside her. "Mommy, Daddy, I'm sorry if I hurt you. I seem to have done a great job of hurting everyone. I can understand if you're ashamed of me. I was too busy thinking about myself to worry about anyone else and you taught me better than that. I didn't mean to be so selfish." Mrs. Johnson took Nicole's hand. "I didn't mean to hurt anyone. I'm sorry," Nicole cried. She called across the room, "I'm sorry, Carol. Please forgive me."

"Nicky, it's all right," her mother said. Mr. Johnson nodded his head in agreement as he held Nicole's hand with his wife.

Carol looked over at them. She felt sorry for Nicole. She didn't really believe that she didn't care about Mark. On the contrary, she knew she did, but she was angry with her for lying to her, for thinking she could not trust her, and mostly for putting Mark through all the changes she had, when he had always loved and taken care of her without asking for anything but her love in return.

"Nicky, everybody makes mistakes," her father said. "No one is perfect. Everybody at some time or another is going to hurt or be hurt by someone they love. It doesn't mean you don't love that person or that they don't love you. You're only human, baby. There's no reason for you to be ashamed or to feel guilty. We know you didn't mean to hurt anyone and we all forgive you. Right?" He looked at Carol when he asked that.

"Right," Mrs. Johnson answered right away.

Carol looked at Mr. Johnson, then at Nicole who stole a glance at her. Carol grumbled, "I guess."

"And no one is ashamed of you, baby. We all love you and we know you love us."

Nicole looked into her father's eyes and saw a deep, understanding love. She put her arms around him and hugged him as she said, "I love you, Daddy."

He held her and whispered, "I love you, too, baby."

It was after midnight when Dr. Boswell and the surgeon that performed the bypass on Mark emerged from the operating room. When Nicole caught sight of them, she jumped out of her seat and rushed over to them. "Dr. Boswell . . ."

He cut her off before she could ask anything. "Mrs. Peterson, the surgery went very well. Although it's still too early to be sure, I think he has a better than average chance of recovering. We'll have to keep a close watch on him over the next seventy-two hours but I think he'll be just fine."

Nicole started crying again, this time from relief. "Can we see him?"

Carol stepped up behind Nicole. Dr. Boswell looked at her as he spoke. "Unfortunately, only his immediate family will be allowed to see him until he's out of intensive care."

"I'm his sister," Carol said. "I can see him, right?"

"Yes, you can. But he's still in the O.R. He'll be out in about a half hour. I'll let you see him in the recovery room, but only for five minutes. You're not supposed to be in there at all, but since you've been here all night, I'll bend the rules a little," Dr. Boswell said.

"Thank you," Carol said.

"Thank you, doctor," Nicole said as she hugged him and kissed his cheek.

He blushed slightly and said, "You're welcome. Mark is a strong man and he obviously has a strong will to live. Without that, he wouldn't have much of a chance, because that's one thing we can't give him."

They were all very happy the surgery had gone so well. Dr. Boswell seemed to be very optimistic about Mark's recovery and that gave them all hope.

As they turned back toward the waiting room, Carol grabbed Nicole's hand. Nicole turned to her, instantly steeling herself against another attack. "Nicky, I'm sorry I yelled and said those things to you. I didn't mean them. I was just so worried I guess I had to unload on someone. I'm sorry it had to be you. I know you want the same thing for Mark that I do, that he comes out of this okay. Do you think you can forgive me?"

Nicole was happy to hear Carol speak those words. She hugged her sister-in-law and said, "You had every right to say what you did. I was wrong. I shouldn't have lied to you. I hope you can forgive me for that. I'll never underestimate your friendship again, Carol. I promise. We are still friends, aren't we?'

Carol hugged her and said, "Of course we are. And family."

Chapter Eight

When Mark was brought out of the operating room, he was taken right to recovery. Since his doctor had given Carol and Nicole permission to see him for five minutes apiece, Nicole decided to go in last.

The nurse in charge of the recovery ward was very upset that Dr. Boswell told them they could see Mark, and she made no bones about her displeasure. "Can't you read? The sign says 'No Visitors.' You can't just come in here and disturb my patients," the nurse grumbled.

Nicole said with a plea in her voice, "He's my husband. We've been here for hours."

"I don't care who you are or how long you've been here, you're not supposed to be in there."

Carol, fed up with the nurse's insolence, said, "Dr. Boswell said we could see him, so we're going to see him. You can complain about it all you like. Knock yourself out!" she exclaimed, and walked into the room.

To Nicole, who was waiting outside with her parents, the five minutes that Carol was in with Mark seemed like five hours. When she came back out, she was crying. Her tears scared Nicole. "What's wrong, Carol? What's wrong?"

Through her sobs, Carol answered, "There are so many tubes and things all over him and he looks so pale."

Nicole's heart dropped. *Oh God, Carol, it sounds like he's dying.* She walked to the door of the room but hesitated a moment before she pushed the door open slowly. There were three other occupied beds in the room. One was covered with what looked like a huge plastic bag. Mark's bed was the first one on her left as she entered. "Oh my God," she moaned as she recognized him. There were, like Carol said, tubes everywhere. They were in his nose and mouth. They were in his arms and there was an enormous bandage on his chest from the surgery.

"Mark," she lamented softly. "Oh, Mark." She cried quietly as she watched him lying motionless. If not for the monitor reading his heartbeat, she would not have been able to tell if he was alive. She walked over to his bedside. Nicole leaned over and kissed his cheek; she got a chill when she noticed how cold he was. She caressed his head and face as she whispered to him, "I'm sorry, Mark. Please get better. I love you. I don't want to lose you. I can't lose you." She laid her head next to his on the pillow and gently kissed his face over and over. She held his limp hand in hers.

As she watched him, her life with him flashed before her eyes; their meeting on her first day of employment at his firm, their meeting in Jamaica, the first time he kissed her, their wedding day and honeymoon, the birth of Tiandra and the look on his face when she discovered him with his ex. All of these visions came to her within the space of a few seconds. She knew she could never live without him. He was everything that she lived for.

"Your five minutes is up! You have to leave, now!!" The irritating nurse was standing in the doorway ready to evict her. Nicole was too upset to tell her what she really felt. Mark's health was more important to her than some insensitive nurse's attitude.

Nicole kissed him on his forehead and whispered, "I love you, Mark. I'm leaving now but I'll be back in the morning, honey. Don't worry, I'll never leave you."

She kissed him again and slowly walked out.

Mark was in the intensive care unit for five days. He was unconscious the entire time. Nicole and Carol were at the hospital with him every day. Although they were worried because of his unconscious state, Dr. Boswell assured them that his condition was improving steadily. Since there was no damage to the brain, he assured them there was little reason to worry.

On the sixth day after his surgery, when Nicole arrived at the hospital, Mark was no longer in the ICU. She went to the nurses' station to find out where they had moved him.

The nurse on duty explained, "Oh, don't worry, Mrs. Peterson. He woke up early this morning so they've taken him downstairs for testing. They'll probably be bringing him back up in about an hour or so."

"Oh, good. Thank you." Nicole was excited that Mark's condition had improved so much and that she would be able to apologize to him soon. She couldn't wait to tell him that she, too, wanted them to spend the rest of their lives together. While she waited for Mark to be brought back to the floor, she called Carol and her parents to tell them the good news.

When Mark's tests were completed, he was placed in a private room.

Carol had arrived while Nicole was waiting for him to be brought back upstairs. Dr. Boswell spoke to Nicole and Carol before they went in to see Mark. He told them Mark was doing very well and that his recovery was progressing better than expected. He also said that if Mark continued on the same positive course, he would be able to go home in a week and continue his convalescence there.

After speaking to Dr. Boswell, they went in to see him together. When they entered his room, Mark was sitting up in bed. His eyes were closed but he was awake. The tubes that had been in his nose and mouth had been removed. Considering all that he had been through, they both thought he looked well.

"Hi, Mark," Carol said as she stepped over to his bed and kissed his forehead.

He opened his eyes and smiled weakly at the sight of his sister.

"How are you feeling?" she asked.

"Okay, I guess," he said softly. He didn't notice Nicole right away. When she spoke, his body visibly stiffened.

"Hi, Mark." Nicole started to move closer to his bed but the look in his eyes stopped her in her tracks.

"What are you doing here? You couldn't wait until I got out of the hospital to tell me again that you're leaving? Did you think I'd forgotten? I didn't forget. Why don't you just go? Just get out of here!" Mark yelled as loudly as his condition would allow.

Nicole was stunned. "Mark. I'm sorry, I love you."

"You don't care about me! Are you scared that I might live long enough to change my will and you won't get anything from me? Is that it?"

"Mark!" Nicole cried, shocked by his accusation.

"Mark!" Carol chorused, equally shocked.

"Get her out of here, Carol. I don't want her here."

"Mark, she said she's sorry," Carol said, defending Nicole.

To Nicole, Mark said, "I don't need you feeling sorry for me. I don't want your damn sympathy. I just want you to get the hell out of here."

"Mark, calm down," Carol urged.

Nicole was distraught. She didn't know what to do or say. She could not believe Mark was saying these things to her.

"Get her out of here!" Mark yelled again. His breathing was becoming labored.

Nicole could see that he was having difficulty catching his breath. "Mark, please take it easy," she begged.

"Get her out of here," he ordered Carol.

Carol turned to her with watery eyes and said, "Nicky, please wait outside."

Nicole ran from the room in tears.

"Mark, calm down. You're not supposed to get excited like this."

"I don't want her here."

"Mark, she's sorry. She knows what she did was wrong and she wants to make it up to you," Carol said, pleading Nicole's case.

"She walked out on me. I didn't leave her. She told me it was over. Now, all of a sudden 'cause she thinks I m dying, she's changed her mind. No!"

"Mark, please calm down," Carol said, crying for Mark as well as for Nicole.

"After all I've done for her. I never asked her for anything. Never. This is the thanks I get. I don't need it. Do you hear me, Carol? I don't need this crap."

"Can't you give her another chance?"

"Give her another chance? Have you forgotten how she totally disregarded my feelings and assumed the worst about me? Why should I give her another chance?"

"Don't you love her anymore?"

"What's love got to do with this?"

She didn't know what to say to that. She knew Mark was upset already and she did not want to upset him any more. "All right, Mark, let's drop it. You're not supposed to be getting all worked up like this."

"Then keep her out of here."

Carol stared at her older brother sympathetically. He would not look at her, though. She could see he was fighting back tears. Her heart was breaking for him and Nicole. They were both so stubborn and so proud that they hurt themselves by trying to hurt each other. She wanted to talk to Mark and try to make him understand this, but she could not risk exciting him anymore. That would be too dangerous for him. She knew Nicole would be devastated when she told her that Mark did not want to see her. It was bad enough that Nicole already felt she was to blame for Mark's heart attack. This would really kill her. Carol hated being the bearer of bad news.

When Nicole ran from Mark's room, she went straight to the ladies' room. As she sat in the stall crying her eyes out, she realized she had made the biggest mistake of her life by not giving Mark the chance to explain what had happened in Jamaica. She knew, too, that because of her selfishness, she had lost the best man she had ever known. How could she ask him to give her another chance? She had walked away from him when he asked her to hear him out.

"Nicky, are you in here?"

Nicole recognized Carol's voice. She was too embarrassed even to face her. She did not answer but when she tried to choke back a sob, Carol heard her and said, "Please come out."

Nicole stayed in the stall, crying.

"He doesn't mean what he said, Nicky. You know he doesn't mean to hurt you. He loves you," Carol tried to convince her.

"Maybe he used to, but he doesn't anymore."

"Nicky, come out, please?"

Nicole did not really want to be alone, so she unlatched the door to the stall.

"Come here," Carol beckoned to her. She did not want to see Nicole and Mark break up. She knew the love they had for each other was good for both of them. Mark had never been as happy before as he was since he met Nicole. She had changed him, probably without even trying. Granted, outwardly he seemed to have it all, but Nicole brought out the best in him.

When Nicole walked out on Mark, he had wanted nothing more than for her to come back to him. Now, even though it seemed that Mark's heart attack triggered a longing in her, Nicole wanted to come back and Mark would not hear of it.

Carol had comforted Mark when Nicole deserted him, now she was comforting Nicole because Mark would not have her. She hated being in the middle, but she loved both of them and wanted them to be happy. She knew the only way they would be was if they were together.

"Carol," Nicole cried as she moved into her outstretched arms, "he hates me."

"He doesn't hate you, Nicky. He loves you," Carol said through tears of her own.

"I don't want to leave him. I didn't mean all those terrible things I said to him. Can't you tell him that for me? Tell him I didn't mean to hurt him. Tell him I love him and I don't want to live without him."

Carol didn't know how to tell her that Mark did not want to hear anything about her right now. She didn't want to upset him either, and take a chance on him having another attack.

"Do you think I could see him tomorrow? I know he doesn't want to see me now and I understand why, but do you think he'll talk to me tomorrow?" Nicole asked hopefully.

"Maybe you should wait until he goes home before you try to talk to him. You know how Mark can be sometimes," Carol said, trying to gently tell her that he didn't want to see her.

Nicole looked into Carol's eyes for a moment before she spoke. "He won't talk to me at all, will he?" When Carol did not answer, Nicole stepped over to the sink and turned on the faucet. She pulled a paper towel from the dispenser and wet it and began to wipe her face. Carol stayed where she was. "I don't blame him, you know," Nicole said quietly. "I don't blame him if he never speaks to me again. He always took such good care of me and I really hurt him." Although she was wiping away the tears on her face, their flow did not slow down. "I love him, Carol. I've never loved anyone as much as I love him. I don't know how I'm going to live without him. I took him for granted. I guess I just figured he'd always love me."

"Mark does still love you, even if he won't admit it now. When he goes home and sees you're not there, he'll realize that he needs you just as much as you need him. You know how stubborn he is. He's got so much pride, Nicky, that sometimes it blinds him. When he's home alone with time on his hands, he'll think about how much he misses you and he'll ask you to come back to him," Carol said, believing it to be so.

"No, he won't. The only thing he'll call me for is to bring Tiandra to him. He'll want to see her, not me."

"Nicky, don't give up hope. Do you think he'll be happy without you?"

"He'll learn to be if he's not already," Nicole assured Carol.

"You're giving up."

"What do you want me to do? You saw how he reacted when he saw me. Couldn't you see the hate in his eyes? He'll never forgive me and I can't expect him to. I wouldn't forgive him, I wouldn't listen to him, I wouldn't even let him touch me when he begged me. He begged me, Carol, but I wouldn't. I know how much pride he has. He was willing to take me back once, but not anymore."

Carol did not want to believe Nicole was right, but she thought she knew Mark better than Nicole did and she had him pretty well read. He would be hard-pressed to give her another chance.

"At least I have Tiandra. Even if Mark never wants to be with me again, I'll always have a part of him in her," Nicole said sorrowfully.

"I'll talk to him, okay?" Carol said as she put her arm around Nicole's shoulder.

Nicole did not respond. She knew it would do no good.

Chapter Nine

With the threat of Mark dying and the realization that she did not want to live without him, Nicole gave up the apartment she had been planning to move into. When Mark came home from the hospital, Nicole was at the penthouse to greet him even though he would not see her while he was hospitalized.

Yvonne and Lucien had come up from Jamaica a few days before to visit Mark. Lucien and Carol escorted him home from the hospital. Yvonne had stayed with Nicole and Tiandra.

Yvonne was sitting in the living room holding Tiandra when they arrived. Nicole was in the bedroom getting dressed. "Hi, guys," Yvonne said. "Welcome home, Daddy."

Mark's face lit up at the sight of Tiandra. In the past five weeks or so, he had seen her for a total of about ninety minutes. Seeing her now brought tears to his eyes.

"Mark, sit down," Carol said as she led him to the sofa.

Yvonne walked over and handed Tiandra to him. She kissed him on his cheek and asked, "How are you, Mark?"

He smiled at her and said, "Much better now."

He kissed Tiandra on her forehead and hugged her. He smelled her hair and kissed the top of her head. "You smell so sweet, Tiandra. God, it's good to hold you, baby,'' Mark said as he hugged her tighter. ''I've missed you so much, precious.''

''Mark, would you like me to fix you a drink or something?'' Carol asked.

''Yeah, a scotch and soda,'' Mark answered, knowing what her response would be.

''No alcohol, Mark. You know that,'' Carol scolded.

''I was just kidding, sis. A glass of water is okay, right?''

''Yes, you can have water. Yvonne, do you want me to get you anything?''

''No, thanks, Carol.''

''Lucien?''

''No, thanks.''

Nicole was very nervous about seeing Mark. She was unsure how he would react to her so she stayed out of view and listened a moment to try to get an idea of the kind of mood he was in. When she heard him joking with Carol about a glass of scotch, she decided he was probably approachable now, so she made her presence known.

Yvonne saw her enter the room, but Mark was playing with Tiandra and Lucien had his back to her, so they did not know she was there until she spoke. ''Welcome home, Mark.''

Mark's body tensed immediately at the sound of her voice, and he was slow in turning to face her. Carol had not told him Nicole was there and he knew she had kept that from him intentionally. He made no attempt to hide his displeasure upon finding her there.

Lucien looked from Mark to Nicole and cracked a nervous smile. ''Hey, Nicky. How are you doing, sweetheart?''

''Hi, Lucien. I'm fine.'' Nicole answered, never completely taking her eyes off Mark, who still had not responded to her.

Mark straightened himself on the sofa. Tiandra was lying beside him. He turned to face her. His face was expressionless but his eyes were as cold as ice. "What are you doing here? You told me you were moving out. Why haven't you gone?"

Nicole faltered but tried to remain calm as she said, "I gave the apartment up."

"Well, maybe you should find another one," he said, looking her square in the eye.

Nicole's resolve was quickly fading. "I thought you might need some help. Dr. Boswell said you have to take it easy for a while."

"I don't want your help, Nicole. I don't want anything from you."

Carol had returned by then. "Mark, Nicky's just trying to look out for you."

He turned to her and said, "Mind your business. This doesn't concern you, Carol."

"But, Mark . . ."

"Mind your business!" he said, with a look that eliminated further discussion.

"I love you, Mark," Nicole said with tears falling unrestrained.

Mark looked at her and for a brief moment, his heart softened. The next instant, however, he was again as cold as ice. "Save it."

Nicole lost all of her reserve and pleaded, "What do you want from me? What do you want me to do?"

Without hesitation, he answered, "I want you to leave. That's what you wanted before, now it's what I want."

"I said I was sorry, Mark. Can't you forgive me?"

"Do you hear what you just said, Nicole? Do those words sound familiar to you. What was your response to them, huh? Can you tell me that?"

"Where am I supposed to go?"

"Where were you when you walked out on me before? Go to your sister's house. That's where you ran before. Go cry to her because I really don't want to hear it!"

"Mark, take it easy, man," Lucien said. He could see that this was getting very heavy. He was embarrassed about being there as he knew Yvonne and Carol were, also, but he had to stop Mark before he got too worked up.

Mark turned to Lucien and said, "Take it easy? Get her out of my house!"

Nicole was crying hysterically. Yvonne went to her and took her back to the bedroom. Carol followed. Tiandra was also crying now as if she knew her parents were being torn apart.

Mark picked her up and tried to comfort her. "I'm sorry, Tiandra. I'm sorry. Shh, don't cry, baby. Daddy's sorry," Mark whispered to her. As he held her, he got up and walked to the other end of the room. His back was to Lucien, who was at a loss for words.

He tried to think of something to say to Mark to make him see that being unforgiving like Nicole had been was going to cause more pain than good. Nicole knew she had been wrong not to forgive Mark and she was paying for it, but now he was doing the same thing. Lucien could not see any good coming out of this.

Since Mark's back was to him, Lucien could not see that Mark was already in pain. Not physically, but emotionally. As he tried to comfort Tiandra, tears streamed down his cheeks. He loved Nicole beyond reason, but she had hurt him in a way he had never allowed anyone to hurt him and she had to pay for that. He couldn't let her think she could treat him any way she wanted and get away with it. He had never begged anyone for anything in his entire life, but he pleaded with her to give him a chance to explain and she just ignored him like he was a nobody.

He could not let her control him. He would never allow any woman to control him. She was the only woman he had ever let get close to him. She had been like an extension of him. He cried with her, to her and for her. *Never again.* When he thought of how he had let her inside his heart, he became angry.

He had trusted her never to hurt him and she almost destroyed his ability to think when she left him. *NEVER AGAIN!* He wanted to hate her, but he couldn't. Even after all the pain she caused him, he still loved her, but he would never tell her that again.

Nicole lay across the bed she had shared with Mark and cried uncontrollably. Carol and Yvonne tried consistently to comfort her, but nothing they did or said seemed to do any good. Naively, she'd thought Mark would be happy that she had changed her mind, but now she knew he would never love her again and for that she was very sorry. They'd had a wonderful life together. He'd given her everything she had ever wanted. Her heart would melt a little every time he told her "I love you," and he told her quite often. He said he didn't want to ever have her wondering if he loved her or not, so he refreshed her memory every day. Her life with Mark had been heaven. She knew life without him would be hell.

Suddenly, she sat up on the bed and wiped her eyes. Carol and Yvonne were on either side of her. She looked from one to the other. Both of them had been crying, too, she saw. She tried to smile at them, but it was more like a grimace of pain. Her heart was in pieces. "I guess I asked for this. Mark always did give me whatever I asked for," Nicole said, trying to choke back a sob.

Neither Yvonne nor Carol knew what to say to her.

"I'd better start packing." She rose from the bed and walked to the closet and took out a suitcase and placed it, opened, on the bed.

Yvonne and Carol looked at one another.

Nicole went to the bureau and began to remove her clothing from the drawers. She walked back to the bed and placed the items in her arms down on it. Very meticulously, she began to fold the items and lay them in the suitcase. Tears fell steadily from her eyes. "I remember the first time I came here. I was so shocked by the size of this bedroom. Now, for some reason, it seems so small."

Yvonne and Carol still did not say a word.

As Nicole packed, she continued to ramble about herself and Mark and things they had done since they had been together. She did not get a response from either girl, but she did not really want one. Sometimes during her rambling she would chuckle about something she said, but she never stopped crying.

Yvonne sat there listening to Nicole's heart breaking and she, too, cried.

"I guess I'll go to my mother's house for a while," Nicole said suddenly.

Carol finally asked, "Nicky, are you all right?"

She smiled through her tears and bravely said, "Oh, yeah, don't worry about me. I'll be fine." She wiped her eyes and said, "I'll be right back." She started toward the living room but paused before she reached the entranceway and took a deep breath before continuing.

Mark was still holding Tiandra, but now he was sitting at the bar. Lucien was standing on the other side. Neither man spoke. Mark felt Nicole's presence and turned to look at her. She stood where she was, not able to speak for fear that she would start to cry again. She returned his stare, although his was one of icy indifference while hers was filled with sadness.

Finally, she broke the silence. "Are you going to take her from me?"

Mark was slow in answering. "No."

Nicole wanted to run to him and beg his forgiveness. She wanted to tell him she would do anything he asked if he would take her back. Thinking this made her tears flow unbound.

Mark misunderstood her fresh tears and said, "I'd like her to stay with me for a few days since I haven't seen her in so long."

Nicole, trying hard to regain her composure, asked, "Can I just hold her for a minute?"

Mark got up and walked over to her. As he handed Nicole their sleeping daughter, he felt a sudden urge to hold her and tell her that everything would be all right. But he didn't.

When she took Tiandra from him, Nicole looked into Mark's eyes and read his thoughts. She saw the love there but only for an instant before he put the wall back up.

Nicole held Tiandra to her breast and kissed her on top of her head. She turned away from Mark so he would not see her crying. "I love you so much," she whispered in Tiandra's ear, but the words were meant for Mark as well. When she handed Tiandra back to him, she whispered, "Thank you."

Mark remained silent.

Nicole went back into the bedroom and walked straight into the dressing room. She put on her leather jacket then grabbed her pocketbook. Yvonne and Carol were still there and they looked at Nicole questioningly. She walked over to the bed, closed the suitcase and began to lift it off the bed.

"Nicky . . ." Carol began.

"Thank you both for being here. I've got to go now," Nicole said, her eyes watering again. "I'll call you. Bye." She picked up the suitcase and started out.

Yvonne got up from the bed and called after her, "Nicky, wait."

"I'll be all right, Yvonne. Don't worry," she said through her tears. She walked to the front of the apartment and put her suitcase down in the foyer. "Bye, Lucien."

Lucien walked over to her and hugged her. "Take care, beautiful. Be strong."

She hugged him back, clinging to him for a few seconds before she released him. "Good-bye, Mark," she said, trying hard not to cry.

"Where will you be?"

"At my mother's house." He was glad she was not going back to Desiree's house.

"Do you need any help?" Lucien asked.

"No, thank you. I'll make it."

She turned and walked back to the foyer to leave. Mark followed her. She picked up her suitcase and placed her hand on the doorknob. She turned back to Mark, who stood at the foot of the stairs in the living room and said, "I'm sorry, Mark." Then she walked out.

After Nicole left, Mark took Tiandra into the nursery and laid her down. He then went back into the living room, through the terrace doors and stood against the railing. As he looked out over the city, he wondered if he had made a mistake. The look in Nicole's eyes when she turned back to him made his heart break. He had never seen such dejection and hurt before in his life. He was suddenly very depressed. He did not like hurting her. *Why did she have to be so stubborn when I asked for forgiveness?*

"Do you think it was wise to let her go?" Lucien asked as he joined Mark on the terrace.

Mark did not respond right away. He wished Lucien would leave. "What should I have done?" Mark asked, never turning to face him.

"Talk to her."

"I tried that once."

"So try again."

"She chumped me, man! Nobody chumps me," Mark exclaimed as he turned to Lucien.

"Mark, we're not talking about some babe you just had a fling with. She's your wife."

"Yeah, that's right. She's my wife and I'm her husband. So why did she put me through all of those changes? She couldn't even find it in her heart to listen to me, why should I be any different?"

"Because she was hurting, man."

"And I'm not?"

Lucien took three steps toward him. "Come on, Mark. What would you have done if you'd walked in and found her the way she found you?"

"I didn't do anything wrong except make an error in judgment and I apologized for that."

"And that makes it all right?"

"Look, she didn't want to hear anything I had to say. She wouldn't talk to me about it. She wouldn't listen to me. She just ran off. Was that all right?" Mark said, trying to justify his reasoning.

"No, she was wrong to do that, but she's apologized for that, too."

"Only after she thought I was going to die," Mark said defensively.

"Yeah, and she realized the mistake she was making," Lucien countered.

"And if I'd never gone into the hospital, she'd still be gone," Mark answered.

"You don't know that."

"You weren't there. You don't know what happened."

"I know she's sorry she put you through all of that and you know it, too." Mark didn't reply. "Why don't you put your pride aside and go get your woman, man."

"That's all you think it's about, right? It's not about pride. I gave her everything and I never asked her for anything. One time I do something stupid like this and she's ready to leave me without even listening to what I have to say. I never even touched that woman but would she believe me? No! She doesn't even trust me. I know I'm not perfect but neither is she. I need someone I can count on, who'll have my back, good or bad!"

"She's down for you, Mark. You know that."

"Maybe once, but I've already seen where she is when the chips are down."

"Who was at that hospital with you every night? Who was

there when you opened your eyes for the first time in a week? How much more down can the chips be if you're so close to death that no one knows if you'll live or die? Doesn't that count for something?''

"Look, I don't want to talk about her anymore."

"Mark, don't ignore it."

Angrily, Mark exclaimed, "I said I don't want to talk about her, so drop it!"

Lucien had hit a sore spot. He knew the reason Mark did not want to talk anymore was because Lucien was telling it true, and the truth hurt. "All right. I'll drop it." Lucien immediately left the terrace to get Yvonne.

She and Carol had been listening to them arguing.

Lucien said, "Come on, baby. Let's go."

Yvonne hesitated. She studied Mark on the terrace. His back was to them. His posture was deflated. Mark, who always stood tall and proud, was a picture of sadness. She walked over to him and put her hand on his shoulder.

"Mark." He turned to her and the pain in his heart was evident. "Take care of yourself. Call us if you need anything, all right?" she asked softly.

He nodded.

She kissed his cheek and said, "See ya."

"Mark, do you want me to stay?" Carol asked him from the terrace door.

"No, I'm kind of tired. I'd like to be alone for awhile."

"All right." Carol walked over and hugged him. She kissed him, too, and said, "Call me if you need me."

"I will," Mark said softly.

As Carol and Yvonne turned to rejoin Lucien in the living room, Mark caught Lucien's eye. Lucien did not say a word but he didn't have to. His eyes said, "You're making a mistake."

He shifted his gaze elsewhere. Once they were gone, he went back to the nursery. He sat in the rocking chair across from Tiandra's crib and studied his sleeping daughter. She was a dream come true for him. Nicole always told him Tiandra was his spitting image, but he thought she favored her. As he looked at her now, he saw Nicole. They had been so happy together. *What happened?* As he looked around him, he saw Nicole everywhere. She had decorated this room by herself while she was still pregnant. He had wanted to hire someone to do it, but she would not hear of it. She said she wanted the baby's room to have a "loving touch" a stranger could not give it. She had done an excellent job of it, too. She had been so proud of herself. He had been proud of her, too. He missed her. Lucien did not understand. No one understood how he was feeling. He had never been so alone in his life.

Chapter Ten

A week later, Nicole called Mark. She had wanted to call him every day since she'd left but could not stand the idea that he might hang up on her, or worse, tell her he wanted a divorce. She had spent the last few days crying her eyes out merely at the thought.

She had waited until she was in her parents' apartment alone. She sat down in the kitchen and picked up the receiver. She held it in her hand with her finger on the switchhook for close to five minutes before she decided to go through with it.

By the third ring there was still no answer and she was about to hang up when a female voice she did not immediately recognize answered. "Hello." Nicole thought, *he's found someone else already.* "Hello," the woman said again.

Nervously, Nicole responded, "Hello."

"Who's this?"

"This is Nicole. Who's this?" she said, more firmly.

"Hi, Nicky. This is Carol. You don't recognize my voice?"

Nicole let out a deep breath. "Hi, Carol. No, I didn't recognize it at first."

"How're you doing?"

She could hear the concern in Carol's voice. "I'm okay. How are you?"

"I'm fine," Carol said.

"How's Tee?" Nicole asked of her daughter.

"She's fine. I just finished feeding her. Mark's here, do you want to talk to him?"

"Not if he's busy," she said, trying to avoid the inevitable.

"He's not. He's right here."

Mark was changing Tiandra's diaper when the telephone rang. Carol had just come from the kitchen after putting the remainder of her bottle in the refrigerator. She had been coming by every day, helping him with Tiandra, although Angie was there. The only thing that bothered him about her coming over was that she would talk about Nicole constantly. He did not want to hear anything about Nicole. It was not because he didn't miss her; he did, but he didn't *want* to and the more he thought about her or heard about her, the harder it was to forget her.

He wanted to forget how to love her and want her and need her. He wanted to forget the sound of her laughter, but he couldn't. He wanted to forget the feel of her body beneath his, but he couldn't. He wanted to forget the softness of her skin, and the scent of her hair, but no matter how he tried, he couldn't. As if she was standing right before him, he could see her smile and the twinkle in her eye that always accompanied it. She was everywhere he looked. He wanted to forget how he had made a fool of himself by loving her the way he did. He wanted to forget that she could not, or would not, forgive him. He wanted to forget that she was the most important person in his life.

He finished changing Tiandra and walked into the living room with her. Carol was still on the phone. He heard her saying, "He's right here."

"Who's that?"

"It's Nicky."

He paused. He didn't want to talk to her.

Carol covered the mouthpiece and held the receiver out to him. "Here, Mark, talk to her."

He took the receiver from her and Carol took Tiandra from him. He hesitated before he put the phone to his ear. "Hello."

Nicole heard Mark asking who was on the line. She also heard Carol's answer. *Why is it taking him so long to come on the line?* She figured he probably did not want to talk to her. She should have known. She knew it would be a mistake to call him. If he had wanted to talk to her, he would have called. She was about to hang up when she heard his voice on the line. Her stomach did a somersault. "Hello, Mark," she said nervously.

"Hello, Nicole."

"How are you?"

"I'm fine. How are you?"

"I'm fine," she lied.

Silence.

"Is something wrong?" he asked finally.

"What?" she asked, puzzled.

"I asked if something's wrong? You called, I thought maybe something was wrong."

"Oh, no. No, everything's all right. I was just calling to see how Tiandra was doing," Nicole said quickly.

"She's fine."

"Is she giving you a lot of trouble?"

"She's no trouble at all."

"That's good. I miss her." Mark did not respond. "So how are you feeling?" she asked.

"I'm doing fine. No problems."

"That's good." *I miss you, too,* she wanted to say. "Well, I guess I'll let you go back to what you were doing. Sorry if I bothered you," she said, regretting her decision to call him.

"Okay, bye."

"Bye," she whispered.

Mark was grateful that Carol had left the room when he took Nicole's call. Hearing her voice made his blood stir. He was glad she'd called, even if it was only to inquire about Tiandra. He wanted to tell her that he needed her, but he remembered how she responded the last time he told her that. She had not cared. He was glad he did not have to see her. He was not sure he would be able to control his emotions if he saw her, and he had made a promise to himself that he would never let his heart rule his thinking again.

Chapter Eleven

A week later, Mark decided to go to Jamaïca. He had not gotten the chance to meet with his people the last time he was there because of the scene with Nicole and Diane. His doctor did not want him going to work, but he never said anything about him visiting his resort. Besides, Mark figured while he was there he could relax and maybe get Nicole off his mind.

He thought about her constantly. He tried to keep himself occupied but there was only so much he could do sitting up in his apartment. If not for Tiandra, he would probably go stir crazy. He was glad she was there with him. She occupied most of his time and, although she slept a lot, he would hold her while she slept and that was always comforting to him.

He knew he would have to call Nicole to tell her of his plans because he wanted to take Tiandra with him. He was not sure whether she would give him a fight about it, but he was determined to take her nevertheless.

When he called her mother's house that Thursday afternoon, he was caught off guard when she answered. She sounded quite cheerful. *Maybe she doesn't miss me at all,* he thought. "Hello, Nicole. This is Mark." Silence on the other end. *Maybe she does miss me.*

"Hi, Mark," she said quietly.

"Listen, I'm calling to let you know that I'm going to be flying to Jamaica on Saturday. I want to take Tiandra with me, if it's all right with you."

"Oh. How long will you be gone?"

"I'm not sure yet. Probably a couple of weeks."

"Did Dr. Boswell say it was okay for you to go?" she asked with genuine concern.

"I didn't ask him, but there shouldn't be any problems as long as I take it easy."

"Is that why you're going? For a vacation or to work?"

She knows me too well. "Well, I'll probably be meeting with a few of my people while I'm there, but mainly for a vacation."

"You're leaving Saturday?"

"Yeah."

"I won't see Tiandra before you go, will I? I miss her."

"I'll bring her by later this evening. I won't be leaving until Saturday afternoon anyway."

"Are you going alone?" Nicole then asked.

"What?"

"Are you going alone? Is anyone going to be helping you with Tiandra?"

"No. She'll be okay. She's no trouble."

"But what about when you're at your meetings?"

"I'll ask Yvonne to watch her for me then. There won't be that many. I told you I'm going down to relax."

"I just thought if you needed some help with her while you were busy, I wouldn't mind going down to help you."

He wanted to say yes, but instead he said, "No, that's not necessary. We'll be fine."

Of course you will. You don't need me anymore. Trying to sound as nonchalant as he did, Nicole asked, "What time will you bring her over tonight?"

"Around seven o'clock."

"Fine. I'll see you then," was her response before abruptly hanging up the phone.

He was surprised that she had offered to come with him. He had almost said yes, but then he would have been letting his heart rule his mind once again.

When Mark brought Tiandra to the Johnsons' house that evening, Nicole was not there. She had purposely found a errand that needed tending to so she would not be there when he arrived. She still was not quite ready to face him without tears.

"Hello, Mark," Mrs. Johnson said as she opened the door when he arrived.

He kissed her cheek. "Hi, Mom. How are you?"

"I'm fine. How are you? You're looking well."

"I'm doing better, thanks."

She turned her attention to Tiandra. "Hello, precious. Come to Grandma." She took Tiandra from Mark and walked into the living room and began to remove her outer clothes.

"Come in, Mark. Sit down."

"Thank you. Is Nicole here?"

"No, she's not," Mrs. Johnson said.

"Oh." He couldn't hide his disappointment at not seeing her.

As Mrs. Johnson removed the last of Tiandra's outer garments, she held her up and kissed her cheek. "My goodness, you're getting so big, Tiandra. My goodness gracious."

"Would you tell Nicole that I'll be here around two o'clock on Saturday to get her?"

"All right. I understand you're taking her to Jamaica with you."

"Yes."

"Shouldn't you be taking it easy?"

"Well, I'm going down there basically for a vacation."

Mrs. Johnson looked at Mark with skepticism. "I hope you won't be pushing yourself, Mark. You've got plenty of people down there that can take care of that place for you."

"I'm not pushing myself. I feel fine."

She continued to look at him skeptically.

Mark was beginning to feel very uncomfortable under his mother-in-law's scrutiny.

Mrs. Johnson could contain herself no longer. "Mark, what's going on with you two?"

Mark looked at Nicole's mother and swallowed deeply. He was in no mood to discuss the events of the past weeks with her or anyone else. "Mom, please, I'd rather not discuss it."

"I think you owe me an explanation."

Mark could not believe his ears. "Why?"

"Because my daughter, who by the way happens to be your wife, is living in my house, when she belongs in yours. I find it puzzling that you don't think I'm entitled to an explanation." She held Tiandra and bounced her on her knee the whole while. She did not raise her voice, although she was steaming at Mark *and* Nicole.

Mark got up. He was trying to control his temper, that he felt rising to the surface. "She wanted to leave, so I let her."

"That was before you went into the hospital. You know she didn't want to leave once you took ill," Mrs. Johnson reminded him.

"I'm not a yo-yo. You can't just tell me something one day and turn around and change your mind the next and expect me to change mine."

"Come on, Mark. How'd all of this start? I'm sure you remember."

Mark was furious that she would bring this up. He could not say to her what he wanted to, out of respect for her being Nicole's mother. He took a deep breath instead. "I thought you made it your business not to get involved in your children's marital disputes?"

"Well, since she's run here for shelter, I am involved. You and Nicole are making me sick with this stupidity. First her, then you. Why the hell did you get married in the first place if you're not going to live together?"

"This was her idea, not mine!" Mark said, his anger now apparent in his voice.

"Oh, and I guess you're too much of a man to try and rectify it, right?"

He was fuming.

"Neither of you are taking your daughter into consideration in any of this," she said, her anger also very apparent.

To keep from saying something to Mrs. Johnson that he might later regret, Mark waved his hand and said, "Look, I'm outta here." He started toward the door.

"Running away is really big of you. Mark."

He turned to her and said, "Mrs. Johnson, you don't understand anything about what's happening. You don't understand anything about what I've been going through and until you can put yourself in my shoes and live my life for me, I think you should mind your business. Why don't you talk to your daughter? Why don't you ask her why she's staying here?"

"I know why she's here," Mrs. Johnson yelled at him.

"No," Mark said, shaking his head. "It's obvious, Mrs. Johnson, that you don't know anything!" He turned and walked out, slamming the door behind him.

* * *

On Saturday, when Mark came by to pick Tiandra up for their trip to Jamaica, Nicole was waiting for him. "Hello, Mark," she said as she stepped aside for him to enter.

"Hi. Is your mother here?" he asked right away. Nicole looked at him questioningly before she answered. Mark clarified. "I wanted to apologize to her. I'm sure she told you I lost my temper the other night when I was here."

"She said you'd had an argument."

"Yeah."

"She's in the kitchen."

"Can I go in?"

"Sure."

Mark walked into the kitchen. Mrs. Johnson was on the telephone. When she noticed him standing in the doorway, she told the person on the line that she would speak to them later and hung up. "Yes?" she said coolly.

"Hi, Mom. I wanted to apologize to you for my behavior the other night. It was totally uncalled for. I hope you'll accept my apology," he said humbly.

"Thank you, Mark. I do. And I hope you'll accept mine. You were right, I should mind my own business."

"Your daughter should be your business."

She appreciated that comment.

"I didn't want to leave and have this hanging over me because I know I wouldn't be able to enjoy my vacation if I thought we couldn't be on good terms. You're Tiandra's grandmother and Nicole's mother and you've always been like a mother to me. I'll never disrespect you like that again."

Mrs. Johnson smiled at him and said, "Thank you, Mark. I wouldn't want us to be on anything but good terms either. I want you to feel that you're always welcome in my home."

"Thank you." He moved closer and gave her a hug and kissed her cheek.

"Have a safe trip," Mrs. Johnson said.

"Thank you."

Nicole was happy that they had made up, even if she and Mark had not. She did not want her whole family to be against him because she would never be. When he returned to the living room, Nicole had Tiandra ready, with her bag packed. "I'm glad that's all straightened out."

"Yeah, me, too. Do you have all of her things ready?" Mark asked, changing the subject abruptly.

Nicole looked at him, but he ignored her.

As she prepared Tiandra to leave, Nicole decided that she'd had enough. If Mark wanted to act as though he'd never cared for her, then so be it. *He wants to get on with his life, well, so will I.*

When Nicole finished wrapping Tiandra in her blankets, she hugged and kissed her before handing her to Mark. He took Tiandra, picked up her bag and turned to the door. Before walking out, he turned to her and said, "I'll see you when I get back." With those words, a feeling of déjà vu swept over him. He brushed it aside.

Nicole crossed her arms over her chest and said, "Have a good trip."

Chapter Twelve

During the two and a half weeks that Mark and Tiandra were in Jamaica, Nicole leased a two-bedroom apartment in Brooklyn Heights. She also figured she had better start looking for a job because once Mark filed for a divorce, which she was sure he would, she would probably have a hard time getting anything from him unless it was for Tiandra. Also, while they were away she went back to the penthouse to get the remainder of her belongings. She knew it was an oversight on Mark's part that he had not asked for the keys.

Nicole was glad he was in Jamaica, but she missed Tiandra. She decided that when Mark returned, she would make some kind of arrangement with her parents so he could go by their house to see Tiandra whenever he wanted. She did not want him to set foot in her apartment and going back to the penthouse was not an option.

Nicole had gotten used to living with Mark, so being in her own apartment again made her a bit apprehensive at first. She did not worry about security. Her building had lobby attendants, closed-circuit TVs on every floor, and was in a decent neighborhood, but the first two nights sleeping there alone, she was extremely lonely.

Mark's trip to Jamaica was a very relaxing one. With the exception of the two meetings he had with his hotel management, he spent his time lazing around either on the beach, by the pool or at Lucien and Yvonne's place. While he was at the resort, his employees waited on him hand and foot. They treated him like a king and he loved every minute of it.

When he first went to see Lucien and Yvonne, he was apprehensive because he and Lucien had parted on less than peaceful terms and he did not know whether Yvonne would bring up his situation with Nicole. When he apologized to Lucien for his inhospitable demeanor, Lucien waved it off and told him the incident was forgotten. He said he could understand that Mark had to work it out for himself. Mark was also grateful to Yvonne because she did not bring up Nicole once. She sensed that he was uncomfortable around her so she went out of her way to make him relax. She offered to keep Tiandra for a few days so he could really relax and he told her it was not necessary, but when she confessed that she wanted to baby-sit so she could "practice being a mommy," he could not refuse her.

* * *

Mark and Tiandra returned from their vacation on Wednesday, October twenty-fourth. The previous Monday, Nicole started a four-week temporary assignment at a bank that was only a few blocks away from the offices of Peterson & Company.

When Mark arrived at the Johnsons' home that afternoon, he was shocked to find that Nicole had moved out. He was disappointed she was not there. He missed her, although he did not let on that he did, and he wanted to see her. "Where is she staying?" he asked Mr. Johnson.

"She's got a nice place in Brooklyn. A two-bedroom apartment."

"In Brooklyn? Why Brooklyn?" he asked, more to himself than to her father.

"Well, it's a very nice building and the apartment is really very nice," Mrs. Johnson said.

"Can you give me her number there?"

"Sure, but she's at work right now," Mrs. Johnson explained.

"At work?" Mark questioned, not believing his ears. "Where?"

"At some bank. I can't remember the name of it right now. She's working through a temporary agency, right, honey?" Mr. Johnson said.

"That's right."

Mark wondered why she had gone back to work. She should know that he would give her anything she needed, even now.

On his way home, Mark thought about the actions Nicole had taken. He was angry that she had gone back to work. He was angry that she had moved into her own apartment. What was she trying to prove?

* * *

An hour before Nicole got off from work, she called her mother. "Hi, Mommy," she said cheerfully when her mother answered the phone.

"Hi, baby. Tiandra's here," Mrs. Johnson said right away.

"Ooh, they're back? Oh, good. How is she?"

"She's fine. She's taking a nap."

"What time did they get back?"

"Oh, I don't know. Maybe about an hour ago. Mark just left about twenty minutes ago."

"How'd he look? Did he look rested?"

"Yes, he did. He said he only attended one meeting with his people down there, the rest of the time he spent with Lucien and Yvonne."

"That's good. I'm glad he wasn't down there overworking himself."

"No, he said he wasn't."

It was eight forty-five by the time Nicole returned to her apartment with Tiandra. Her mother had suggested that Tiandra stay with her for the night since it was so late, and since Nicole would be bringing her back in the morning, but Nicole insisted on taking her home. She had missed her baby and wanted to spend time with her alone, no matter how little time it was.

At nine fifteen, Yvonne called her from Jamaica. "Hi, hon. What's up?"

"Hi, Yvonne. My baby's home," Nicole said happily.

"I know. Lucien and I took them to the airport this morning. How is my little sweetie?"

"She's trying to pull my earrings out of my ears right now," Nicole said, laughing.

"She's getting so big. I can't believe it. It wasn't that long ago since I last saw her."

"I know, she's growing like a weed. Yvonne, how's Mark? Did he take it easy?"

"Yes, he did. He surprised me and Lucien, too. A couple of days, he and Tee stayed with us here. He just lounged around the pool with Lucien. He took a couple of days off to hang out with Mark. I kept Tiandra a couple of days, too. I told Mark I was practicing being a mommy since me and Luce are trying to have a baby.''

''You are? I'm sure you're having lots of fun trying,'' Nicole said wickedly.

''And you know that! Every night.''

''I wish. It's been so long since I've had some, I think it's beginning to shrivel up.''

Both girls laughed.

''You're crazy, Nicky.''

''I'm serious.''

''So, how's the apartment?''

''It's fine. It's a little lonely sometimes, but it's nice.''

''Well, Tiandra's home now, so you won't have much time to be getting lonely,'' Yvonne pointed out.

''That's true.''

''Listen, baby, I hate to cut this call short, but my honey just walked in the door. I'll call you this weekend. I know you want to spend some time with your girl.''

''Yeah. Tell Lucien I said hi.''

''All right. Kiss Tiandra for me.''

''I will.''

Twenty minutes later, her phone rang again. ''Hello.''

''What's up, Nicole?''

''Hi, Mark.''

''You couldn't wait to get your own apartment, could you?''

''What?''

''I said you just couldn't wait, could you?''

''It was getting very crowded in my mother's house. I didn't have any space or privacy and I was getting very irritable.''

''Yeah, I bet.''

''So, how was your trip?'' Nicole asked, trying to change the subject.

He would not be moved, though. "It was fine. I hear you went back to work, too."

"That's right."

"Why?"

"Why? So I can pay the rent. The apartment isn't free, you know."

"You know I want you to be at home with Tiandra."

"I think the circumstances are a little different now, don't you?"

"I can take care of your rent, Nicole. I don't want some stranger keeping her. There are too many nuts running around these days."

"My mother's not a stranger or a nut! She's going to be keeping her while I'm at work!"

"And when will you see her? You won't have any time for her if you're out working."

"I'll have plenty of time for her."

"I can't see how. Or have you become a magician while I was away and you can be in two places at the same time now?"

"Why are you so worried, Mark?"

"Because a mother's place is at home with her children!"

"I'm working so I can take care of her and me. If I can't give her what she needs, it doesn't make much sense for me to be at home with her."

"I told you I can take care of your rent and whatever else you need. I don't want you working. I want you at home with her!" Mark yelled.

"Look! I'm not one of your numbers! I don't want to be kept by you! I'll make my own way, if you don't mind," she said adamantly.

Mark was infuriated by her remark. He started to say something very cruel but held his tongue. Instead, he slammed the phone down in her ear.

* * *

What a lot of nerve he has! She thought he was being totally ridiculous about her going back to work. He acted as though he was insulted. *What does he expect?* He didn't want her staying with him, he didn't want her to do anything for him. Now, because she was trying to do something for herself, he was being totally irrational. She could not believe he would actually think she would want him to pay her rent. She would never ask that of him. He must know she had more pride in herself than to let even him keep her like she was his mistress. If he wanted to take care of Tiandra, that was fine, but she could take care of herself.

She made a point not to forget to go to the bank tomorrow and transfer some money into her checking account to cover the check she would send him for the furniture she had charged on his cards.

The following Monday, Mark received a check for sixty-seven hundred dollars from Nicole. He had no idea what it was for. He had not spoken to her since they had argued about her going back to work. He was hurt and angry that she did not want his help. He was still her husband and he still felt a responsibility to her. He wanted to know she had everything she needed and he felt obligated to give her whatever that was.

He had gone by her parents' house that Friday and spent the day with Tiandra. The way Nicole sounded on the phone the other night, he figured if he wanted to see Tiandra, he had better do it while she was at work. He didn't think she would welcome him at her apartment. When he called her that night to inquire about the check, he did not expect the coldness in her voice when she recognized his. "Hello, Nicole."

"Hello."

"How are you?"

"Fine."

"How's Tiandra?"

"Fine."

"What's the matter?"

"Nothing. What did you want? I'm very busy."

Her icy tone angered him, but he tried to keep it out of his voice. "I got a check in the mail today from you. What's it for?"

"It's for the furniture I bought when I moved in here. The check should cover the bill you get for it."

He could not believe his ears. "Have I ever asked you for money for any of the bills I've gotten for your cards?"

"That's not the point. I wanted to pay for it myself."

"Don't be ridiculous, Nicole."

"I'm not being ridiculous, Mark!"

"Don't be so proud, Nicole, that you can't take anything from me. One day you might need something and I'll be the only one that can give it to you."

"I'll worry about that when *and if* that day comes."

"Nicole, I'm sending this check back to you."

"I told you to keep it. If you send it back, I'll only send it back again. Save yourself some postage and keep the check, Mark."

"Why are you so stubborn?" Mark asked, no longer able to control his anger.

"Maybe it's a trait I learned from you."

He did not say anything.

"Look, I've got to go. Good-bye," she said and hung up.

Mark held the phone and stared at it for a few seconds after Nicole hung up. He sat back at his desk and picked up the check and stared at it. He had never been so insulted in his life. She had to be the most stubborn woman he had ever known. *How dare she assume that I would stoop to asking her for money for anything? How dare she assume that I would take any money from her?* As if he had a grudge against the check itself, he tore the document to shreds.

Although Nicole still loved Mark, she felt an overwhelming anger toward him now. She was angry he didn't want her to live with him but that he wanted to take care of her as if nothing had changed. *How could he be so two-faced?* He acted as if she should be thrilled that he would offer to pay her rent. He even had the audacity to act as if he was insulted when she refused him.

MEN!!!

Chapter Thirteen

Since Mark and Nicole were on less-than-peaceful terms, they did not speak to each other very often in the following weeks. When Mark saw Tiandra, she was at her grandparents' house. He spent a good deal of his time with his sister and her two children, too. He was lonely living without Nicole, but his pride would not allow him to ask her to come back to him again.

By the middle of November, Mark started his Christmas shopping. He tried very hard to get in the spirit of the season but he really did not look forward to spending the holidays alone. Two days before Thanksgiving, while he was shopping for Tiandra, he ran into Ashlei Brown. He had not seen or spoken to her since before his heart attack.

"Mark!" she called to him.

"Hey, stranger. How are you?"

They embraced each other in greeting.

"I'm fine. How are you? I heard you had a heart attack," she said with a worried expression on her face.

"Yeah. A couple of months ago."

"Are you all right?" she asked with genuine concern.

"Yeah, I'm doing okay. Trying to take it easy, you know."

"I've been meaning to call you. I've been so busy lately; I just got back yesterday."

"Oh? Where've you been?"

"Well, I've been working in California. I'm remodeling an old house in San Francisco. I've been there since early October. Before that, I was in Atlanta. I've been running so much that I haven't had time to keep up with what's going on at home. But you're okay, right?"

"Oh, yeah, I'm fine."

"Well, you're looking well."

"You don't look too bad yourself," Mark said, openly giving her the once over.

She blushed and said, "Flattery will get you everywhere, Mark."

He laughed.

"So what are you doing, Christmas shopping?" she asked.

"As a matter of fact, I am."

"Did you get me anything?" she asked coyly.

"What would you like?" His loneliness was getting the best of him.

"Anything you want to give me."

"I can't handle that one, doctor's orders."

"Mark! Don't be fresh," Ashlei said, feigning embarrassment. *Is he flirting with me?*

"I told you, doctor's orders. I can't be."

"You're too much," she said, laughing.

"I try."

"I'd better change the subject. So, how's Nicole and Tiandra?"

Mark looked past her. "Tiandra's fine. I guess Nicole's okay, too."

"What do you mean, you guess she's okay?"

"We're separated."

"Oh, I didn't know. What happened? I mean, it's really none of my business, I know, but I thought you two were so happy."

"It's a long story. I'd rather not go into it."

"I'm sorry."

Mark shrugged his shoulders and said, "What can you do? I guess that's just the way of life. One minute you're happy, the next you're wondering what happened."

Ashlei noticed that Mark looked very unhappy when he spoke of Nicole. "You don't see her at all?"

"Naw. We try to avoid each other."

"Why?"

"To keep from arguing. It seems like every time we see each other now, we're at each other's throats," Mark said sadly.

"That's a sign of love."

"So is making love. Personally, I prefer the latter."

"Doesn't everyone?"

"I thought so."

Ashlei looked at her wristwatch. Noticing the time, she quickly said, "Oh my God, I'm late. I'm standing here running my mouth like I don't have anything to do. I was supposed to be meeting a client five minutes ago."

"Well, don't let me hold you up any longer. You go and take care of your business. It was good seeing you."

"You, too, Mark."

They exchanged kisses on cheeks.

"Give me a call sometime. Don't be such a stranger," Mark said.

"I won't. Take care of yourself. I don't want to hear about you having any more heart attacks. You're too young for that kind of nonsense."

"Yes, ma'am. Take care, beautiful."

As Ashlei hurried down the street, Mark looked after her for a moment, then smiled. Seeing her cheered him up considerably.

She was a good-looking woman with a good head on her shoulders and it was no secret that she was interested in him. She even made him forget about his loneliness for awhile. *Maybe I'll give her a call sometime.*

Chapter Fourteen

Nicole's birthday was a week and a half after Thanksgiving. When she got up that morning and looked out her window, she was shocked that all she could see was white. It was snowing pretty heavily outside and appeared that it had been all night. When Tiandra woke up a few minutes later, Nicole washed her up and gave her some cereal for breakfast. When she was finished feeding her, they sat down on the living room rug to play. It seemed that Tiandra was already trying to walk although she was just seven months old. She never wanted to sit, she was always pushing herself up on something. It also seemed to Nicole that she was developing her own little personality. She was pretty stubborn at times, a trait Nicole attributed to her father. She never attributed any of her less-than-pleasant traits to herself.

Nicole had not spoken to Mark since Thanksgiving day. She knew he had seen Tiandra at her mother's house since then though, because he went by there almost every day while she was at work. It seemed that he always made a point to leave before she got there. She figured he was purposely avoiding her. *Well that's his problem,* she thought in a huff. As she was thinking about him, her phone rang. "Hello."

A gentle "happy birthday" flowed through the telephone line.

"Thank you," she replied, taken aback. Her heartbeat had doubled its pace. She had not expected to hear from him.

"How are you? I haven't talked to you in a while," Mark said.

"I'm fine. How are you?"

"I'm hanging in there. How's my girl?"

"She's fine. She's right here. Do you want to say hi to her?"

"Yeah, put her on."

After a couple of minutes of trying to make Tiandra acknowledge Mark, Nicole finally sat her back on the floor and put the receiver back to her own ear. "She's not talking today."

"Yeah, I see. Makes me feel kind of silly."

Nicole laughed.

It was the first time Mark had heard her laugh in months. It sent a shiver up his spine. "It's good to hear you laugh, Nicole."

She didn't say anything. She didn't know what to say.

"So what are you doing for your birthday?" Mark asked, trying to ease the tension he felt coming through the line.

"Nothing. I'm just going to stay inside and watch TV. It's too messy outside."

"Yeah, I guess so. It's been snowing all night. I got caught in it last night."

"Oh, yeah?"

"Yeah. I was out with some clients."

"Oh."

After a pregnant pause, Mark said, "Well, I'm not going to hold you. I just wanted to call you and wish you a happy birthday."

"Thank you, Mark."

"You're welcome."

"And thanks for calling," she cooed.

"You're welcome, again."

"Bye."

"Bye, beautiful. Enjoy your day."

* * *

Although Mark and Nicole seemed to be relating to one another much better in the last few days than they had in the last couple of months, they still had not seen each other since early October. They talked on the phone much more frequently, albeit briefly, and since her birthday they had not found a single thing to argue about.

Christmas was approaching fast and the closer it got, the more depressed Mark became about having to spend it away from Nicole. Being that they seemed to be getting along so much better than before, he figured he would take a chance and ask her if he could come to her apartment on Christmas to see Tiandra instead of going to her parents' house.

Christmas was two days away and Nicole was planning to spend the day with her family. Yvonne and Lucien had come up from Jamaica to spend Christmas with Yvonne's mother. Nicole had just stepped out of her apartment on her way to pick up Yvonne for some last-minute shopping when she heard her telephone ring. She ran back inside to answer it, figuring it was Yvonne wondering why she was taking so long. She picked up the telephone. "I'm on my way."

"Great. I'll be here."

"Mark? I thought you were Yvonne. I was just walking out the door to go get her."

"Oh. Well, go ahead. I'll . . . I'll talk to you another time." He was nervous about asking her if he could come over.

Nicole sensed that he wanted to say something, so she said, "Was there anything in particular you wanted to tell me?"

"Oh, no," he answered quickly. Then, "Well, yes. What are you doing on Christmas?"

Nicole's heart skipped a beat. "I was planning to go by my parents' house for dinner, that's about it," she answered, anticipating his next words.

"About what time?"

"Oh, I don't know. I guess about three o'clock."

"Well, I was wondering if you'd mind me coming by your place to bring Tiandra's gifts instead of taking them to your mother's house. I figured I could save you the trouble of transporting them. I sorta went overboard," he chuckled nervously.

"Oh," she sighed. She was excited about the prospect of seeing him. It had been too long. "Sure, you can bring them by here."

Mark breathed a sigh of relief. "What time should I come?"

"How about twelve? Is that too early?"

"No. That's fine. Twelve is fine."

"All right."

"I'll be there at twelve," Mark said.

"Okay."

"Well, you go on, don't let me keep you. Tell Yvonne I said hi, and ask Lucien to give me a call, will you?"

"Sure."

"I'll see you later, Nicole. And thank you."

"You're welcome, Mark. Bye."

As she hung up the phone, a broad smile crossed her face. She could not wait to tell Yvonne.

On Christmas Eve, Mark paid a visit to Dr. Boswell. After a thorough examination, Mark asked the doctor, "So, what's the verdict, Doc? Will I live another forty years or what?"

Dr. Boswell laughed and said, "I can't guarantee another forty but I can say that if you do drop dead before then, it shouldn't be because of any heart failure. You're doing fine."

"Can I go back to work?"

"After the first of the year. But take it easy. Just because you're doing so well doesn't mean you should dive in head first. Ease back into it. Don't overwork yourself."

"And the most important question of all, can I have sex now? I'm dying from a lack thereof," Mark commented.

Dr. Boswell grinned and shook his head, "Yes, Mark. You can engage in sexual intercourse again, but like I said, just don't . . ."

"I know, don't dive in head first," Mark said, cutting him off. "But what if I can't see where I'm going?"

Dr. Boswell laughed and said, "Get out of my office, Mark."

Mark smiled and offered his hand, "Thank you, Doctor."

As he was leaving, Mark stuck his head back in the door and said, "Hey, Doc, do you think you can give me that in writing? You know how women get once you've had a heart attack."

"Get out of here!"

Christmas morning, Nicole got up at ten o'clock. She immediately jumped into a warm tub of bubbles and when she got out she put on the lavender silk lounging pajamas she bought when she was shopping with Yvonne the other day.

Tiandra woke up right after Nicole got out of the tub so she gave her a bath, too, and put on her red and white Santa pajamas complete with a pompom cap. Nicole then sat her in front of the Christmas tree with one of her stuffed animals and took some pictures of her.

At eleven thirty, Nicole began making breakfast. She hoped Mark had not eaten because she was making enough for both of them. Assuming he was probably on a very strict diet, she prepared a fresh fruit salad, that she knew Mark loved. She decided to wait until he arrived before she cooked their vegetable omelets made with egg-whites. Her kitchen table was set with the placemats she had bought for the occasion. She wanted everything to be perfect when he arrived.

Mark arose at ten o'clock that morning, also. He got right up and shaved and showered. He was hoping Nicole would not mind him staying until she left for her parents' house, because he was planning to go straight to Carol's for dinner when he left her. He splashed on Nicole's favorite cologne and wore the gray suit she had given him last Christmas. Mark always took special care when grooming himself, but on this morning he took extra pains to make sure he looked his very best. He was going to see his two favorite girls.

He arrived at Nicole's apartment at exactly twelve o'clock.

When he rang her intercom from the lobby to announce his arrival, Nicole became a little nervous. She looked around the apartment to make sure everything was just so. She ran to her bedroom quickly to look at herself in the mirror one final time. Her hair was combed and the pj.'s looked very elegant, if she did say so herself.

When the doorbell rang, her heart dived into her stomach. "Calm down, Nicole, calm down," she said to herself as she walked to answer the door. "Who is it?"

"Mark."

She took a deep breath then unlocked and opened the door.

"Merry Christmas," Mark said with a smile.

Nicole smiled shyly and said, "Hi. Merry Christmas. Come in."

He stepped inside the apartment. He wanted to kiss her but he decided against it. "How are you?" Mark asked as he put down the bags he was carrying.

"I'm fine. How are you?"

"Pretty good! I went to see Dr. Boswell yesterday and he gave me a clean bill of health."

"That's great," she said. "Oh, give me your coat."

"Thanks," he said as he removed his coat and handed it to her.

Nicole noticed right away that he was wearing her suit and her favorite cologne. "Sit down."

"Thank you."

She went to the closet to hang up his coat. As she reached for a hanger, she put the coat to her face and inhaled the sweet fragrance of him. She was so excited that he was there. When she walked back into the living room, she asked, "Mark, have you had breakfast?"

"No."

"Oh, good. I know you're not supposed to eat the way you used to, but I put a little something together that I think you might like. Would you like to eat?"

"You didn't have to go to any trouble for me, Nicole."

"It was no trouble. I was going to make breakfast anyway. I figured since you were coming over, I'd just wait until you got here."

Mark smiled and said, "Well, if you're going to eat, then I'll eat with you."

"Okay, just give me a few minutes. I'll be right back," Nicole said. She walked into the kitchen to cook the omelets.

Mark watched her as she walked away. *Damn, she looks good.* He loved her pajamas. Watching her walk in them gave him an erection; he was glad he was sitting. It had been so long since he had made love to her that he knew if he did not focus on something else, he might make a total fool of himself. "Nicole, where's Tiandra?"

She called back from the kitchen, "Oh, she's in her crib. You can go back and get her."

Mark got up and walked to the back of the apartment. It was a nice place, he noted. He was glad she had found an apartment in such a nice neighborhood. The building looked pretty secure, too. He felt better knowing that she and Tiandra were safe living away from him.

Tiandra's bedroom was the first room he came to when he entered the hallway. Nicole had it decorated it beautifully. Almost as nicely as she had decorated her room at the penthouse. Tiandra was lying awake in her crib when he entered. "Hey, precious. How's my baby?" He picked her up. "Merry Christmas, Tiandra." He kissed her face. "Wow, I like your p.j.'s, Tee, they're really something." She smiled at her daddy, exposing her first two teeth, as soon as she saw him. "Santa

Claus was really good to my girl this Christmas. He told me to bring you all of these nice presents. You want to see them?''

Mark took her into the kitchen where Nicole was preparing their breakfast. ''I like these pajamas, Nicole,'' Mark said of Tiandra's night-clothes. Where'd you get them?''

''Huh? Oh, I don't remember the name of the store. I bought them the other day when Yvonne and I went shopping.'' At first, she thought he was talking about her pajamas.

He must have read her mind. ''I like yours, too,'' Mark said, openly admiring her.

Nicole blushed and said, ''Thank you.''

Mark smiled. ''It's good to see you, Nicole.''

When she looked at him, she realized that she would never love anyone else the way she loved him. ''It's good to see you, too, Mark.''

''You look good,'' he said, nodding his head. ''Very good.''

She blushed again and said, ''Thank you. So do you.''

He stood in the doorway of the kitchen holding Tiandra and stared at her for a couple of minutes. He wanted to hold her and kiss her and make love to her so bad he could almost taste it.

''You can sit her in her high chair while we eat. I already fed her,'' Nicole said, breaking the spell.

''All right.'' Mark placed Tiandra in the high chair and buckled her in. Then he kissed her on top of her head. He took a seat at the table with Tiandra. As Nicole was fixing his plate, he said, ''I like your apartment, Nicole.''

She smiled and said, ''Thank you. I'm glad you do.''

''Is the doorman there twenty-four hours?''

''Yes. He makes everyone sign in, too.''

''Yeah, I noticed. That's good. This looks like a pretty nice neighborhood.''

''It is. A lot of rich white folks live in this area, so there are always a lot of policemen patrolling,'' Nicole informed him.

''That's good.''

She placed a plate in front of him and placed hers on the table opposite him and sat down.

"Smells good."

"Of course, I made it," she said, smiling.

He laughed. *She's beautiful,* he thought.

Nicole said grace and they ate. When they were finished, Mark offered to help Nicole wash the dishes, but she refused him. She told him to take Tiandra into the living room and sit down. She would join them in a minute.

When she had finished washing the dishes and joined Mark and Tiandra in the living room, he had already started opening Tiandra's gifts and showing them to her.

Nicole sat at the other end of the sofa and watched as Tiandra tried to play more with the wrapping on her gifts than with the toys themselves. She suddenly remembered a gift that was under the tree. She leaned over (Mark's eyes immediately went to her backside) and grabbed the gift. When she sat back down and looked at Mark, he had a silly grin on his face and was shaking his head.

"What?"

Mark sighed and said, "Oh, nothing."

She looked at him questioningly, then shrugged it off. "Here, this is for you," Nicole said, handing the box to him.

He was genuinely surprised. He smiled brightly and said, "Thank you."

"It's from Tiandra," she clarified.

"Oh. Thank you, Tiandra," Mark said, never taking his eyes off Nicole.

"You can open it now, if you want."

"No, I'll wait till later."

Mark had brought two shopping bags full of presents. He was almost down to the last one when he pulled out a box and handed it to Nicole. "This one's for you."

Nicole blushed and said, "Thank you."

"It's from Tiandra," Mark said, echoing Nicole.

She smiled and said, "Thank you, Tiandra."

"Open it."

"Now?"

"Yeah. Tiandra wants to see what she got you," Mark said, smiling.

Nicole chuckled and said, "All right."

As she unwrapped the gift, her fingers trembled. She opened the box and folded back the tissue paper. Inside was the most beautiful emerald green dress she had ever seen. "Oh, it's beautiful." Her eyes started to water. "Thank you." She leaned over and kissed his cheek.

He smiled and said, "Don't thank me, thank Tiandra."

Tears were in her eyes as she picked Tiandra up and kissed her. "Thank you, Tiandra. It's beautiful. I love it."

Mark was overjoyed. "Why don't you try it on?"

"Right now?"

"Sure. Tiandra wants to see how it looks on you, don't you, baby?"

Nicole giggled, "All right." She got up and hurried into her bedroom.

Mark picked Tiandra up and sat her on his lap. "She likes it, Tee. I knew she would."

As she was zipping the dress up, Mark appeared in the doorway. "Need any help?"

He startled her. "Oh! Yeah. Would you zip me?"

"My pleasure," Mark said as he casually strolled over to her.

"Where's Tiandra?"

"She's in the crib. She fell asleep," he said with a devilish grin.

"That fast?"

"Yeah. That fast," Mark said nonchalantly.

She was not sure about that, but she let it go. She turned back to the mirror and smoothed the dress over her figure. The dress was simply styled with long sleeves, a princess neckline and cummerbund waistband above a straight, knee-length skirt with a small slit in back, but the color and silk fabric were spectacular.

"It looks good. Tiandra said it would," Mark said coolly.

"Oh, she did?"

"Yeah, she did."

Nicole smiled and shook her head.

"Do you like it?"

"I love it. Thank you."

"You're welcome."

They stood quietly for a moment, neither of them knowing quite what to say to the other. Mark was intoxicated by being this close to her. He wanted nothing more than to hold her in his arms. Nicole wanted to take the dress back off, but she did not want to do it in front of him, but she didn't want to tell him to leave the room either.

Mark broke the silence. "What are you doing New Year's Eve?"

Her heart skipped a beat. "Nothing."

"I'm having a little get-together. Why don't you come?"

"I was planning to just stay at home with Tiandra."

"Bring her. If she gets sleepy, you can put her in the crib."

"You don't think it would be too noisy?"

"No, I'm not inviting that many people over."

Nicole thought for a moment. "I don't know. Maybe." She had been hoping he would have asked her to go out with him. She really did not want to be at a party where people would be asking a lot of questions about them.

"Well, think about it. It'll be fun."

"Okay, I'll think about it."

From then, until about two o'clock, when Nicole started to get dressed to go to her parents' house for dinner, they talked about insignificant things. They avoided talking about themselves. They laughed and kidded each other though, like they used to when they were alone together. They were more comfortable with each other than they had been in a very long time.

When Nicole started to get dressed, Mark volunteered to dress Tiandra. They were ready to leave by three thirty.

Nicole had a bag full of gifts that she was taking with her for her family. Mark asked her, "Were you planning on driving?"

"Uh-huh."

"How're you going to get from the car to the building with all this stuff and Tee?"

"I'll take Tiandra upstairs first then come back down and get this."

"Why don't I drop you off. I can help you take these things upstairs so you don't have to make two trips."

"You don't have to. I don't want to put you out of your way."

"You wouldn't be putting me out of my way, Nicole. Besides, even if you were, I wouldn't mind," he said sincerely.

"But how will I get home?"

"Call Bobby. He can pick you up and drive you home," Mark said of his chauffeur.

"But it's Christmas. I don't want to bother him today."

"I pay him to be available whenever I need him. It won't kill him to take a couple of minutes to drive you from your mother's house to yours. Just page him."

"Are you sure?"

"Yes."

She thought about it for a moment, then agreed.

When she arrived at her mother s house with Mark, everyone was surprised. They thought he and Nicole had reconciled and were getting back together. No such luck.

Ten minutes after they arrived, he left to go to Carol's. Nicole walked him to the door. "Thanks, Mark, for the ride and for coming over. You can come by any time you want to see Tiandra."

Only inches separated them when he responded tenderly, "Thank you. I had a great time today. It was good seeing you."

"It was good seeing you, too."

As he gazed into her brown eyes, he took her chin and gently lifted her head up to meet his. He kissed her lips softly. He didn't part his lips but the gentle pressure he exerted let her know how much he truly missed her.

"Merry Christmas, Nicole," he murmured before he walked out.

"Merry Christmas, Mark."

As expected, for the remainder of the evening, although they were apart, Mark and Nicole were in excellent moods. Neither of them had been as happy in months.

When Mark returned home that night, he was exhausted. He was at Carol's house until almost one o'clock in the morning. His sister was ecstatic that he and Nicole seemed to be getting along so well. She was sure they would be together again very soon.

Once home, Mark took a shower and went straight to bed.

When he arrived at Nicole's house to see Tiandra, it was late. When she opened the door to let him in, she was nude. "Hi, Mark. I was hoping you would come over tonight," she said seductively, he noticed.

"Where are your clothes?"

"Why do I need clothes? All you're going to do is take them off, anyway, right?" she said, moving closer to him.

"Where's Tiandra?"

"She's asleep. Come on, Mark, let's go to bed. I want you to make love to me. It's been too long," she purred as she grabbed his hand.

He allowed her to pull him into the bedroom. He never took his eyes off of her backside as it swayed sensuously in front of him. His hunger for her was so intense, and he was so hard he felt as though he would bust through the fabric of his pants.

She turned to face him once they were in the bedroom and

said, "Come on, baby, give it to me. Love me good like you always do."

He could not contain himself any longer. He grabbed her and kissed her hungrily, urgently. He cupped her butt in his hands and picked her up. She wrapped her legs around his body. She was attacking him ardently, but he did not want her to stop. He needed to be buried in her warm chamber of love that he knew so well and missed so much. He couldn't get his pants off fast enough. When he was finally able to release his throbbing manhood from its prison, she did not hesitate for a moment. She lowered herself onto him and before he could stop himself, he exploded inside her.

Mark was sweating feverishly when he woke up although he had slept in the nude. He looked at the clock on his nightstand. It read five thirty-six a.m. "Damn!" The dream had been so real, so vivid that he was disappointed when he looked over and realized that Nicole was not there with him.

It had been months since he had been with his wife. Seeing her yesterday in those silk pajamas had turned him on right away. He needed her good loving, but he couldn't ask her to sleep with him. Not yet. Not until things were correct between them. As much as he wanted Nicole, he would never use her just to satisfy himself. When he made love to her again, he wanted it to be forever.

As he sat on his bed trying to fight the feeling he had in his loins, he tried to think of what he could do. Against his better judgment, he picked up the telephone and began to dial.

Chapter Fifteen

Ashlei had wanted Mark Peterson since she first laid eyes on him at the dinner party where they met almost two years ago. Before meeting him, she had heard about his shrewd business tactics and his devil-may-care attitude with the ladies. Until the moment they met, she would have never considered involvement with a man with his reputation. Seeing him in the flesh, however, changed her view. She knew she would do anything to spend one night with him.

Ashlei arrived at Mark's apartment at seven p.m. on New Year's Eve. She had come directly from her office. She started to stay home that morning as she had gotten home late the night before from visiting with her father over the Christmas holiday. Although she had given her people the day off, she knew there were a number of things she had to take care of before the new year began. She liked to start her new year with a clean slate.

She was delighted that not only had Mark invited her to his little get-together, but that he had asked her to assume the roll of hostess. That bolstered her confidence in the notion that he would finally be her man since Nicole was out of the picture.

When she arrived at Mark's place, his chauffeur Bobby answered the door.

"Hello," Ashlei greeted him pleasantly.

"Mark said to go on back," Bobby said disparagingly, not bothering to acknowledge her greeting.

Ashlei got the distinct impression that he was not happy about her being there. She wondered why. Little did she know, Bobby strongly disapproved of Mark's involvement with her.

He had started to tell Mark as much, too, when Mark told him to send her to his room when she arrived. Bobby stilled his tongue when Mark looked at him incredulously, almost as if he could read his mind.

When Ashlei entered the bedroom, Mark was sitting in his recliner, reading the paper.

"Hi," she said, as she walked into the room.

"Is that what you're wearing tonight?" he asked with a frown, despite the fact that he saw her lay a garment bag on his bed.

"Boy, you don't believe in formalities, do you?" He cut his eyes at her over his paper. "No, Mark. I brought a change of clothes," she said before he could say anything.

Mark was not in a good mood. Bobby had really pissed him off earlier. When he told Bobby to send Ashlei back to his bedroom when she arrived, Bobby had actually looked at him like he was crazy. He had even opened his mouth to say something about it, Mark was sure. One look, though, shut him up before he could get the words out.

Mark knew Bobby liked Nicole and that he would bend over backwards to do anything for her. For that, Mark was grateful. He was glad they had become friendly, but Bobby was still his employee.

Mark hadn't been able to reach Ashlei when he called her the morning after Christmas. He figured later that it was probably for the best that he hadn't. He was surprised, however, when she called him later that day to wish him a Merry Christmas. Without hesitation, he invited her to his New Year's Eve get-together and asked her to come by a little earlier than everyone else. He had planned to take her up on the offer she had made him last year, but Bobby had put such a damper on his mood that sex was now the last thing on his mind.

Bobby's disapproval of Ashlei was of no concern to Mark. He did not pay Bobby for his opinion. That he would even think about making a remark about it to him was stepping too far out of line. He would have to put Bobby in check later.

The guests for Mark's New Year's Eve get-together began to arrive at ten. Ashlei fell into the role of hostess naturally. Mark was somewhat tickled by this. He watched her as she paraded around the room, going from person to person, making sure everyone had a drink and was comfortable. He hated to admit it, but he was glad she was there. He wished Nicole was there, though. He really didn't expect her to come, but he'd had to invite her, anyway.

By eleven forty-five, most of Mark's guests had arrived. The party was going strong and he was feeling no pain. Although his doctor had specifically told him to lay off the alcohol for a while, Mark had been drinking since nine o'clock.

Bobby was thoroughly disgusted with Mark and that woman, Ashlei. She walked around the penthouse like she owned the place. He felt bad for Nicole. Bobby knew how much she missed Mark. She had told him so, but it seemed that Mark did not feel the same. It seemed as though he had forgotten all about her.

At eleven fifty-five, when Bobby opened the door and saw Nicole standing there, a smile split his face and lit his eyes.

"Hi, Bobby," Nicole said as she tiptoed and kissed his cheek. "Happy New Year."

"Hi, Nicky. Same to you. You look beautiful, as always," Bobby said brightly.

"Thank you. I'm late, right?" Nicole said uncertainly.

"No, you've still got five minutes," Bobby said as he glanced at his watch.

"I started not to come."

As he took her coat, he said, "I'm glad you did."

She was wearing the dress Mark and Tiandra had given her for Christmas. She also wore the ermine he had given her when she went to her first formal dinner party with him before they were married.

As she entered the living room where everyone was gathered, she looked around for Mark but she didn't see him. She saw a number of guests that she knew and she spoke to several as a waitress came around with a tray of champagne-filled goblets. She took one.

As Nicole continued to scan the room looking for Mark, she spotted Ashlei Brown. She hadn't seen her since Mark's hotel had opened. She was surprised to see her now.

Nicole could remember when she thought Mark was fooling around with her. She had been so sure but Mark had finally, after much talking, convinced her that he wasn't. She could remember how silly she felt afterwards and apologized to him numerous times for being so insecure, but Ashlei was so beautiful and successful and smart, that at the time, she intimidated Nicole, especially since she knew that Ashlei had designs on Mark. She had always figured that Ashlei was Mark's type.

It was a minute to twelve when Nicole finally spotted him. He looked incredible in his ecru wool slacks and silk turtleneck sweater of the same hue. Her eyes began to water as she thought about this night, in this very room, two years ago. They had been married right here. She wanted to go to him and wish him "Happy Anniversary." Although it wasn't the happiest of anniversaries, they were still married and it was still a special day to her.

As she started over to him, the clock struck twelve. Everyone began yelling, "Happy New Year!" and kissing and hugging. Nicole was caught up in the excitement and was glad she had come after all.

As she continued through the throng of guests, she caught sight of Mark again, but what she witnessed made her stop in her tracks. Nicole stood frozen for a few seconds before she turned and quickly walked away.

Someone called to her, "Happy New Year, Nicole!"

She ignored them. She was too ashamed to face anyone with tears in her eyes. She went straight to Tiandra's room. She didn't know where else she could go to be alone.

When the clock struck twelve, Ashlei grabbed Mark and kissed him full on the mouth. She was beside herself with glee because she finally had him all to herself. Mark was quite drunk and his body responded as she rubbed hers against him. He knew she had nothing on underneath her dress but a thong and that turned him on all the more. He grabbed her behind and squeezed until she moaned with pleasure.

He was so filled with lust for her that he could have taken her right there, but suddenly, he felt someone's eyes burning into him. He didn't like the feeling. He looked up then, right into Nicole's tear-filled eyes. She was standing across the room watching them.

NO! his mind screamed. *When had she arrived?* He had not known she was there. He hadn't even expected her to come. He released Ashlei immediately.

"What's wrong?" she asked. He did not speak. He just stared straight ahead. She turned to see what he was looking at but did not notice anything peculiar. "Mark, what's wrong?"

He still did not answer. He stepped around her and followed Nicole.

Nicole stood at the window of Tiandra's nursery and cried as she looked out. *What could I have been thinking? Why did I come here? I should have known he didn't really want me here. He was just being polite by asking me to come,* she told herself.

She felt like a fool for believing she and Mark could ever be together again. *I should have known better,* she thought.

When Mark reached the hall, he heard the door to the nursery close. He dreaded going inside but he knew he had to. *What can I say to her?* He cursed himself for causing her such pain. He loved her more than anything, but he had hurt her again. He opened the door and stepped into the nursery, closing the door softly behind him. She stood across the room with her back to him. He wanted to go to her and hold her and apologize for his brazen-faced behavior. He figured by now, though, she was probably through with him.

Nicole took a deep breath and straightened her spine. She would face him like an adult. She would not carry on like a spoiled child. *Be strong, Nicole,* she told herself. *Be strong.* She turned to him. "Happy New Year, Mark."

He was caught off guard.

"Aren't you going to wish me the same?" she asked boldly.

"H-Happy New Year," he said uncertainly.

"Sorry I was so late. I got here at five to twelve. It looks like everyone's having a good time, though."

"When I didn't see you, I . . . I didn't think you would come," he said softly.

"I started not to, but I figured, why not?" she said with a shrug of her shoulders. "I didn't have anything else to do."

He noticed then that she was wearing his dress. His heart started breaking all over again and his shame overwhelmed him. "I'm sorry, Nicole."

She tried to laugh it off as she said, "You have no reason to be sorry. I shouldn't have been staring."

He felt lower than a snake.

"You look nice," she said to him.

"Thank you. You look beautiful in your dress."

She feigned modesty as she said, "You think so?"

"Yes."

"Thank you. I wasn't sure if I should wear it tonight or save it for another time."

"I'm glad you're here."

"Well, I can't stay," she said lightly. "I just wanted to come by and say Happy New Year, you know. Maybe have one drink. I'm driving so I don't want to get too fired up."

Mark's high had dissipated upon seeing her. His head had never been more clear in his life.

Although Nicole was genuinely hurt by seeing him with Ashlei, she could see he was very sorry she had witnessed them together. He looked extremely uncomfortable and she hated to see him like this. With more nobility than she would have ever believed she could muster, Nicole said, "Listen, Mark, don't worry about it. I was upset at first but I don't want you feeling bad about it or anything. You have the right to see whomever you choose or be with anyone you want to be with. I don't hate you for that. I don't want you to feel like you have to act any differently around me than you would any of your other guests here. If I make you feel uncomfortable, I'll leave. This is your party, you should be able to enjoy it without any hassles."

Mark could not believe his ears. Her humility in the face of his indiscretion was more than he could bear. A tear fell from his eye as he looked at her.

She stepped over to him. She reached up and wiped the tear from his face, then gently kissed him on the cheek. "I'm going to go now."

He could not move or speak.

She walked past him but when she reached the door, she turned back and said softly, "I still love you, Mark. I probably always will."

As she walked out, he lowered his head and cried softly in the emptiness of the room.

* * *

Ashlei wondered what was going on with Mark. One minute he was all over her, then suddenly he just walked away from her without a word.

He was the strangest man she had ever known. He made her so angry sometimes that she wondered why she even bothered with him. What bugged her the most though, was that he did not seem to care. It wasn't like she couldn't get a man. She had more than her share of suitors, but Mark was an enigma. One could never tell what he was really thinking. He was so secretive yet outspoken at the same time. He was quick to tell you what he wanted, but equally quick to tell you not to do anything for him. She felt as though she had to prove to the world that she could get inside of him and find out what the real man beneath the tough outer shell was really like. Little did she know, Nicole was the only woman who had ever gotten that close to him and she was the only woman who ever would.

After a few minutes when he did not return, Ashlei went to find him. Just as she was about to walk up the stairs and out of the living room, Nicole appeared. *When did she get here?* Ashlei wondered.

Nicole turned suddenly and looked right at Ashlei. Ashlei was visibly shaken. Nicole, on the other hand, was the picture of nonchalance. ''Hello, Ashlei.''

''Hello.''

''Mark's in the nursery,'' Nicole said as she donned her coat and immediately left.

As Ashlei proceeded to the nursery, Mark emerged.

''Mark, I didn't know Nicole was here,'' Ashlei said quickly.

''Where is she?''

''She left.'' Ashlei did not notice, but Mark flinched. ''When did she get here, Mark?''

''I don't know. Look, she's gone, right? Don't worry about

it,'' Mark said. He walked back into the living room and his party as if nothing had happened.

Chapter Sixteen

The last of Mark's guests left at five thirty that morning. Everyone had had a wonderful time, except Mark. After Nicole left, Mark set out to drown his sorrows. By five thirty, he was wasted. He sat sprawled on the sofa as Ashlei bid everyone farewell. Bobby and the other hired help went around removing dirty glasses and trying to straighten up.

After letting the last guest out, Ashlei stood at the base of the stairs and looked at Mark. She had never seen him like this before, she could not believe she was seeing him this way now.

"What da' hell you lookin' at?'' Mark suddenly yelled at her in a drunken slur.

She walked over to him and took the empty glass he was holding out of his hand. "Come on, Mark. I think you'd better go to bed.''

"Don' tell me what t'do! Who d'hell you think you are?'' His speech was slurred by the many glasses of scotch he had drunk in an attempt to dull the memory of what he'd done to Nicole.

"Mark, come on, baby. I wasn't trying to tell you what to do. I just thought you might feel better if you got some sleep.''

"I'ont pay you ta think f'me. D'only thing I wan' from you is unner dat dress,'' Mark said with a scowl.

Ashlei was shocked and hurt by his words. She began to cry.

Bobby witnessed this, and although he was not happy that Mark was seeing her, he didn't feel she deserved such blatant disrespect, either. He walked over and said, "I'll take him to bed."

Mark looked up at Bobby and said, "What d'hell you doin' here?"

Bobby ignored Mark's verbal abuse. "Let's go, Mark. You've had a few too many."

"You know, das da' secon' time t'day you try ta tell me sum'n bout what I'm doin'. Who you think you are? You work f'me . . . boy, not . . . da' udda way round. You got a big mouf an . . . if you keep talkin', I'ma haf . . . ta shut it f'you," Mark slurred. Needless to say, he was still sprawled on the sofa. Bobby bent over to pick Mark up. "Git ya' hands offa me!"

Ashlei cried harder but Bobby was undaunted.

Suddenly, Mark swung at Bobby. Due to Mark's drunkenness, the blow only glanced his face. Bobby hit Mark back, but much more solidly. Ashlei was now at the point of hysteria.

Bobby's blow knocked Mark down and almost out. It slowed him enough that Bobby could pick him up and carry him to bed. Once in the bedroom, Bobby dropped him on the bed. He removed Mark's shoes and placed them in his dressing room. He then took the comforter on the bed and pulled it up from the foot of the bed and threw it across Mark's semiconscious form.

"Is he all right?" Ashlei asked nervously.

"Yeah, he's fine. He'll have a hell of a headache when he wakes up and he'll probably fire me for hitting him, but other than that, he'll be all right."

"I won't let him fire you, Bobby."

Bobby looked at her. *What makes you think you have any influence on Mark outside the bedroom?* But he did not say a thing. He simply walked out of the room and left her with him.

Mark awoke at five o'clock that afternoon. When he picked his head up from the pillow, it felt like a fifty-ton block of cement was holding it down. He grabbed his head in both hands and moaned. He had not felt this crappy in years. He tried to roll over slightly but found that he was wrapped up in the comforter somehow. Slowly, he turned over on his back. That was when Ashlei moved. She turned over and faced him. "How're you feeling?"

"Lousy." She reached up and turned on the bedside lamp. "Turn that light off!" he yelled, then cursed himself because the sound of his own voice reverberated inside his head.

"Sorry," Ashlei said timidly.

Mark lay where he was a few minutes more, then slowly swung his legs out of the bed and sat up as he held his head in his hands. He was still fully dressed with the exception of his shoes. He stood up slowly, supporting his weight by holding onto the nightstand beside the bed. Using the side of the bed for support, he made it to the bathroom. His head was spinning and his stomach was turning in the opposite direction. He made it to the toilet just as the contents of his stomach decided to make an appearance.

Ashlei lay in the bed and listened to Mark throwing up in the bathroom. She started to cry quietly as she thought about what he'd said to her that morning. She told herself that he didn't really mean it, it was just the alcohol talking.

When Mark was finished throwing up, he walked to the sink to wash his face. He took one look at himself in the mirror and swore he would never take another drink of alcohol for as long as he lived. "You look like crap," he said to his reflection. Cold shower. That was what he needed. An ice cold shower. He opened the medicine cabinet and took out the bottle of aspirin. He popped three into his mouth and put his hand under the faucet to catch enough water to push them down. He then stripped, leaving his clothes in a pile on the floor, and walked to the shower stall and turned on the cold water, full blast. He stepped in and immediately yelled upon feeling the icy water hit his body.

Ashlei heard his scream in the bedroom and came running. "Mark, what's the matter?"

Mark ignored her. *Why hadn't she gone home,* he wondered. He certainly didn't feel like having her around tonight.

"Mark? Are you all right?"

"Yes."

Slowly, Mark added hot water to the spray. He was as awake as he would ever be now. After fifteen minutes, he turned off the water and stepped out of the shower and began to dry himself off. He walked back into the room, ignoring Ashlei. He put on his robe, sat on the bed and picked up the telephone.

First, he called Bobby. "Get up here, now." He listened for a moment then said, "Bring me a turkey sandwich on rye bread. Dry." He hung up.

He picked up the telephone again but hesitated before he dialed. He listened as the phone rang in his ear. Five. Six. Seven. Eight rings. He hung up. Then he dialed another number. "Happy New Year. This is Mark. Is Nicole there?" He listened to the response. "Is she coming by there tonight?" Again, he listened. "Ask her to call me when she gets there. It's urgent."

As Mark was hanging up the telephone, Ashlei asked him, "Mark, do you want me to get you anything?"

"No." He was sitting with his back to her. Suddenly, he turned around to face her and said, "Look, Ashlei, you're going to have to go home. I feel like shit right now and there are a few things I have to do since I'm supposed to go back to work tomorrow. I'm really not in the mood for company."

She fought back tears as she got up and carried her things into the bathroom.

Mark lay back on the bed and thought about Nicole. He wanted to see her so he could apologize to her again and tell her how much he loved her. Ashlei was the last person he wanted to see right now. She reminded him that Nicole was not with him like he wanted her to be.

When Ashlei came out of the bathroom twenty minutes later, she was fully dressed. She walked to the door of the bedroom and started to leave, but she could not go until she found out if he meant what he had said to her that morning. "Mark?"

"What?"

"Did you mean what you said?"

He looked at her, not knowing what she was referring to, but he saw tears in her eyes, so he figured it must have been pretty bad. He sat up. "What did I say?"

"You said the only thing you wanted from me was . . . sex!" she spat the word, like it was painful to say.

Mark got up from the bed. As he walked over to her, he could see how he had hurt her by his callous remark, and although that was how he felt, he had never planned to tell her that. He put his arms around her. "No, Ashlei. I didn't mean that," he lied.

She cried from relief as she held him tightly. She did not want to leave. "Can't I stay with you tonight, Mark?"

Not tonight, Ashlei. "Not tonight," he vocalized his thoughts.

She was sure he planned to spend the night with Nicole. "When can I see you again?"

"I'll see you soon. I'll call you tomorrow, all right?"

Although she did not want to wait until tomorrow, she said, "All right."

He walked her to the door and let her out. As she was leaving, Bobby was coming off the elevator. Bobby looked at Ashlei indifferently, then at Mark. He walked into the apartment without saying anything to either of them.

Mark closed the door behind her. He turned to Bobby, who stood in the living room, and asked, "Was I dreaming, or did you hit me?"

"Yeah, I hit you, but you hit me first," Bobby answered.

"Well, I obviously was drunk."

"Well, I wasn't."

Mark walked into the living room, past Bobby. Bobby turned to face him. "You got my sandwich?"

"It's in the bag," Bobby said, referring to the bag on the bar.

"You know, you pissed me off yesterday, Bobby." Mark was referring to Bobby's reaction when Mark told him to bring Ashlei back to his bedroom yesterday evening.

"Yeah? Well, likewise, I'm sure."

Mark walked to the picture window and looked out. He wanted to explain to Bobby why Ashlei had been there. For some reason, he felt as though he owed him an explanation since he had always looked out for Nicole. He turned to Bobby and asked instead, "How'd I get in the bedroom?"

"I carried you." Bobby wanted to tell Mark how angry he had made him. He had been ready to quit. He decided to wait, though, and see what Mark had to say first.

"You know, for a moment, I thought about firing you."

"For a moment, I thought about quitting."

"So what do you want to do?"

"It's your call."

Mark and Bobby stared each other down; neither of them wanted to relinquish the hold. After a few seconds, Mark decided it was not worth it. He turned away and walked back to the bar and opened the bag to remove his dinner. "I'm going to work tomorrow. Be here by seven."

"You owe me an apology, Mark."

Mark looked at him in disbelief. Bobby did not flinch. He thought about what Bobby said, though. He and Bobby had always had a good working relationship. Bobby had put up with a lot of flak from him over the years but he had always stuck with him. He had never let Mark down, either. Never. For Bobby to say he owed him an apology meant he must have really went overboard. Mark looked over at Bobby once again. Bobby's stare never wavered. "I apologize."

" 'Nuf said. See you in the morning," Bobby said. He turned and walked out.

* * *

When Stephanie hung up the phone after Mark's call, she turned to her sister and said, "Mark said to call him. He said it's urgent."

Nicole knew what he wanted. She did not want to hear any more apologies from Mark. She was really surprised she had been able to keep her composure when he came to apologize to her. She had been devastated when she saw him kissing Ashlei so lustfully. *Was he seeing her when he came to my house on Christmas?* Nicole decided that evening she had to get away from him. Seeing him, especially now, would be more than she could bear.

Chapter Seventeen

When Mark arose on the morning of January second, he was feeling better than he'd felt in weeks. The idea of going back to work was exciting. He missed being at his office, running things. Although he had been in constant contact with his people throughout the course of his recovery, he had basically been a spectator. There were a few projects that had been put on hold while he was out and he knew he would have his hands full once he got back, but he was ready, and more than willing, to face any challenge.

Bobby was at the penthouse at seven a.m. to pick Mark up. The incident of the night before was forgotten by both of them. "Good morning, boss," Bobby said.

"Good morning, Bobby. I'm ready to roll."

Bobby had Mark at his office before seven thirty. When he stepped off the elevator, the feeling of being back in control immediately overwhelmed him. He smiled to himself as he walked back to his office. There was a sign taped to his office door. It read, *WELCOME BACK, MARK*. It was good to be back.

He walked into his office, hung up his coat and went straight to his desk. Before starting on the pile of mail that awaited him, he picked up the telephone to call Nicole. The phone rang ten times before he hung up. *Where is she? Why hasn't she returned my call?* He decided to go by her place when he left the office that evening. Now it was time to take care of business.

Nicole called her travel agent and asked if there was a cruise from anywhere to anywhere that she could reserve a cabin on as soon as possible. As luck would have it, the agent informed her of a twenty-one-day Caribbean cruise that was leaving from Florida in two days with plenty of cabins available. Nicole told her, "Book it. You know what I like. And book me a flight out first thing Friday morning."

The agent jokingly said, "Sounds like you're trying to run away."

In all seriousness, Nicole answered, "I am."

Mark did not leave his office until eight o'clock that evening. He was tired, but he felt good because he had gotten a lot done on his first day back. He had scheduled meetings with his staff for the next two days so they could update him on what had been going on in his absence. He had been in touch with most of his clients, if only for a couple of minutes, to let them know that he was back on the scene. He had been pleasantly surprised, too, when he met with his vice president, Dave Green, and was told they had landed a big contract Mark had been shooting for when he went on disability.

That evening when Mark got home, his exhaustion caught

up with him and he decided to wait until tomorrow to call Nicole. He showered and went to bed.

Nicole spent all day Thursday shopping and packing for her trip the following day. She had gotten up very early and dropped Tiandra off at her mother's house along with a suitcase that was half-packed. She was grateful that her parents were so understanding of her need to get away, and they cheerfully agreed to keep Tiandra while she was gone. Her brother Reggie volunteered to watch her apartment while she was away so she gave him her keys Thursday night. She spent the night at her parents' place so she could be with Tiandra before she left, and also because her father was taking her to the airport in the morning.

Mark was as busy at the office on Thursday as he had been the day before. He decided that instead of trying to squeeze in a few minutes over the phone with Nicole, he would wait until Saturday to go by and see her and try to explain to her that nothing was going on with Ashlei. He just hoped she would hear him out this time.

Nicole's flight left on schedule Friday morning. She landed in Miami about two and a half hours later. The ship was not scheduled to leave until four thirty that afternoon, so she had a couple of hours to kill before she boarded. Since her bags were being transferred from the plane to her ship and she did not have to carry them around, she took advantage of the time she had and did a little shopping. She was amazed at how good she felt already. Not having to worry about whether she would run into Mark or Ashlei on the street, or even picking up the telephone and having to listen to his voice, took a load off her shoulders.

When she boarded the ship to leave on her three-week vacation, she went straight to her cabin and lay down until the ship disembarked. Once on the open sea, Nicole began to feel a little queasy from the rocking motion of the ship. For that reason, she decided to skip dinner. She took some pills for motion sickness and went straight to bed.

Saturday morning she awoke feeling refreshed. She took a shower and put on a pair of leather slacks and a wool sweater, since it was still chilly outside, and went upstairs to have breakfast. As she was stepping out of the corridor onto the deck, she bumped into a man that was entering the corridor.

"Excuse me. I'm terribly sorry," he said politely.

"That's all right," she said with a smile.

He held the door for her and said, "After you, ma'am."

"Thank you."

Gosh, he's cute, she thought. As she walked down the deck, she turned and looked back in the direction she had come from. He was still standing there holding the door. He smiled and waved. Nicole waved back. That was when she knew this was going to be a wonderful cruise.

Mark got up at ten thirty Saturday morning, got dressed and went to see Nicole and Tiandra. He was trying to think of what he would tell her when he arrived at her building. He knew he had to tell her how much he loved her. He had decided they had played this game long enough. He was sure she would be reluctant to come back to him since she had seen him kissing Ashlei, but somehow he had to convince her it would be the best thing for all of them if she did.

Reggie Johnson opened the door for Mark when he rang. "Hey, Mark. Happy New Year! What's happenin', man? Long time, no see," Reggie said, offering his hand.

"Happy New Year, Reggie. How ya doin?" Mark asked, shaking his hand.

"I'm all right, I guess. Just cooling out, that's all. Come on in," Reggie offered as he stepped aside to let Mark into the apartment.

"Is Nicole here?"

"No. She didn't tell you she was going away?"

Mark stopped in his tracks. "No. Where'd she go?"

"She went on a cruise, for three weeks. She left yesterday morning. She asked me to watch her place while she was gone. That's why I'm here."

Mark was hurt that she had left and not said anything to him. "For three weeks?"

"Yeah."

"Did she take Tiandra with her?"

"No, my mom's keeping her. You can go by there and see her."

"Damn!" Mark exclaimed.

"I can't believe she didn't tell you," Reggie said truthfully.

Mark sighed and said, "I can. I wanted to talk to her. I did something really stupid the other night and I wanted to apologize to her. She probably took this trip to get away from me."

Nicole was scheduled for the late dinner session Saturday evening and, although there were other travelers dining at the same table, the two seats on both sides of her were left vacant.

Nick Latargia noticed the young lady he had bumped into that morning the moment he walked into the dining room. She appeared to be traveling alone. *Perfect*. He thought she was gorgeous. After he had almost knocked her down that morning, he watched her as she strolled down the deck. The way her hips swayed in those leather pants stirred a desire in his loins. When she turned back and saw him staring at her, he smiled and hoped she could not read his mind. If she had, she would have come back and slapped him. Seeing her now, though, just reinforced the desire he felt earlier. After dinner, he decided he'd ask her to join him for a cocktail.

Nick was president and chief financial officer of NL Import-Export Company, Inc. which was based in Miami. He was thirty-five years old and worth close to twenty million dollars. His wealth had, some said, come through questionable means. There was talk that he had connections with Colombians in the drug trade, but no one had ever been able to prove that.

He was a handsome man with a very fair complexion and naturally wavy hair. His fairness of skin was because his father was white and his mother was a light-skinned black. When it was necessary, he could, and did, easily pass for one or the other.

On this night, he sported an elegantly tailored dinner jacket and black tie and slacks. He wore black patent leather tuxedo moccasins, and on his left pinkie he wore a ring with his initials in diamonds totaling three carats in weight.

He sat at a table across the room from the young woman that had captured his eye, and tried to be inconspicuous as he watched her. He wondered why a woman that beautiful was traveling alone. Hopefully, she would not be getting off at any of the islands to meet anyone. He could very easily picture himself spending his time on this cruise with her.

When Nicole finished her dinner, she immediately excused herself and got up to leave the dining room. Nick saw her getting ready to leave and rose from his table. Before Nicole reached the exit, he had caught up with her. As she was about to open the door to leave the dining room, he reached past her to open it for her. She turned to see who was behind her. She recognized the man from that morning and smiled. "Thank you."

"You're welcome."

She stepped through the door but did not slow her pace. He stepped beside her. "You look very lovely this evening."

"Thank you." She was wearing one of the many cocktail dresses she had purchased when she was in Paris on her honeymoon. Since the dress bared her shoulders, she wore a lightweight fur stole over them.

"May I ask your name?"

She blushed and said, "Nicole."

"Nicole? What a coincidence."

Being in a humorous mood, she said, "Why? Is your name Nicole, too?"

He laughed. As he looked into her smiling eyes, he knew she was the woman for him. "My name is Nicolas. Nicky, to my friends," he said as he offered his hand.

She took his hand. "Hi, Nicolas, Nicky to your friends. My friends call me Nicky, too."

He brought her hand up to his lips and gently pressed it to them. "I bet they call you beautiful, too."

Nicole blushed.

"I was going to take a walk to the lounge for a cocktail. I'd be honored if you would join me," he said.

"That sounds like a nice idea. Thank you. I think I will."

As they walked to the lounge, Nicole could not believe she had met such a gorgeous guy already. It was only the second day of the cruise. There were still nineteen days to go.

They took a table near the back of the lounge and a waitress came over to take their drink orders. Nicole ordered a piña colada. Nick ordered a whiskey sour.

While waiting for their drinks, Nick noticed the wedding band on Nicole's finger. "You're married."

"Separated," she clarified.

"Oh, so I guess he won't be joining you."

"He doesn't even know where I am."

"Do you always travel alone?"

"Not usually. I just needed to get away for awhile. Things have been kind of crazy in my life lately."

"Your husband?"

"Yes."

"How long have you been married?"

"Two years."

"And you're already separated?"

"He felt it necessary to sleep around," Nicole said, certain now that he had been unfaithful to her.

"How long have you been separated?"

"Four months."

"Do you plan to divorce him?"

"I don't know. We have a small daughter."

"Oh, how old is she?"

"Eight months."

"She's just a baby."

"I know."

"Your husband must be a fool. If I had a wife as beautiful as you at home and in my bed every night, I would never, ever sleep anywhere else," Nick said emphatically.

"That's what he told me, too," she said sadly.

Nick surmised that she must be lonely. To cheer her up, he said, "Listen, let's talk about something else. I can see you don't want to talk about him. I'm sorry for being so nosy."

She smiled and said, "That's all right. I would like to talk about something else, though."

Damn, she's beautiful, he thought as he looked at her. He was glad the dumb sucker she was married to didn't know what a good thing he had because he sure knew what to do to make her smile.

Nick and Nicole stayed up that evening talking, first in the lounge, then strolling on deck, until well after three a.m. They learned a lot about each other in those few hours and found they each enjoyed the other's company very much.

Their first stop on the cruise was to be Jamaica. Nicole told him she would be getting off there to visit her best friend. When he offered to go along, she told him it would not be a good idea for her to bring him there since their husbands were friends. He agreed without any hassle, but made her promise they would tour the other islands on the cruise together.

When Nick walked Nicole to her cabin that night, he started to kiss her good night on her cheek, but she turned her head so the kiss landed on her lips. Nick looked into her eyes and saw the loneliness there and put his arms around her and kissed her softly. Nicole responded maybe a tad too eagerly, but he understood her need and did not take advantage of her because of it.

When their lips parted, Nicole looked into his eyes and saw something there that made her want to cry. She had a feeling she would be safe with him. "Thank you," she whispered.

"Good night, beautiful," he said, as he hugged her one final time.

For the next five days, with the exception of the one spent with Yvonne in Jamaica, Nicole spent most of her waking hours with Nick. She was having the time of her life with him. He was open and honest and he kept her in stitches. He made her feel wonderful. He never asked her anything about Mark, but told her if she wanted to talk about her situation, he was more than willing to be her sounding board. They ate breakfast, lunch and dinner together every day, went dancing every night, and when they docked at the different ports, they toured the islands together, with Nick refusing to allow her to spend a dime.

Nicole found that she was becoming infatuated with him. At the end of their first week together, Nick asked her if she would join him for dinner in his stateroom. She readily accepted. At seven o'clock that evening, Nicole went to his cabin. A valet answered her knock.

Nick came out of the other room and greeted her with a kiss. "Hello, beautiful."

Nicole hugged and kissed him in return. "Hi."

"I'm glad you could make it," Nick said sincerely.

"Did you think I wanted to eat alone?"

"I hope not."

They kissed again, more passionately than before. Nick murmured, "I could fill myself up on your sweet kisses, you know."

"Do you want to try?" she asked seductively.

Nick looked into her eyes. He liked what he saw there. He whispered, "I'm going to make love with you tonight, if you'll allow it."

Although she truly wanted to be with him, too, when he spoke the words she felt a knot of apprehension tighten in her stomach. Nevertheless, she replied, "I will."

He kissed her hungrily but stopped suddenly because he could feel himself getting carried away. "Let's eat before this delicious food gets cold," he said.

"We could always have it warmed back up."

"I know you could, but that would be indecent."

She laughed and playfully punched him in the arm.

There was a dining alcove in his suite and the table was set for two. A single rose in a bud vase and two lighted candles adorned the table. Nick led her to one of the chairs and seated her, then went back across the room and turned off the overhead light. "A little atmosphere."

Nicole smiled as he joined her back at the table. "I know, that was corny," he said.

"No, it wasn't. I think it was sweet."

"No, you're sweet," he said as he softly caressed her cheek.

As if on cue, his valet appeared, carrying a bucket of chilled champagne.

"Would you like some champagne, Nicole?"

"Yes, thank you."

The valet poured for them both, then sat the bucket on a stand beside the table. He asked Nick, "Shall I serve?"

"Yes," Nick answered, never taking his eyes off Nicole. The valet left the room.

"Do you always travel with a valet?"

"Usually. I very rarely travel alone. I'm spoiled."

"Nothing wrong with that. Being married to Mark, I became spoiled and I loved it."

"As beautiful as you are, you should be spoiled. I'll spoil you rotten if you let me. Then no other man will be able to handle you."

Upon hearing his words, Nicole visibly shivered.

Nick noticed and asked, "What's wrong?"

"Nothing. I just got a chill," she said, trying to force a smile. Mark had said the same words to her when they first started seeing each other.

The valet re-entered, pushing a cart with their dinner. First, they had soup, lobster bisque.

Nicole told him, "I love lobster."

"Somehow, I knew you would."

Their main course was broiled stuffed lobster, sliced carrots and wild rice pilaf. Through dinner they made small talk. When she was finished eating, Nicole said, "That was excellent."

"I'm glad you enjoyed it. Would you like some more?"

"Oh, no, thank you. I'm stuffed."

"Would you like more champagne?"

"Yes, thank you."

He refilled her glass.

Again, as if on cue, the valet appeared and began to clear the table. Nick led Nicole to the sofa where she sat with her legs folded under her.

"Nick, you don't mind if I take off my shoes, do you?"

"Of course not. Make yourself comfortable."

He walked over to the wall unit, that held a tape deck, CD player and radio, and asked her, "Do you like jazz?"

"Yes."

He put a disc on the CD player then joined her on the sofa. He looked into her eyes, then took her hand and kissed her palm. "You are beautiful."

"You flatter me too much."

"I don't believe in flattery. You are a very beautiful woman. I don't mean just your face, I'm referring to your inner beauty. When you smile, I see a light in your eyes that will never die. I love looking into your eyes. They tell me so much about you. When you laugh, I see joy but I also see pain. I know you're going through a rough time right now but if I can, I want to help erase the pain. I won't push you, Nicole, but I don't want you to feel as though you have to hide what you're feeling, either. I'm here for you, if only for a short time. You can lean on me."

Nicole was touched by his words. She smiled, but he noticed a sadness in her eyes. Nick moved closer to her and put his arms around her. She was comforted by his embrace.

The valet finished clearing the table and came back into the room. "Anything else, sir?"

"No. You can go."

"I'm sorry, Nick. I've never been too good at hiding my feelings. I try to forget about what happened but it's hard. Sometimes I get so angry at myself because I let so much get to me. I wish I could just turn my feelings off at times."

Nick put his hand under her chin and made her look at him. "But don't you see, that's why you're so beautiful, because you're so warm and sensitive. These are the things that make you who you are. I know, sometimes people you love hurt you and they don't always mean to, and even knowing this doesn't make the hurt any less painful. It's good to let your feelings show, Nicole. People become bitter from pent-up frustration. Besides, if they see how they're hurting you and they really love you, they'll make an effort not to hurt you that way again. If no one knows you're hurting, they'll make no move to change it."

Nicole looked into his eyes as he said this. She wanted him to put his arms around her again. "Will you hold me?" He embraced her gently, lovingly. "I'm so glad I met you. You make me feel safe," she said in his ear.

"You are safe with me, Nicole."

"I wish we didn't live so far apart."

"Distance won't keep me away from you."

Nicole looked into his eyes and could see he meant what he said. She kissed his lips softly, then his forehead, his cheeks, his nose and his lips again. Nick held her tighter and kissed her passionately, pushing his tongue into her mouth. Nicole reciprocated.

He began to caress her shoulders and back as he continued to kiss her, never reducing the fervor with which he did. He leaned back on the sofa and Nicole moved with him as one, until they were fully horizontal and she was on top of him. He continued to stroke her body gently, but moved his hands to her backside and squeezed it softly while pressing her pelvis to his erection. He looked into her eyes as he kissed and fondled her and saw the yearning for the love he so wanted to give her.

Slowly, in the small space of the sofa, he turned her over so that she was on her back and he was on top of her. He continued to kiss her but now began to stroke her breasts and she rubbed his backside and pressed closer to him. The feel of his erection rubbing against her center, pushed her to the pinnacle she hadn't been to in too long. As the wave overtook her, she bit down on her bottom lip to stifle the cry she felt rising in her throat.

Nick knew she was in the throes of orgasmic delight. He was in ecstasy. Her body was warm next to his. He could feel the desire in her. It overwhelmed him. He began to unbutton her blouse as she kissed his neck and face. He buried his face in her neck and gently nibbled at her flesh. This sent her to orgasmic heights once more.

At the very instant the second climax shook her to the core,

Mark pervaded her mind. "Wait," Nicole said suddenly. He did not stop. "Nick, wait." She tried to push him off of her.

He raised up slightly and looked in her eyes. "What's wrong, sweetheart?" he asked in a tone as soft as a caress. He could see the apprehension in her eyes.

"I can't do this. As much as I want to, as much as my body is aching for you, I can't."

Nick sighed. Her body felt perfect under his and he was so ready for her. "Why, Nicole? I can feel how much you want me."

"I didn't mean to tease you and leave you hanging but I . . . I still love my husband."

"Nicole, he cheated on you," Nick reminded her.

"He said he didn't."

"Of course, he's going to say that."

She shook her head and gently urged him off of her. "It doesn't matter. I can't do this now. I can't make love with you while he's still in my heart and mind. I'm sorry." She sat up on the sofa and began to refasten her blouse. Nick reached for her hand to stop her. "I try to forget everything that's happened and move on with my life, but I can't. Not yet."

"I won't hurt you, Nicole," he said.

"I don't believe you would, but I didn't come on this cruise looking for some torrid affair. I took this cruise so I'd have an opportunity to decide where I want my relationship with Mark to go. I don't believe if I let myself get caught up in anything with you now that I'd be able to make a totally rational decision about my marriage and I have to at least give him the benefit of the doubt. The way you make me feel already . . . I know I won't be able to and I don't want to hurt you either, Nick."

Nick bowed his head momentarily, letting her words sink in. He wanted her in a way that he'd never wanted any woman, but he had to give her credit for at least trying to be more mature than her husband obviously was. He felt a new respect for her. When he looked into her eyes, he smiled and said, "I want you, Nicole, but I can wait. I don't want to confuse you. I just hope he has the good sense to wake up and see the caliber of woman he's married to. Of course, if he doesn't, I know how to treat a good woman like you. I hope I get an opportunity to show you.''

While Nicole was away, Mark divided the majority of his time between his office and Tiandra. He was at the office almost every night until after seven, but he loved being there so the length of his workday did not bother him. In the evenings, before returning to his penthouse, he usually went to the Johnsons' house to see Tiandra. That was, of course, the high point of his day. He was so proud of her that he would sometimes catch himself bragging about his "beautiful" daughter. He did not mean to come off as conceited, but as far as he was concerned, she was the most beautiful baby alive.

On Friday evenings, he took her home with him and kept her until he went back to work on Monday. He knew he was spoiling her but he couldn't help himself. She was the only daughter he had, and the way things had been going lately with Nicole, Tiandra was likely to be the only one he would ever have.

He avoided Ashlei during the three weeks Nicole was away. She called him practically every day, but most times he had his secretary run interference for him. He liked her well enough, but uppermost in his mind was being with Nicole again. As far as he was concerned, if he saw Ashlei now, especially after the New Year's Eve incident, it would be like stabbing Nicole in the back.

He missed her terribly. He would be glad when her cruise was over.

Chapter Eighteen

On the final night of the cruise, as Nick and Nicole shared a slow dance, she whispered, "I've had a wonderful time with you, Nick. Thank you so much. You've made this cruise very special."

"You talk as if you don't think you'll ever see me again."

Nicole was embarrassed. She honestly believed that to be the case. "But you live in Florida and I live in New York."

"They aren't that far apart. Only a couple of hours away. Besides, I do a lot of business in New York."

"Mark is there," she said.

Nick did not respond immediately. He knew she still loved him and the last thing he wanted was for her to be hurt, but he would be lying if he didn't admit to himself that he secretly hoped things would not work out between her and her husband. He looked into her eyes, but she shifted her gaze. He stopped their dance and took her chin in his hand and tilted her head up so he could look into her eyes. "You still love him very much, don't you?"

As Nicole looked into his eyes, she saw a hint of sadness there. Her eyes began to water.

He hugged her close and whispered, "It's all right, Nicky. I understand. I don't expect you to just forget him because you've met me. I hope everything turns out the way you want it to. But you must know I care for you tremendously. I hope you won't forget me."

Nicole looked at him and said, "I'll never forget you, Nick. You will always be very special to me. I wish it could be different for us."

"I'll tell you something, Nicole, if things don't work out with your husband, I'm ready to step in and take his place."

She looked into his eyes, then kissed him softly. She was grateful to him for being there when she needed someone to just be there. She was exceedingly grateful he accepted her terms for their relationship without trying to persuade her to change her mind. She genuinely cared about him. He was a very sweet man and he had been wonderful to her in the past three weeks. She could not have asked for more.

Chapter Nineteen

As Nicole walked through the airport to the baggage claim area, she smiled as she thought about her vacation with Nick. She decided she would call him as soon as she got back to her apartment.

"Nicole!" She heard the familiar voice call her name, and she froze in her tracks. She turned and was shocked to see Mark standing near the terminal exit. As he began to walk toward her, she wondered what he was doing there. *How did he know I'd be back today and now?*

"Hi," he said, leaning down to kiss her.

"Hello."

"How was your trip?"

"Fine."

Suddenly, she thought, *something's happened to Tiandra.* "Where's Tiandra?" she asked nervously.

"She's with your mother."

"Is she all right?"

"Yes, she's fine."

"Why are you here?"

"I figured you'd need a ride home," he said as he took the totebag she was carrying.

"How did you know when I was coming in?"

"Reggie told me. Why didn't you tell me you were going away?"

"Because I knew you would try to stop me."

"Why would I try to stop you?"

"Because you were the reason I had to leave. Didn't you know that?"

Mark didn't know what to say to that. He knew he had hurt her at the party, although she tried to pretend he hadn't. He felt terrible knowing she felt she had to run away from him again. "I'm sorry, Nicole. I wish you would have come to me . . ."

"And said what? It's not like we were living together like a married couple. You can do whatever you want. You don't have to explain anything to me."

"Then why'd you run away?"

"Because it took me to be away from you to accept that it's really over between us. Seeing you on Christmas gave me hope that things would change, but now I know they won't."

"But that's why I'm here, because they can change. We belong together, Nicole. Let's stop playing this silly game."

"Silly game? This was your idea, Mark," she said angrily. "You wanted me to leave. I only did as you asked. No, excuse me, as you ordered me to do. After seeing you with Ashlei, it's not easy for me to forget how happy you are without me."

"But I'm not happy without you. I need you," he admitted with a slight plea in his voice.

"It's too late. I've come to accept things as they are. I'm not a yo-yo. I can't change my feelings from one moment to the next with your words. Before I saw the two of you together, I would have been very receptive to your way of thinking, but it took you hurting me again before you realized you wanted us to be together. I don't want you to hurt me anymore, Mark. I don't want to hear you telling me how sorry you are for hurting me. I'm tired of crying over you."

"I'll never hurt you again, Nicole," he vowed.

"Never say never."

"Baby, just hear me out. Just give me another chance. That's all I'm asking."

"Look, I'm tired. I've got to get my bags," she said as she started toward the claim area.

Mark stood where he was and watched her walk away from him. *Please,* he prayed, *don't let it be too late.*

They rode in relative silence from the airport, caught up in their own thoughts. After fifteen minutes, Nicole said "Take me to my mother's house, Mark. I want to get Tiandra."

She's probably asleep by now. Why don't you wait until tomorrow to pick her up?"

"I don't want to wait until tomorrow. I've been away from her long enough."

"One more night's not going to make a whole lot of difference."

"To me, it will."

"I was hoping we could sit down and try to work something out between us."

"I'm tired. I just want to get Tiandra, take her home and go to sleep, if you don't mind."

Mark sighed. He could tell she was on the verge of getting angry again. That was not what he wanted. He decided to take her to get Tiandra instead of arguing with her. He was sure he could get her to listen to what he had to say once she was home.

When they arrived at Nicole's apartment, she took Tiandra straight to her room and put her to bed. She had been asleep when they reached her mother's house and Nicole had hated waking her, but she had missed her so much that she had to see her right away.

Nicole went to her bedroom after she put Tiandra back to bed and began unpacking, ignoring Mark completely. She was angry that he had assumed she would be happy to see him. On the contrary, he was the last person she wanted to see right now.

She was tired of being treated like a rubber ball, thrown away one minute, only to be retrieved then thrown away again. She would not stand for it. She didn't have to. She realized that she had been naive to think she should be grateful that someone like Mark would want her to be his woman, lover and wife. She had been stupid to actually believe he was perfect and that he could do no wrong. Those days were over. That way of thinking was dead. He was a man just like any other and she was a woman, a good woman who deserved the best, and his careless treatment of her was far below what she deserved and she would not tolerate it any longer.

Since Nicole did not return to the living room, intentionally, Mark decided to stroll back to the bedroom to see what was keeping her.

"Nicole, why are you ignoring me?"

"If I was ignoring you, you wouldn't be here."

"Look, can't we work this out? I'm tired of living alone."

"So move Ashlei in. I'm sure she'd be more than happy to live with you," Nicole said, never stopping her unpacking.

"I don't want to be with Ashlei. I want you. You're my wife. We belong together, not living apart like this."

"Like I said before, this was your idea. I've gotten used to it and it's not so bad."

"What about Tiandra?"

"What about Tiandra? She's not suffering. She knows who her parents are."

"Come on, Nicole. Don't tell me you like living this way. I know you've got to be lonely. You haven't been going out or seeing anyone, you told me that yourself. I know you, baby. I know you need to be loved sometimes."

Nicole was infuriated by his assumptions. She stopped unpacking and turned to him. "What makes you think I'm so lonely because you're not here? For your information, Mark Peterson, I'm not as lonely as you think," Nicole said adamantly.

Mark was patronizing her when he said, "All right, all right. So you're not as lonely as I said. You just spent three weeks on a ship by yourself. I guess you weren't lonely then either, right?"

That was it. "For your information, I was not alone! I met a man on the cruise. A very nice man and I spent the entire time with him. We had a ball," she said defiantly.

Her outburst shocked Mark. *She's lying.* "Is that why you got off the plane alone?" he asked smugly.

"He lives in Florida and I plan to see him again."

"Don't hold your breath," he sneered.

"You hate the idea that I might be interested in someone else, don't you? You can't bear to think of me with anyone but you. You're not the only man on this earth, Mark. My world doesn't revolve around you. I've grown up. I've seen the light. I had a wonderful time on that cruise with Nick and not once did I think about you!"

Now it was Mark's turn to be angry. "Why are you bragging about some chump you met on your cruise? So what! He screwed you and now he's gone. That's nothing to brag about, Nicole. You don't seriously think you'll see him again, do you? He probably pegged you right from the start. He figured since you were by yourself, you would be an easy target and obviously, he was right. You didn't do anything that great. He made a fool of you and you're standing here bragging about it."

"You'd love to believe that, wouldn't you?" She wasn't about to tell him that she hadn't slept with Nick. If he wanted to believe she was that easy. . . . "Well, you know what? You can believe what you want to, Mark, and while you're at it, you can get the hell out of my house!"

He glared at her for a few seconds, then turned and strode out of the room and the apartment, slamming the door behind him.

Mark could not remember having been this angry in years. *How dare she throw me out of her house?* He had convinced himself that she was lying about this guy Nick she claimed to have met on the cruise. *Hmph, does she think she can make me jealous just by inventing some guy's name? She couldn't even be more imaginative than to come up with something other than Nick. And that crack about her world doesn't revolve around me, where'd she get that mess from?* He knew he was the best thing that had ever happened to her and now she wants to play hard to get. *Well, two can play that game, if that's what she wants. We'll see who comes running to who first.*

Nicole didn't hear from Mark for the rest of the week. She was glad, too, because she was tired of his holier than thou attitude. He had some nerve telling her she had been made a fool of. He was just jealous because she'd told him about Nick. She hadn't wanted to throw it in his face like that, but what was she supposed to do? He was so certain her life was miserable without him, and he was so arrogant about it, she had to let him know that life goes on and she was trying as hard as she could to deal with that reality.

She spoke to Nick twice that week. She had been ecstatic when he called. Although she would never admit it to Mark, she had been apprehensive about whether she would hear from him again. She was a little ashamed for doubting Nick's truthfulness. She could hardly wait to see him again, and she told him as much when they talked.

Chapter Twenty

The Saturday following their fight, Mark called Nicole to tell her he was coming over to see Tiandra. As much as she didn't want to see him, she gave him the okay because she had promised that she would never keep Tiandra from Mark again.

When Mark arrived, he barely said two words to Nicole, but she had no conversation for him either. He went into Tiandra's room and stayed there playing with her the entire time he was there. She went about her business of cleaning house.

Nicole knew the way she and Mark were behaving was childish, but she refused to be the one to always give in when something went wrong. It was Mark who put the wheels in motion on this emotional roller coaster when he invited his ex-girlfriend into his hotel room. Now they seemed destined to ride it forever.

While Nicole was busy cleaning her apartment and Mark was busy entertaining Tiandra, Nick Latargia was in the lobby of Nicole's building trying to persuade the doorman to let him upstairs.

He had come up from Florida the night before for a meeting with some business associates and decided to stay over so he could see Nicole before he flew back. He'd spoken to her on Thursday, but didn't tell her he was coming to New York because at the time he hadn't been sure if he would have time to see her. Once he reached the city, however, he knew there was no way he could leave without seeing her. She had been on his mind every day since their cruise ended.

Instead of calling to let her know he was in town, though, he decided to surprise her. When he got to her building, he had not expected to find a doorman that would not let him upstairs.

Finally, Nick decided the only way he could get this guy to ease up was to offer him some cash. *Money talks,* Nick thought. The doorman reacted exactly as Nick figured he would to the crisp fifty-dollar bill he slid across the desk. The man discreetly took the bill off the desk and slipped it into his pocket. "Sign in."

When he reached Nicole's front door, Nick hesitated for a moment before he rang the bell. *Maybe I should have called first,* he thought. Maybe she wasn't even home. Well, the only way to find out, he figured, was to ring the bell. He did.

"Who is it?" Nicole asked from the other side of the door.

He smiled when he heard her voice. "Nick," came the answer.

Nicole thought she was hearing things. "Who?"

"Nick. Latargia. Have you forgotten me already?" he called through the door.

Nicole's heart hit the floor. Nick. *What is he doing here?* She unlocked the door as fast as she could, forgetting she was wearing a pair of beat-up jeans and a beat-up T-shirt. Her hair was not combed but she didn't think about that either. She could not believe Nick was actually at her door.

"Hi, beautiful. Surprise!"

"Hi!" Nicole said, grinning like a schoolgirl on her first date.

"Aren't you going to invite me in?" he asked with a smile.

"Oh, yes. I'm sorry," she said quickly, a little embarrassed.

He stepped inside and Nicole closed the door. Suddenly, she remembered how she was dressed and cursed herself for not being more presentable. As she turned around to apologize for her appearance, Nick stepped up to her, wrapped her in his arms and kissed her before she could get a word out of her mouth. As quickly as she remembered what she was wearing, she forgot and returned his embrace, giving herself up to his sweet kiss.

"It's good to see you, sweetness," Nick whispered to her when their lips parted.

"It's good to see you, too. Why didn't you tell me you were coming up when I spoke to you Thursday?" Nicole asked, still wrapped in his embrace.

"I didn't know if I'd have time to see you."

"You mean you would have come all the way up here and left without stopping by?"

"I'm here, right?"

She smiled and said, "Yes. I m glad you are, but you still could have called me."

"I wanted to surprise you.

"Well, you did. I look terrible, too. At least if you had called, I could have put on some decent clothes and combed my hair," Nicole said, running her hand across the crown of her head.

"You don't look terrible, you look beautiful," Nick said. He gave her a quick kiss.

"Yeah, right."

"So how've you been, gorgeous? You know, I missed you," Nick whispered sweetly.

Upon seeing Nick, Nicole momentarily forgot that Mark was in the apartment. As fate would have it, Mark emerged from Tiandra's bedroom at that moment. When he entered the living room and saw Nicole locked in an embrace with this stranger, he almost lost it. He hadn't heard anyone come into the apartment and for Nicole to have the gall to stand there like she was, rubbing up with this guy while he was there, was too much for him to handle.

Nicole's back was to him, so she did not notice Mark, but Nick did, the moment he entered the room. He knew, too, that the obviously furious man standing there was Mark Peterson, Nicole's estranged husband. "You have company," he stated as he took a step back.

Nicole froze instantly. When she turned to look at Mark, she saw a look of rage on his face unlike any she had ever seen. She didn't know what to say at that moment. She was fairly positive, however, that he did not want to be introduced to Nick.

Mark was livid. He wanted to hurt this man. He wanted to hurt her, like he was hurting from seeing her with him. *How could she do this to me?* There were so many things he wanted to say and do at that moment, all of which he knew he would later regret, so instead he strode past them, purposely bumping into Nick as he went to the door, and stormed out of the apartment.

When Mark bumped him, Nick started to retaliate but he refrained for Nicole's sake.

Nicole moved away from Nick and slowly started across the room. She hadn't wanted this to happen. She knew she had hurt Mark and she was sorry for that.

Nick was filled with disillusion and self-reproach. He should have called first like he started to. Obviously, there had not been as much conflict between them as Nicole had led him to believe. Otherwise, Mark would not have been there, would he?

"I'm sorry, Nicole. I should have called. I had no idea he would be here," Nick said.

Nicole turned to face him. "That's all right, it's not your fault. I didn't know he'd be here today, either. He just called this morning to say he was coming over to see Tiandra. I haven't spoken to him all week," she said softly.

"I didn't want to cause any problems for you with your husband."

"I know. I didn't want that to happen like this, either."

"He looked really pissed. Maybe I'd better go. I'll call next time, before I come."

She didn't want him to leave. She did not want to be alone now. "Please don't go, Nick. He won't be back. You came all this way and I'm not sorry you're here. I'm just sorry you two had to meet this way."

He went to her and put his arms around her and held her close to him. She was comforted by his embrace. "I'm sorry," he said sincerely. "I should have been more thoughtful and less selfish. I just wanted to see you so bad I didn't think about anyone else."

With a sad smile, she said, "Don't worry about it. It's not as though we were getting along that great, anyway."

"Yeah, but I didn't have to come along and add fuel to the fire, either."

"Well, he would have met you sooner or later. I already told him about you."

Nick was surprised. "You did?"

"Yeah." She stepped out of his embrace and moved across the room. With her back to him, she continued, "We had a fight last weekend when I got back. I didn't tell you, but he was waiting for me at the airport when my plane landed. We had an argument and I told him about you. He thought I was making the whole thing up, though. I know that. He just made me so angry. I didn't mean to use you to get back at him, but I didn't know what else to say to him, so I told him I'd spent the entire cruise with you."

Nick did not appreciate being used as a tool of vengeance against Nicole's husband, but he did appreciate her honesty in telling him as much. He wondered what was really going on with them. Were they playing a game of tit for tat or was this marriage over?

"Nicky, how do you feel about your husband? Do you love him or what?"

"I'm not sure anymore." She turned to face him. "He's hurt me so many times and I'm tired of being hurt. I'd put him on a pedestal, which wasn't fair because nobody's perfect. But things just kept happening that seemed to be tearing us apart. I didn't want our marriage to end but something happened on

New Year's Eve that made me see things differently. That's why I took the cruise. I needed to be away from him to decide what I wanted to do for myself. By the time I got back, he'd changed his way of thinking and expected me to just fall in line with his plans, but I wouldn't. That's why we had the fight. Right now, I don't want to be with him because the hurt is too fresh in my mind and my need to heal myself is more important to me. I've gotten used to living by myself and I'm beginning to feel good about myself once again. For a while, I was so down I just figured everything that was going wrong in our marriage was my fault. But I don't feel that way anymore. I've got to think about what's best for me before I can work on what's best for Mark and me.''

"What do you want from me?" Nick asked.

Nicole took a seat on the sofa. She was thoughtful for a moment before she answered him. "Your friendship, your companionship, whatever you're willing to share with me. You're special to me, Nick. The time we spent together was special. I enjoyed that time. I needed it. If you don't want to be here, I'll understand because my life is kind of crazy right now. I want you to know, though, that I don't want to hurt you, ever, and if we can be friends, I'll give you the best of my time and myself. That's all I can promise you.''

Nick studied her face as she said these words to him. He cared for Nicole. She said she wanted to be friends. Was that what he wanted from her, though? He was not sure. He was sure he did not want to give up on her already. The time they spent together on the cruise, he felt, was the beginning of something he was sure could be so much more. They had something magical between them.

"What happens if you decide you made a mistake about Mark? Where will that leave me?"

"I can't see the way I feel changing any time in the near future. I can't give you any guarantees about me or us, but you won't get that anywhere. I know how I feel right now. I want us to be friends, Nick, but only if you want that, too. I'm not going to promise you how it's going to be a year from now. All I can vouch for is the present.''

Nick walked across the room and took her hands in his. He pulled her to her feet, looked into her eyes and smiled at her. In that instant, he realized he was falling in love with her. ''We'll take it a day at a time, okay?'' Nick said to her.

''Okay,'' she answered with a smile.

Nick spent the rest of the day with Nicole and Tiandra. The following morning, however, at a few minutes of eight, Nick was at Nicole's door once again. When he left the night before, he inadvertently forgot his appointment book. He had a nine thirty flight back to Miami, so on his way to the airport he stopped by to pick it up.

Nicole was in the middle of brushing her teeth when he rang her doorbell. With her toothbrush in hand and toothpaste foaming in her mouth, she mumbled, ''I'll be right back, Nick,'' after she let him in. As she headed back to the bathroom, the telephone rang.

''Nick, would you pick that up for me?'' she called to him.

''You sure?'' he asked.

''Yeah.''

He picked up the extension on the wall in the kitchen. ''Hello.''

There was no response on the other end. Then the line went dead.

''Who was it?'' she asked as she entered the kitchen.

''Must have been a wrong number. They hung up.''

Nicole shrugged and put the call out of her mind.

Mark was hurt to see that she had found someone else. He thought she still loved him. That's what she'd said on New Year's Day. *Had she lied to me?* He wanted to explain to her why Ashlei had been there. He wanted to tell her that Ashlei meant nothing to him. He wanted to tell her that he loved her, too. They had been through so much together, he couldn't imagine that their marriage could really end. He didn't want to accept that, but she obviously didn't want to be with him anymore. Seeing her with her arms around that man was something he could not fathom. *Doesn't she know how much I need her? Doesn't she know I don't want to live without her anymore?* He knew his selfishness had been immature and pushing her away had just been a way of easing his wounded pride, but he never meant for it to go this far. He never thought she would take it to heart and turn to someone else.

He couldn't let this happen. She was his wife and he loved her and needed her. If it took a fight to claim what was rightfully his, he would fight. He could not let her get away.

He picked up the telephone to call her. He was willing to throw away his pride, beg her forgiveness and ask her to give him one more chance to make everything right, the way it should be. He only hoped she would not hang up on him. He hoped she would listen.

He listened to Nicole's phone ring three times in his ear.

"Answer the phone, Nicole." he said into the receiver. At that moment the receiver was picked up. A man's voice said, "Hello."

Mark was thrown for a loop. He thought, *I must have a wrong number. What was a man doing answering her phone?* Then it hit him. He was still there. *She let that bastard spend the night!* Mark slammed down the receiver. *How could she do this? How could she let him sleep there?* She was his wife and now she was behaving like a tramp, letting this guy sleep over.

Mark ceased to think rationally upon hearing the man's voice on the line. All he could think of was getting to Nicole's apartment and physically removing the man from the premises.

* * *

"I'll give you a call when I get home to let you know I made it in one piece, all right?" Nick said as he was leaving.

"All right," Nicole said with a smile.

He kissed her softly on the mouth and said, "Be good, sweetheart. I'll see you in a week."

"Okay."

Nick left Nicole's apartment at eight fifteen. Mark arrived thirty minutes later. He was in such a rage that when he reached the building, he did not stop at the desk to sign in or call to see if he could even go upstairs. The doorman called after him trying to stop him, but Mark paid him no heed. All he saw was red. All he heard was that man's voice on her phone. When he reached her door, he did not use the bell. He banged on the door like a man possessed.

The sound of banging on the door scared Nicole and caused Tiandra to cry. Nervously, Nicole went to the door and asked, "Who is it?"

"Mark!"

What's he doing here, she wondered. She unlocked the door but before she could even open it all the way, he pushed it open with a bang. He barged into the apartment and walked straight to the bedroom. Nicole ran behind him.

"Mark, what's wrong? What are you doing?"

"Where is he?" Mark yelled.

"What?"

"Where the hell is he, Nicole? Where's the bastard you have answering your phone?"

"What are you talking about?"

"You know good and well what I'm talking about," Mark said between clenched teeth. "You let that bastard spend the night here, didn't you?"

"What are you talking about?" Nicole asked.

"What do you mean, what am I talking about? I know he spent the night here! You had him answering the damn phone for you this morning."

Nicole didn't even remember the phone ringing earlier. "You didn't call here this morning."

"Yes, I did call and he answered the phone! What did he do, screw you and leave you again?"

Now she was beginning to anger. "For your information, Mark Peterson, no one slept here last night but me and Tiandra. But you know what? You've got a lot of nerve barging in here, talking about people spending the night. Nothing kept you from sleeping with Ms. Ashlei Brown, so don't you dare preach to me about anything."

He didn't tell her that he'd never slept with Ashlei. "You let that man sleep here and my daughter is here! You didn't even have the decency to take her to your mother's house while you were screwing. If you don't care any more about her than that, I'll take her off your hands and you won't ever have to bother with her again, then you can screw whoever you want."

"What are you talking about?" she asked, her tone questioning whether he had lost his mind or not. "He didn't spend the night here. What do you think I am?"

"I used to think you were a lady. But now I'm not so sure. You meet this guy, you don't know anything about him, you let him come here and you screw him while my daughter's here; then he leaves. What does that make you?"

Nicole looked at him in disgust. "You're losing your mind," she sneered. "You kill me, talking about 'your daughter'. She's my daughter, too, or have you suddenly forgotten that? You can't come into my house, acting all high and mighty and tell me anything. You don't pay my bills. You're not doing anything for me. If you've got a problem with my friends, then don't come around when they're here!"

"Is he paying your bills, baby? How much money did he give you for your services?"

Mark's implication was the last straw. Without thinking, Nicole hauled off and slapped him, hard, in the face. The impact of her blow snapped his head to the side.

Instantly, she knew she had made a mistake.

Seconds later, when he turned his head back to look at her, a chill went through her body. His eyes were like ice, cold and hard. It was as if there was no longer any feeling inside of him.

He stepped closer to her, his stare never wavering. Nicole winced, suddenly very afraid.

Mark was in shock. He couldn't believe she had actually hit him. He took several deep breaths before he was able to speak. He knew if he had acted on impulse to the slap, he would have hurt her.

When he was certain that he was in control of his emotions, Mark smiled at her. Nicole shivered; he suddenly looked quite maniacal. In a barely audible voice he said, "I know you just had a mental lapse and because I know that's what's happening, I'm going to forget what you just did and leave while I still can. But I swear, Nicole, if you ever put your hands on me like that again, if you ever even think about hitting me again, I'll . . ." He paused abruptly in his speech, stilling his tongue before he said something he knew he would never be able to take back. Instead, he turned without another word and walked out of the apartment.

As he left the building and walked back to his car, a tear slid down his cheek. He opened the door to his car and sat behind the wheel, but he made no move to start the vehicle. He was too upset. *How can you be so stupid? Why did you say those things to her? No wonder she doesn't want to be with you.* He knew he had gone overboard this time. No wonder she'd slapped him like that. They'd had arguments before, very heated arguments. They both had fierce tempers and they had both said things to one another they later apologized for when

making up, but never before had the idea that she would actually
strike him ever cross his mind.

Mark's hand instinctively went to his cheek. He rubbed the
spot where she let him have it. *Damn,* he thought, *she hits
pretty hard.* If she had been anyone else, he would have laid
her out. But he knew he deserved this. He was never more
sorry for anything he had done in his life. She said she hadn't
slept with him, that he hadn't spent the night. Then why had
he been there that morning? Where was he now?

After a few minutes, Mark took a deep breath and started
his car. As he drove, he thought about Nicole and what he told
her after she slapped him. He was glad he'd restrained himself.
The words he'd bit back would have done irreparable damage.
But he had never been so angry or hurt in his life.

He'd never known that loving someone could be so painful.
He'd never known what it was like to live for someone's love.
Believing that she was giving her love to someone else was a
circumstance he did not want to face. Even though they hadn't
been on the best of terms before this, it was easier to believe
that eventually they would both see how silly they were behaving and realize they belonged together.

He wanted to blame her for this, but he knew in his heart
this whole mess was his fault. In the beginning it was nowhere
near as serious as it was now. But they had let it snowball into
something that was now bigger than both of them. Instead of
stopping and listening to each other, they just yelled and
screamed about the injustices they had done to one another.
Instead of trying to patch up the little rift between them, they
had each taken turns pulling it farther and farther apart. Now
they were no longer one but two, separate and individual. Even
having Tiandra between them could not mend the tear in their
relationship now.

He wanted to hate her for hurting him, but more so, he hated
himself for his weakness and selfishness. She had always been
a good wife, mother and friend. She had always been there for

him when the chips were down and he couldn't turn to anyone else. And when he needed her the most, after his heart attack, his pride would not allow him to forgive her for running away from him, when it was his carelessness that pushed her away in the first place. Instead, he'd pushed her farther away.

Knowing he had pushed her into the arms of another man ripped his soul in two. He knew he would never find another woman like her. He knew he would never know true love and happiness again like he had when they were together.

Nicole cried, too, when Mark left, although, not for the same reasons. Yes, she was upset that their marriage was, without a doubt, a thing of the past and, yes, she was upset that it had to end this way, but she cried mostly from relief.

He had never looked at her with such vivid rage and she never wanted to see anyone look at her like that again. At the very moment he threatened her, she believed in her heart that he would hurt her. She now wondered if he really could.

She hadn't meant to slap him, but when he implied that she was sleeping with Nick, for money no less, she had been so insulted and shocked by his words that she reacted purely on impulse. He didn't even hear her when she told him that Nick had not spent the night. He just continued with his tirade as if she hadn't said a word.

She cared for Nick because he was such a wonderful man. She knew he genuinely cared for her simply because he had been willing to wait until she was ready to be with him, but she was sorry that she and Mark would never be together again. Even after seeing him with Ashlei, Nicole never stopped believing that eventually he would realize there was no one else who could love him the way she did and they would be together once again, happy together, like they had been in the beginning.

Nicole got up from the sofa and went to take Tiandra out

of her crib. Mark had awakened her when he banged on the door and Nicole had meant to go to her then, but he had been so irate that Nicole forgot about her for a moment and Tiandra had gone back to sleep.

How could he think such terrible things about me? He might as well have called me a whore outright. Suddenly, Nicole thought about Mark's heart. What if, in his enraged state, he had another heart attack? She still felt responsible for the first one.

Thoughts of his heart attack made her angry once more. How dare he preach to her about Nick? He was the one that had been unfaithful to her in the first place, no matter how much he denied it. If he hadn't been found with that woman in his hotel room, it was probable that none of this would have ever happened.

Then there was Ashlei. He obviously didn't know how much it hurt to see him with her. Did he think she had no feelings? As she removed Tiandra from her crib and held her, tears filled her eyes once more. They had been so perfect together. Tiandra was proof of that. She was perfect and had been made from their love. Nicole asked herself what more could she be to Mark than what she had been?

Chapter
Twenty-One

Two weeks later, since the temp agency she was registered with didn't have any assignments that appealed to her, Nicole decided she would go to Florida and spend a few weeks with Nick. The day before her planned trip to Miami, she went by

Mark's office to tell him of her plans. She didn't want to see him at all and hadn't seen him since their fallout, but she knew she had to tell him where she would be in case of an emergency, since she was taking Tiandra.

Mark was standing in front of his desk holding the telephone at his ear when Nicole entered his office. She tapped on the open door to get his attention. He turned at the sound and was surprised to see Nicole standing in the doorway. He stared at her for a moment before he gestured for her to come in.

She looks great, he thought. He felt a stirring in his loins as the thought of making love to her involuntarily entered his mind. She was wearing a short, dark brown mink jacket and matching skull cap. The brown suede pants she wore showed off her exquisite figure. She wore red leather riding boots and a red angora sweater. To Mark, she was still the most beautiful woman in the world. He wished he could tell her as much.

While Nicole waited for Mark to finish his call, her thoughts were very similar to his. She had always loved to see him at work. He was always so impeccably dressed. Even when he was just in a shirt and tie, as he was now, he was still sharp as a tack. While he spoke into the phone, he turned his back to her once more and faced the window. Just like the first time she'd seen him, her eyes were automatically drawn to his backside. She used to love pinching his behind, especially if he was not expecting it. He used to call her a "bootie bandit" and she would get a real kick out of catching him off guard. At that moment, she felt a strong urge to squeeze his cheeks, but she let the urge die. Their time of fun and games was over.

Mark completed his call and replaced the receiver on the phone. He sauntered around the desk and sat down. She stood in the middle of his office, facing him. "What can I do for you, Nicole?" Mark asked casually, as he looked up at her.

Responding in kind, Nicole said, "I just came by to let you know that I'm going to Miami tomorrow. I'll be there for a few weeks. I just thought I'd let you know where I'll be staying in case of an emergency.'' She took a piece of paper from her pocketbook and handed it to him.

He stared at her for a moment before he reached for the slip of paper she held in her hand.

As he read the address printed on the note, Nicole said, "I'm taking Tiandra with me so if you want to see her before I leave, you can come by tonight."

"Why can't you stay in a hotel?" Mark said softly, knowing the address was Nick's.

"Why should I?"

"I'd rather you stayed in a hotel since you're taking Tiandra with you."

"What difference does it make?"

Raising his voice slightly. Mark said, "It makes a lot of difference."

"To you, not to me."

They stared at each other defiantly.

"What's his full name, Nicole?"

"Nicolas Latargia. Why?" she asked with a frown of skepticism.

"Latargia? What is he, Italian?" he said with a smirk as he scribbled the name on a notepad on his desk.

Nicole didn't think this was funny, so she turned to leave.

"What do you know about him?"

She turned and said, "I know all I need to know."

"Yeah, that's what I figured," he said as he rose from his chair. "You don't know anything about him. I'd rather you didn't take Tiandra with you on your little expedition."

"Well, that's too bad, because I'm taking her whether you like it or not!"

Mark's temper was rising. He stepped from behind the desk. "What does he do?"

"What do you mean, what does he do?"

"What line of work is he in?" Mark clarified.

She hated being grilled like this, but she knew if she didn't tell him, he wouldn't let her take Tiandra. "He owns an import-export business," Nicole said arrogantly.

"Import-export business? What does he import and export? Oranges or drugs?"

Nicole was shocked by his accusation.

Before she could answer, Mark said, "Latargia sounds like an Italian name. Was he adopted by someone in the mob?"

"That's what you'd like to think, that he's doing something illegal. You don't know anything, Mark. You just can't stand to think of me with anyone but you," she sneered.

Mark chuckled and said, "Don't flatter yourself, baby. You're not that hot."

Nicole's eyes were beginning to water. *Don't cry,* she told herself. *Don't let him see you cry anymore!* She pulled herself together quickly and said, "Look! I didn't come here to argue with you and I don't have to justify anything I do or that Nick does. I'm leaving tomorrow and I'm taking Tiandra. If you want to see her, you'd better come by tonight. Otherwise, you'll see her when I get back!" With that, she turned and proudly strode out of his office.

Mark was furious. *How dare she come into my office and speak to me like that? She doesn't know who she's dealing with, but that's all right.* He knew he could find out everything he needed to about Nick Latargia. Something in his gut told him this guy was up to no good.

He picked up the telephone and dialed. "Detective Sandra McAllister, please."

"One moment," the voice on the other end said.

A few seconds later . . . "McAllister, here. Can I help you?"

"Hey Sandy. How you doin'?"

"Mark? What's up, stranger?" she asked.

"Ain't nothin', baby. What's good?"

"You, I'm sure."

"Would you like to find out?"

''No, thanks. I'll just wonder. I wouldn't want to spoil the fantasy.''

''Still playing hard to get, huh?'' he asked good-naturedly.

''Always. That's what makes it so much fun.''

''I beg to differ.''

''So, what's up? What can I do for you?''

''I need the services of your vast range of information.''

''Talk to me.''

Becoming serious, he said, ''I need information on someone. A guy named Nicolas Latargia. He lives in Florida. Miami, to be specific. I have an address if it'll help.'' He gave her Nick's address. ''He owns an import-export company and I think he might be connected to the mob. He might also have an address in New York, but I'm not sure.''

''White guy?''

''Naw, he's black.''

''With a name like Latargia?''

''Yeah, believe it or not. He's probably a half-breed. I'm not sure. He's very fair-skinned. Would you try to find out whatever you can about him and let me know?''

''Sure, Mark. What's up?''

''A friend of mine has gotten hooked up with this guy and I'm just looking out. I don't want to see her get into any trouble with him.''

''Okay, baby. Listen, how soon do you need it?''

''As soon as possible, but don't put yourself in a bind over it.''

''All right. Give me a couple of days and I'll get back to you.''

''Good enough. Thanks, Sandy. I owe you one.''

''You owe me two, turkey.''

Mark smiled and said, ''Whatever you say, beautiful. I'll talk to you later.''

* * *

While Nicole was in Florida, Mark took a trip to Jamaica. The resort was doing great and Mark was pleased at how well it and a few other ventures he was involved in were doing. If only his private life ran as smoothly, he wouldn't have a care in the world.

While he was there, he paid a visit to Yvonne and Lucien. Mark had not spoken to either of them in quite a while and they were glad to see him when he showed up at their house.

Yvonne greeted him with a hug and kiss. "Hi, stranger. How are you?"

"Hi, Yvonne. I'm fine. How are you? You look great." He had always been very fond of Yvonne and living in the islands definitely agreed with her.

"Why, thank you, sir. You look quite good yourself. It's good to see you."

"You, too. How's my man?"

"He's fine. He's out back," she said as they held each other around the waist and started through the house. "He'll be glad to see you. We were just talking about you yesterday."

"I hope it was good.'

"It was all right," Yvonne said with a smile.

"Well, that's better than nothing."

They walked through the kitchen to the backyard. Lucien was working in his vegetable garden. "Luce, look who's here," Yvonne called as she stepped through the door.

Mark followed her. At the sight of his friend, a big grin crossed his face.

"Wow!" Lucien exclaimed, "I thought this guy was dead, it's been so long."

Mark laughed and said, "All right now, don't start none, won't be none."

Lucien walked across the yard to greet Mark. They shook hands and embraced.

"How you doin', guy?" Lucien asked.

"I'm hangin' in there. How about you?"

"You know me, tough as nails, man. It's good to see you," Lucien said sincerely.

"You, too."

"Come on inside."

As they walked back into the house, Yvonne asked, "How's my gorgeous goddaughter?"

"She's fine, Yvonne. She's in Florida right now with Nicole."

"Nicky's in Florida?" Yvonne asked.

"Yeah. She didn't tell you she was going to see her boyfriend?"

"No, that turkey." Yvonne ignored the 'boyfriend' comment.

"Yeah, well, you know how people keep things to themselves when they're unsure about what they're doing, that way they don't have to listen to anyone telling them something they don't want to hear," Mark declared.

Yvonne also let that comment ride without any of her own. "When did she leave?" she asked, instead.

"Friday."

"When's she going back home?"

"I don't know. She said she was going to stay for a few weeks. Your guess is as good as mine," Mark said, shrugging his shoulders.

"Mark, what are you drinking?" Lucien asked, trying to change the subject.

"Scotch. On the rocks."

"Mark, you're going to stay for dinner, right?" Yvonne asked.

"Come on, Yvonne. Me, leave and not eat any of your

exquisite cooking? What do you think, I've lost it or something?''

"Yeah, that's right, soup me up.''

Lucien had an extensive collection of old jazz albums and after dinner, he and Mark went into the den to listen to a few of them.

After cleaning up in the kitchen, Yvonne came into the den to tell Lucien she was going next door to visit with their neighbor. "Mark, if you're not here when I get back, take it easy," she said as she leaned over his chair to kiss him.

"All right, beautiful. You, too. I promise it won't be as long in between my next visit."

"It better not be, or we're going to fight."

"Well, since you put it that way, I'll make sure it's not. I know I don't stand a chance against you."

"See ya'," Yvonne said, grinning. She walked over and kissed Lucien. "I'll be back in a few."

"All right, sweets."

Once she was gone, Lucien felt he could speak freely to Mark about Nicole. He broached the subject very carefully. "Mark, what's up with you and Nicole?"

Mark knew this was inevitable. He was surprised it had not come up earlier. "Nothing."

"Is that what you want?"

"It's what she wants, so it's what I want."

"Come on, man. This is me. You can tell me how you really feel."

Mark gave Lucien a cynical look. "What makes you think that's not how I really feel?"

"Because I know you and I know Nicole and I know how you two are together. There's no way you can sit there and tell me you're happy with your situation."

"See, Lucien, that's where you're wrong. I am happy,"

Mark said, wanting desperately to believe it. "Maybe I wasn't at first, but hey, life goes on, right?"

"That's a cop-out, man, and you know it."

"Hey, look, she's doing what she wants and I'm doing what I want. I don't need her."

"You're telling me that you don't love Nicole anymore?"

"That's right."

"I don't believe you," Lucien said with a wave of his hand.

Mark rose abruptly from his seat. "I don't care whether you believe me or not, Lucien. I'm sick and tired of people telling me they know what I want or what's good for me or how I feel. Nicole is history! End of story! Life goes on, man. Life goes on."

Lucien looked up at Mark with sadness. He could see the hurt that Mark was trying so desperately to cover up. "How do you feel about this guy she's been seeing?" Lucien then asked.

Mark paced the floor. "I don't care about who she's running around with. She's a grown woman. She can do what she wants."

"Is that why you barged into her apartment like a madman, looking for him?"

Mark was becoming aggravated. "Why can't you leave it alone? Why can't everybody just leave it alone? Why is it that everywhere I go, I have to listen to this crap? First, Carol, now you. It's over!" It was just a week ago that he'd had a similar conversation with his sister.

"Mark, why are you running away from your feelings. Nicole is a beautiful woman. Whatever she's doing is because she's hurting, man, and she doesn't know what else to do. She's missing you and this guy is just a substitute. You know it and I know it. You've got a beautiful wife, man. It's a shame that you don't realize how beautiful she really is," Lucien said quietly.

Mark moved to the window and stared out at the sea. He

This fall, BET Arabesque Films will create 10 original African-American themed, made-for-TV movies based on the Arabesque Romance book series.

The list includes some of the best-loved Arabesque romances, including Francis Ray's *Incognito*, Donna Hill's *Intimate Betraya* Bridget Anderson's *Rendezvous*, Lynn Emery's *After All*, Felicia Mason's *Rhapsody*, Monica Jackson's *Midnight Blue*, Dianne Mayhew's *Playing with Fire*, Donna Hill's *A Private Affair*, Jacquelin Thomas' *Hidden Blessings, and* Donna Hill's *Masquerade*.

And now BET is offering you the chance to win a cameo appearance in one of these upcoming productions! Just think, you can join some of today's hottest African-American movie stars—like Richard T. Jones, Loretta Devine, and Holly Robinson—in the creation of a movie written by, and for, African-American romantics like yourself! All you have to do is complete the attached entry form and mail it in. Just think, if you act now, you could be in one of these exciting new movies! Mail your entry today!

PRIZES

The **GRAND PRIZE WINNER** will receive:
- A trip for two to Los Angeles.
  Think about it—3 days and 2 nights in L.A., round-trip airfare, hotel accommodations.

- $500 spending money, and round-trip transportation to and from the airport and movie set...sounds pretty good, right?

- And the winner's clip will be featured on the Arabesque website!

- As if that's not enough, you'll also get a one-year membership in the Arabesque Book Club and a BET Arabesque Romance gift-pack.

5 RUNNERS-UP will receive:
- One-year memberships in the Arabesque Book Club and BET Arabesque Romance gift-packs.

WIN A CHANCE TO BE IN A BET ARABESQUE FILM!

Yes! Enter me in the BET Arabesque Film Sweepstakes!

NAME _____

ADDRESS _____

CITY _____ STATE _____ ZIP _____

TELEPHONE _____ AGE _____

SIGNATURE _____

(MUST BE 21 OR OLDER TO ENTER)

Visit our website at www.arabesquebooks.com

ARABESQUE FILM SWEEPSTAKES
P.O. BOX 8060
GRAND RAPIDS, MN 55745-8060

AFFIX
STAMP
HERE

wished he could go somewhere where he could just forget about her, but everywhere he went someone had to remind him that she was out of his life. They all thought they had the answers, but no one knew what he was feeling. Why couldn't they just mind their own business and let him be?

"There's no reason to be ashamed of how you feel about her. I know if I lost Yvonne, . . . I know I'd be lost without her," Lucien admitted.

"Don't patronize me, Lucien," Mark said, turning to face him. "You can stand there and tell me 'what if' all night. You can't possibly know how I feel. I'm trying to deal with this the best way I know how but every time I turn around I have to listen to people telling me things they don't know anything about. No! I'm not happy she's in Florida with this guy. Is that what you want to hear? But what am I supposed to do about it? I'm not going to chase her. I tried to talk to her when she came back from that damn cruise she went on but she wouldn't talk to me! What should I do, beg her? No! I won't! If she wants to be with him, so be it. There's nothing I can do about that. I can't make her love me," Mark said with tears glistening in his eyes.

Lucien felt sorry for him. He had known Mark for many years and could remember when he first met Nicole and the look in Mark's eyes when he saw her. He'd been in love with her then and he had never even touched her. It broke his heart to see his friend in such turmoil. "I just thought maybe you'd like to talk about it. I'm sorry for prying into your business. You're my friend and I hate to see you like this. I'm sorry," Lucien said sadly.

A tear fell from Mark's eye and he wiped it away quickly in embarrassment. He knew Lucien meant well but he just didn't understand. No one did. This was something he would have to work out by himself. "Listen, I'm going to cut out. I've got a lot of work to do tomorrow and I'm kind of tired. Tell Yvonne I said thanks for dinner."

"Mark."

Mark had walked to the door of the den to leave. Reluctantly, he turned to face his friend. "What, Lucien?"

"You're right. It is easy for me to talk because Yvonne is here. But man to man, I guess I'd feel pretty much the same way you do now if I were in your shoes. Don't give up, bro. You know what's best for you."

Mark looked at Lucien for a long moment but made no comment. He simply turned and left. Thinking about Nicole on the long drive back from Lucien's caused him to reflect on everything Lucien, Carol and Nicole had said to him. He felt crippled at times because he loved her so much. He hated feeling this way and he fought with himself to remove the feeling from his heart, but no matter how he tried, there was no relief in sight.

Chapter Twenty-Two

Nicole stayed in Miami for almost three weeks. The majority of the time she was there, she lazed around Nick's twelve-room mansion, spending days by the pool or horseback riding (he had a stable with ten beautiful horses). There were a couple of times when she offered to cook for him, but he would not let her to do any kind of housework. He had an abundant household staff and he told her that whatever she wanted or needed, all she had to do was ask for it.

Nick put Nicole and Tiandra up in a beautifully decorated guest room, complete with private bath. Every night of their first week together, Nick tried, though not too insistently, to persuade Nicole to make love with him. She was relieved when he finally let the matter drop.

He gave her money and had a car available for her whenever she wanted to go anywhere, despite her reluctance to become more intimate with him. Twice, in the three weeks she was there, Nick had gone out of town overnight on business and left her, telling Nicole that his house was her house. Do as she pleased.

She enjoyed being there with him, too. He treated her like a queen and he made sure all his people treated her the same.

Nick took her out in the evenings to elegant dinner parties, some so extravagant they rivaled the ones she had attended with Mark. He took her dancing and to the theater. He owned a seventy-five foot yacht, and their first weekend together he took her sailing.

Nick showered her with gifts; jewels, clothing, perfumes, so many things that Nicole felt as though she would drown from his outpouring of generosity. He told her he was just so happy to have her there with him that he didn't know how to act.

The only thing about Nick that really bothered her was that he never talked about his work with her. Granted, he told her about owning his own business, but when she asked what kinds of products he imported and exported, he had been very vague and just told her "produce." Although she loved being at his house, she was slightly nervous about all the bodyguards he had around him. There were people all over the grounds and in the house.

One morning she awoke early and strolled onto the terrace in his bedroom. Nick was out of town on business. She saw a man on the back lawn carrying an automatic weapon. He was just standing there but when he realized he was being watched, he stared up at her, making her very uncomfortable. She turned and went back inside, closing the terrace doors and pulling the drapes together. She could not help but think about the accusation Mark had made about Nick being involved with drugs.

She didn't want to believe that was true, but deep in her heart she had little pangs of doubt.

Upon her return to New York, Nicole called Mark to let him know that Tiandra was back. He called her the next day and told her he would be by later that evening to see his daughter.

It was nine o'clock when Mark arrived at Nicole's apartment. When she opened the door to let him in, he stood just outside the door, giving her the once over before he stepped inside. She was beautifully tanned although it was only the middle of March. He noticed that she looked very well-rested. He started to say as much but decided not to pay her any compliments lest she think he was getting soft. He wasn't.

Nicole purposely looked at her watch and said, "I thought maybe you'd changed your mind. It's almost nine o'clock. I was putting her to bed."

"I had a few things I needed to take care of before I left. Is she asleep?"

"No, not yet."

"Then what's the problem?" Mark asked arrogantly. He strode past her and went to Tiandra's room.

Nicole glared at him as he walked out of the room. *He makes me so angry.* She sat down on the sofa and resumed watching the television. Mark was with Tiandra for a half hour before he came back into the living room.

"I'm going to come by on Friday to get her for the weekend. Have some of her things ready for me when I get here," Mark said.

"Why? She has clothes at your house, doesn't she?"

"In case you've forgotten I haven't seen her in a while. She's grown since you took her to Florida. There may be a chance that the clothes she has at my house are too small. Should I wait until I get her there and I'm dressing her to find out they are?" Mark asked sarcastically.

Nicole looked at him with a frown. She rolled her eyes and went back to looking at the television.

"Have something ready for me to take when I get here Friday," Mark said again.

"Don't worry. What time will you be here?"

"Around six. I'll call you if I'm going to be later than that."

"How thoughtful," Nicole said with a hint of her own sarcasm.

Mark looked at her with disdain. He didn't like her attitude. *Fine,* he thought. *Two can play that game.* Being spiteful, he asked, "So how was your trip, Nicole?"

"Just fine, thank you."

"Was it? Did you find out any more about him than you knew when you left?"

She quickly turned and looked at him. "What's that supposed to mean?"

"I don't think that question is so difficult to understand. I asked you if you know anything more about him than you did when you left. What's so confusing?"

"I told you before, I know all I need to know about Nick," she said defensively.

"Really? Did you know his father is a soldier in the Mafia? Did he tell you that?"

"So what? That has nothing to do with him."

"No? You don't think so, huh? Did he tell you he'd been indicted on a number of occasions for drug smuggling and racketeering? The only reason he's still walking around a free man is because they've never been able to find any solid evidence to convict him. He's very slick, Nicole, very lucky. The FBI's got a nice fat file on him. Did he tell you that?"

"You're a liar, Mark. You just have to make something up about him to make him seem like a bad person," Nicole said.

"You'd like to believe that, wouldn't you? I've got the proof on paper, baby."

"How could you have proof of anything that he's doing?"

"I've got a lot of connections, Nicole. You know that," Mark said coolly as he slipped one hand in the pocket of his pants. "I don't have any reason to make up things about your friend. I'm just trying to look out for you. I'd hate to see you get caught up in some mess with a creep like him. He can't be about anything good if he's smuggling drugs into the country. Think about it."

"You're wrong. He's not doing that," Nicole denied, with a fear she wasn't able to hide.

Mark looked at her pitifully. He knew that she knew he was telling the truth. If she chose to ignore it, he would do whatever he had to do to make her see the light. "Since you choose not to believe what I'm saying and I assume you plan to continue seeing him, then I have to tell you I don't want him around my daughter."

"What?"

"I don't want him around Tiandra."

"What do you think, that he'd hurt her? He would never hurt her," Nicole cried, defending Nick.

"You don't know what he'll do. You won't even acknowledge the truth. How can you tell me what he won't do. If you want to see him, that's your business, but you keep him away from my daughter," Mark said emphatically.

"She's my daughter, too!"

"Well, you obviously don't care enough about her to keep this slime away from her."

"What am I supposed to do, hide her when he comes here? You're being unreasonable."

Mark shouted, "I don't give a damn what you do, just keep him away from her!"

"Why are you doing this, Mark?" Nicole asked anxiously.

"I'm trying to protect you, Nicole, but you're a grown woman and you're going to do what you want regardless of what I say. Tiandra is a different story. You keep him away from her." He paused for effect. "If you don't, I'll take her away from you."

"You can't take her from me!" Nicole yelled.

"Yes, I can," he said as he moved slowly across the room. "There's not a court in this land that would deny me custody of her if they knew the type of people you're associating with."

Nicole fought back hysteria at the thought of Mark taking custody of Tiandra. "You can't do that! C'mon, Mark. You can't take her from me. She's all I've got."

He hated doing this to her but he felt he had no other recourse. Nick was too deeply involved in the drug trade. The report Sandy had given him was undeniable proof of this. He could not let Nicole put Tiandra's life in jeopardy because she wanted to be with Nick.

"Keep him away from her, Nicole," Mark said, outwardly showing no sympathy for her feelings. "Or I'll keep her away from you." He turned and quietly walked out of the apartment.

Nicole was a nervous wreck after Mark left. She couldn't imagine what she would do if he took her baby from her. She asked herself why he would want to do this to her. She didn't feel she deserved such an act of loathing. Was it because he just didn't want her to see anyone? Could he be angry because of that? It had to be more than just Nick. Why wouldn't he want her to have someone if he was not going to be with her? After all, she was sure he was seeing Ashlei regularly now.

What frightened her the most was that she knew he was serious. Did he hate her so much that he would take from her the only thing she had in this world that she loved more than her own life? He knew she would never let anyone, not even him, hurt Tiandra, just as she knew he wouldn't.

Nicole went to Tiandra's room and stood by the crib and watched her sleep. She was so beautiful. Nicole couldn't imagine what her life would be like without her. Gently, trying not to wake her, she lifted Tiandra from her crib. She hugged her close and kissed her softly on her nose. She carried her into her bedroom and laid her under the covers in her bed. She undressed and turned off the bedside lamp, then slipped into bed beside her. She gently picked her up and laid her on her chest. "I love you, Tiandra," Nicole whispered to her sleeping daughter. She held her that way and cried herself to sleep.

Chapter Twenty-Three

For the next month, Mark and Nicole saw very little of each other. They spoke on the telephone occasionally, usually to arrange for Mark to visit Tiandra or, if she was with him already, to make arrangements for Nicole to get her.

When they spoke, their conversations were short and to the point. Mark was very cold to her, but instead of responding in kind as she normally would have, Nicole picked her words very carefully when talking to him. The threat of him taking action to gain custody of Tiandra loomed large in her mind. She tried hard not to make him angry and although she would become angry herself because of his unnecessarily cruel manner, she tried to remain calm when she spoke to him.

Nicole never told Nick about Mark's threat. She was too embarrassed. She knew he would never hurt Tiandra. He loved her. He played with her for hours on end when he came to visit, letting her climb all over him, no matter what he was wearing, or pull his hair or any number of other playful yet sometimes painful gestures, and he never minded. He was great with her. There was no way Nicole could bring herself to tell him what Mark said. Instead, she made every effort to make sure their paths never crossed.

As fate would have it, one Saturday afternoon in the middle of April, Mark paid Nicole a surprise visit. He never came to her apartment without calling first, so when he rang her intercom from the lobby to announce his arrival, she was shocked and dismayed. Nick was in Nicole's room, stretched out on the bed watching television. Tiandra was asleep on his chest.

Nicole tried to think of what she would say to Mark about Nick. Then she started to tell Nick about Mark's threat, but before she could say anything, Mark was at the door.

"Who's that, baby?" Nick asked.

Nicole swallowed deeply and said, "Mark."

Nick noticed the worried expression on her face. "What's wrong?"

She didn't answer. She simply walked back to the living room to let him in.

"What's up?" Mark asked when Nicole opened the door to let him in.

"Hi," she said cautiously. "I didn't know you were coming by today."

"Well, I didn't plan to but I was in the area so I figured I'd come by and see if you were home. Where's Tee?"

"She's asleep," Nicole said quickly. Mark started to walk back to Tiandra's room. "I wish you had called first," Nicole said, trying to keep him in the living room.

He stopped and turned to face her. "Well, I'm here now, right? I didn't see any sense in spending a quarter when I could walk across the street and ring the bell."

"What if I wasn't here?" she asked, for lack of anything better to say.

Mark looked at her as if she were losing her mind. "If you weren't here, then I'd just walk back to my car and go home. What's the big deal?" He turned and started back to Tiandra's room again.

At the same moment, Nick emerged from Nicole's bedroom carrying Tiandra. He was going to put her in her crib. Mark froze at the sight of Nick holding his daughter. His face turned to stone. Nick stopped in his tracks and returned Mark's stare. But only for a moment. He resumed his initial course and entered Tiandra's bedroom. Nicole stayed in the living room. She was literally holding her breath, waiting for. . . .

"Nicole!" She began to whimper. Mark strode angrily back into the living room and confronted her. "What did I tell you? You think I'm joking, don't you?"

"Please, Mark."

"I told you to keep him away from her! I told you I didn't want him near her, didn't I?" he shouted.

"He didn't hurt her. Mark, he wouldn't hurt her."

With clenched teeth he said, "I didn't ask you anything about him. I told you to keep him away from her!"

"Leave her alone!" Nick was now standing just inside the living room.

Mark turned at the sound of Nick's voice. Barely above a whisper, he said to Nick, "You'd better mind your business."

"She is my business! Now I said leave her alone!"

"What're you gonna do if I don't?" Mark challenged.

Nick did not answer the question directly but he stepped closer to them. "If you don't leave her alone, you're going to find out."

Nicole was afraid now. She didn't want them to get into a fight. She knew one of them would be hurt badly if that happened, and in her heart she felt it would be Nick.

Mark walked right up to Nick until he was standing less than six inches away from him. "Who do you think you are? You think you're tough?"

Nick was trying very hard not to lose his cool. He didn't want to fight, but Mark was making it very difficult for him. "You'd better get out of my face," Nick said, looking Mark squarely in the eye.

"When I'm talking to *my wife* about *our daughter,* you stay out of it. When I have something to say to you, I'll let you know. Till then, you'd better mind your own business.''

"Why don't you stop bullying her?'' Nick said, not backing down an inch.

"If I want to bully her, I will. What are you gonna do about it? You gonna kick my ass?''

Nick looked past Mark to Nicole. She was nervously biting her fingernails. If she hadn't been standing there, Nick would have decked Mark the moment he jumped in his face, but for her, he would try not to resort to violence. "I don't want to fight you, Mark.''

Mark didn't move but said, "That's real smart of you. Now, if you don't mind, I was talking to my wife. Why don't you take a walk.''

"I'm not going anywhere and leave her here with you. If you want to talk to her, go ahead. But you'd better stop hassling her because I really don't want to have to bust you up.''

"Oh! You're gonna bust me up!'' Mark shoved Nick and said, "Come on! You're so bad. Come on!''

Mark assumed a fighting stance and was ready to swing on Nick but Nicole jumped between them in a hurry. "STOP IT!! STOP IT!'' She was hysterical. "Why are you doing this?'' she yelled. "Why are you trying to pick a fight with him?'' she yelled at Mark.

"I told you to keep him away from my daughter!'' Mark said, as he pointed at Nick.

"He's not hurting her! You're hurting her by carrying on like this! You don't have to do this.''

Mark ignored Nicole. "You keep your filthy hands off my daughter or I'll kick your ass. Do you understand?'' Mark said to Nick.

"I'm shaking in my boots,'' Nick responded with balled fists at his side.

Mark tried to lunge at Nick but Nicole blocked his path. She put her arms around him to hold him back. "STOP IT! WILL YOU PLEASE STOP!"

"Get out of my way, Nicole!" Mark ordered.

"No! If you want to hit someone, hit me! He hasn't done anything to you!"

"Let him pass, Nicky. If he wants to fight, I'll fight him," Nick said just as willing to throw down as Mark was.

"No! You won't fight in my house! If you want to fight, you go outside and do it! But don't come back here. I'm tired of this!" she yelled at Nick.

"You'd better stay away from my daughter!" Mark yelled at Nick over Nicole's head.

"Shut up, Mark!" Nicole yelled.

Mark was fuming. "Get off of me, Nicole!"

"No! Mark, please stop. Please," she cried as she held him as tight as she could.

Their arguing had awakened Tiandra, who was now crying hysterically. Nicole moved away from Mark in disgust. "Look what you've done! Both of you! Mark, you're so busy telling Nick to stay away from your daughter, you don't even care that she's in there crying because of your stupid arguing. And Nick, now you're acting no better than him! Both of you make me sick! Why don't you both get out of here. Just get out! You can go outside and beat each other to death. I don't care! Just get out!" She ran from the living room and went to take care of Tiandra.

Nick turned and watched her go. He felt terrible for hurting her this way. Mark, on the other hand, was too angry to feel anything else. "I don't want to see you with your hands on my daughter ever again."

Nick ignored him.

Mark turned and walked out of the apartment, slamming the door behind him.

Nick wanted to go to Nicole, but he knew he had hurt her and he didn't know what to say to her now.

When Nicole got to Tiandra's bedroom, she was standing up in her crib, crying hysterically. She took her up and began to rock her, trying to get her to calm down. Nicole was crying, too. She couldn't believe what had just happened. The men had behaved like two children fighting over a toy.

"Nicole." Nick was standing in the doorway of Tiandra's room. He wanted to go to her and hold her and try to comfort her.

"Why don't you go away?"

"Nicole, I'm sorry. Please, forgive me. I don't know why I said those things. I feel terrible because I made you cry," Nick said sincerely. He walked toward her. He needed to hold her. Before he got too close though, he stopped. "Is she all right?" he asked of Tiandra.

"No thanks to you."

He could understand the bitterness she must feel toward him now. He would accept it. He just needed to know that she still cared for him. "I'm sorry, honey. I just couldn't stand there and listen to him talking to you like that."

"So, what do you do, you threaten him?" Nicole asked angrily.

"I only said that because he said he would hit you. I would never allow him to hit you and get away with it. Even if you refused to ever see me again, I wouldn't let him do that."

"Why couldn't you have just stayed out of it?"

Nick looked at her sadly. What should he have done? She was his lady. He didn't care if Mark was still legally her husband. He didn't have to talk to her like that.

"If you hadn't said anything, he might have just left," Nicole said.

Nick was hurt by her words. "Maybe I should leave."

Nicole looked at him for a moment. She could see he was sorry for what had happened but she didn't care. She needed to be alone with her baby right now. "Maybe you should."

Chapter
Twenty-Four

The next couple of weeks were somewhat hectic for Nicole. Tiandra's first birthday was a month away and Nicole had taken a three-week temp assignment, while also trying to plan Tiandra's birthday party. She still had not told Mark what day she was going to do it, and since the fight between him and Nick, she hadn't spoken to him and was very apprehensive about calling him.

She had called Nick the next day and apologized for her brusqueness toward him. He was understanding and apologized for letting Mark get to him like he had. He told her he was grateful that she still cared for him because he knew his behavior had been very immature.

She told him about her plans for Tiandra's birthday party. He told her to let him know whatever she needed and he would get it for her.

On the morning of Tiandra's party, Mrs. Johnson was at Nicole's apartment by nine o'clock. She and Nicole's youngest sister, Stephanie, were going to help Nicole decorate the room where the party would be held. By two o'clock, they were downstairs in the Community Room of her building waiting for their guests to arrive. Tiandra was dressed in a beautiful red velvet dress with a white lace pinafore, white tights and white patent leather baby doll shoes. Nicole had combed her hair in two pigtails, parted from ear to ear across the crown of her head with red ribbons tied on each.

"Look at my baby. Isn't she gorgeous?" Nicole said proudly to her mother and sister.

"She sure is," said Stephanie, picking up Tiandra. "You look so pretty in your red dress, Tiandra. Can I borrow it when it gets too small for you?"

Tiandra laughed as if she knew her aunt was telling a joke. Nicole and her mother thought Tiandra's timing was very funny, too.

By three o'clock, the majority of the children invited had arrived. All of Nicole's nieces and nephews were there and they were running around making a lot of noise and generally having an all-around good time.

Mark had not arrived yet. Nicole wondered if he was going to come. She told him she didn't care one way or the other, but if he didn't show up, he would never hear the end of it. Nick hadn't arrived yet, either. Nicole was very disappointed. He'd told her he would be there. She knew he was in the city because she had been with him the day before. If he didn't come, he would never hear the end of it, either.

Carol had arrived early and was trying to organize a game of musical chairs. The kids were running around so much though, that Nicole knew Carol would give up before long, and Nicole wouldn't blame her. Tiandra was trying to keep up with the older children, running behind them and playing with the balloons that had already been snatched from the walls. Nicole smiled as she watched her because Tiandra looked as if she was having the time of her life.

At three thirty, Mark arrived carrying a huge box wrapped in white paper with red hearts and a big red bow. When he walked into the room, Mark looked right at Nicole, held his gaze for a moment then turned away without saying anything to her. He scanned the room as if he was looking for someone, his face wearing a scowl. Upon spotting Tiandra, though, the scowl was immediately replaced by a big smile.

He walked over to where she stood, curiously watching as one of her cousins tried to blow up a balloon. Mark squatted next to her and put his arms around her and kissed her cheek, nuzzling her as he did. When she turned to him, her face lit up and she put her arms around his neck to be picked up.

"Hi, precious. Happy birthday!" Mark said to Tiandra. "How's my baby, huh? How's my sweet baby? You look so pretty. Daddy missed you. I'm sorry I haven't been by to see you, Tee. Do you forgive me?"

Tiandra paid no mind to what Mark was saying to her. She was just happy to see her Daddy. She hugged him and laid her head on his shoulder. Nicole watched them and her eyes began to water. No matter what else Mark may be, she could never say he did not love their daughter, and although Tiandra was still just a baby, she knew who her father was and clearly loved him more than any other man in her life.

Mark was friendly to everyone at the party except Nicole. He still hadn't acknowledged her. In truth, he came in and started acting as though the party was his doing instead of hers. This infuriated Nicole because he hadn't contributed a dime nor had he lifted a finger to help her with anything. Nick had given her the money for food and decorations, even though she hadn't asked for it or needed it, and with Mark now here, Nick's absence seemed all the more obvious. Nicole wondered where he was.

At a quarter to five, Nicole began making preparations to serve dinner. Mark got up from where he was sitting and walked over to the kitchen area. Nicole hadn't seen him approach and was caught off guard when he leaned over her shoulder and asked, "So, where's your friend?"

She turned quickly and said without thinking, "Don't worry, he'll be here."

"When? When the party's over?" Mark taunted.

"Why are you so worried?"

"I'm not. It just seems funny that he's not here. He was invited, I assume."

Nicole didn't answer immediately. She was embarrassed that Nick was not there and angry because he hadn't called to say he wasn't coming. Now Mark was teasing her about it. "Look, I don't need you to worry about my friends for me," Nicole finally said.

"Oh, I'm not worried," Mark said nonchalantly. "It's a shame that you've been stood up, though. I thought you said he was a nice guy. A really nice guy wouldn't have stood you up. He would have at least called, don't you think?"

"How do you know he didn't?"

"If he had, you wouldn't be so defensive about me asking where he is."

It was clearly evident that Mark had touched a sore spot. Nicole felt her eyes begin to water and she quickly turned away from him. She didn't want him to see that he had upset her. "What do you want in here?" she suddenly asked as she resumed the task of preparing the food to be served.

"I just came to get something to drink."

"Then get your drink and leave me alone, please. I have too much work to do to stand here discussing my personal business with you," Nicole said, irritated.

"What's the matter? Did I hit a sore spot?"

"Just get away from here, will you?" she said angrily.

Mark grinned at her and turned to pour himself a glass of punch. He stood by the punch bowl and drank the contents of his cup, never taking his eyes off her. She tried to ignore him as she continued with her task.

After a few minutes, Mark walked away without saying anything else to her. Nicole let out a sigh of relief when he did. She wished she hadn't told him anything about the party. She would have been happier if he hadn't come.

Ten minutes later, someone else snuck up on her. "Boo!"

She turned quickly again, but this time to her sheer delight there stood, "Yvonne!!" She quickly embraced her.

"Hi, babe," Yvonne said, hugging Nicole back.

"Oh, Yvonne, I'm so glad you're here," Nicole said as tears sprang to her eyes. "I didn't know you were coming. Why didn't you call me?"

"I wanted to surprise you. Did you think I'd miss my god-daughter's first birthday party? No way!"

Nicole was happy that Yvonne was there. She needed her at that very moment. She held Yvonne at arms length and gazed at her. She loved Yvonne so much. Tears she could not check fell as she thought about the many years they had been friends and the many times, like this one, when Yvonne had been there when she needed her. "I'm so happy you're here, Yvonne. How'd you know I needed you?"

Yvonne hugged Nicole close once more and softly said, "I could feel it."

Nicole was embarrassed because she couldn't stop crying. She released her hold on Yvonne and tried to stem the flow of her tears. She tried a weak smile.

Yvonne could see that she was troubled.

"How long are you going to stay?"

"Until you get tired of me."

"I guess you'll be moving back to the States, huh?"

Yvonne laughed.

"Where's Lucien?"

"I left him home," she said with a wave of her hand. "No, seriously, he couldn't come. He's working."

"Oh. How is he?"

"He's fine. He's driving me crazy, but he's fine."

Nicole smiled.

"Where's my baby?" Yvonne asked.

Nicole looked across the room and saw Tiandra sitting on her sister's lap. "Shelly's got her."

"Let me go see my baby," Yvonne said, walking off in that direction.

Nicole looked after Yvonne as she walked away. She was relieved that her best friend was there. Yvonne was her strength when she felt she had no more. Maybe with her there, Mark wouldn't pick on her so much.

After seeing Tiandra and saying hello to Nicole's family and friends, Yvonne came back to help Nicole in the kitchen.

"Where's Mark?" Yvonne asked.

"He's around here somewhere. He must have gone to the bathroom."

"Where's your friend Nick?"

Nicole shrugged her shoulders and said, "I don't know."

"He didn't come?"

"No," she said sadly.

"He didn't call you either?"

"No, and of course, Mark loves that. He came over here a few minutes before you got here and asked me where he was. He said, 'It's a shame he stood you up, Nicole.' He makes me so sick, Yvonne. I wish he wasn't here."

"He's picking on you?"

"Of course. That's how he gets his kicks."

"He's jealous. He can't stand you being with anyone else. That's all," Yvonne said knowingly.

"I don't know why. He's messing around with Ashlei."

After witnessing them together on New Year's Eve, Nicole was certain that Mark was still involved with Ashlei, but he wasn't. In truth, he wasn't seeing anyone, and that made Nicole's relationship with Nick all the more painful for him.

"Are you sure?"

"Yes, I saw them together, remember?" At that moment, she spotted Mark coming back into the room. "Speak of the devil."

Yvonne turned in his direction. She smiled and walked over to him. "Hello, stranger."

He turned and with a look of surprise on his face said, "Hey, Yvonne, how're you doing? I didn't know you were coming." He embraced her and kissed her cheek.

"I wanted to surprise you guys so I didn't tell anyone I was coming and I made Lucien promise not to tell you when he spoke to you the other day. I didn't want you spoiling my surprise."

"Now, would I do that?"

"Yes."

Mark chuckled. He loved Yvonne. She always made him laugh.

"So tell me, big guy, how does it feel to be a bully?"

"I'm not a bully."

"That's what I hear."

"Is that what your friend told you?"

"She said you've been picking on her. How come?"

"I haven't really been picking on her. She's just upset that her friend stood her up, that's all."

"Oh, is that all? Well, I beg to differ. I think you like messing with her."

With a mischievous grin he answered, "Well, to be honest with you, Yvonne, I do."

"Why? Why would you want to upset her?"

"Because she looks so cute when she's angry. Haven't you ever noticed that?"

Yvonne playfully punched him in the arm and said, "Listen, buster, you'd better leave her alone or you're going to have to deal with me and I don't think you want to do that. I'm a black belt. I know kung fu. Don't force me to use it on you."

Mark laughed. He threw up his arms in mock surrender and said, "Whoa! I won't mess with you. I know I wouldn't stand a chance."

"Seriously, Mark. Leave her alone. Why do you want to make her unhappy?"

"I'm don't want to make her unhappy, Yvonne. I just don't like this guy she's running around with."

"Why should it matter to you? You're seeing Ashlei, right?"

"Wrong, and I never have," he said. "But this guy she's seeing is no good. Seriously."

"Would you be happy if she was seeing someone else? And don't lie."

"No, Yvonne, 'cause I still love her. But if you knew what I know about him, you wouldn't want her fooling around with him either. I have a friend in the Police Department that gave me some info on him. They've got a file on him this thick," he said, gesturing with his thumb and index finger. "He's deep in the drug scene."

Yvonne pondered this information. Nicole had never said anything to her about this. "Does Nicky know about this?"

"I tried to tell her but she thinks I'm making it up."

"I'll ask her about it later. Meanwhile, you leave her alone."

"I'll try. It might be kind of hard, though, she's really fun to pick on."

"You're mean, Mark," Yvonne said as she walked away from him.

Mark laughed as she did.

Later in the evening, after she had opened Tiandra's presents and everyone had sung 'Happy Birthday' to Tiandra, Nicole was trying to straighten up the kitchen area when Mark came over to her once more.

"So, I guess he couldn't make it, huh?"

Nicole cut her eyes at him angrily. "Don't you have anything better to do than mess with me?"

"I was just curious, Nicole. What do you see in this guy?"

"None of your damned business! Now, why don't you get out of my face!"

Mark was taken aback by the intensity of her anger toward him. "There's no reason to yell at me. I didn't yell at you."

"If you left me alone, I wouldn't say anything you. But

since you insist on messing with me, I'll continue to talk to you any way I want to.''

"I'm not your little street thug, Nicole, and I won't stand for you talking to me like one.''

She continued to yell. "No, you're acting more like a spoiled child! I'm not bothering you. Why don't you just get away from me?''

"Stop yelling at me.''

"Why? What are you going to do?'' She was furious now and because of her anger, she boldly challenged him.

"Get out of my face, Nicole.'' He did not like her arrogance in the face of his machismo.

"Why don't you drop dead, Mark?''

He couldn't believe his ears. He stepped closer to her, as close as he could without physically touching her. She did not back down.

"Don't you ever say that to me again.''

Nicole looked boldly into his eyes and once again, with more emphasis this time, said, "Drop dead!''

Mark was furious. "What are you trying to do, Nicole? You trying to see how far you can push me?'' Mark asked as he fought to control the rage that suddenly engulfed him.

Nicole was past the point of caring about the circumstances of anything she said. "I don't have to push you. I already know you're very easily persuaded,'' she said. Instinctively, he knew she referring to Ashlei.

Mark couldn't believe she had actually gone there.

Neither of them realized that at this point, they had an audience. They were so wrapped up in their heated, pointless debate, they had forgotten where they were.

Mark was about to respond to Nicole's last dig when Mr. Johnson quickly intervened. "Stop it, dammit! Just stop it!!'' he yelled. "What the hell is wrong with you two?''

Nicole said, "He started it.''

"I don't care who started it! Can't you stop this stupid

bickering for one day?'' he said, clearly disgusted with them. ''It's your daughter's birthday. Do you care so little about her that you can't put aside your differences for her? Do you have to ruin her day with your foolishness?''

''But, Daddy . . .''

''Shut up, Nicole.''

Nicole quickly shut her mouth.

''You're both acting worse than children! You're supposed to be adults. What kind of example are you setting for these kids? You both make me sick!'' he spat as he turned and walked away from them.

Nicole had never been so embarrassed in her life. Tiandra was crying and Mrs. Johnson was holding her, trying to calm her. She gave Nicole a look of utter disgust.

Mr. Johnson had also made Mark totally ashamed of his behavior. He wanted to go somewhere and hide. He stood frozen to the spot. It seemed that everyone in the room had stopped talking. He suddenly noticed, too, that the music had stopped. It was utterly silent in the room except for Tiandra's crying. *Damn,* he thought, *I've done it again.* Twice he had hurt his baby by being thoughtless and selfish. *What kind of father am I?* He looked at Nicole. Tears slid down her cheeks. He knew he owed her an apology. There had been no reason for him to pick on her like he had. He was sorry for it now. He owed her mother and father an apology, too. But mostly, he knew he had to make this up to Tiandra. She was still small and didn't understand what was happening, but he had made her cry and that ate at his insides like an ulcer.

He walked over to Mrs. Johnson. ''May I take her?'' he asked softly.

Reluctantly, she handed Tiandra to Mark. Tiandra reached for him and immediately hugged him and laid her head on his shoulder. Mark held her tight. To Mrs. Johnson he said, ''I'm sorry.'' But she didn't respond. Instead, she simply turned and walked away. He sat down and placed Tiandra on his lap. She put her thumb in her mouth and leaned her head on his chest. Within minutes, she was fast asleep. Mark didn't move from that seat until everyone except Yvonne and Nicole was gone.

When they had finished the cleanup, Yvonne said, "Okay, you guys, that's it. Let's move 'em out," trying to lighten the tension in the room.

Nicole walked over to Mark and said, "I'll take her upstairs now."

He looked at her eyes as he handed Tiandra to her. They were very sad and she wouldn't look at him. He felt very small at that moment. "I'm sorry, Nicole."

"That's all right," she said. "I'll see you."

"Nicky, would you like me to fix you a drink?"

"Yes, please."

"What do you want?"

"Anything, just make sure it's strong."

They were in her apartment. She had undressed Tiandra and put her to bed, then changed her own clothes, putting on a pair of shorts and a T-shirt.

Nicole was feeling very depressed because of the incident at the end of the party. Her father's words echoed loudly in her ears. The whole thing had been senseless. She had yelled at Mark for picking on her, but she should have ignored him. If she had, he would have probably left her alone. Instead, she behaved just as childishly as he had. They were both responsible for upsetting Tiandra this time. She could not fault Mark.

She plopped down on the sofa and put her feet up on the coffee table.

"Here," Yvonne said, handing her a glass of vodka and orange juice.

"You should have saved the orange juice. I feel like drowning my sorrows tonight."

"Believe me, honey," Yvonne said as she joined Nicole on

the couch. "The orange juice is just for coloring. There's not enough in there for you to even taste it."

They sat a few minutes in silence. Yvonne wanted to ask Nicole about the things Mark had said about Nick, but she decided to wait for a more suitable moment. She knew Nicole was feeling down right now and the mere mention of Nick might depress her even more. She didn't want to do that.

"You think I'm silly, don't you?" Nicole suddenly asked.

"No. I probably would have done the same thing, but sooner."

"I should have just ignored him."

Yvonne shrugged.

"Why couldn't he have just left me alone? I didn't say anything to him. When he walked in the door, he looked at me like I was dirt and didn't even speak. Why couldn't he have just left it like that?"

"Nicky, let me tell you something Lucien told me a long time ago. You know he's known Mark for a long time. He said he was familiar with a number of women that Mark was involved with. He said there were a few, like that woman Diane that you found him with, for instance, that Mark genuinely liked. Some were just hangers-on and he would use them for his own satisfaction, but the ones he liked, Lucien said, he was good to. He said Mark would never actually show them his true feelings though, he'd sort of hide behind this tough exterior. But before you guys were even married, Mark told Lucien that you were the only woman he had ever known that he felt he could be totally honest with about his feelings. He said he didn't worry about appearing soft or weak if he told you how much he really cared for you. And that's what he did. He let himself go, showing you the real Mark, a Mark that no one ever sees. Lucien says he thinks that's why Mark has been carrying on the way he has. Lucien thinks he's angry with himself for letting his guard down. He thinks Mark's embarrassed because he's shown you that he's not as tough as he'd like everyone to believe, but that he's really just a pussycat.

"Personally, I think Mark's problem is that, yes, he's in love with you unlike he's ever been before. This is probably a totally new experience for him and he can't just brush it aside. You've done something to his heart and mind that no other woman has been able to do, and this, to him, is probably unthinkable. You know Mark, he's big and strong and more than anything else, Nicky, you know he has a tremendous amount of pride. Maybe too much for his own good. He still loves you and he's trying to fight it, but since he's losing the battle, he has to strike out at you. He has to try to hurt you to assuage his own sense of pride. You know it's killing him that you're seeing Nick. That he could still be in love with you and you're not with him is more than he's willing to accept, so he has to pretend he doesn't care."

"Do you think I don't love him?"

"No. I know you do."

They were silent once again.

"I told you what happened on New Year's Eve, right?"

"Yeah."

"I was so excited because he'd asked me to come to his party. I was dumb enough to think he wanted me to be there with him. When I got there and saw him with Ashlei, Yvonne, I wanted to die. It was worse than when I found him with his ex. There were all these people that knew me and knew I was his wife and there he was, kissing her and feeling her up like no one else was there. If it wasn't for him, I probably would have never met Nick. I had to go on that cruise just to get away from him. I was tired of him hurting me. If he loves me so much, why does he keep hurting me?"

"A lot of times, men don't think about what they're doing and who they're hurting. They just act and later apologize and expect to be forgiven," Yvonne said, trying to rationalize.

"How many times should I have to forgive him for hurting me?"

"I know."

"He's said things to me, Yvonne, that I would have never thought he could say to me. Cruel things. I can't see how he could love me and say these things. He threatened to take Tiandra from me. It would kill me if he did that. He knows that."

"He wouldn't do that, Nicky. I think he's just trying to scare you."

"But why?"

"Maybe because he's scared. Maybe he feels like he's pushed you too far and he's afraid that his chances of being with you are gone and he doesn't want to face that. I don't know."

They sat together in silence once again. There were tears streaming down Nicole's face.

"You know what Lucien told me a few weeks ago? You know when you went to Florida, Mark came down to Jamaica for a few days. He came by the house and had dinner with us. After he left that night, Lucien told me Mark feels like the situation between you and him is out of his control. Things are happening and there's nothing he can do about them, and he doesn't like that. You once told me that Mark likes to be in control of everything he's involved in. Well, your relationship with Nick is something he can't control. He can't control what you do, so to spite you, when in actuality he's spiting himself, he tries to make your life miserable."

"He's doing an excellent job of it," Nicole commented.

"He's miserable without you. Misery loves company, Nicky."

"He's just jealous of Nick."

Yvonne contemplated this. She believed Mark was jealous of Nick, too. But she also believed that Mark was genuinely worried about Nicole because of the information he had obtained regarding Nick. Yvonne suddenly felt this was the opportunity she was looking for to ask Nicole about those accusations. "Nicky, what's Nick really like?"

She looked at Yvonne for a moment, wondering why she was asking about Nick all of the sudden. "What do you mean?"

"I mean, what kind of guy is he? I know you told me he's really sweet and funny and stuff, but what's he really like?"

"He is really sweet and funny," Nicole said, suddenly very defensive of Nick.

"You guys don't argue or anything?" Yvonne asked incredulously.

"No, but we'll probably have one the next time I see him because he didn't show up today, but that doesn't mean he's not a sweet person."

"I know that." Yvonne chose her next words very carefully. "Mark says he's involved with the mob."

Nicole tensed visibly. "That's a lie. He made that up because he's so jealous of him."

"He said the police have a file on him."

Nicole quickly looked at her friend. Yvonne was looking her square in the eye. Nicole averted her eyes. She got up from the sofa and walked across the room. "How can you believe anything Mark says about Nick? He doesn't even know him. He's just jealous because I want to be with Nick and not him."

"I don't think he would make something like that up, Nicky. He's worried about you. I believe he's jealous, too, but to say something as serious as this and that you could just as easily check out, I don't think that's like Mark at all. Do you?"

"I never thought Mark would say a lot of things that he's said to me, so what does that mean?"

"But, Nicky, the things that Mark told me, he says he has proof of. Do you really know what Nick does? You told me he lives in a huge mansion with armed guards and everything. Do you think he needs all of that if he runs a legitimate business?"

Since Nicole had seen the guard in back of Nick's house with the machine gun, she had a nagging suspicion in her gut that he was involved in something more than he was telling her. When Mark informed her of the indictments against him, the suspicion grew, but she never mentioned any of this to Nick. She didn't want to believe that he could be involved in the terrible things Mark accused him of. Now Yvonne was questioning her, too, because Mark told her about them. Nicole knew he would never hurt her. Those things couldn't be true.

Nicole turned on Yvonne. "I don't believe you! You're supposed to be my friend. Why are you taking sides with Mark? What proof could he have?"

"Nicky, he said there's a file on him. If you don't believe him, why don't you check it out for yourself?"

"I don't have to check it out. I know who Nick is and I know what he does. Mark is a liar!"

Yvonne realized that she would get no accurate information out of Nicole. She was too involved to be levelheaded. Yvonne only hoped she wasn't intentionally putting on blinders to hide from the truth. The way she was carrying on, it seemed to Yvonne that Mark was telling the truth about Nick and Nicole knew it but didn't want to face it. She knew Nicole was lonely, but she hoped she wouldn't sacrifice her and Tiandra's safety just to be with this guy.

"All right, Nicky. Let's drop it. I'm sorry I said anything about it. You're probably right. I'm sure he's a very nice man," Yvonne said, not meaning a word of it.

Suddenly, Nicole didn't want to talk anymore. "Look, Yvonne, I'm tired. I'm going to go to bed. You can sleep in the bedroom and I'll sleep on the couch."

"Oh, no. I'm not going to put you out of your bed. I'll sleep out here."

"It's no problem."

"Exactly, it's no problem for me to sleep out here. I know you must be tired. You've been up all day getting the party together, so you go and sleep in your bed. I'll stretch out right here."

"You sure?"

"Positive," Yvonne said and smiled.

Nicole smiled weakly and said, "Okay. I'll see you in the morning."

"Okay, babe. Sleep tight."

Nicole walked back to her bedroom.

Yvonne sat up a while longer and thought about Nicole. She was worried about her. Now, with the likelihood that Nick was a criminal, Yvonne felt she had to really try to keep an eye out for her.

Two days later, Nick showed up at Nicole's house. He had never called to explain why he didn't come to Tiandra's party.

Yvonne was out when he came by. She had taken Tiandra over to her mother's house for the day. Nicole wished she was there because she wanted Yvonne to meet Nick to see for herself what a sweetheart he was. On the other hand, though, she was glad Yvonne was out because she was very angry with Nick and she planned to let him know that in no uncertain terms.

When she opened the door for him, her scowl was met with a big grin.

"Hi, beautiful," Nick said as he walked into the apartment and kissed her.

"Where have you been?"

"I've been busy, baby, takin' care of business."

"You were so busy you couldn't pick up the telephone to say you wouldn't be at Tee's party?"

He turned to her and with a devil-may-care attitude said, "Hey sweetheart, sorry 'bout that. How was it, anyway?"

She was very upset that he was taking this so lightly. "It was terrible."

"Aw, come on. It couldn't have been that bad just because I wasn't there. Didn't Tiandra have a good time?"

"Mark was there and he found it necessary to bother me the entire time. We had a big argument that might not have happened if you had been there. He thought it was very humorous that you stood me up," Nicole said angrily.

Nick's attitude quickly changed. He finally realized how upset Nicole actually was. He stepped closer to her and put his arm around her waist. "What happened, baby?"

Nicole moved away from him and said, "What difference does it make now? You weren't there so you can't really care what happened."

He put his arms around her again and held her close. "I'm sorry, Nicky. I meant to be there but something came up that I had to take care of right away."

"You couldn't call me and tell me you were going back to Miami?"

"I didn't go back home."

"You were here in the city all this time and didn't call?" Nicole said in disbelief.

"No, I wasn't in New York. I had to fly out to L.A."

"For what?"

"I told you, business."

Nicole moved away from him. Suddenly, the information Mark had laid on her about Nick's drug dealings moved to the forefront of her mind.

Gingerly, she asked, "What kind of business, Nick?"

"What do you mean, what kind of business?"

Nicole knew she couldn't back down now. She had to ask him if what Mark had told her was true. She had to know. She watched his face closely as she said, "I mean just what I said. Mark told me you deal in illegal drugs."

For a split second, she thought she saw something in his eyes that registered surprise, but it quickly disappeared, replaced by humor. He began to laugh. "Is that what he told you? That's really funny, Nicole. Really funny."

She didn't think so.

Nick turned his back to her and walked across the room. She studied his movements, trying to determine if he was being truthful. "Mark said you're involved with drug smuggling and racketeering. Is that the business you were taking care of?"

Nick turned back to her, smiling a weak smile, and said, "Where does he get his information? Your husband obviously has a very wild imagination, Nicole. Maybe he should see somebody about that."

"Mark knows a lot of people. He has a lot of connections. Some in the Police Department. He told me that you've been indicted a number of times for drug smuggling and racketeering," Nicole said calmly. She was beginning to believe Mark. She was becoming very disillusioned with Nick.

"Do you think if all of that was true, I'd be standing here talking to you? Don't you think I'd be in prison right about now?"

"He said the only reason you aren't is because they couldn't find any solid evidence to convict you. He said he has the proof, Nick. Is it true? Don't lie to me."

Nick looked at her for a moment and was about to say something, but noticed the serious look in her eyes and thought for a moment. He decided to tell her what she needed to hear, which was not necessarily the whole truth. "Did he give you any dates as to when all of this occurred?"

"Why?"

Nick assumed he hadn't. "Since you must know, Nicole. All of that happened a very long time ago."

"So it's true."

"Partially. Look, baby, when I was a lot younger, I was involved with drugs and a number of other unlawful activities. I never hurt anyone, if that's what you're thinking. I was young and I wanted to make fast money. But that's in the past. I was not indicted a number of times like Mark claims, but only once. I wasn't convicted because my father was able to pull a few strings, but that's all. I've never had any dealings with the mob. I don't now. What I do is strictly legitimate. I didn't tell you before because I didn't think it was necessary.'' Nick paused and looked into her eyes to see if she accepted his explanation. ''I hope you won't hold against me what I did five years ago. I love you, Nicole. I didn't mean to lie to you at first, but I don't want to lose you, baby. You mean so much to me.''

He moved close to her and held her hands in his. He looked into her eyes and saw the anger and disapproval dissipate. He kissed her softly on her lips. Nicole released his hands and put her arms around him. She then kissed him passionately, and he embraced her and responded in kind.

''I'm sorry I didn't believe you. I told Mark he was wrong. I guess I was just upset about the other day,'' Nicole said. ''Can you forgive me for doubting you?''

''No apology is necessary, baby. I can understand how you were feeling. I'm sorry I let you down. I promise it'll never happen again. Okay?''

She looked into his eyes and smiled, ''Okay.''

''Do you love me?''

''Yes, I do. Very much.''

''I love you, too. Very much.''

Yvonne stayed with Nicole for a week. Before she left, she did have the opportunity to meet Nick, but only briefly. She wanted to sit and talk to him and try to feel him out, but she caught him as he was leaving and she was coming in.

Chapter Twenty-Five

The week after Tiandra's birthday party, Mark flew to Los Angeles to attend a real estate conference. He had originally planned to skip the conference but decided at the last minute that he needed to get away from New York. He was still smarting from the sounding off he received from Nicole's father at the party.

He still felt terrible about making Tiandra cry because of his petty jealousy. He knew it had been totally unnecessary to continually harass Nicole the way he had, but he was still in love with her and she didn't seem to reciprocate his feelings any longer. That hurt him. What hurt more, however, was the knowledge that his behavior over the past several months was more than likely directly responsible for her lost affection.

Many times he considered going to her and telling her how he really felt, telling her how much he needed her, how much he wanted her back. But his pride always got in the way.

He really wished, though, that there was something, anything, he could do to get her away from Nick. The thought of her with him left a bad taste in his mouth. He probably wouldn't be happy with anyone that Nicole was involved with, but he would at least feel better if she was seeing someone who didn't have Nick's background.

The Sunday Mark returned from his trip, he called Nicole to let her know he was back. When he got no answer at her apartment, he called her mother's house. He was then informed that Nicole had gone to Miami for a few days. He was grateful to learn that she hadn't taken Tiandra this time and that she told her mother if he wanted to take Tiandra home with him, she would pick her up from there when she got back.

Nicole was in Florida for five days. She went by the penthouse to pick up Tiandra at approximately eight p.m. the day she returned. Although it was still May, it was extremely hot that day so Nicole was wearing a silk top with spaghetti straps, matching silk shorts and sandals on her feet. Mark thought she looked very cool and extremely sexy.

Nicole was feeling satisfied. She'd had a fantastic time with Nick while she was in Florida and she was planning to inform Mark that the information he had about him was false. She relished the idea of telling Mark he was wrong.

Once she was seated, Mark asked, "How was your trip?"

"Very nice, thank you. How was yours?"

"Very boring."

"Sorry to hear that. Where's Tee?"

"She's asleep. If you had called, I would've told you that you didn't have to come for her today. I'm off tomorrow for Memorial Day."

"How long has she been asleep?"

"Since about five thirty."

"Well, she'll probably be up in a few minutes. Do you mind if I wait?"

"No, not at all. Can I get you anything? Would you like a drink?"

"Sure, why not. Just some wine.

"White?"

"Yes. Thank you."

"You're welcome," he said as he gazed into her eyes.

She shifted her position on the couch. His stare made her uncomfortable.

Mark poured her a glass of wine and one for himself. He walked over and handed her the drink.

"Thank you."

He smiled and said, "No problem."

She took a sip of the wine then placed the glass on the table in front of her. Suddenly, she got a strong feeling of déjà vu. She was at once reminded of the first time she had come there. She quickly shook it off. "It s hotter here than it is in Miami," she said.

"Yeah, it's been like this for the past two days. Summer will probably be a bitch."

She took another sip.

"You've got a nice tan," said Mark.

"Thank you."

Innocently, Mark said, "I appreciate you not taking Tiandra with you this time."

"Oh yeah, you were wrong about Nick. I told him what you said and he told me the truth," Nicole said haughtily.

"He told me that he'd been indicted once on drug charges but that was a long time ago. He's a legitimate businessman, Mark, not a hood like you said."

Mark sighed and shook his head. He couldn't believe she was being so gullible. "How long ago did he say it was that he'd been indicted?"

"What difference does it make? The past is the past. You told me yourself that you've been in trouble with the law before. No one's holding that against you."

"I was a kid. You know that. How long ago did he say it was?"

"He didn't say, but then, I didn't ask him. It doesn't matter to me."

"It should. Would you like to see the report I have on him?

It has the dates, plural, dates he was indicted. Not once, but three times, Nicole." He held up three fingers for emphasis.

"I don't care about that report," she said, becoming a bit ruffled by Mark's insistence.

"Well, I'm going to show it to you anyway," he said as he walked over to the bar. He reached up into an overhead cabinet and removed a manila envelope. He walked back to her while removing the contents. He stood over her and shoved the report under her nose. "Look at it, Nicole. Right there," he said, pointing to an entry on the page. "The last indictment was last year. November. His case was thrown out because of a lack of evidence."

Nicole turned her head away. Mark physically turned her head back. "Look at it! He's lying to you! The proof is right here. Why won't you accept it?" Mark said.

Nicole quickly got up from the couch. "That's all a lie! He told me the truth. Why can't you accept it?"

Mark looked at her, shaking his head. "What do I have to do to make you see? I wouldn't lie to you. I've never lied to you. He's no good for you, Nicole. I don't want to see you get hurt over this guy," Mark said, pleading with her. "Please, leave him alone. Please."

Nicole started crying. "You don't know him, Mark. All you know is that garbage you're reading on those papers. That's not him. He told me the truth. He's not doing that anymore. He's not!" she said, trying not only to convince Mark but herself as well.

"Nicole . . ."

"No! I don't want to hear anymore," she said. She ran out of the apartment.

After Nicole's hasty exit, Mark plopped down on the sofa in defeat.

Why won't she listen, he wondered. *What is this guy doing to her? What is he telling her?* She was behaving almost as if she had been brainwashed. Couldn't she see the kind of person he was? He could not believe she intentionally averted her eyes when he tried to show her the proof. Was she doing this to spite him? He couldn't figure it out. He was certain he had to do something to make her see, something that would really shock her into believing that he had only her best interest in mind. The only thing he could think to do was the last thing he wanted, but he couldn't see any other way to bring her back to reality.

The following evening at nine o'clock, Nicole was just hanging up the telephone when her doorbell rang. "Who is it?" she asked as she looked through the peephole.

"Mark."

Good, she thought happily, *my baby's home.* She quickly opened the door. "Hi."

"Hello," Mark said blandly.

Immediately noticing Tiandra's absence, Nicole asked, "Where's Tiandra?"

"She's at my apartment."

"Why didn't you bring her? You were supposed to be bringing her home today."

Mark stood near the door. He had no intentions of staying longer than it would take to tell her why he had come. "You still insist on seeing Nick, am I correct?"

"Yes, I do!" Nicole stated, a bit too indignantly.

"Fine. Until you decide to leave him alone, Tiandra will be with me," he said coolly.

It took a moment for his words to register. "What?! What are you talking about?"

"I told you once before that I didn't want her around him. You thought I was playing a game with you but you should know, Nicole, I don't play games when it comes to Tiandra. Since you insist on being with him, you've forced my hand. I don't want to take her from you but I won't have her life placed in jeopardy because of some silly crush you have on this creep.''

"You can't take her from me! Please, Mark? You don't know him. He's not like you say he is. He loves me and he loves Tiandra. He would never do anything to hurt us. Please, bring her back." Tears were streaming down her face.

"You can come by and see her whenever you like. I won't keep her from you, but I have to know that she'll be safe. As far as I'm concerned, she's not as long as you're seeing him and he's coming here. For all you know, someone could have it in for him and they're following him here. You don't know, I don't know. For my own peace of mind, I have to do this.''

"Why do you hate him so much?"

"I don't hate him, Nicole. If he wasn't into this mess that he's involved in, I wouldn't be bothering you at all. But since he is and you choose to be with him, I have to act accordingly and look out for the welfare of my daughter. I've got a bad feeling about him. Maybe I'm being insecure, but I've got to go with my feelings. I'm sorry if you can't understand that."

"I wouldn't let anything happen to her. I love her just as much as you do, Mark."

He remained the picture of cool. "That's not the point. You don't know from one day to the next what's going to happen with this guy. I don't want to see anything happen to you, Nicole, but if you're not going to face the truth, there's nothing I can do about it. Tiandra is a baby. I can't be as certain about her safety as you seem to be. I have to do this. I'm sorry."

"You're not being fair! You can't give me ultimatums about my life. Why should I have to be alone just because you say so?"

Mark could not continue his cool demeanor any longer. "What the hell is so special about this guy? What is he telling you? You're acting as if he's got you brainwashed!"

"I love him!" Nicole cried. "Can't you understand that? I love him."

Her words cut him like a razor. The idea that she was in love with Nick was more than he could bear. That she would feel this way for him was something Mark had never anticipated.

He quickly turned to leave. As he opened the door, he turned back to her. His eyes were filled with pain. "She'll be with me. If you want to see her, you know where I live."

As he walked aimlessly from the building, the realization that she was truly out of his life now hit him like a brick. Mark was devastated. Her words kept echoing in his brain. "I love him!" *She doesn't know what she was saying. She's delirious. Yes, that's it*, Mark told himself. *She's delirious.*

When he reached his car, he opened the door and sat behind the wheel, but made no move to start the engine. *How could she do this? Doesn't she know I still love her?* A wave of emotions flooded his mind. He was angry, hurt, disappointed and jealous, but most of all, he felt sorry for himself.

Before her confession of love for Nick, Mark never worried that they would not be together again one day. He just took for granted that she would always, even if they were separated like now, be his. He took for granted that deep in her heart, even if she wouldn't admit it, she was still as madly in love with him as he was with her. But now, all of that had changed. He had taken too much for granted. He had pushed her too far away. Now he was paying for it.

Nicole immediately noticed the painful look in Mark's eyes when she told him that she loved Nick. Seeing his pain made her want to take back her words.

Do I really love him or is it gratitude? After all, Nick had been there when she needed to get away from Mark after her painful discovery of him and Ashlei. He had been very patient when she needed someone to talk to. He had been understanding when she became overwrought. He comforted her when she needed it and he told her that he loved her. But now that she had actually spoken the words, she wondered if it was love or just infatuation.

The next evening, Nicole went by the penthouse to see Tiandra. As beautifully furnished as it was, and as costly as all the furnishings were, Mark allowed Tiandra to have the run of the place. He didn't care if she walked across his white leather sofa, or tried to climb on the glass cocktail table in front of it. As long as she didn't hurt herself, she could do whatever she liked.

When she arrived and Mark let her in, he was very brusque.

Nicole felt as if she were stepping into a freezer. His attitude was chilling. Before she went into the living room to see Tiandra, she said, "I really wish you would reconsider what you're doing."

Mark simply turned and walked into the back of the apartment without saying a word to her.

Angie, Mark's housekeeper and their daughter's nanny, was in the living room with Tiandra. "Hello, Angie," Nicole said.

"Hi, Mrs. Peterson. How are you?"

"I'm fine, thanks, and you?"

"Fine. Look, Tiandra. There's Mommy."

When Tiandra noticed Nicole, she quickly crawled off the couch and tried to run to her, but her little legs just would not carry her as fast as she wanted and she tripped and fell.

"Careful," Nicole said as she squatted to pick Tiandra up from the floor.

Tiandra put her arms around Nicole's neck and cooed, "Da da."

"No, Tee, not da da. Mommy. Say Mommy."

"Da da," Tiandra repeated.

"Mommy," Nicole said again.

"Da da da da da," Tiandra sung.

Angie laughed and said. "I think all children like to irritate their mothers by saying 'da da' first."

Nicole laughed and said, "I think you're right."

"Are you going to stay for dinner, Mrs. Peterson?" Angie asked.

"No, thanks. I just came by to see Tiandra," she said with a note of sadness.

"Okay. Then, I'll leave you two alone."

"Thank you," Nicole said.

Nicole plopped down on the floor and hugged Tiandra. "How's my baby, huh? Mommy misses you. I wish you were at home with me, don't you?" she said to Tiandra.

Tiandra smiled and hugged Nicole tighter.

Nicole sat on the floor and played with Tiandra for about thirty minutes. It was a beautiful day and Nicole figured Tiandra would like to go outside and run around for a while, so she decided to take her to the playground in the park. She took Tiandra into the kitchen to stay with Angie while she went to tell Mark.

Mark was in his study. The door was cracked a bit so she pushed it open without knocking. Mark was sitting at his desk. There was a woman she didn't know sitting in the chair beside the desk. Angrily he asked, 'Don't you know how to knock?"

"I'm sorry. I thought you were alone."

"What difference does it make? The door was closed."

Nicole's embarrassment was clearly evident. "I'm sorry."

"What do you want?" Mark asked impatiently.

Nicole did not want to talk in front of this woman, but Mark made no move to excuse himself nor her. "I just wanted to tell you, I m going to take Tiandra to the playground across the street."

Mark moved as if he had been struck by lightning. "You're not taking her anywhere!" he said angrily as he rose from his seat.

Nicole was shocked by his outburst. "What?"

"I said, you're not taking her anywhere. You're not slick, Nicole. What do you think, I'm stupid?"

"What are you talking about? I just want to take her outside. It's so nice out, I thought she might like to run around in the open air, that's all."

"She can run around right here."

Nicole could not believe her ears. "Do you think I'm going to run off with her? Is that what you think?" Nicole asked incredulously.

"Why can't you just see her here? Why do you have to take her anywhere?"

Nicole stared at him for a long moment. Her eyes began to water. Mark became visibly uncomfortable by her stare. He could no longer look her in the eye.

"I can't believe you actually think I would do something to hurt her," she said with poignant sorrow.

Mark was silent.

Nicole turned away for a moment. She couldn't understand why he was behaving this way. She turned back to him. "I don't know what I've done to you to make you hate me like you do, but whatever it is, I'm sorry. I never wanted it to be like this, Mark. I won't take her anywhere if it makes you feel better, all right? I'll just leave. I'll try to see her another time," Nicole said as tears fell freely from her eyes.

She turned and walked from the room. She was so heartbroken she didn't even go to the kitchen to say good-bye to Tiandra. She just walked out of the apartment.

Mark had overreacted. He knew she would never hurt Tiandra. He also knew that she wouldn't run off with her again. He was so mixed up because of the love he felt for her. The pain of not being with her was becoming unbearable to him. It was causing him to act without thinking, and that was a trait he despised in others.

Chapter Twenty-Six

It was June nineteenth. Tiandra had been staying with Mark now for three weeks. Nicole now made a point of visiting Tiandra during the day, before Mark came home from the office. She could not bear being around him since he had carried on so about her taking Tiandra to the playground. Of all the things he had ever said and done, none hurt more than the look in his eyes when he told her she could not take Tiandra anywhere. She would never forget that look.

On this particular evening, Nick was taking her to the opera. Nicole didn't really care for the opera, but she loved the pageantry and glamour associated with it. She liked dressing up in beautifully tailored evening gowns and going out and mingling with high society. This was something she had come to love when she and Mark were first married.

Mark hadn't seen Nicole since that first time she had come by the penthouse to see Tiandra. He knew she was avoiding him and, truthfully, he couldn't blame her. He felt terrible about the way he had behaved that day and no matter how he tried, he could not erase the picture of her pain-stricken face from his mind.

Of all the things he had done or said to her, he knew in his gut that this was the lowest he had sunk. He owed her an apology, no doubt about that. But would she accept it? Would she even see him now?

His actions of three weeks ago weighed very heavy on Mark's mind on this day. At three different times during the day, his secretary had come into his office and interrupted his musings about Nicole.

He thought about calling her, but figured she would probably hang up on him the moment she heard his voice. But he needed to talk to her.

Nick told Nicole to be ready by seven o'clock because the opera started at eight. By seven thirty, however, he still had not arrived. Nicole did not like to be kept waiting. The only thing she hated more was being stood up. She did not want to think Nick would stand her up, but the longer it took him to show, the angrier she became, and in a situation like this she always thought the worst.

While Nicole was wondering where Nick was, Mark was wondering if she would see him if he went by her apartment unannounced.

By eight o'clock, Nicole was furious. Nick was an hour late and hadn't called. She knew they would not be going to the opera now. She called the hotel where he was staying, but when they rang his room, there was no answer and he had left no messages at the desk.

She would read him the riot act when he did show up, that was for sure.

At eight o'clock, Mark was standing across the street from Nicole's building, debating whether or not he should take a chance and go up to her apartment.

* * *

By eight thirty, Nicole was so angry that she was in tears. She could not believe Nick had actually stood her up again.

Finally, Mark decided he really had nothing to lose by going by and ringing her bell. She was already out of his life.

When he entered her building, the doorman must have recognized Mark from his previous visits, so he just had him sign in and told him to go on up.

Mark was surprised when, after he rang her bell, she did not ask who it was, but instead just opened the door.

At eight thirty-five, Nicole's doorbell rang. She was in her bedroom when she heard it. She quickly wiped her face and tried to hide the fact she had been crying.

"It's about time," she whispered to her reflection as she fixed her face.

She hurried to the front door and without checking to see who was there, she opened the door and said, "I thought you'd never get here!" Then she froze. It was not Nick at the door. It was Mark. "What are you doing here?"

Mark had anticipated her coldness and had prepared himself to deal with it, but being faced with it was another matter. The humble attitude he had when he rang her bell quickly dissipated. "I didn't come to stay. I just came by to get a few things for Tiandra," he lied. It was the first lie he ever told her.

"She doesn't have any clothes at your house?"

"Just put some things in a bag for her and I'm gone," Mark said indignantly.

Nicole cut her eyes at him and Mark knew if looks could kill, he would be dead. She had not invited him in and she suddenly turned to walk back into the apartment. She let the door go and if he hadn't caught it, it would have slammed in his face.

A few minutes later, she emerged from the back of the apartment with a tote bag filled with clothes for Tiandra. "Here!" she said, shoving the bag toward him.

He took it from her before it hit him in his chest. "Where are you going all dressed up like that?"

"None of your business!" She moved to the door and pulled it open. "Now, if you don't mind, I'd appreciate it if you did like you said. Her things are in the bag, why aren't you gone?"

Mark glared at her. He did not like her insolence, regardless of the reason. As he turned to leave the apartment, he said, "Next time, ask who's at your door. Somebody might come in here and knock you upside your head if you keep opening your door like that."

"That's my problem, not yours!" she said, slamming the door.

Now she was really angry. Not only had Nick stood her up, but Mark had the audacity to come to her house without calling, like he was a welcome guest.

At ten thirty, Nicole was sitting in the same spot on her sofa as when Mark left. She was no longer waiting for Nick, though. She was just too heartbroken to get up. She kept telling herself that he would call. Even if he didn't come, he would call. But he never did.

By eleven o'clock, she had cried herself to sleep right there.

Mark slept poorly that night. He was ashamed of himself for being such a coward and not apologizing to Nicole like he had intended. He'd known she wouldn't be happy to see him. He had prepared himself for that, but deep inside he still wished that she might have forgiven him and when he saw that she hadn't, his irrepressible pride once again took control.

At six a.m. the next morning, the ringing of his telephone

brought him fully out of his troubled sleep. "Yeah," he grumbled when he picked up the receiver.

"Mark? Sorry to wake you."

"Who's this?"

"Sandy McAllister."

Mark attempted to sit up at the mention of her name. "Hey, Sandy. What's up?"

"I'm sorry I woke you. I figured a big-time executive like you would be up making money by now."

"I should be, since I slept like hell last night."

"Oh? What's wrong?"

"It's a long story. You'd better tell me yours, we've probably got more time for it."

"Okay. Is your friend still seeing that guy, Nick Latargia, you had me run that check on?"

"Yeah, unfortunately. Why?"

"Well, the love affair is over."

"He's been busted," Mark stated.

"Yeah, by that big police officer in the sky."

"What?"

"He's dead. He was killed yesterday in a sting along with six others, including three men who were each wanted for murder, and two Feds. Word is he was the man at the heart of the whole thing. There was over twenty million dollars in cocaine confiscated, over ten million dollars in cash and an arsenal that could wipe out a small country."

Mark was silent on the other end.

"Mark? Are you there?"

"Yeah. I'm here."

"Is something wrong?"

"No. Listen, Sandy, thanks for the info. I owe you. I'll talk to you later."

"All right. See ya'."

Damn, he thought. *Nick's dead.*

He would never have to worry about him hurting Nicole or

Tiandra again. He would never have to face the man that was making love to his wife again. He would never again have to feel jealous of the relationship Nick had with Nicole. Nick was finally out of their lives.

Then why wasn't he happy?

Nicole doesn't know. She had been waiting for him last night when he went by her apartment. She thought he was Nick when she opened the door for him. She was probably thinking he had stood her up.

"Damn!" he muttered.

He had wanted Nick out of their lives, but not like this. He did not wish death on anyone, especially a violent death like Nick's. Mark was in shock, too, at the magnitude of Nick's involvement in the whole thing. He knew Nicole would have a very hard time accepting the fact that Nick had died as he had.

Mark got up from the bed and went into the bathroom. He shaved and showered quickly, then went to his dressing room and got dressed for work. He then went to the nursery and woke Tiandra. He hated waking her, but he decided he would have to tell Nicole what had happened and he thought she might need Tiandra around to take her mind off of it somewhat. He washed her quickly and dressed her and had Angie feed her before they left.

Since Mark usually left home by seven thirty for the office, Bobby was downstairs waiting when he came down with Tiandra. "Bobby, take me by Nicole's place."

"Sure thing," Bobby said as he held the door for Mark. "Hello, beautiful," he said to Tiandra as he pinched her cheek.

During the ride Mark was trying to think of how he would break the news to Nicole. He hated being the bearer of bad news but he felt obligated to tell her, and he certainly did not want her to find out by turning on the television and hearing it on the news.

When they reached her building and Bobby had parked in

front, Mark sighed deeply, then reached for Tiandra. "Come on, baby. Let's go see Mommy," he said as he picked her up and carried her out of the car. This time, however, when Mark entered the building, he insisted that the doorman call up to Nicole to let her know he was there.

Nicole woke up at about three a.m. and got up from the sofa, went into her bedroom, undressed and got in bed. She was very hurt and angry that Nick had stood her up again. The last time was at Tiandra's birthday party. He claimed then that he had business to take care of. If he came this time and told her that, she would scream.

When she climbed into bed, she was crying once again. *Why do men always have to hurt me,* she asked herself. *Why can't I find someone that will love me and not hurt me, too?*

At seven fifty-five, she was awakened by the buzzing of her intercom. As she groggily got up to answer it, she glanced over at the clock on her night stand. *Probably Nick,* she thought as she lumbered to the speaker. "Yes?"

"Mark Peterson is here to see you," the doorman's voice came through the intercom.

Nicole was puzzled. *What is Mark doing here this early in the morning?* She really did not feel like being bothered by him already. She was in no mood to be arguing with him about anything. "Send him up," she said reluctantly. Maybe it was something important. Maybe it had something to do with Tiandra, she thought.

She went to the bathroom and hurriedly washed her face and put on her bathrobe. She came back and waited for him to ring the bell. *What's taking him so long,* she wondered as a big yawn escaped her. Although only a minute and a half had passed since he rang her intercom, to Nicole it seemed like five. She was anxious to know why he was here.

Finally, her bell rang. Without asking who it was, she opened the door for him. When she saw Tiandra, her face lit up with joy. "Hi, Tee!" Nicole said happily. "How's my baby?" She took Tiandra from Mark's arms and hugged her. "How are you, sweetness? Mommy's so happy to see you."

After a few moments, she acknowledged Mark. "Hello."

"Hi."

Nicole noticed that he looked very anxious about something, but she did not comment on it. "Thank you for bringing her home," she said humbly.

Mark just nodded.

Nicole put Tiandra down and she immediately ran away from them.

Mark stared at Nicole sadly. He didn't know how he was going to do this.

Although her back was to him, Nicole felt his gaze upon her. She turned and looked at him curiously. Suddenly, a chill ran through her body as she watched him, and she visibly shivered. "What?"

Mark swallowed deeply then sighed. "I have some bad news to tell you, Nicole."

She didn't want to know what it was. She turned away from him and walked over to the sofa and sat down. She concentrated on Tiandra, who was sitting on the floor playing with a magazine.

"It's about Nick," Mark said as he moved a few steps closer to her.

Nicole quickly turned to look at him. A feeling of dread permeated her body. She didn't want to hear anything Mark had to say about Nick, but she did not say that. She didn't say anything. She gripped the arm of the sofa, trying to steel herself against what was coming next.

Reluctantly, he continued. "I received a phone call this morning from my friend in the Police Department who gave me that information I have on Nick."

Nicole still did not speak. She sat stark still and waited for his next words.

"Nick is dead, Nicole."

His eyes immediately told her he was telling the truth. She had not expected this. She'd expected to hear that he had been arrested or something like that, but not this.

"He was killed in a sting operation," Mark added. He watched helplessly as the blood drained from her face. It hurt to have to tell her this. It hurt more to watch her face as he told her. She looked up at him, her eyes pleading with him to tell her it was not true. But he could not do that. "I'm sorry," he said sincerely.

She still did not move or speak. She just stared straight ahead.

"If there's anything that I can do, Nicole, please let me know."

Nicole felt as if she were drowning. *This cannot be happening,* her mind screamed. She leaned her head on the back of the sofa and looked up at the ceiling. Tears spilled from the corners of her eyes. *Why did he have to live that way,* she asked herself.

Finally, she rose and faced Mark. The tears fell unrestrained from her eyes. She studied his face.

He felt very uncomfortable under her scrutiny.

"I guess you're very pleased by all of this."

Mark was hurt by her words. He frowned when he said, "I didn't want this for Nick. No matter what I might have said or felt about him, I never wanted this to happen. I wouldn't wish death on anyone, Nicole. I'm sorry if you think I would."

She tried to keep her composure but she felt it slowly giving way. She knew Mark was not a malicious person and what she said to him was not called for, but she was hurting now and she was angry and he was the only one she could lash out at. "Was there something else you wanted to tell me?"

"No."

"Well then, you've delivered your bad news. I would appreciate it if you left now. I'd like to be alone."

Mark could see how hard she was trying not to break down in front of him. He felt totally useless at that moment. *I've caused her nothing but heartache. She probably hates me now.* "If there's anything I can do to help, please let me know."

"Thank you, there's nothing you can do," Nicole said in a trembling voice.

When Mark reached his office that morning, his mind was a thousand miles away. He had not wanted to leave Nicole alone. He wished there was something he could do for her. With regret, he reasoned that if he had not been such a coward last night and had told her he was sorry like he had planned to, things might be different now. She might have willingly accepted consolation from him. But it was too late for that now.

Finally, after a few hours of trying to think of a way to get close to her, he decided to call Yvonne. She picked up the telephone on the second ring.

"Good morning," she answered cheerfully.

"Good morning, Yvonne."

"Mark? Hi. How are you?"

"Not too good. How are you?"

She did not answer his query but asked, "What's the matter?"

"Nick is dead, Yvonne."

"What?" Yvonne said in shock.

"Yeah. My friend who gave me that information I told you about, called me this morning to tell me he'd been killed. I went by Nicole's this morning to tell her. I didn't want her to find out about it by reading the papers or hearing it on the news."

"Oh, God, how's she taking it?"

"Not too good," Mark said sadly.

"Oh, God."

"She thought I was happy about it. Yvonne, I never wanted this to happen. I'm not going to lie and say I liked him or anything. I didn't even know him. I was jealous of him because she was in love with him and not me."

"She wasn't in love with Nick. She was infatuated. There's a difference."

"Regardless, she didn't want to be with me, so I disliked him for that. I never tried to make it easy for her, but I never wanted anything like this to happen. If you could have seen her face . . . She turned pale. I thought she was going to faint for a moment. I wanted to hold her, but she looked at me with such loathing that I knew she would never let me get close to her. I know she's at home right now, probably crying her eyes out and I want to help her, but she won't let me. I feel so helpless. I hate thinking about her up there all by herself. Would you call her and talk to her, see how she's doing, then call me back and let me know?"

"Sure, Mark. I'll call her right now, then I'll call you back."

"Thanks. Call collect."

"Don't worry about it. I'll talk to you in a few."

"All right, bye."

Yvonne called Mark back in thirty minutes. "Mark, it's Yvonne."

"Hi. Did you talk to her?"

"Yeah."

"How is she?"

"Not good. She's very upset and not just because Nick's dead. She's angry because he lied to her. She's really talking crazy and not making a whole lot of sense."

"Damn," Mark muttered.

"I told her you were worried about her. She thinks you're

happy that Nick's dead. I told her that was ridiculous and that she wasn't being very fair to you."

"I wasn't very fair to her when he was alive."

"That's what she said."

"I wish I could go to her and try to help her through this, but I guess I'm the last person she wants to see right now," Mark said sadly.

"Mark, she's upset now and she feels like Nick deserted her. She hasn't taken the time to think about what's happened. When she does, she'll see how ridiculous it is to think that you'd be happy about this and she'll realize that you're there for her. She just needs time. I guess you'll just have to be patient with her."

Mark sighed deeply. "I guess so," he said with resignation.

"Does Mrs. Johnson know?"

"Not unless Nicole's told her."

"I don't think she has. Maybe you should call her and ask her to go over to Nicky's house. At least that way she won't be alone."

"Okay, Yvonne. I'll do that."

"Don't worry, Mark. She'll come around. She still loves you," Yvonne said.

"You think so?"

"I know so."

Mark could not be as certain as Yvonne was, so he did not say anything.

"Listen, I'll call Nicky again tonight to see how she's doing, okay? Then I'll call you and let you know."

"Okay."

"Don't worry. She'll be all right."

"Yeah," he said half-heartedly.

"Call me anytime if you need me, all right?"

"All right, Yvonne. Thank you."

* * *

The next evening, Nicole went by Mark's apartment. Mark was not expecting her but was very pleased by her visit. "Nicole, I'm glad you came by. How are you?"

"Okay."

She was carrying Tiandra. She was asleep in her arms.

"Come, sit down," Mark said. "Let me take her." He reached for Tiandra.

Because Nicole had not mentioned right away why she was there, Mark just assumed that she had come because she wanted to be with him. "How are you feeling?"

"I'm fine."

She still had not accepted his offer to sit, so he repeated it. "Sit down, Nicole."

"No, thank you. I'm not staying. I only came by to ask if Tiandra could stay with you for a few days. I'm flying down to Florida for the funeral tomorrow."

Mark's joy immediately turned to sadness. "Oh."

"Is it all right?" Nicole asked again.

"Huh? Oh. Yeah, yeah sure," Mark answered, disheartened.

"The funeral's not for a few days still, but I want to go down to see if there's anything I can do to help," she explained.

Mark simply nodded his head.

There was an awkward silence for a few seconds, but to each it seemed like hours. The air was thick with tension. Finally, Nicole said. "Well, I'll go now. Thank you for keeping her."

"You don't have to thank me. She's my daughter."

She looked at him as if she was about to say something but decided not to. "Well, then, I'll see you later," she said.

As she turned to leave, Mark had an almost irresistible urge to tell her he loved her and that whatever she needed, he would give, but her cool demeanor made it clear to him that a confession of love would not be well-received at this time. Instead, he said, "Call me when you get back."

A week after Mark informed Nicole of Nick's death, she returned to New York from Miami where she attended his funeral. On that trip, Nicole learned more about Nick than she cared to remember.

When she arrived in Florida five days earlier, she went straight to his mansion. Once there, she was shocked to find that it had been sealed and that the police were not allowing anyone to enter. When she asked an officer on the premises, she was told there was an investigation underway and until it was over, no one would be allowed inside.

Nicole was very disillusioned and disappointed when she arrived at the funeral parlor for the service. His parents were there, of course. She had never met either of them, but she recognized them from a picture she had once seen when she was staying with him. When she approached them to introduce herself and offer her condolences, she was treated with indifference, like all of the other women that showed up crying over Nick's corpse.

She was also very upset to find out that Nick had two teenage daughters and a wife. She learned this by reading Nick's obituary in the program given out at the service. She felt like a fool. How could he have lied to her so easily? She had believed everything he told her. When she cried at his funeral, no one knew she was also crying for herself.

When the congregation was given the opportunity for a final viewing of Nick's remains, she started not to participate. But when her row was called up to pay their last respects, she rose and walked up to say good-bye, nonetheless.

She could not help thinking as she looked down at him that he looked very peaceful. He did not look as if he had died violently as he had. She wanted to be angry with him for the lies he told her, but she couldn't be. While he was alive, he had always been good to her, she could not ignore that. She had not known about his other life and maybe that had been for the best. Regardless of the lies, she would still miss him. Their relationship, to her at least, had been a special one, one that she would not easily forget. She would not curse him in his death for being untruthful in his life.

With tears streaming down her face, she bent over and kissed his lips. "Good-bye, Nick. Rest in peace."

Chapter Twenty-Seven

Nicole was home for two days before she got the envelope. As she opened her mailbox that afternoon to remove the assortment of mail that had accumulated over the past week, she noticed the manila envelope right away because it lacked a return address and her name and address were scrawled on the front with a felt-tip pen, as if someone had done it in a hurry. When she got upstairs, though, she forgot about it for a few hours as she began to prepare something for her and Tiandra to eat for dinner. Afterwards, they shared a bubble bath, then she dressed them both for bed and sat Tiandra up in bed with her and read her a bedtime story until she fell asleep.

It wasn't until Nicole had placed Tiandra in her crib and walked into the living room to make sure her front door was locked that she remembered to look at her mail. Then she remembered the envelope. She took the collection of magazines, bills and other items into her bedroom and placed them on the nightstand beside her bed. As she sat on the bed, she picked up the envelope with her address scrawled sloppily across the middle of it and looked at it with a frown creasing her forehead. She wondered who it was from. As she thought this, a chill ran through her body and she shivered. For some completely inexplicable reason, her heart beat at a phenomenal rate as she slowly tore the envelope open. Her hands trembled as she removed the contents. Inside were two letter-sized envelopes. One had her name typed in the center, the other had a document inside with her name typed and showing through the window. She opened that envelope first. As she pulled the document free, she noticed immediately that it was a check. She read the face of it. It took a few seconds for the numbers to register in her brain. When they did, she inhaled loudly and her eyes bulged from shock. She tossed the check away as if it had suddenly scorched her fingers, then, she covered her mouth. *This is not real. It can't be. I'm dreaming. Yes, that's it. I'm dreaming.* Who did she know that would send her a cashier's check in the amount of three million dollars?

She began to cry. She didn't know why, but she didn't know what else to do. *Who would do this to me?* She knew this had to be some kind of joke. Of that she had no doubt. *But why would anyone play a trick on me like this? What were they trying to do, give me a stroke?*

"Oh, God," she moaned. She jumped up from her bed and began to pace, back and forth, back and forth. Then she remembered the other envelope. She quickly picked it up from the bed. *This will explain everything,* she hoped. She removed the paper inside and unfolded it. As she began to read it, she immediately recognized Nick's handwriting.

"Nick," she whispered breathlessly.

She held the paper against her breast as fresh tears welled in her eyes. She sat down on the bed and tried to collect herself. She inhaled and exhaled deeply three times, then proceeded to read his letter. It began:

Dearest Nicole,

If you are reading this letter, then I am no longer of your world.

She stopped then and cried, "Oh. Nick. Nick."

She dropped the letter on the bed as she got up and went to the bathroom to get a tissue to wipe her eyes. She blew her nose and discarded the tissue, then retrieved another. She stood in the door of her bedroom for a moment eyeing the letter Nick had written. Slowly, she returned to the bed and sat down. She picked up the letter and started again.

Dearest Nicole,

If you are reading this letter, then I am no longer of your world.

There are so many things I want to say to you but unfortunately, all I have is one sheet of paper so I will try to tell you all that I can right here. First, I want to thank you for your time, your friendship, your smile, your love. Without them my world was a very empty place. You hold a very special place in my heart and I will love you forever. While we were together, you brought me tremendous joy and happiness and for those times that I unwillingly caused you to cry, I apologize and hope that you can forgive me for my weaknesses.

I loved being with you and your beautiful daughter, Tiandra. You are blessed to have one so loving and carefree in your midst. The times I spent with you and Tiandra were some of the happiest of my life. I wish I could be with you now to gaze into your beautiful eyes, to touch your hand, to kiss your lips. I treasure every moment I had with you. I wish I could be there to take care of you, to see that you have everything in this world that you'll ever need and want. But since I can't be, I leave you this. Maybe it will help you to achieve some of what you want in life. The enclosed check is for you to use however you please. It was drawn from funds that were earned by me through totally legal channels. It's yours.

However I leave this world, be it in my sleep or at someone's hand, I want you to know that I never wanted to cause anyone pain. I never told you about my "extra-curricular activities" because I never wanted to involve you in that. You were my escape from that world. I didn't mean to lie to you when you asked about it but I had to protect you from that. I hope you understand and forgive me.

Nicole, I love you. I will always love you. No matter what you may learn about me after I'm gone, know that my love for you is and always has been true. Take care of yourself and take care of Tiandra. One day, we will meet again and never part.

Forever,
Nick

P.S. Don't be too hard on Mark. I feel in my heart that he's a good man. I know in my heart that he loves you and that he'll take good care of you. Give him another chance. Sometimes the people we love the most are the ones that inadvertently hurt us the most.

Nicole read the letter twice before she put it down. She sat on the bed and cried for the better part of thirty minutes. Finally, she picked up the check again. *Is this real?* she wondered. Logic told her that Nick would not send her a counterfeit check. But why would he leave her three million dollars? It was evident from his letter that she was not to receive it until after his death. *Had he known that his life would be over so soon?* She was nervous about having that much money in her apartment. Should she tell her mother about it, she wondered? Probably not. Her mother would probably tell her to report it to the FBI, then that would be the end of it, she was sure. She had to tell someone, though. She couldn't keep something like this to herself. She would explode from the pressure. But who to tell? She couldn't tell any of her sisters or brothers because they would most likely tell her mother and father. She wished Yvonne was near; Nicole was much too paranoid to tell her about the money over the telephone. There was really no one else she trusted to tell. Strangely though, one person kept coming to mind, but she repeatedly ignored the thought, not wanting to acknowledge what she knew to be the answer.

She had absolutely no idea what she would do with the check. Could she just walk into a bank and deposit it with no explanation? She knew she would have to put it in the bank or invest it somehow, but how? She had no knowledge of investment tactics. She wouldn't even know where to begin. She could call an accountant but she didn't know any. *Call Mark.* A little voice in the back of her head kept telling her to call Mark. She hated to admit it, but he was the only person she felt she could trust enough to tell about this. Besides, he could probably tell her how to invest it or at least put her in touch with someone trustworthy to handle it for her, and he could probably tell her whether it was legal to receive such a large gift, especially with Nick's background.

She thought about calling Mark that night. Then she remembered how she'd treated him the last time she had seen him. He told her to call him if she needed him for anything, and she maliciously told him she did not need his help. How could she call him and ask for his help now? He had every right to tell her to get lost.

Once again, she reread the letter. She missed Nick terribly. She had been angry when she found out he was married and that he was most likely seeing a number of other women present at his funeral. Now she felt bad because of the loathsome thoughts she had about him. He had always behaved as a gentleman with her. He had always gone out of his way to make her happy. Although he was now dead, he was still looking out for her, it seemed.

She folded the letter and placed it and the check in her night table drawer. She turned out the lamp on her night table and lay down, but she could not sleep. She really wanted to call Mark but she was afraid to. She had not spoken to him in a civil manner in who knew how long. Maybe he wouldn't want to talk to her. If that was the case, she didn't know what she would do.

The next day . . .

"Good morning, Mark Peterson's office."

"Good morning. May I speak to him, please?"

"Can I tell him who's calling?"

"Yes. Nicole."

"Oh, hi, Nicky. This is Denise."

"Hi, Denise. I didn't recognize your voice."

"Yeah, I've got a little cold. Hold on a moment, I'll tell him you're on."

"Hi." His voice sounded like a caress.

Her heart skipped a beat. "Hi," she said shyly.

"How are you?" he asked tenderly.

"I'm okay. How are you?"

"Fine. How'd everything go?" Mark asked, referring to Nick's funeral.

"Oh, okay, I guess."

"Are you feeling all right?" He was genuinely concerned.

"Yes, I'm okay."

"That's good. Remember what I told you. If you need anything, let me know."

That's my cue, she thought. "Okay."

There was an awkward silence between them then. Nicole

broke it. "Mark, the reason I called was because, well, I know you just got back from a trip but I thought, maybe, if you want you could come by tonight to see Tiandra."

Mark was taken aback by Nicole's offer. He smiled when he said, "I'd love to. I was planning to call you to find out when I could come by to see her. How is she?"

"She's fine. I was just getting ready to feed her."

"Give her a kiss for me."

"Okay," she said. She leaned over to kiss Tiandra. "That's from Daddy."

"What's a good time to come?"

"You can come right from work if you want to. I thought I'd fix something for dinner and you could eat with us if you like."

"That would be nice."

Nicole was smiling when she said. "Okay, then I guess I'll see you tonight."

"Right. I'll probably be leaving here at around six."

"That's fine. We'll be here. I'm not going anywhere."

"Okay. Then I'll see you later."

When Mark hung up the telephone, he sat back in his chair and replayed in his mind the conversation he had just had with Nicole. He smiled. He was pleased that she seemed to want their relationship to take a turn for the better. *Maybe just maybe,* he thought, *this could be the start of a new beginning for us.* He hoped so.

He arrived at Nicole's apartment at a quarter after six with a bottle of Nicole's favorite wine. "Hi," he said with a big smile when she opened the door.

"Hi. Come in," Nicole said as she opened the door wider to let him in.

"How are you, Nicole?" he asked as he gazed into her eyes.

She blushed from the intensity of his stare and said, "I'm fine. How are you?"

"I'm okay."

"Sit down."

"Thank you. Oh, here." He handed her the bottle of wine. "I thought you might like this."

When she saw that it was her favorite, she smiled at him. "Thank you, Mark." She was flattered that he remembered. "We can have this with dinner. I made spaghetti and meatballs. Is that okay?"

He smiled and said, "You know I love your spaghetti and meatballs."

She blushed. She hadn't been this nervous around him since he'd come by on Christmas. "Tiandra's sleeping. She should be waking up soon, though," Nicole said, trying to draw attention away from herself.

"Do you mind if I go in and take a peek at her? I promise not to wake her."

"I don't care. You can wake her if you want."

"Naw. I'll let her sleep. I just want to look at her."

"Go ahead. I'll fix our plates so we can eat."

"Okay."

By ten o'clock, Mark and Nicole had eaten dinner, washed and dried the dishes, fed Tiandra and put her to bed. They'd drank more than half the bottle of wine. As a result, Nicole was much more at ease. They laughed and talked about a number of different subjects easily.

Mark paid special attention to Nicole as she spoke. He noticed that although she appeared to be carefree, there was something bothering her. He could not put his finger on what, so he said nothing about it. He figured if there was something she wanted to talk to him about, she would talk about it. He did not want to push. He was very pleased with their rapport, and did not want to do anything to ruin it.

Suddenly, Nicole's mood changed. She became very contemplative. She got up from the sofa where she had been sitting next to Mark and ambled over to the window. She stood looking out for a moment until Mark spoke.

"What's wrong, Nicole?"

She slowly turned to face him. She looked into his eyes, then quickly lowered her head. Unable to look at him, she said, "I owe you an apology, Mark."

He rose from the sofa and went to stand before her. He took her chin in hand and gently raised her head so she was looking at him. "Why?" he asked softly.

"Because when you came by to tell me about Nick, I was very rude. I'm sorry."

"That's all right. Look, it wasn't as if I had anything good to tell you."

"Yeah, but I didn't have to react like that," she said shamefully.

"Nicole, don't worry about it. To be honest, I owe you an apology. The night that Nick died, when I came by I was coming to apologize to you for my behavior when you came by to see Tiandra that day. I was totally out of line and I'm very sorry for that. I hope you can forgive me."

She gazed up into his eyes and saw the warmth and love there that she had seen the first time he told her he loved her. "I forgive you."

He looked into her eyes. He wanted to kiss her but he refrained. He knew there was much healing that had to be done before they could be intimate again.

Nicole suddenly felt the urge to pour out her heart to him. "You know when I went down for Nick's funeral, I found out some things about him that greatly disillusioned me. Granted, you tried, on many occasions, to tell me about his drug dealings and I didn't want to listen."

"Nicole . . ."

"No. Please, listen. I have to tell you this. You were right to some extent about Nick. He lived a very fast and dangerous life. I never knew how much so. He kept me away from that. But while I was with him, I was happy. I knew he'd never hurt me or Tiandra. But he lied to me about other things, too. I found out that Nick was a married man. He has two teenage daughters and he probably had other women besides me. Needless to say, when I found this out, I was hurt and angry. I felt like a fool for falling for him.''

She took a deep breath and walked aimlessly across the room. Mark was silent, waiting for her to continue.

''When I got home, I tried to concentrate on getting him out of my mind. It's been hard. Sometimes I feel so alone. Anyway, yesterday I finally went and got the mail out of my box from when I was away. There was this big manila envelope with no return address on it. I can't explain it, but before I even opened it, I was nervous about what it might contain.''

She stopped then and her eyes became moist. ''You're not going to believe this, Mark,'' she said, on the verge of tears. ''Come here,'' she said to him, reaching for his hand. He took her hand and allowed her to lead him to the bedroom. Once there, she went straight to the night table drawer and removed the envelope. ''This is what came for me,'' she said as she handed the envelope to him. Mark reached into the manila envelope and removed the contents.

''Open the one with the window first.''

He pulled the check from the envelope and read the face of the document. ''Holy cow!'' he exclaimed.

''Mark, what am I supposed to do with this?''

''Who's it from?''

''Nick.''

''Nick?''

''Yes. Open the other envelope,'' she then said.

Mark took the letter and started to read it. When he read the salutation, ''Dearest Nicole,'' he stopped and looked at her questioningly.

''You can read it,'' she said when she saw his hesitation.

''You sure?''

She nodded her head.

Mark quickly read the letter. He was moved by it. He also

felt guilty all of the sudden. "Wow. I've been very unfair to you and Nick."

"Mark . . ."

He cut her off. "No, Nicole. I never even gave him a chance. You said it yourself, he kept that stuff away from you. That was always his intention, not to be deceitful but to protect you. But I had to stir things up. I never gave either of you a chance. I'm sorry. You were right when you said that I never knew him. I was wrong to judge him. Can you forgive me?"

"Yes," she said with watery eyes.

"He must have cared for you very much to have done this."

"But what am I going to do with it, Mark? Can I just take it to the bank and deposit it?"

"Yeah, you can, but it would probably do you better to invest it," Mark said, simply.

"How? I don't know anything about that kind of stuff. I wouldn't even know where to begin," she said, helplessly.

"I'll help you. The first thing you need is an accountant. He can tell you how to turn this into tangible assets. You're going to have to report this to the IRS. Damn! If you don't invest it properly, they'll kill you in taxes. You also need a lawyer."

"But I don't know any accountants or lawyers."

"I'll tell you what, I'll speak to Bruce. You know Bruce Silverman, my accountant. He can tell you everything you need to know. He can advise you on how to invest this, how to spread it out so you don't get hit by the IRS on the whole thing in one shot. I'll see if I can set up a meeting with him for you, okay?"

"Would you come with me?"

"Sure, I'll go with you," he said as he gently caressed her arm.

"Thank you." Then, "Are you sure it's good?"

"Yeah. This is a cashier's check. This is just like cash," Mark said with certainty.

"When I opened the envelope and saw this, I almost passed out," Nicole confessed.

"I can understand that."

"I was trying to figure out who to tell. I didn't want to just tell anybody."

"That's smart. Who'd you tell?"

"You."

"No one else knows about this?"

"No. You were the only person I felt I could trust and who I thought would be able to help me figure out what to do with it."

He smiled at her and took her hand. "I'm glad you feel you can trust me. That makes me feel good. Thank you."

They smiled at each other, each wanting to kiss the other but both apprehensive about making the first move.

"Come on, let's put this away," Mark said. They put the envelopes back in Nicole's night table drawer, then returned to the living room.

"You know, one thing you should do is invest in real estate," Mark suggested. "That's where the money is."

"I've always wanted to buy a house. Do you know of any nice ones for sale?"

"I can find out for you."

"Would you?"

"Sure. You probably should take a trip, too. A nice long vacation."

"Yeah. That would be nice. Maybe I'll take my mother somewhere."

"That would be nice." He smiled at her. He felt good about being with her but he didn't want to wear out his welcome. "It's getting late. I'd better be going."

"Are you driving?"

"No, I'll get a cab. Thanks for dinner."

"Thanks for coming when I needed you."

"Call me any time you do. I'll be here," he said sincerely.

"I will," she said with a smile. She walked him to the door.

"I'll call Bruce first thing tomorrow, then I'll let you know when we can get together with him, all right?"

"All right."

Mark decided to take a chance. He leaned forward and kissed Nicole gently on the lips. "Thank you," he whispered. He opened the door and stepped out. "Good night, beautiful."

"Good night, Mark. Be careful."

"I will."

When she closed the door, she stood against it for a moment, smiling and thinking about how much she really loved him. She had a feeling they would be together again. Soon.

The next morning at ten o'clock, Nicole's telephone rang. Her instincts told her it was Mark. She answered the phone very cheerfully. "Good morning."

"Good morning. You sound nice and cheerful this morning. Was it something you had for breakfast?"

Nicole laughed. "No, I think it was something I had last night."

Mark smiled at this. "Something I missed?"

"I don't know. Did you?"

He chuckled. "I don't know if I should answer that. I might be setting myself up."

She said, "No comment."

"Okay. Moving right along. I spoke with Bruce a few minutes ago."

"Oh? What did he say?" she asked excitedly.

"He said we can come by his office this evening."

"Is that good for you?"

"Yeah, I'm free tonight."

"What time?"

"How's five?"

"Five is good for me. Where should I meet you?"

"Uh, let me see," Mark said, contemplating how to hook up with her. "Listen, why don't I have Bobby come by your place and pick you up at about four fifteen, four thirty, then he can swing by here and we can go from there."

"Okay. I'll be ready. Should I bring anything?"

"Just your sweet face."

She smiled and said, "Okay. Then I'll see you later."

"Definitely," Mark said enthusiastically.

Nicole put on a vibrant, yellow linen suit to wear to her meeting with Mark and his accountant. She wore sheer off-white pantyhose and cream colored pumps. She wanted to look her best for her meeting with Mark.

Bobby was in front of her building at four twenty when Nicole went downstairs. When he saw her leave the building, he got out of the limousine and came around to open the door for her. He hadn't seen Nicole in a very long time and was pleased to see her looking so well.

"Hi, Bobby," Nicole said as they exchanged kisses on cheeks.

"Hi, Nicky. How are you? You look great."

"Thank you. I'm fine. How are you?"

"Not bad. It's good to see you. It s been too long," Bobby said, smiling at her.

"It's good to see you, too. Do I look okay? Do you think Mark will like this suit?"

"If he doesn't, then he's got a serious mental deficiency."

Nicole laughed. Although Bobby was one of Mark's employees, Nicole had always considered him a friend.

She climbed into the car and settled into the back seat. When they arrived in front of the building that housed the offices of Peterson & Company, Nicole's stomach became a bit nervous. They were there only a couple of minutes when she spotted Mark coming out of the building toward the car. *God, he looks so good,* she thought. He had on a tan cotton suit, white shirt and a tan paisley tie. He was the picture of professionalism as he walked toward them.

When Bobby opened the door for him to enter the car, Nicole, unconsciously, held her breath. The first thing Mark noticed when he bent to get into his limo was her legs. As far as he was concerned, she had the best pair of legs this side of the planet. Then he looked into her face. *Damn, she's beautiful.*

"Hi," she said, smiling.

"Hi," he responded with as big a smile. As he sat down next to her, he automatically leaned over to kiss her. But pleasantly and just as automatically, she did the same. "How are you?" he then asked.

"I'm fine. How are you?"

"Not bad. Not bad at all," he said with a mischievous grin.

"What?" she asked, wondering why he was looking at her that way.

"You look very nice."

"Thank you. So do you."

They arrived at Bruce Silverman's office fifteen minutes later. Bobby got out and came around to open the door for them and Mark stepped out, then held out his hand to assist Nicole. As she stood next to him, he held on to her hand and whispered in her ear, "Did I ever tell you you have the sexiest legs I've ever seen?"

She blushed and said, "Thank you."

"You're welcome. I like your suit. That color looks great on you."

"Thank you."

Then he held out his arm for her to hold and said, "Shall we?"

She put her arm in his and said, "We shall."

They spent a little more than an hour with Bruce Silverman. Nicole was grateful for the information he provided her with. He advised her on how she should split up her newly acquired wealth into different investments. He advised her to hire a lawyer to oversee all transactions having to do with any investments she might care to make. He also advised her on how she should report the money to the IRS and told her he would be happy to handle the reporting of it. He suggested she put some of the money into a money market account or IRA, and also purchase some municipal bonds, tax-deferred bonds, etc. She told him she would like to put some of the money into a trust account for Tiandra. He told her that would be a wise decision.

When they left Bruce's office, Nicole was feeling much more confident about how she would deal with her newly acquired wealth. She was grateful to him and offered to pay him for his time and advice but he refused. He said if she decided to hire him as her accountant, he would worry about it then, but for now there was no charge.

As they left the building, Mark asked Nicole, "So, do you feel better now that you've spoken to Bruce?"

"Oh, yes, much. Thanks for arranging this for me."

"Any time. If you like, I can put you in touch with a good lawyer."

"I'd appreciate that."

It was almost six thirty. Mark was hungry. He asked Nicole, "Are you hungry?"

"A little."

"Would you join me for dinner?"

"Sure."

They went to Mark's favorite restaurant, Maxwell's. After placing their drink orders, they shared an easy silence for a while, then they made small talk for the next few minutes until their drinks arrived and they ordered dinner.

Nicole lifted her glass and said, "Cheers."

Mark lifted his glass and said, "Here's to doubling your money."

"I'll drink to that."

They each sipped their drinks, then placed them back on the table.

''Do you really think I can?'' Nicole suddenly asked.

''What?''

''Double my money.''

''Oh, yeah. If you follow Bruce's advice, I'm sure you can do better than that.''

''I think I'll take my mother on a trip.''

''Where to?''

''I don't know. I'll ask her. Wherever she wants to go. I know I'd like to go to Spain.''

''Spain is a beautiful country.''

''I know.''

''Your mother would probably like Spain, too.''

''I think so. If she doesn't want to go there though, we can go somewhere else.''

''How long would you go for?''

''Probably three weeks to a month.''

''Do you plan on taking Tiandra?''

''Probably.''

''Oh, man. You mean, you're going to take my baby away from me for a whole month? How will I survive?'' Mark said, teasing her.

''You'll manage. When we come back, I'll send her to stay with you for a month to make up for it.''

Mark gazed at her lovingly for a moment, then said, ''It's good to see you, Nicole.''

She smiled and said, ''You sound like you haven't seen me for a long time.''

''I haven't, like this.''

She looked into his eyes and smiled. ''It's good to see you, too, Mark.''

He shook his head thoughtfully and said, ''We've been through quite a lot together, haven't we?''

''To say the least,'' she said, smiling.

"Yeah. I'm really sorry for all the headaches I've caused you."

"That's all right. I'm sure I've caused you a few."

"No. Mine were mostly my own doing. When I look back at what a hard time I gave you about Nick, I feel really . . . I'm very ashamed of myself," Mark said.

"Mark, I never planned to get involved with Nick or anyone else for that matter. To be honest with you, we were nothing more than friends. When I met him on that cruise, I was still smarting from finding you with Ashlei, and the last thing I wanted was an intimate relationship with anyone. I was able to talk to him about it and he was always willing to listen. I needed to talk to someone that was totally unbiased and he didn't know me, or you, so he couldn't make any rash judgments or anything. He just let me speak my mind."

"I was wrong to judge him, Nicole. I didn't know what kind of person he was, or anything. I just went by what I was told, what I'd read. I was afraid for you. I didn't want to see anything happen to you because of what he was doing. I was so quick to try and convict him that I never considered that maybe he was keeping that from you for your safety. If I hadn't said anything, who knows, maybe things would have been different."

"I don't think so. He lied to me about everything, and I would have found out sooner or later. I don't think I would have understood if I'd found all that out while he was still alive," Nicole said.

"But you were in love with him, weren't you?"

"I don't think so. I think I was more in love with the way he treated me. He went out of his way to make me happy, it seemed. I was always able to talk to him, even about you. I couldn't understand why you were so totally against him."

"I think the reason I hassled you and him so much was because I thought maybe I could chase him away. Granted, I didn't like what he was doing and I genuinely worried that you might get caught up in something bad, but I was jealous that you wanted to be with him, plain and simple. I really got crazy when I saw that my antics weren't working," Mark confessed.

"He was stubborn," Nicole said with a smile. "Like you."

"You've got a thing for bullheaded guys, huh?"

"I guess so."

"I'm really sorry he had to die like that. I know that was very painful for you."

Her eyes began to water a little. She averted her eyes. "It was," she said quietly.

"I hated having to be the one to tell you, but I didn't want you to pick up the newspaper and read about it, or turn on the television and find out like that."

"I appreciate that. I don't think I would have been able to handle that."

They were both silent again, this time for a much longer period of time.

Finally, Mark said, "I'm glad we're able to talk like this. I hope this means that you'll consider me a friend you can talk to, if you ever feel the need."

She smiled at him and said, "I'd like that. I think that's what we were missing before."

"You're probably right."

"I think we were both in too much of a rush to take the time to get to know each other."

"That was my fault. I didn't want to let you get away," Mark confessed.

"It wasn't entirely your fault. You didn't put a noose around my neck and force me to marry you. I was in as much of a rush as you were. I didn't want you to change your mind."

"I wouldn't have," he said sincerely.

They studied each other for a few seconds. Nicole smiled meekly and looked away first.

Mark wanted to tell her he hoped they could work things out between them and get back to being a family again, but he refrained. He didn't want to press his luck. He knew where he had messed up before. He would take his time with her this time and do it right.

After dinner, they went to Nicole's parents' house to get Tiandra, then they drove back to Nicole's house. Mark carried Tiandra upstairs and into the apartment. He took her straight to her room, undressed her, changed her diaper, put on her pajamas and put her back to sleep. When he finished he went back into the living room.

"Can I get you something to drink, Mark?"

"No, thanks, baby. I'm going to cut out. I've got an early meeting tomorrow and I have to go over a couple of files at home to prep myself."

"All right. Thanks for hooking me up with Bruce."

"It was my pleasure."

"And thanks for dinner, too."

"Any time. We have to do this again sometime," he said.

"Soon."

"Soon," he agreed.

They walked to the door and Mark unlocked and opened it. "I'll call you tomorrow if I can hook up with my lawyer friend and let you know when you can get together with him."

"All right."

He was standing in the doorway, holding onto the knob on the outside. Nicole moved closer and grabbed the doorknob on the inside. Mark leaned forward and kissed her lips softly, sensuously. She responded in kind. They parted slowly, reluctantly it seemed, and he gently caressed her cheek.

"Good night, beautiful," he said softly.

She gazed into his eyes and whispered, "Good night."

Chapter
Twenty-Eight

A week later, Nicole called Mark at work to tell him she was cruising to Spain.

"That's great! You're taking your mother, right?" he asked.

"Yup. I was telling her about it and before I could even finish, she said, 'I don't care. I'll go anywhere you like.' "

Mark laughed. "When are you leaving?"

"Saturday."

"This Saturday?"

"Yeah."

"Wow, you're not wasting any time, huh?"

"Well, I think I need to get away for a while. I'm still kind of a mess and I think the sooner I get away for some R&R, the sooner I'll be back to my old self."

"Well, now that you mention it, your old self is kinda nice."

Their ship was scheduled to sail at four p.m., Saturday. Mark picked Nicole up and took her and Tiandra to the pier. Tiandra had stayed with Mark from the previous Monday night until that day.

When they reached the pier, Mr. and Mrs. Johnson were already there. "Hi, Mommy, hi, Daddy," Nicole said as she walked up to them, hugging and kissing them both.

"Hi, sweetheart," said Mr. Johnson.

"Hi," Mrs. Johnson said. "You all ready for our cruise?"

"You know I am."

"Hey, Bill, how're you doing?" Mark said, reaching out to shake his father-in-law's hand.

"Hey, Mark. Hi, precious," Mr. Johnson said to Tiandra, kissing her cheek.

"Hi, Mom. Ready for your trip?" Mark asked as he kissed Mrs. Johnson's cheek.

"Oh, yes, Mark. I've been waiting for this for a long time."

"You'll love Spain. It's a beautiful country. Especially at this time of the year."

"I'm sure it is. I can't wait to see it."

"Come on, let's go on board," Nicole said excitedly.

"They can't come on board with us, Nicky," Mrs. Johnson said.

"No? Why not?"

"Only ticketed passengers are being allowed on board," Mrs. Johnson informed them.

"Oh," Nicole said sadly.

"No bon voyage party, huh? I guess we'll have to say goodbye right here," Mark said.

Suddenly, Nicole did not want to leave Mark.

"Here, Mark, I'll take Tiandra," Mrs. Johnson said, reaching for her granddaughter. "Are you ready for our trip, honey?"

Tiandra smiled and put her arms around Mrs. Johnson's neck and hugged her.

"I guess she is," Mark said with a smile. He leaned over to kiss Mrs. Johnson and Tiandra. "Have fun."

"Tiandra, say, 'We will, Daddy,' " Mrs. Johnson said.

Mr. Johnson kissed Nicole and said, "Have a good trip, baby. Be careful."

Nicole hugged her father. "I will, Daddy." Tears were falling freely from her eyes.

Mr. Johnson kissed his wife on her lips and said, "Have fun, baby. I'll miss you. You, too, Tiandra."

"I'll miss you, too, sweetheart," Mrs. Johnson said. "I'll bring you back something nice."

"Okay."

Nicole was avoiding Mark's eyes.

"Nicole," Mark said.

"Huh?"

"Don't cry, baby, you should be happy." He put his arms around her gently and she melted into them. She put her arms around him and held him tight. Mark lifted her head with his hand and looked into her eyes. "I'll miss you."

"I'll miss you, too," she muttered.

"Will you bring me something back?"

"What?"

"Your sweet face."

New tears fell at this request.

"Aw, baby, I wish I was going with you. Maybe next time, huh?"

She could only nod her head.

"Have a good time, sweetheart. Don't think about me too much."

Nicole looked into his eyes and before she realized what she was doing, she reached up and put her hands behind his head and kissed him. Mark's embrace tightened around her waist as he reciprocated her kiss.

When they released each other, Mark's eyes were also wet, but he smiled and said, "Have fun, baby. I'll see you when you get back."

"Bye," she said weakly.

"Bye, beautiful. Tiandra, take care of Mommy for me."

Their first night on the cruise, they went to bed soon after dinner. Nicole and her mother were both very tired and they wanted to be fresh for their first full day on board their beautiful ship.

After laying awake for more than an hour thinking about Mark, she began to cry softly. She did not realize her mother was still awake in the next bed and could hear her sniffling. "Nicky."

Nicole did not answer, she just continued to cry.

Mrs. Johnson got up from her bed and went to sit on Nicole's. She gently turned her over until she was lying on her back.

"What's wrong, baby?"

"I miss Mark already."

Mrs. Johnson smiled and nodded her head. "I miss your father, too. This is the first time I've been on a trip without him in years."

"Mommy, I want him back. I don't want to be without him anymore," Nicole cried.

"Then tell him how you feel."

"But . . ."

"But, nothing. He's still your husband and you still love him, right?"

"Yes."

"I'm sure he still loves you, too. Tell him how you feel."

"You think I should?"

"Yes."

"Sometimes I think about telling him that I still love him, but I don't want to hear him say that it's too late."

"I don't think you have to worry about that. I saw the way he was looking at you today."

"He means so much to me."

"I know, baby," Mrs. Johnson said as she hugged her daughter. "I know."

They sat in silence for a few minutes, holding on to each other for comfort and support.

"I'm sorry I woke you, Mommy."

"You didn't wake me. I was laying there thinking about your father."

They held each other quietly for a few minutes more.

"Thank you, Mommy. I think I'll try to sleep now."

"Okay, baby. Sleep tight," Mrs. Johnson said as she kissed Nicole's forehead.

"I love you."

Mrs. Johnson smiled and said, "I love you, too, sweetheart."

Chapter
Twenty-Nine

Their cruise ended four weeks later on a Friday. The ship docked in Manhattan at seven fifteen p.m. It was almost nine o'clock when Nicole, Tiandra and Mrs. Johnson disembarked. As they were coming through the ship's terminal, Mrs. Johnson was the first to spot their welcoming committee which consisted of her son and son-in-law. "Hi!" she called as she waved. "There's Billy and Mark."

"Where?" Nicole asked. She did not see them.

"Over there," Mrs. Johnson pointed.

Nicole looked in that direction. When she spotted Mark, a big smile crossed her face. She waved to him. He waved back. "I didn't know he would be here," she said.

"I'm not surprised."

In addition to the bags and trunk Nicole had taken on the trip, she now had another small suitcase to carry. She and Mrs. Johnson had done an enormous amount of shopping while in Spain. Aside from the items they bought for themselves, they each bought a souvenir for every member of the family, from Mr. Johnson down to the youngest grandchild. And of course, Nicole had souvenirs for Mark.

"Hi," Billy said as they approached the gate near the terminal exit.

"Hi," Mrs. Johnson and Nicole called simultaneously.

Mark and Nicole's eyes locked and they smiled at each other. She stepped up to him and he did not hesitate for a moment. He put his arms around her as she held Tiandra and hugged her close while he greeted her with a big kiss.

"I'm glad you're home," he said, for her ears only.

"I'm glad I'm home, too. I missed you."

"I missed you, too." He kissed her again. "Hi, precious," he said, kissing Tiandra, although she was asleep.

"Hi, Mark," Mrs. Johnson said.

Mark released Nicole and turned to his mother-in-law. "Hi, Mom. How are you? How was the cruise?" he asked as he kissed her cheek.

"It was fantastic! I loved it. Spain is the most beautiful place I've ever seen," she said enthusiastically.

"Hey, Nicky," Billy said.

"Hi, Billy. I'm sorry. I didn't mean to ignore you," Nicole said as she hugged her big brother.

"I know. I understand. Did you have fun?"

"Oh, yes. It was great. It was really great. You've got to go to Spain, Billy. Right, Mommy?"

"Yes. It's a beautiful, beautiful country. And everyone is so nice."

"Right! Especially on the ship. The crew fell in love with Tiandra."

"Oh, yeah. Every day, at least one crew member wanted to kidnap her," Mrs. Johnson said, laughing.

"You should see the pictures we have of her. Some of them are really funny."

Mark was smiling at Nicole as he listened to her tell of her trip. He was glad to see she had enjoyed herself so much. She looked rested and at peace. "So, Nicole," Mark said.

"Huh?"

"Did you bring me anything?"

"Of course. I brought something back for everyone. I think you'll like what I got you, too. I hope so."

"I'm sure I will," Mark said as he gazed at her.

Bobby had driven the limousine to the pier to pick up Nicole and Tiandra. Billy had also driven so he and Mrs. Johnson said their good-byes to Nicole, Mark and Tiandra at the pier.

When the limo reached Nicole's apartment building, Bobby removed Nicole's trunk and carried it in while Mark carried her other bags up to her apartment. She and Tiandra followed. Once they were settled, Bobby went back down to the limo to wait for Mark.

"Nicole, do you mind if I take Tiandra home with me? I missed my baby and I'd like to keep her with me for a few days."

"Of course, I don't mind. As a matter of fact, that'll probably give me a great opportunity to get some rest. I am so tired. It'll be nice to sleep on solid ground again, too."

"I'm sure," Mark said with a chuckle.

Nicole yawned and stretched. "Gosh. I'm whipped."

"You don't look whipped. You look great," Mark said with a smile.

"Thank you. I feel a lot better. After I get some sleep, I'll be ready for anything."

"I'm sure you're ready for anything right now," he said suggestively.

"Not anything. I'm too tired," she said, laughing.

He laughed with her. "So where're my souvenirs?" Mark asked in jest.

"Oh, they're in the trunk. You'll have to wait until tomorrow, though. I'm not even going to open that sucker tonight. When you walk out that door, I'm jumping in bed. I might not even take off my clothes."

"I was just teasing."

"Oh, but I have a couple of things for you."

"Yeah?"

"Yeah." She yawned again. "I'm so tired. I hate to be antisocial, Mark, but you've got to leave," she said, giggling.

"I'm outta' here," he said, smiling.

She walked them to the door. "Bye, Tee. See ya' later, baby," Nicole said to Tiandra. "Gimme kiss."

Tiandra leaned over in Mark's arms and puckered her lips to be kissed.

Nicole kissed her and said, "Ooh, that's good sugar. That's some good sugar."

Mark leaned over and kissed Nicole, open-mouthed. He said, "That's some good sugar!"

Nicole smiled and said, "And you know that."

They smiled and looked into each other's eyes with mutual adoration.

"I'll see you later, baby. Sleep tight," Mark said.

"I'll try. Be careful."

"I will."

Nicole did not get out of bed until almost one o'clock the following afternoon. When she got up though, she felt totally refreshed and decided to play Santa Claus and deliver the souvenirs to her sisters and brothers and nieces and nephews.

As she was packing the gifts in her tote bag, she decided to take Mark's gift to him also. She had his gift-wrapped while in Spain to add to the excitement of watching him open it. She tried to call him to tell him she was coming over, but his line was busy both times she tried, so she decided to just go on over. When she reached his building, she knew the doorman would have allowed her to go upstairs unannounced, but she had him call up anyway.

Angie answered the intercom. Mark was on the terrace. Carol was visiting with her kids, and Ashlei Brown just happened to be visiting, also. Angie went to the terrace door and said, "Excuse me, Mr. Peterson."

"Yes, Angie," Mark said, giving her his full attention.

"Mrs. Peterson is on her way upstairs."

"She is?" Mark asked, surprised.

"Yes."

"Great."

Carol said, "I haven't seen Nicky in a while. How is she?"

"She's doing great."

"Since she met that guy, Nick, she's forgotten about everyone else," Carol said in jest.

"Nick is dead, Carol. I hope you won't say that to her," Mark said, not appreciating her sense of humor.

"I wouldn't say that to her, Mark," Carol said, slightly hurt that he thought she was so unfeeling.

Ashlei had been a regular chatterbox since her arrival, but she had not said a word since they were informed that Nicole was coming upstairs. She was the last person Ashlei wanted to see.

Angie answered the bell right away when Nicole rang.

"Hi, Angie," she said cheerfully.

"Hello, Mrs. Peterson. How was your trip?"

"Oh, it was fabulous. Very, very nice."

"That's good. Mr. Peterson is on the terrace."

"Thank you."

As she was walking through to the terrace, she stopped to say hello to Mark's niece and nephew. While greeting the children, Carol came off the terrace and said, "Hi, stranger." She was holding Tiandra.

Nicole smiled and said, "Hi, Carol. How are you?" She walked over to her and they embraced.

"I'm fine. How're you?"

"Fine," Nicole answered. "Hi, sugar baby," she said to Tiandra.

Carol said, "You look great. What a tan!"

"Thanks."

"So, how was your cruise?"

"Oh, it was fantastic! I can't remember having that much fun in a very long time. I needed this," Nicole said matter of factly.

"Well, you look great."

"Thanks, so do you. I just came by today to bring the souvenirs that I bought for Mark in Spain. He's out there?" she asked, gesturing toward the terrace.

"Yeah. Ashlei's out there, too."

"Oh." Nicole's heart seemed to plunge. She certainly didn't want to see Ashlei, especially here. "I tried to call him but the line was busy. I should have kept trying."

"Don't worry about it. He was very happy when Angie told him you were coming upstairs," Carol informed her.

"Well, I won't stay. I'll just do my business and leave."

Carol deposited Tiandra on the floor so she could play with her cousins, but she stood near the terrace doorway to keep an eye on them.

"Hello," Nicole said as she entered the terrace.

"Hey, baby," Mark said enthusiastically, walking over to her and kissing her on the lips. "How're you doing?"

"I'm fine. Hello, Ashlei."

"Hello," Ashlei said dryly.

"Brought my Christmas presents?" Mark asked, peeking into her bag.

She slapped his hand and said, "Maybe. Have you been a good boy?"

"Of course I have" Mark said with a big grin.

"Yeah, I bet. But I did bring your presents. Here," she said, handing him one flat square box and a smaller jewelry box.

"Both for me?" he asked, clearly surprised.

"Yes."

"Oh, wow. Thanks," he said, grinning.

"Mark, you look like a little boy at Christmas," Carol said, shaking her head.

"You didn't have to wrap them," Mark said to Nicole.

"That's to add to the suspense."

Mark sat down in one of the lounge chairs and proceeded to remove the wrapping from the big box first. He looked up at Nicole and smiled in anticipation. Although Carol and Ashlei were present, Nicole suddenly felt like she and Mark were alone. He had eyes only for her and vice versa.

When he had removed all the wrapping, opened the box and noticed the contents, he beamed. He lifted the gift out of the box and held it up for everyone to see. It was a burgundy eelskin briefcase, inscribed with his initials, MP, in twenty-four karat gold letters.

"That's beautiful," Carol said sincerely.

"Isn't it?" Mark agreed.

He stood up and examined the bag, running his hand along the side, feeling the smooth texture of the grain. He walked over to where Nicole stood and kissed her again, on the lips.

"Thank you, Nicole. This is beautiful," Mark said, smiling brightly.

"You're welcome," she said. She wished they were alone. "Do you really like it?"

"Oh, most definitely."

"Good. I was hoping you would."

Ashlei sat there watching Mark fawn over Nicole's gift. She did not understand what the big deal was, it was only a briefcase. Her unceasing jealousy of Nicole was quickly rising to the surface.

"Open the other one, Mark," Carol said enthusiastically.

"Okay."

Mark laid the briefcase on the table beside his chair, sat back down and picked up the smaller box.

Ashlei promptly got up from her chair. "I'm going to the ladies' room." Mark paid her no mind. Nicole was really the only one that noticed. She couldn't help feeling a bit triumphant.

When Mark opened the second box, he was rendered speechless for a moment as he gazed at the contents of the box. He looked up at Nicole, his eyes filled with love and appreciation. In a voice filled with awe, he said, "This is beautiful. Thank you."

"You're welcome," Nicole said softly.

"Let me see," Carol cried.

Mark paid her no heed. He rose from his seat and, without taking his eyes off Nicole for a moment, walked over to her and kissed her gently on her lips. He gazed into her eyes and said, "Thank you, Nicole."

Nicole looked up into his, also in a near trance, and said, "You're welcome, Mark."

"Let me see!" Carol exclaimed.

Mark slowly turned to Carol, then was totally brought out of the daze he was in a moment ago. He handed her the jewelry box.

When she saw the watch inside, she sucked in her breath in awe. "Oh, Nicky, this is beautiful."

It was an eighteen-karat gold watch, with four diamonds totaling a carat in weight, on the face. The wristband was a rich black suede. It was truly an elegant watch.

When Nicole came out of her trance, she remembered Ashlei. "Mark, I didn't know that Ashlei would be here. I tried to call you before I came, but the line was busy," she explained.

"That's all right, baby. You're welcome here anytime."

She smiled weakly and said, "Well, I'm not going to stay. I have to go to my mother's house. I have things for my brothers and sisters in the car, anyway."

"You don't have to leave, Nicole."

"Yes, I do."

"No, you don't."

"Yes, Mark, I do. Don't worry about it. I'll talk to you later on in the week." She wasn't about to spend any time having casual conversation with Ashlei. "See ya', Carol. I'll call you," Nicole said, kissing her cheek.

"Okay, Nicky. Take it easy."

She started toward the door. "Bye, kids," she said to Mark and Cherie.

"Bye, Aunt Nicky," they said.

She picked Tiandra up from the floor and said, "Bye, sweetness. I'll see you later." She kissed her daughter and placed her back on the floor, then continued to the door.

Mark followed her. "You really don't have to go, Nic."

"Yes, I do. I don't want to be here with her."

"Then she can leave."

"No, Mark, that's alright." She reached for the door and Mark grabbed her other hand. "Thank you for the gifts," he said sincerely.

She smiled and said, "You're welcome."

"You know you didn't have to do that."

"I know. I wanted to."

"Thanks for thinking about me."

"I always think about you."

They stared at each other lovingly until Nicole blushed and looked away. He touched his hand to her face and bent to kiss her once again.

"I'll call you tomorrow," Mark said.

"All right. Bye."

"Bye, baby."

The next morning, Mark called Nicole.

"Hey, beautiful," he said when she picked up the receiver.

"Hey, handsome," she responded.

"Oh, so you know who this is?"

"Of course. You're that good-looking guy I met on the cruise, right? Um, let me see, what's your name again?"

"Very funny."

"Oh!" she exclaimed, feigning surprise. "Mark? Oh, I'm sorry. I thought you were someone else."

"Right."

Nicole cracked up.

"That wasn't funny."

"Aw, come on. Can't you take a joke? I knew it was you."

"Did you?"

"Of course, I did. I didn't give any strange men my telephone number on that cruise."

"I hope not. Remember the last guy you picked up on a cruise."

"Yeah, right. Thanks to him, I'm rolling in dough."

Mark chuckled. "Listen, Nic, that's what I was calling you about. I don't know how I forgot to mention it to you yesterday. I guess I always get excited when a beautiful woman gives me presents."

"How many beautiful women give you presents?" she asked curiously.

"Actually, just one. You."

"Uh-huh," she said skeptically.

He chuckled again. "Seriously, though. While you were away, I saw a house that I think you might be interested in taking a look at."

"Where?"

"It's in Westchester. It's a beautiful two-story house. Full, finished basement, walk-in attic. Three, no, four bedrooms. The master bedroom has a private bath. There's also another bathroom on the second floor, a full bathroom. There's a full bathroom on the ground floor and a half bath in the basement, you know, sink and toilet. There's plenty of land in front if you want to start a garden or something and there's a nice big porch with an awning. The backyard is tremendous. I mean, really big. Plenty of space for Tiandra to run around. The property is fenced off, too. There's a two-car garage, attached. Big living room and dining room. The kitchen is huge, too, and there's a nice size family room with a working fireplace and there's a room off the family room that can be used as an office, or whatever. Um, let me see, what else?"

"Wow! That's enough. It sounds fabulous. How much is it going for?"

"Three fifty."

"Is that a good price?"

"I think it's a steal, Nicole. But you've got to see it. I think you'll like it, but maybe you won't."

"When can I see it?"

"I'll call the broker and find out. When are you available?"

"Whenever. I'm open."

"All right. I'll tell her that. I really think you'll like this place. I like it, but that's me."

"I'll probably like it, too. You know what I like."

"I like to think so."

She smiled at this. "So, call me when you get in touch with the broker and let me know when I can go up there. Are you going to come with me?"

"Sure. I'd like to see your reaction when you see it."

"It's that nice, huh?"

"Yes. Very nice."

"Why don't you buy it?"

"I would if you promised to live there with me."

Nicole was caught off guard by Mark's comment. She did not know what to say.

"That's what I thought. That's why I'm telling you about it."

"You set me up," she said softly.

"I know. I'm sorry."

"I'll get you for that."

Mark smiled and said, "Promise?"

"Yes."

"I look forward to it."

"Look, stop trying to flirt and just find out when I can see this house, thank you."

"Yes, ma'am," Mark said, laughing. "I'll call her now and call you right back."

"All right."

"How's Saturday for you? Ten o'clock?" Mark asked when he called Nicole back later that day.

"Ten o'clock's fine. Should I pick you up or will you come and get me?"

"Doesn't matter. Whatever you suggest."

"Well, since we're going to go north, I'll come and get you, that way you won't have to come all the way out here then have to go back through the city."

"All right. That's fine. You should be here by nine, though. It's a pretty good drive."

"No problem. We'll be there. You just be ready."

"Aren't I always?"

"Oh, yeah, that's right."

When Nicole pulled up in front of Mark's building Saturday morning, he was waiting, just as he said he would be. She jumped out of the car. "Hi!"

"Hi, baby," he said as he stepped off the curb.

"You drive, since you know where the house is."

"Okay."

As they walked around the car, Nicole to the passenger side and Mark to the driver's side, Mark grabbed her and kissed her on the mouth. She was a bit stunned by the intensity of his kiss, and she was unable to hide her surprise.

"You've always been irresistible to me in the morning," Mark said.

"Well, at least I haven't lost it."

Mark looked her square in the eye and said, "You'll never

lose it, Nicole.'' This time he kissed her forehead softly, then continued on to the driver's seat.

She hesitated a moment and looked at him as he climbed into the car. He winked at her as he got in. Suddenly, as she got back into the car, she felt slightly nervous. *Was he suggesting something,* she wondered. *Isn't he seeing Ashlei?*

''Where's Tee?''

''Shelly came by last night and took her home. She's taking her to a birthday party today.''

''Oh, so I've got you all to myself today,'' he said, stealing a sideways glance at Nicole.

She blushed, but did not comment.

''I love it when you blush.''

Of course, this remark caused her to blush once more.

Mark chuckled and said, ''Am I making you uncomfortable?''

''Somewhat.''

''I'm sorry.''

They stopped at a traffic light and Mark turned to her. ''You look very pretty this morning.''

''Thank you.''

''You're welcome.''

Nicole looked over at him. The look on his face was one of genuine love and affection. Her heart skipped a beat and she felt her eyes begin to water. She quickly turned to look out the window.

Mark reached over and took her hand. ''I know we've got a long way to go, Nicole, but I want you to know I'm willing to do whatever I have to do to get back on the right track.''

Nicole sighed. Her heart was doing flip-flops. Her feelings were so mixed up at that moment, she was afraid to speak lest she say something foolish and make him think she was an idiot.

Mark could feel her apprehension about discussing their relationship, so he decided to change the subject. ''I really think you're going to like this house.''

Nicole looked at him graciously. "You think so?"

"Oh, yeah. It's a very, uh . . . homey. I think it would be a perfect place to raise kids. There's a lot of land around the house and the neighborhood is well above average."

"What about schools?"

"I asked Karen about that and she said there's a public elementary school four blocks from the house, and about six blocks in the opposite direction is a private elementary school."

"Karen's the broker?"

"Yeah."

"I'd really like to send Tee to a private school when she starts."

"Me, too."

"What about stores? Are there any grocery stores or anything nearby?"

"There aren't any in walking distance, unless you just like to walk. It's about a mile into town but there's a big shopping mall with a large supermarket, pharmacy, liquor store, etc. It's a five to ten minute drive away."

"That's not too bad. So it's entirely residential?"

"Uh-huh. It's a quiet block. The houses in the area are all pretty large and they all have a good amount of land surrounding them so they're spread far apart, you know, not all on top of each other. Karen said the neighbors are very friendly and they all take a great deal of pride in keeping the neighborhood nice. They look out for each other. If a family is away for a few days on vacation, or whatever, they keep an eye on that family's house and make sure there's no trouble or anything like that."

"That's good."

"Yeah, and although no one on the block actually has any say in who the house is sold to, they'd like it if a person or a couple with kids moves in, someone that has the same basic values about family and property and things like that."

"That's understandable."

"Sure."

"It sounds nice."

"Oh, it is. It really is. I'm sure you'll love it," Mark said confidently.

Nicole looked at him and smiled, "I'm sure I will."

When they reached their destination, Karen Walter was waiting for them. It was five after ten. Mark was a stickler for punctuality, so he immediately jumped out of the car and called to Karen, "Sorry we're late."

She waved it off and said, "Don't worry about it. I just got here myself."

Mark walked over and shook her hand. "How are you?"

"Fine, thanks. How are you?" Karen asked.

"Fine."

Nicole had joined them by then, so Mark introduced them. "Karen, this is my wife, Nicole. Nicole, this is Karen Walter."

"Hi," Nicole said. "Nice to meet you."

"Hi. It's nice meeting you, too. I didn't know Mark was married."

"We're separated," Nicole clarified.

Mark looked a little embarrassed by Nicole's frankness, but Karen did not notice.

"Oh, well, at least you're not fighting like some couples I know that are separated."

"We've been through that," Nicole said.

"Oh, I see."

Mark just shrugged.

"Is this the house?" Nicole asked, changing the subject.

"Yes, it is," Karen said, at once transforming herself into the attentive salesperson. "As you'll notice, there's an abundance of land in front where you could plant a flower garden and in back . . . Would you like to see the backyard?"

"Sure," Nicole said.

"Follow me."

An hour later, after having gone through the entire house,

they all returned to the first floor. "So, what do you think?" Karen asked.

"I think it's beautiful. I love it," Nicole said, looking at Mark. It was everything Mark had told her and more.

"I thought you might," he said.

"How much is it going for?" Nicole asked.

"Three hundred thousand. That's down from three fifty," Karen said.

Nicole stood where she was and looked around her. She thought about all the things she could do with the house, the different ways she could furnish it and so on. Her mind was working overtime on decorating schemes.

"This is a beautiful, beautiful house," she said dreamily.

"Have there been any other people by to look at it?" Mark asked.

"Yes. I showed it to a couple yesterday. They made an offer but the owners really didn't take it seriously," Karen said.

"So then it's pretty much spoken for, huh?" Nicole asked, disconcertedly.

"No, not at all. The owners are looking for serious buyers. What that couple offered was far less than they would ever consider," Karen pointed out.

"Can I look around one more time?"

"Sure, Nicole. Take your time," Karen said.

"Come with me, Mark?"

Once they were out of Karen's earshot, Nicole asked Mark, "What do you think?"

"You know what I think. What do you think?"

"I really like it, Mark," she said sincerely.

"I figured you would."

"Do you think I should buy it?"

"I can't answer that," he said honestly.

"Would you buy it?"

"Probably."

"You're not being much help."

Mark laughed and said, "Listen, baby. I'm not going to tell you to buy it or not buy it. If you want my opinion, I think it's a beautiful house. I think it's a sturdy house. I know what they're asking for it is well below what it's worth. The land alone is worth at least two hundred thousand. If you decided to buy it and sell it in a couple of years, you could make back every dime you put into it and then some. I think the neighborhood is a good one for raising kids, and even though it's a good distance from your family, it's not unreachable. The railroad comes right into town from Grand Central Station.

"Now, you might want to look at other houses, maybe you don't want to make a decision right now since this is the first house you've seen, but if you really like this one the way I think you do, you might look elsewhere and not find anything that you like as much, and when you decide this is the house you want after all, it may be too late. Someone else might have snatched it up."

"I know. I was thinking about that," Nicole said. She walked over to one of the windows and looked out into the backyard. "The backyard is so big. I could have all the kids over and they could run around and go crazy back there," she said. "I could put some swings and a seesaw and sliding board back there. Get a little wading pool for them, and later, a big in-ground. We could have cook-outs on the holidays." She sighed. "It's so hard to decide."

"I know, baby. But maybe this will make it easier. Go with your first instincts. Whatever you felt you wanted to do first, whether it was buy it or not, do it. I guarantee if you do, you won't regret it," Mark said.

She looked at him, contemplating what he just said. It was a beautiful house. Everything she wanted in a house, actually. Mark was probably right, too. If she decided to look around at other houses, she might not see anything she liked as much and would probably lose out on this one. She would hate for that to happen because something told her she would not find another house for a long time that took her breath away like this one did.

"Let's go," she said, starting back towards Karen.

Once they had rejoined Karen in the living room, Nicole said, "Karen, I'd like to make an offer on this house." She pulled out a notepad from her pocketbook and wrote a figure on the top sheet. "Do you think they'll take this seriously?" she asked as she showed the paper, first to Mark then, after a "go ahead" nod of his head, to the agent.

Karen beamed. "Certainly, Nicole. Most certainly."

"Oh, Mark! I'm so excited," Nicole said, deliriously happy that she would soon own her own home. They were driving back to the city. "Do you think there'll be any problems with me getting the house?"

"I don't see why." He was happy for her. He realized, too, that they had been separated for so long he had actually forgotten how beautiful she was when she was happily excited about something. As he drove them back to Manhattan, Mark listened attentively as Nicole rambled on and on about the many things she planned to do with the house; it was like music to his ears. She was pouring out her heart to him, sharing with him her plans and dreams, things one would only divulge to a trusted friend, and he was drinking it all in. He was happy for her but he was also very happy for himself. He had a strong feeling their separation would soon end.

When they reached Manhattan, they stopped at a restaurant in midtown and had lunch. Nicole was still going on about the house and Mark, as patient as ever, although by now, he really was not absorbing anything she was saying, commented affirmatively or negatively at all the right times.

When they were seated, Nicole finally realized she had been monopolizing the conversation from the time they started back.

"Mark, why didn't you tell me to be quiet?" Nicole asked, embarrassed that she had not let him get a word in edgewise.

"Why should I have?"

"I've been running my mouth all the way back and you didn't say anything. I'm sorry. I know you must be tired of listening to me go on about this house."

"No, I'm not. I'm happy that you're happy. If you want to talk about the house, you go right ahead. I'm more than happy to listen."

"But, I know I must be boring you."

"I don't think there'll ever come a day when you could bore me," he said truthfully.

Nicole saw something in his eyes that made her stomach do a flip. She blushed. "Well, I'll tone it down, anyway, so you can talk."

"Nicole, I'm happy that you feel good enough about me to share with me all your dreams about the house."

She gave him her best smile and said, "I'm glad I'm not boring you."

Mark laughed. She did, too. As she watched him, at that moment she knew she would never be happy with anyone else. She loved him so totally that the feeling consumed her entire being. And she knew now that he still loved her, too.

"Thank you, Mark."

"For what?"

"For everything," she said softly.

"You're welcome, whatever it is."

"I owe you so much."

"You don't owe me anything."

"Yes, I do."

"No, you don't. You don't owe me anything."

"But you've helped me so much."

"And I'd do it all again. And not for any reward or payment or debt. On the contrary, Nicole, it is I that owe you."

"For what? What have I done?"

"You've changed my life entirely for the better. You've given me a new outlook on life. A much brighter one. My life is richer because of you. You didn't know that, did you?" he asked her matter of factly.

Nicole was speechless. What could she say after that?

It was almost five o'clock when Nicole dropped Mark off at his apartment building. They had spent the entire day together, talking and laughing and just enjoying each other's company. Mark was still driving, so when they pulled up, they both got out of the car. Mark waited by the door on the driver's side for Nicole to come around.

Neither of them paid any attention to the cab that pulled up behind Nicole's double-parked Jaguar. As fate would have it, the passenger was Ashlei Brown.

As Mark stood holding the door partially open, Nicole stepped up to him and said, "Thank you, Mark, for taking me up to see the house."

"You're welcome, baby. You know you can call me anytime for anything and I'll be there," he said as he looked deep into her eyes.

"I'll let you know if I hear from Karen."

"Oh, I'm sure you will."

"Thanks for lunch, too. I had a great day with you."

"Likewise, I'm sure."

They stood looking at each other for a moment, Mark smiling easily, Nicole smiling shyly. When she moved to step around him to get back in the car, he grabbed her arm gently to stifle her movement. When she looked up into his eyes, he kissed her. Immediately, forgetting they were standing in the driveway, she touched her hand to his waist and he put an arm around hers and pulled her close. For a few seconds, they were lost in that kiss, but as Ashlei witnessed the entire scene unbeknownst to them, she moved quickly to intercede. "What perfect timing," she said as she stepped up to them.

Nicole recognized her voice and quickly, as if she had been caught cheating, released Mark and moved away.

Ashlei noticed, happily, how flustered Nicole was. "How are you, Nicole?" Ashlei asked, not really caring.

"Fine," Nicole answered, but Ashlei had already started speaking to Mark.

"I've been trying to reach you all day."

Mark was very displeased at Ashlei's sudden appearance. He could see how uncomfortable she made Nicole and he did not like that. In answer to her question, he simply said, "I was out."

"Did you forget about tonight?" Ashlei asked him.

Mark looked very uncomfortable. "No, I didn't."

Upon noticing his discomfort, Nicole figured it was time for her to leave. "I have to go. I'll see you later," she said as she hurriedly got into her car.

Mark was so upset by the timing of the whole situation that he turned and strode toward his building. Ashlei quickly followed him.

When Mark reached the elevator to take him up to his penthouse, Ashlei was right on his heels. "What's the matter with you?" she asked.

"Look, just forget about it. What time is this thing, anyway?" he asked. Although there was nothing between them, Mark had accepted an invitation to escort Ashlei to a dinner party with one of her clients because it was an excellent networking opportunity for him. After seeing how upset her sudden appearance had made Nicole, however, he did not want to go anywhere with Ashlei now, but the businessman in him could not pass on this opportunity.

"It starts at seven o'clock," she answered.

"Just give me a few minutes, then we can go."

Chapter Thirty

A week later, on Friday morning, Mark got a call from a business associate. He was a personal friend of Kenneth "Babyface" Edmonds and had front row tickets to his concert that evening. He told Mark something had come up and he would have to go out of town that day. He offered Mark the tickets and offered to have them sent to Mark's office that morning by messenger, if he wanted them. Mark told him he would gladly take the tickets off his hands. Before he hung up, Mark told his friend, "I owe you one." He immediately thought of Nicole. She loved Babyface's music. He wondered if she was already going to the show. Mark picked up the telephone and dialed her number.

She answered on the second ring. "Hello."

"Hi."

"Hi," Nicole said.

"How're you doing?"

"I'm fine. How are you?"

"Fine. How's Tee?"

"She's fine."

"I'm sorry about the other day, Nicole."

"That's all right. It was no big deal."

They were silent on the line for a few seconds.

"Listen, um, what are you doing tonight?"

"Nothing."

"I've got two tickets to the Babyface concert at the Music Hall. Front row. Would you like to go?"

Nicole was caught off guard. *Is he actually asking me out on a date?* "You do?"

"Yeah. A friend of mine gave them to me. I know how much you like him. I figured, if you didn't already have tickets, you might like to go."

"I'd love to," she said happily.

"Great. The show doesn't start until eight. I figured maybe we could have dinner first and then go on to the Music Hall from there. How's that sound?"

"That sounds fine. Should I meet you somewhere?"

"No. I'll come and get you. I'll be there at five thirty, how's that?"

"That's good."

"Okay. So, I'll see you then," Mark said, feeling much better.

"All right."

They were about to hang up when Nicole called into the receiver, "Mark?"

"Yeah?"

"Thank you."

He smiled. "You're welcome, beautiful. See you tonight."

Nicole was ecstatic. She and Mark were actually going on a date. They hadn't been out together in a year.

"Oh, God, what am I going to wear?" She was so excited she couldn't even think. *Wait until I tell Yvonne. She's going to be so happy.* She decided to call Yvonne right away and tell her the good news.

Just as she expected, Yvonne was delighted about Nicole's news. They talked about the possibilities of what this could mean . . . of what it could lead to for Nicole and Mark. They were going on about it for more than fifteen minutes when a cloud suddenly invaded Nicole's happy thoughts.

"Yvonne, wait."

"What?"

"What if it's not like I think? What if the only reason he's taking me is because Ashlei couldn't make it? Damn! How could I be so stupid? That's probably it. He hasn't been taking me out anywhere, why all of a sudden?''

"Nicky, you're crazy. What are you talking about? Mark's not seeing Ashlei.''

"Yes, he is. He was with her last weekend. She came up on us right outside his building after he took me to see that house.''

"Lucien told me he's not seeing her.''

"Lucien's in Jamaica. Ashlei is here. I saw them together.''

"Yeah, well, even if he is, he invited you. And no matter what you think, Nicole, Mark loves you. Why don't you give him a chance?''

"I don't know," she hedged. "I think I'm going to call him and tell him I can't make it.''

"You'd better not! Nicky, don't be silly. You know he loves you.''

"I don't want him to hurt me anymore, Yvonne.''

"Nicole, stop it!''

Finally, Nicole confessed. "I'm scared, Yvonne. What am I going to say to him?''

"What do you mean? You'd talk to him any other time. It's no different.''

"Yes, it is.''

"No, it's not. Look, just go have dinner and see the show. Don't think about it being a date. You spent the day with him last weekend when he took you to see the house. Think of it like that. If you'd just relax, everything'll be fine.''

"But . . .''

"Don't you want to see Babyface? I know how much you love him.''

"Yeah, but . . .''

"But, nothing. Go and see the show. I don't want to hear any more foolishness. You go and have fun. Call me tomorrow and let me know how it went.''

Nicole sighed. "I wish I could be as confident about this as you are.''

"Don't worry about it. Go and buy yourself something sexy to wear. Take your mind off of it. I bet if you wore something really hot, you'd really feel good and you'd see that he is totally interested in you!"

"You've got all the answers, don't you?"

"Not all, believe me. But I know how you feel about Mark and I know how he feels about you. And I know you two are a couple of the most miserable people when you're not together," Yvonne said, breaking into hysterical laughter.

Nicole had to laugh, too. "I'm sorry I'm bugging you," she said.

"You're not bugging me, baby. I just want to see you guys together again, that's all."

"Well, I hope you're right about this."

"Don't worry, you'll see I am," Yvonne said confidently.

After taking Tiandra to her sister's house and shopping for a new dress, Nicole returned home at four fifteen that afternoon. She had a little more than an hour to get ready. She quickly jumped into the shower and washed her hair and body as fast as possible. Once out, she lotioned herself from head to toe with his favorite fragrance. She slipped on a pair of lace string bikini panties and sat on the bed to put on her pantyhose. She sat at her vanity table and quickly, but carefully, polished her nails. As she waited for them to dry, she pulled one of Babyface's tapes from her rack and slipped it into her cassette player.

She danced around her bedroom to the music, warming herself up for the evening ahead and, at the same time, blowing and fanning her nails to speed them in drying. Once she was confident that her polish would not smudge, she removed the black patent leather sling back pumps she had just purchased from their box. She slipped her feet into them and paced around the room a few times to stretch them. She certainly didn't want to have to worry about her feet hurting her tonight. Finally, she removed the dress wrapped in tissue paper from the box on her bed. It was a simple tank dress, a mini to be precise, cut low to a V in front to reveal a hint of cleavage. Aside from the fact that it was purple washed silk, there was nothing special about it when you saw it on a hanger. Of course, Nicole was no hanger. When she put the dress on once again, as she did in the store's dressing room, she felt electricity in the air as she spied her reflection in the mirror. The dress had been made for her. She knew this dress would knock Mark off his feet.

She smiled as she thought about what his reaction would be when he saw her in it. It fit her like a glove, although it wasn't tight. It was perfectly proportioned for her body. Purple had come to be one of her favorite colors just with this purchase. Seeing the dress on her body, anyone would understand why.

She combed her hair. Because she still wore it cut short, this was no great task. She put on a light touch of makeup, something she did only on special occasions. She grabbed her black patent leather clutch purse and put her keys, wallet, lipstick, tissue and a few other nonessential items in it.

When she was absolutely certain she had taken care of everything necessary, she stood back and gave herself the final once over in her bedroom mirror. She was pleased with what she saw. She smiled and said, "Don't hurt him, baby."

It was five twenty. At five twenty-five, her intercom rang.

When Nicole opened the door to let Mark in, she was taken aback. She had forgotten how good Mark looked when he dressed to go out. Of course, he always looked good in a suit. He wore them every day to work, but when he went out at night, there was a totally different effect.

He was wearing a salt-and-pepper, raw silk suit, a white shirt with the collar open and black snakeskin loafers. His hair was freshly cut, his mustache expertly trimmed and she could smell his cologne, Givenchy's Insensé. He stood outside her door with his hands stuffed in his pockets, a bouquet of roses tucked under his arm.

"Hi," Nicole said, as she took in the sheer masculine beauty of him.

As if seeing her for the first time, Mark was jarred out of his cool demeanor and was at once aware of her beauty. He quickly pulled himself up to his full height, took his hands out of his pockets and grabbed the bouquet as a young boy would that had been scolded for forgetting the proper way to greet a lady. His face lit up with his smile as he said, "Hello."

Nicole stepped back to open the door fully for him to come in. As he entered the apartment, he devoured her with his eyes.

"You must have left work early to get here by now."

Mark didn't hear a word she said. He continued to stare at her.

Nicole was aware he had paid no attention to what she said. She was flattered that her dress was having the effect on him that it was. "Mark?"

He came out of his trance. "Huh? I'm sorry, what did you say?"

"I said, you must have left work early today."

"Oh, yeah, I did," he said with a silly smile. Then he remembered the flowers. "Oh, these are for you," he said, handing her the bouquet.

She smiled and said, "Thank you. They're beautiful."

"You're beautiful, Nicole."

She blushed. "Thank you."

He stood there, gazing at her.

"I'll go put these in some water. You can sit down."

Mark just nodded. *Damn, she's beautiful.*

Nicole felt a little self-conscious now. Maybe she should have worn something else. She felt as if he was undressing her.

When she came back into the living room with the roses in a vase, Mark said, "Nicole."

She turned to him, "Yes."

"You look beautiful."

"Thank you," she said demurely.

"I love your dress. It looks like it was made for you."

"Thanks." She placed the vase on the coffee table. "Can I get you something to drink?"

"No, thank you. I'm fine," Mark said, still staring at her. "You're fine, too."

Nicole blushed again. "We can leave then, if you want," she said.

"Whenever you're ready."

"I'm ready." She reached for her pocketbook and grabbed a black short-waisted jacket from the closet in case it got cool later that night.

Nicole walked to the door and opened it for him to leave. He held it, however, and said, "After you, gorgeous."

When they left the building, Nicole had expected to see Bobby, but Mark was driving his new BMW Z3 sports car tonight. Nicole hadn't known he'd bought a new car. It was a beauty, black on black leather.

"When'd you get this?" she asked as they stepped up to the car.

"At the end of May."

"It's gorgeous, and very you."

"Would you like one?"

She smiled at him but did not answer.

He unlocked the door on the passenger side and held it open as she got in. Before he closed the door, he leaned in and said, "You really look beautiful, Nicole."

"Thank you, Mark." She was as nervous as if this was their first date, but she noticed that Mark seemed to be a bit nervous, too.

When he got into the car, his eyes immediately traveled to Nicole's legs. He smiled to himself. As he turned the key in the ignition, he looked over at her lasciviously and said, "You know, if looking good was a crime, you'd get a life sentence."

She grinned and said, "Will you stop it. Flattery will get you nowhere."

"Well, I'm glad you told me that. I'll save the flattery for someone else. But, you know, I'm not one that just throws compliments at everyone. I'm just telling it like it is. You look good, Nicole."

"Thank you."

"You've got great legs, too. Can I touch them?"

"No!"

Mark laughed. "Can't fault me for trying."

Nicole sighed and shook her head. "You're crazy, do you know that?"

"About you."

She looked at him for a few seconds, wondering how true his words were. She could not resist saying, "You probably say that to all the girls."

"Don't believe it," he said seriously.

He took her to a new seafood restaurant on the east side of the city. He had been there once before with a client and was very impressed by the service, the food and the atmosphere.

When they were seated, Nicole commented on the restaurant. "This looks like a nice place."

"Yes, it is. I've only been here once before, but I liked it so much I thought I'd share it with you."

She smiled and said, "Well, that's sweet of you."

A waiter walked over to their table at that moment. "Good evening. My name is Tony. I'll be your waiter this evening," he said as he placed a water glass in front of each of them. "Would either of you like to order a cocktail?"

"Yes," Nicole said. "I'd like a frozen margarita, no salt."

"All right. And you, sir?"

"I'll have a vodka martini. Very dry, no olive."

"Yes, sir. I'll be right back to take your orders," Tony said.

"I'm glad you decided to come with me tonight," Mark said sincerely, once their waiter had left them.

"Well, to tell you the truth, Mark, I started having second thoughts about it."

"Why?"

"A lot of reasons," she said, looking down at her hands.

"Talk to me. I've got time."

Nicole looked up at him. She was trying to decide if she should tell him of her doubts about why he asked her out tonight. He looked as if he genuinely wanted to know. "I don't want to start anything, Mark."

"If you have reservations about me, I want to know why. Maybe there's something I can do to dispel them."

Tony returned to the table with their drinks.

"Would you like to order your dinner now or shall I come back?"

"No, we'll order now," Mark said. He wanted him out of the way so he could talk to Nicole without being interrupted.

Once Tony had taken their orders and left the table, Nicole said to Mark, "Wow, this is a big drink. I hope I don't get too drunk after this."

"Don't try to change the subject, Nicole," he said sternly. "What's bothering you?"

Nicole looked at him and saw there was no way she was going to get out of telling him what she felt. "Why did you invite me to the concert?"

"Because I thought you would enjoy it. I know how much you like Babyface. I thought you might like to see him in person."

"It wasn't because Ashlei couldn't make it?" *There, I said it. Now, let's see what he says.*

He looked at her in amazement. "Ashlei? Of course not!"

"Don't say 'of course not' like it's a total impossibility," Nicole said discordantly.

"Nicole, I'm not seeing Ashlei."

"You were with her last weekend, remember?" she said shortly.

Mark explained that his date with Ashlei last weekend had been strictly business. Nicole wasn't sure if she believed him, but she said, "Yeah, well, you haven't been asking me out."

"Maybe because I didn't want to hear you turn me down."

She looked deep into his eyes to see if he was being sincere. "You're going to tell me that not once after this guy gave you these tickets did you think about calling Ashlei, or anyone else, before you called me?"

"That's right."

They sat in silence for a few minutes. Mark was trying to think of how he could make her believe that he loved her, and Nicole was trying to find the courage to say what was on her mind.

Finally, she decided she had nothing else to lose so she asked, "How many women are you involved with, Mark?"

Mark was surprised by her question. "I'm not involved with anyone and Ashlei and I are just friends, Nicole. That's all, and we've never been anything more."

She took a deep breath and let it out loudly. She looked up and past him, trying hard to keep her composure. Annoyingly, she felt her eyes begin to water. "You have a short memory, I see."

Mark frowned. He knew what she was referring to. "Nicole, you know I love you. I always have and I always will. Nothing can change that."

"You sure have a strange way of showing it."

"What was I supposed to do? Up until Nick died, you didn't seem to want anything to do with me."

"That's because you seemed to be already tied up and I didn't want to interfere with anything you were doing, so I decided to get on with my life like you were."

"What are you talking about? Nicole, when you came back from that cruise, I told you I wanted to make things right between us. You didn't want any part of me, remember?"

"Because you'd already hurt me enough, Mark. I didn't want

to give you the opportunity to hurt me anymore. How do you think I felt when I walked into your apartment and saw you all wrapped up with Ashlei, touching her like there was no one else in the room? How do you think that made me feel?'' she asked angrily, tears now rolling freely down her face.

"I know and I'm sorry for that. I was drunk . . . I know that's no excuse but when you weren't there by a quarter to twelve, I figured you weren't coming and I was hurt. I guess I tried to hide my pain by drinking, and with her being there . . . and willing, I just . . . I don't know, I guess I just forgot about everything else. When I saw you standing there, Nicole, you've got to know, I felt lower than a snake. I felt as if I was in the middle of a bad dream and I couldn't wake up. I never wanted you to see that. I . . . Then when you told me that you still loved me anyway, I felt so ashamed and . . . I didn't know how I would ever be able to face you again.

"I tried to call you the next day but you weren't home. I even called your mother's house looking for you."

"I was there when you called. I didn't want to talk to you. There wasn't anything you could tell me," she confessed.

"I can understand why you felt that way. I never meant to hurt you, Nicole. I swear. I never, ever wanted to hurt you." He reached across the table to take her hand, but she pulled away. He winced at her reaction.

"No matter what you might think, I've never been intimate with Ashlei. After what happened that night, she was the last person I wanted to be with."

He paused a moment to collect his thoughts before he continued.

"Nicole, I've experienced emotions with you that I've never felt with anyone else. You make me see things that I never . . . The most important things in my life had always been things I could put my hands on, material things, not feelings. Certainly not other people's feelings. But you changed all of that. All I wanted was to be with you, to make you happy, to make you want to be with me. Material things took on less and less importance in my life. Having your love and respect was all that mattered.

"I know you didn't believe me and maybe you still don't, but I swear, I never touched Diane either. I never invited her to my room. She was there for all of five minutes when you knocked on the door. I had just told her she had to leave before I went to let you in. It hurts like hell that you thought I would do something like that to you." He paused again as he lowered his head and sighed. "When you left me after I, . . ." He looked into her eyes once more, ". . . . after you found me with her, I couldn't deal with that. I couldn't handle your rejection, Nicole, so I had to turn it around. I tried to convince myself that I didn't need you since you didn't want me. I couldn't stand to think that you didn't want me anymore. When you moved out of your mother's house, it was like you were telling me that you didn't need me anymore, and I couldn't deal with that.

"When the holidays came around, my loneliness really started to get the best of me, but I couldn't ask you even then to take me back because I couldn't bear to hear you say no. Spending Christmas with you and Tiandra made me feel that maybe there was a chance for us. Seeing you then gave me a spark of hope that maybe you still loved me. I needed to know that. That was why I wanted you to be with me on New Year's Eve. Aside from it being our anniversary, I wanted to start all over with you."

"Why did you invite her?"

"I don't know. She called me the day after Christmas and I just invited her." He sighed heavily. "I was horny and I figured she'd be easy," he confessed. "I wanted you, but I knew I couldn't ask you for sex, knowing how things were between us."

Nicole noticed that his eyes were watering.

"I got so drunk that night, I don't even remember what

happened after you left. When I woke up the next day, she was still there but I sent her home. I didn't see her again until a couple of months later, and that's only because I decided to stop ducking her.

"When you told me you weren't interested in trying to patch things up, I got angry and I was hurt, but I figured it was probably because of what had happened at the party. I was pretty sure that if I gave you some time, you'd come around. Then Nick showed up. I didn't believe you when you told me about him and I couldn't bear to think of you with him . . . or with anyone. When I found out what he was doing, I figured I'd use that to get him away from you. When that didn't work . . . Well, I don't have to tell you."

"I didn't take that cruise because I was looking for someone else," she said. "But when I met Nick, he was nice to me and I guess I felt like I needed someone to make me feel good about me. He was always good to me and he knew how I felt about you all along."

Mark reached across the table again to take Nicole's hand. This time she didn't pull away. They looked into each other's eyes for a long moment.

"I love you, Nicole. I'll always love you."

"I love you, too," she said in a shaky voice.

"I want it to be the way it used to be," Mark said.

"It's not that easy."

"I know. Look, I know I'm responsible for what's happened between us and I know that's not something you can easily forget, but I want to try to make things right with you if you'll let me. I know I've got a long way to go, but I'll do whatever I have to," Mark told her earnestly.

Nicole was becoming tearful. She did not want to sit there in front of everyone in the restaurant, crying. "I have to go to the ladies' room," she said as she quickly got up and walked away from the table.

Mark was worried. He had thrown too much at her too fast.

He picked up his drink, which, up until that time, had been untouched. He drank it down in one swallow. Tony brought their food to the table. Mark ordered another martini. Suddenly, he was no longer hungry.

Nicole did not return to the table until Tony had brought Mark's second martini and he had drank it. She sat down and took a deep breath. She looked across the table at him and said, "I'm sorry."

"Are you all right?"

"Yes," she said, nodding her head. "You know how I get. I wish I wasn't so mushy."

Mark smiled and said, "That's all right, baby. There's nothing wrong with a little mush."

She laughed and said, "Yeah, but I'm a big mush."

"Just more of you to love, that's all."

She smiled at him. "Mark, I'd like for it to be the way it was in the beginning, too, but that's something that we both have to work on. I think the first thing we have to do is to be friends. Not just talk about being friends, but actually doing it. I'll respect your feelings and you respect mine. That's what friendship is all about, right?"

He nodded.

"I know it won't happen overnight, but if we make a conscious effort, I don't think it's an impossibility. Do you?" she asked.

"I know it's not. I know that together, we can do anything. I think this is a pretty good start. What do you think?"

"Yes. I think so, too."

Mark's appetite suddenly returned and the remainder of their dinner went like clockwork. They were both more relaxed because they had gotten so much out into the open. Before, they'd both kept their true feelings hidden. Now, they easily asked and answered questions that had plagued them about each other during the time they were apart, and both were eager to dispel any doubts or fears the other may have been having.

Mark had noticed that Nicole had never removed her wedding band. He asked her why.

"Because, I always felt . . . Well, I always hoped that we'd be together again and I felt that if I took it off, that would jinx it and I didn't want to do that. I like being married to you. When we were together, that was the happiest time of my life. I felt that as long as I kept the ring on, you'd see that I still wanted to be your wife."

He was pleased that she felt this way and he told her as much.

After they had finished dinner and were waiting for the check, Mark asked Nicole, "So, are you excited about seeing the Face Man?"

"Yes. I've never seen him in person before."

"Well, I'm glad I'm the one that's taking you, then. Maybe this will be a night you'll never forget."

"I'm sure it will be."

As they left the restaurant, Mark took Nicole's hand. It was very warm outside that evening and, since he had parked in a garage and the concert hall was less than ten blocks from the restaurant, they decided to walk the distance.

"Mark, can I ask you something?" Nicole said as they walked hand in hand to the show.

"Sure."

"Did you ever consider divorcing me? I remember when you were in the hospital, you mentioned that you thought I was there because I was afraid you might live long enough to change your will."

Mark chuckled. "That was silly, wasn't it?"

"I don't know. Not if that was how you felt."

"Well, you know I was a little delirious while I was in the hospital. I was scared. I thought that was it for me. I was upset because you'd told me you were leaving me. I didn't know what I was saying. I've never felt that you wanted me for my money. You're the only woman I've ever known who couldn't care less about that.''

''But did you ever consider divorcing me?''

''No. I was not willing to let you go that easily. Not even after you hit me.''

''I was surprised you didn't hit me back.''

''I was too much in shock,'' he said. He snickered and said, ''You know, you pack a powerful wallop. My face was stinging for a good while after that.''

''I didn't realize what I was doing until I'd done it,'' she admitted. ''As soon as I did though, I knew I'd really messed up. I was waiting for you to knock me out.''

Mark smiled at her and put his arm around her shoulder and squeezed her. ''I would never hit you.''

''I know you thought about it, though.''

He chuckled. ''For a moment. But I knew what I'd said to you was pretty low. I deserved it. The only reason I said it was because . . . Well, because I didn't know what else to say. I was upset that you'd let him spend the night with you.''

''But he didn't spend the night. He came back that morning because he'd forgotten his appointment book,'' Nicole explained.

''Why'd you let him answer the phone?''

''Because I was brushing my teeth. I was never intimate with him.''

''Oh,'' he said sheepishly. ''Well, I guess I really deserved that slap then, but when I heard his voice on the line, I hung right up and left my house, because I had every intention of coming into your apartment and physically removing him. No one's ever made me crazy like you do. I don't want to share you with anyone. Ever. I'm very insecure about where I stand with you. I've never been insecure about a woman before in my life. That's why I say you do things to me that no one has ever done.'' He stopped in his tracks and faced her. ''My life is empty without you, Nicole. No one can take your place.

That's the truth. I could never love anyone the way I love you," Mark confessed.

Nicole looked into his eyes and smiled. "We've got some serious work to do, you know that, right?"

"I know."

They stood looking into each other's eyes for a few seconds, neither saying anything. Finally, Mark put his arm around her shoulder and said, "Come on. Let's go see this man."

She put her arm around his waist and they walked on.

After the concert, Mark asked Nicole, "So, do you want me to take you home or would you like to go somewhere and have a drink with me?"

Nicole contemplated this for a second, then said, "Let's go have a drink. I'm kinda thirsty."

Mark drove them to a night club in the village. There was a jazz band performing and they took a table in the back, where the lights were the dimmest. They stayed there until almost three o'clock in the morning. Nicole was feeling no pain because on top of the margarita she had at dinner, she had ordered two more at the club.

She and Mark were very affectionate toward one another, touching hands, legs, cheeks, etc. while listening to the band and conversing. Occasionally, they even shared little pecks on noses or foreheads. It was like they were rediscovering each other.

When they left the club, they slowly walked to where Mark had parked his car. Nicole locked her arm in his and held him tightly while holding her head on his shoulder. The drive to her apartment was made in peaceful silence. When they reached her apartment building, as they walked up the stairs to her floor, Nicole began to tell Mark about Tiandra's latest escapades. They were both laughing exuberantly when they reached her door.

As they tried to catch their breath, Nicole caught Mark's eye for a split second and their laughter simultaneously stopped. They gazed into each other's eyes and Nicole said softly, "Thank you, Mark. I had a wonderful time with you this evening."

"Likewise. Thank you for sharing it with me," he said softly.

She blushed suddenly and began fumbling in her pocketbook for her keys. When she had taken them out, she turned to unlock the door.

While her back was to him, Mark asked, "Can I come in with you for a little while?"

As tempting as that was, Nicole said, "Not tonight, Mark."

He understood.

She unlocked the door and opened it slightly, then turned to him again. "Thanks again. I hope we can do this again soon," she said.

"Definitely."

She smiled shyly and said, "Good night."

Mark took her hand and moved closer to her. He tilted his head to kiss her. Nicole instantly moved to close the slight distance between them as she tilted her head up to meet his. He had waited all night to put his arms around her and hold her. He couldn't wait any longer. He enfolded her in his arms and she did the same. They kissed with an urgency that told of the longing they had for one another and the yearning they had to be together again. It was a kiss filled with passion, desire and love. As they kissed, they seemed to be trying to hold one another tighter and tighter, as if to meld their bodies together.

They stood in front of her door and kissed for more than five minutes. They were like teenagers making out after a date. They rubbed against one another, the desire to make love strong in each of them. Mark began to caress her body through the soft silk that covered her and Nicole found her hands moving across his back beneath his jacket.

Although he needed and wanted to make love to her desperately, Mark felt this was not the time. He knew he had to stop before things became, once again, out of control. Reluctantly, he released her.

Tears of joy streamed down her face. Mark's eyes, too, were moist with tears as he said, ''I have to go,'' in a voice filled with emotion.

''Mark, wait,'' she cried.

''No, baby, I have to go,'' he said. He quickly turned and left her.

She stood outside her door and watched him leave. Tears fell as she thought about how deeply she loved him and the joy of knowing he still loved her just as much. She had wanted him to stay with her, but that was a purely physical impulse. They had to take it slow. They could not rush this again. This time it had to be perfect, otherwise everything would be lost.

Nicole was happy and sad at the same time as she undressed for bed. She wanted to make love with him again. It had been a year since she last felt his love. As she lay down to sleep, the desire in her loins made it difficult for her to get comfortable.

When Mark arrived at his penthouse, he, too, knew that sleep would be very hard coming on this night. He had been so close to having her again. But she said no and he had to respect that. For the entire ride home, he'd had to deal with an erection that seemed to have a mind of its own. He tried not to think of her. He wanted her so bad, though. As soon as his lips touched hers and her arms went around him, he knew there was no way he could ever turn back again.

He sat on his bed and took off his shoes. He unbuttoned his shirt, slowly, almost absent-mindedly. He could see her clearly, as if she were there with him. His heart was heavy. Never had he known a love as deep and as engrossing as this. He opened his night stand drawer and took out the picture on top. He had taken it of her on their honeymoon. As he stared at her image now, as he had a thousand times before, he thought of how beautiful she was then and how much more beautiful she was now. His eyes began to water as he realized how much he needed her, how genuinely lonely he was without her. He stood the picture on the night stand next to the telephone. He reached out and caressed the glass.

He finished undressing and turned out the light and got into bed. He lay in the darkness for twenty minutes, thinking of her. He turned over on his side and looked through the darkness at her picture. Almost automatically, he picked up the telephone and dialed her number. He held the phone to his ear as he listened to it ring twice.

"Hello."

Her voice was like music to him. "I love you, Nicole," he said and quietly hung up.

Chapter
Thirty-One

"So, Nicky, how was the date?" Yvonne called Nicole the following morning to see how her evening with Mark had gone.

"It was perfect, Yvonne," Nicole said happily.

"See. Didn't I tell you?"

"Yes. But it wasn't all peaches and cream. At first, there were a number of rough spots we had to smooth out," Nicole clarified.

"But you talked, right?"

"Yes. We did a lot of talking. He told me that he's never

been intimate with Ashlei and that nothing ever happened with that girl in his room.''

''Do you believe him, now?'' Yvonne asked, hoping she did.

''Yes. We've decided to try and work things out between us so we can be a family again.''

''That's great!'' Yvonne said excitedly. ''That's fantastic! I knew if you gave him the chance, you'd see that he really loves you, Nicky. He's a good man, you know that. And he cares about you and Tiandra more than anything else in this world.''

''He didn't bring me home until after three thirty this morning. He asked me if he could come in for a while but I told him no.''

''Why'd you say no?'' Yvonne asked incredulously.

''Because we've got a long way to go before we become physical like that again, Yvonne. If I'd let him stay, I know we would have ended up in bed.''

''So what? He's your husband.''

''I know, but we've never had any problems in the sex department. Our other problems need to be straightened out before we worry about sleeping together.''

''Nicky, come on. It wouldn't have killed you to let him stay.''

''No, it wouldn't have, but we would have lost sight of the real issues, I think. We would have gotten caught up in the physical aspects of our relationship which is not where the problem lies,'' Nicole explained.

''Well, what do you want from him?''

''I want us to be friends to one another.''

Yvonne chuckled and said, ''You're already friends.''

''No, not really. We've never taken the time to be friends. We were in too much of a rush for that. When the time comes for us to be intimate again, it'll have to be all the way. No turning back. When we make love again, we'll be living together.''

* * *

"Hello," Nicole said when she picked up the receive later that day.

"Hi."

A surge of warmth went through her before she responded, "Hi, Mark. How ya doin'?"

"I'm fine. How're you?"

"Good."

"How's my girl?"

"She's fine. We're sitting here watching a Barney cartoon."

"She's sitting still?" Mark asked, knowing how hard it was to get Tiandra to sit still for any length of time.

"Right now she is. There's a commercial on."

Mark laughed.

"Mark?"

"Yeah?"

"I had a great time last night. Thank you, again."

"So did I. I'm sorry I left you in such a rush this morning."

"That's all right. I understand."

"What're you doing tomorrow?" Mark asked suddenly.

"I was planning to take Tiandra to the Bronx Zoo."

"Really?"

"Yeah."

"You know, I haven't been to the Bronx Zoo since I was a kid. I know it's totally different from what it used to be. Would you mind if I came along?"

"No. Not at all. We'd love for you to come, right, Tiandra? Tiandra said, right."

Mark chuckled and said, "Yeah, I heard her. What time are you planning to go?"

"I was going to try to leave here by ten thirty."

"Okay. Well, I'll tell you what. I'll come by and pick you up at ten, how's that?"

"That's good. We'll be ready when you get here. I can make

a couple of breakfast sandwiches and we can eat them on the way up if you like.''

''If you want to, baby. Don't go to any extra trouble for me.''

''I don't mind,'' she said truthfully.

He smiled and said, ''I guess that's why I love you so much.''

''I love you, too, Mark.''

''I'll be at your door tomorrow morning at ten o'clock, okay?''

''Okay.''

''Kiss Tiandra for me. And kiss yourself, too.''

She giggled and said, ''Okay. You do the same.''

''Bye, sweetheart.''

When Mark arrived at Nicole's apartment Sunday morning, he was wearing white jeans, a red and white striped polo shirt and white sneakers. When Nicole opened the door for him, he was tickled to see that she was also wearing red and white.

''I like your taste in colors.''

''Hey, how'd you know I was wearing red and white?'' Nicole asked as she let him in.

''It was the vibes.'' He put his arm around her waist and pulled her close as he kissed her. ''Mmm, how are you?'' he asked as he gazed into her eyes.

''Fine. How are you?'' she asked, holding him by his waist.

''Fine, now,'' he said as he kissed her again.

When their lips parted, he said, ''You know, I could stand here all day kissing you.''

''I could let you.'' They kissed again. ''Mmm, you taste good,'' she said.

''That's because you've added the sweetener.''

She then held him tight as she kissed him more passionately than before. When their lips parted, she whispered, ''I love you.''

"I love you, Nicole."

They held each other close with Nicole resting her head on his chest.

"Where's Tiandra?" Mark whispered.

"In her crib waiting for you to rescue her. She has on red and white, too. People are going to think we belong together."

"We do."

They released each other and went back to Tiandra's room. She was sitting in her crib playing with one of her toys.

"Tiandra," Nicole called as they entered the room.

Tiandra turned immediately at the mention of her name.

"Look who's here, Tee. Daddy's here. Look," Nicole said as she pointed to Mark.

When Tiandra spotted her father, she immediately stood up and held her arms up for him to pick her up.

"Hi, precious," Mark said as he lifted her out of the crib. "How's my baby, huh? How's my sweetheart? Can I have a hug?"

Tiandra put her arms around Mark's neck and laid her head on his shoulder in the semblance of a hug. "Oh, boy, that's a good hug. Thank you, Tee. Thank you. Can I have a kiss?" Tiandra puckered her lips and kissed Mark's. "Oh, thank you. That's some good sugar. Hey, Mommy," he said to Nicole. "She's got some good sugar."

Nicole asked, "Can I have a kiss, Tiandra?" Tiandra leaned over in Mark's arms to kiss Nicole. "Thank you. Ooh, Daddy, that is some good sugar. She's a sweetheart, right?" Nicole said as she and Mark exchanged kisses with their daughter.

They arrived at the zoo at half past eleven and didn't leave until almost five o'clock that afternoon. While there, they toured the entire park. They took Tiandra into all the different animal houses and, although she didn't understand what exactly was going on, Mark and Nicole had a wonderful time explaining the different types of animals to her.

They had lunch in one of the zoo's many eateries, and while strolling through the park they either held hands or walked with arms around one another practically the entire day. They were very affectionate toward one another. It was as if they were in a world all their own. There was no room for anyone outside the three.

Both, in their separate thoughts, were overjoyed at being together this way. They were, if only for this day, a family again and they reveled in this feeling of oneness.

There was a moment in the reptile house when Nicole was reading the information plate outside one of the exhibits and Mark looked at her and a warm feeling spread throughout his body. At that moment, the love he felt for her was stronger than it had ever been. He had wanted to tell her, too, but the feeling was so totally consuming that he was left speechless.

Nicole also had a private moment within herself, similar to Mark's. There was a camel ride in the zoo and Mark wanted to take Tiandra on it. Nicole didn't want to ride because she was afraid of the camel. She really didn't want Mark to take Tiandra on either, but she kept her discord to herself.

When Mark and Tiandra were on the camel's back, she watched closely with love and adoration as he held Tiandra and talked to her while they rode. She always loved to watch him with their daughter. She thought he was the perfect picture of fatherhood. Seeing him with Tiandra gave her a feeling of such joy and pride, it brought tears to her eyes.

When they left the park, Mark suggested they return to the penthouse to have dinner. Unaware that Mark was hoping to persuade her to spend the night with him, Nicole readily agreed. Once they reached his apartment, Mark put Tiandra to bed because she had fallen asleep during the ride home. When he rejoined Nicole in the living room, he said to her, "You know, that was fun. I really enjoyed that."

"Me, too."

"We've definitely got to do that again," he said, then chuckled. "It's funny because since we have Tiandra, we can use her as an excuse to go to the zoo more often."

Nicole laughed and said, "You know, I was thinking the same thing."

"Hey, no one has to know it's her parents that really want to go."

"You don't mind if I pour myself a glass of wine, do you?"

"Of course not. While you're at it, you can pour me one, too."

She went behind the bar and proceeded to fix their drinks.

When she walked over to the couch to give Mark his glass, he said, "Sit down." She sat next to him, her drink in hand. "Put your glass down." She sat the glass on the table in front of them. Mark took her hand and said, "You can sit closer to me than that. I won't bite you."

"I know, but I might," she said with a smile.

"Oh, well, bite me then," he said with a chuckle.

She giggled.

He put his arm around her shoulder and pulled her closer still. When he kissed her, she responded eagerly, putting her arms around him. They sat on the sofa and necked for nearly ten minutes. Mark was already aroused, but holding Nicole and kissing her this way was making it almost unbearable.

He stopped and said, "You know, baby, it'll be a while before Angie has dinner ready."

"I know."

"Why don't we kill some time?"

"How?" Nicole asked, knowing the answer.

"Well, if you'll follow me into the bedroom, I'd be more than happy to show you," he said, smiling like a little boy with a devious plan.

Nicole hung her head. *How can I tell him I'm not ready to go to bed with him without hurting his feelings.*

Mark sensed her hesitation immediately. "What's wrong?"

"I'm not ready for that."

"Why?"

"Because there are so many other things we need to work out before we worry about sex."

"Hey, baby, I'm not worried about sex. I just want to make love to you," Mark said with a grin.

"But I don't want to rush, Mark. I think we should take our time."

"I won't rush. I'll do it real slow."

"Mark! You know what I mean. I want to make sure everything is right between us before we do that."

"Nicole, didn't you have a good time today?"

"Yes."

"I did, too. Don't you want us to be a family again?"

"Yes, Mark."

"Don't you love me?"

"Yes."

"And I love you. I just want to show you how much I love you."

"There are other ways," she said. She would not meet his eyes.

"Nicole, look at me. I can feel it when you kiss me that you want me just as much as I want you. There's nothing wrong with us making love, baby. You're my wife. We belong together. You're the one I should be making love with."

Nicole got up from the couch and walked over to the bar. She was confused because her body longed for his touch but her mind told her there was still a long way to go. "How can I make you understand how I feel? If we make love now, we'll forget about the important things we're lacking in our marriage that we need to make it work."

"I don't think so."

"Yes, we will. We'll make love and you know, Mark, that's one thing we've never had a problem with. I've never been loved as well by anyone as I have by you and I know that once I start feeling good like that I'm going to want you over and over, and everything we said we'd do to make this right will go right out the window.''

"Nicole,'' Mark said as he got up and walked over to where she stood. He took her hands and looked into her eyes and said, "Baby, don't you think I want to make this work, too?''

"Yes, but . . .''

"No buts. I need you. Every time I see you, touch you or kiss you, I want to make love with you. I don't think it will take anything away from what we need to do.''

"Mark, please. I just don't think it's the right time. It's only been two days. We haven't really accomplished much. We've spent today together and I had a wonderful time, but who's to say that the way we related today will be the way you'll feel a few months from now. We've been separated for a whole year. I've changed in that time and I'm sure you've changed. There might be things about me now that you don't like. I don't want to get my hopes up to be let down again. It's hard for me to think with my head when you're making love to my body,'' Nicole confessed.

Mark knew he could not argue her point and get anywhere, so he tried a different approach. "Please, Nicole. Please? I want you so bad. What can I tell you? I just want to hold you and love you,'' he said as humbly as he could.

"Mark.''

"Please? Do you want me to beg? I'm not too proud to beg, baby.''

"I don't want you to beg me for anything, Mark,'' Nicole said seriously.

"What can I do to make you change your mind?''

"Nothing. It's just not the right time. I'm just not ready.''

Mark looked at her sadly. He was greatly disappointed, but he could see it had been difficult for her to turn him down. He figured he might as well hang it up. He knew he would not get his way with her today. "All right," he said, giving up. "I'll cool out. Would you excuse me while I go take a cold shower."

She looked at him with sadness.

He put his arms around her and hugged her, saying, "I'm just teasing, Nicole. Don't worry about it. I'll wait until you're ready, okay?"

She looked up into his eyes to see if he really understood. He smiled at her to let her know that everything was all right.

"I'm sorry, Mark."

"That's all right. You're right, there's no reason to rush. I'm not going anywhere."

She hugged him back, grateful he was so understanding of her feelings.

Then he asked, "Can I ask you one thing, though?"

"What?"

"How long will I have to wait?" he asked, then laughed and said, "Just kidding."

She looked distressed when he said that, but when he smiled at her she saw he was teasing her, although she knew he was very serious.

The following week, Mark and Nicole spent every evening together. One night he took her to dinner and a Broadway play. The other nights he either had dinner with her and Tiandra at her apartment or his.

On the nights that Nicole and Tiandra had dinner at his apartment, Mark would come home, change his clothes and go pick them up, and they would take Tiandra to the playground first. During these times, they had many refreshing and enlightening conversations.

They laughed, teased each other, and generally just had fun sharing their time. They were still very affectionate toward one another, but Mark did not approach her for sex at all.

On Saturday, Mark and Nicole took Tiandra, Carol and her

two children, Nicole's sister Stephanie and her daughter to an amusement park.

When Nicole called Carol on Friday to invite her, Carol was flabbergasted. "Mark is going to an amusement park? I can't believe it," Carol said. "Do you know how long it's been since he's done anything as wild as that? Since he started that company, he never has time for fun things like that. He's become rather boring to say the least. I'm glad you were able to talk him into it."

"I didn't talk him into it," Nicole said. "It was his idea."

"What?"

"Yeah. He called me a little while ago and said he had discount tickets for Adventure Land. He said he always gets them for his employees but he's never used them before. He thought it would be fun to take the kids to the park."

"Damn, Nicky. I still can't believe it. You know why he's doing this, don't you?"

"Why?"

"Because he's trying to . . . I don't know how to put it, but he wants to be more of a family man, I think, than he's been in the past. I guess he figures the more time he spends with you and Tiandra doing stuff like this, the sooner you'll move back in with him."

"I don't know, Carol. Mark has changed, though. I've noticed that he seems more at ease or something. I don't know what it is but I like it. The only problem is that he's asked me to sleep with him and I'm not quite ready for that yet. He didn't get angry when I said no, but I'm not sure when he's going to approach me again or if he'll be as understanding as he was before."

"He'll wait. Even if he doesn't want to, he will. I don't think he wants to blow a chance at reconciling his marriage over a little sex."

* * *

Their day at Adventure Land was great fun for everyone. Like Carol had said, Mark had not been to an amusement park in years. He had the time of his life. They took the kids on all the "kiddy" rides. A couple of times, they had trouble getting Tiandra off the rides because she was having so much fun.

After they had taken the children on all the rides, Mark and Nicole decided they wanted to try a few. The first one they went on was the Daredevil Rollercoaster. Mark wanted to sit in the first car. Nicole didn't, but with a bit of coaxing from Mark, she gave in and had a blast.

They all went on a few rides, then moved on to the arcade games. Before they left that evening at seven thirty, Mark had won stuffed animals for all the children. They stuffed themselves all day on hot dogs, French fries, fried shrimp, popcorn, cotton candy, jelly apples and the like.

On the drive home, everyone fell asleep except Nicole. She was tired, too, but she knew Mark was probably tired also, so she stayed awake to keep him company. It was over an hour's drive back to the city.

"You know, I had a really good time today," Mark said to Nicole on the ride home.

"Me, too."

"I haven't had that much fun since you took me up the Dunn's River Falls in Jamaica," he said, stealing a glance at her.

She giggled and said, "Yeah, that was fun, wasn't it?"

"Oh, yeah."

"I'm glad you had a good time."

"Do you know the last time I went to an amusement park was, damn, over twenty years ago? At least," he added.

"Well, maybe you should do this more often."

"I will. You know, now that I think about it, I must be a really boring individual."

"No, you're not."

"Hey, I never have this much fun at dinner parties. They're like . . . Going to a dinner party is like going to work. I can't get loose or let myself go like I did today. I've got to keep up the facade. Damn, look how much I've been missing out on," he said pensively.

"Well, before I had Tiandra, there probably wasn't much reason for you to do anything like this."

"Sure there was. I could have done it for me, or I could have taken Mark and Cherie. I never take them anywhere. I'm going to try to spend more time with them since their fathers never do. I've got to get back to my family. I've been so busy trying to get that dollar that I never took the time to be with my family."

"You spend time with Carol," Nicole said, refuting his negativity.

"Yeah, because she's here. You've never even met my other sister. I haven't seen Tina in over ten years. That doesn't make any sense. I can travel all over the world anytime I like, but I haven't even made an attempt to go down south to see my sister."

"Were you close to her?"

"No, we were never really close. She's older than me and when we were growing up, because she was older, she was always very bossy. Or if she was doing something that I thought was wrong, and I said something to her about it, she'd give me a lot of flak and because I was bigger than her, I wouldn't let her talk to me any way she wanted, so we were always at each other's throats."

"Sibling rivalry," Nicole stated.

"Intense sibling rivalry," he added. "But we're not kids anymore. I'm forty three years old and I'm not getting any younger."

They rode in silence for a few minutes.

"I spend too much time at that damn office," Mark said, breaking the silence.

Nicole looked over at him in shock.

"It's no wonder my life's so screwed up," he said.

"Your life's not screwed up."

"Oh, no?" he said, looking at her. "You're my wife, right?"

"Yes."

"Then how come you're not living with me?"

Nicole did not answer.

"If I hadn't been so anxious to build that hotel, we'd be together now like we're supposed to be," he said testily. "I didn't need to build that hotel. I was just being greedy. Look at how much strain it put on our marriage."

"It didn't put any strain on our marriage."

"Of course it did. Nicole, you can't tell me that you were happy about all the time I spent away from home while it was being built."

"A few times, though, I was traveling, too."

"I'm not talking about then. There were a lot of times when I was in Jamaica and you were home by yourself."

"But I could have gone with you, you always told me that."

"How many times can you go to Jamaica for two- and three-day stints and not get tired of it. I was working while I was there. I wouldn't have been able to spend any time with you. I never even considered that you might not want me to leave you. I was too interested in building that hotel. Then when Tiandra was born, I didn't even give you a chance to rest up from that. The hotel opened and I wanted you there with me. I've been very selfish. I realize that now. I want to change that," he said sincerely.

Nicole didn't know what to say to Mark, so she just reached over and took his hand.

"Maybe God was trying to tell me something when I had the heart attack. Maybe He was saying, 'You've got to start thinking about other people's feelings with as much passion as you think about your own.' I don't know, baby. I think maybe I should rearrange my priorities. It's not necessary for me to be at the office for twelve hours every day. I've got people there, competent people that can run the place just fine. I told you how well Dave did when I was on disability, right?''

"Yes."

"Maybe I'll delegate more responsibility to him and my other vice presidents. What do you think?''

"I don't know, Mark. Is that what you want to do?''

"I want to be able to spend more time with you and Tiandra and the rest of my family before it's too late," he said as he squeezed her hand.

"We're not going anywhere, Mark."

"But, I might. I don't want to have to endure another heart attack. I don't think I'd make it through another one. There's so much lost time I have to make up for. So much time," he said, his eyes watering.

After dropping everyone off, Mark drove to Nicole's apartment. He parked the car and went upstairs with her. Together, they put Tiandra to bed.

"Mark, do you want me to fix you a drink?" Nicole asked, yawning.

"Just some water, baby."

She went to the kitchen and poured him a glass of ice water. She brought it back to him and sat next to him on the couch. "I'm so tired," she said.

"Me, too."

"I know you must be. You should have let me help you drive."

"That's all right. I'd be just as tired. We had a pretty full day."

"To say the least," she said as she laid her head on his shoulder.

They sat like that for almost an hour. They both dozed off. Nicole woke up first. She had to go to the bathroom. When she came back, Mark was stretched out on the couch. She knew how tired he was and she really did not want him to drive with the chance that he might fall asleep at the wheel, so she left him alone. She went to her bedroom and undressed. She was hot and felt sticky from all the excitement of the day, so she took a shower. When she finished, she went back to her room, put on a baby doll nightgown and got in bed. She was asleep ten minutes after her head hit the pillow.

When Mark woke up on the couch, it was two thirty. He had to use the bathroom. As he stood there, he wondered why Nicole hadn't awakened him when she went to bed. After he flushed, he washed his hands and face. She obviously didn't want him to leave. He knew her well enough to know she would not hesitate to put him out if she were so inclined. He turned off the light in the bathroom and went to check on Tiandra. She was fast asleep. He bent over the rail of her crib and kissed her cheek. "I love you, angel," he whispered. He went to Nicole's room. She was out of it, too. He stood inside the door trying to decide what to do. After five minutes, he walked back into the living room. He went to the front door and checked the locks. Then he turned off all the lights and walked back to Nicole's bedroom.

He stood beside the bed for a few minutes, watching her as she slept. He began removing his clothes. When he had stripped down to his shorts, he got into the bed. He felt foolish because his heart was beating so fast. He didn't touch her at first, he just lay next to her and watched her to see if she would awaken. She stirred slightly when he got into the bed, but she never opened her eyes. *She must be very tired,* he thought, because she had always been a fairly light sleeper.

After a few minutes, Mark turned over on his side and put

his arm across her waist. He moved closer to her and again, she stirred but still did not awaken. He couldn't believe he was actually lying beside her. His aching member was straining for freedom in his shorts. He wanted her so much. He moved closer still and gently kissed her on her forehead. This time, she grumbled slightly in her sleep and turned onto her other side so that her back was to him, but she moved closer to him until her backside was firmly pressed against his erection. *Oh God,* his mind screamed. The feel of her body against his sent a shiver of need through his body. *Is she aware of what she's doing to me?*

He put his arm over her again and pressed his body still closer. He kissed the back of her neck, but she did not move. He inhaled the sweet fragrance of her until once again he was asleep.

Nicole woke up at seven o'clock Sunday morning. While she slept, she dreamt of Mark. She dreamt they had made love. When she opened her eyes that morning, she got the surprise of her life when she looked at his sleeping form in bed next to her. She quickly jumped out of the bed. *What was he doing? How dare he just jump into my bed without my permission? How could he be so thoughtless to try and take advantage of me like that?* ''Mark! Mark, wake up!'' she demanded.

Mark turned over and mumbled incoherently, then went back to sleep.

''Mark! Get up!'' Nicole yelled, this time shaking him.

Mark opened his eyes and shook his head to clear it. ''What's wrong, baby?'' he asked sleepily.

''What's wrong? You know what's wrong.''

''No, I don't. I just woke up. What's the matter?'' he asked, clearly puzzled.

''What are you doing in my bed?''

''What?''

"You heard what I said. What are you doing in my bed?"

"I was sleeping. What did it look like?"

"Did I invite you to sleep with me?" she asked angrily.

Her words brought him fully awake. "Nicole . . ."

"Did I? No! Who do you think I am?"

"What's the big deal, Nicole? I didn't do anything to you while you were asleep. I was tired. I didn't think you'd mind."

"I left you on the couch. Why couldn't you stay there?"

Mark was at a loss for words. That she would be so vehement about him sleeping next to her really hurt.

"I told you I wasn't ready to sleep with you again. You think just because I fell asleep, you can take advantage of me?"

"I would never do that to you."

"If you weren't going to try anything, why didn't you wake me up and ask if it was all right for you to sleep here?"

"It was three o'clock in the morning."

"So what?"

Mark was stunned. He could not believe she was carrying on this way. "Why are you acting like this?"

"Like what?"

"Like I'm some kind of stranger or something. I'm your husband, Nicole. I love you," he said in desperation.

"Yes, you're my husband, but you don't respect my feelings."

"Nicole, I have the utmost respect for you."

"How could you? I told you I wasn't ready to jump into bed with you, but that obviously doesn't mean anything to you, does it?"

Mark was exasperated. "Baby, I wasn't going to try anything. I was just tired," he said with a plea in his voice. "I want to make love to you, Nicole, but not while you're asleep. I want you to be awake so you can enjoy it, like I would."

"How many times do I have to tell you, I'm not ready."

"What are you waiting for?" Mark asked, a little too impatiently.

Nicole did not like his tone. "Whatever it is I'm waiting for, I won't sleep with you until then!"

Mark was becoming very angry. He didn't want to argue with her, though. They had argued enough already. They were supposed to be trying to patch things up.

"Last night you were talking all this stuff about how selfish you've always been and how you want to change. Well, you're still being selfish. You're not thinking about how I feel. All that matters are your feelings," Nicole yelled.

He stared at her. He was angry and hurt and he knew if he did not leave right away, the steps they had climbed toward their goal would be for naught. He threw the covers off his body and got out of the bed. He went to the chair where he had placed his pants and shirt and began to put them on.

Nicole went to the other side of the bed and sat with her back to him.

When he was fully dressed, he went to the bathroom to wash his face. He was hurting so bad he wanted to cry, but he held himself together. He came back into the bedroom and stood just inside the door. "Nicole," he said quietly. She did not answer. "Nicole, look at me," he said sternly. Slowly, she turned to face him.

"You're right. I am being selfish. But only because I love you so much. If I'm wrong for wanting you, then I'm sorry. I won't bother you about it anymore. When you're ready, you let me know, okay? That way, there'll be no problems." With that, he turned and left the apartment.

Nicole sat where she was and sighed miserably. She had gotten what she wanted. But now she felt as though she had pushed him further away.

Chapter
Thirty-Two

In the two weeks that followed, Mark and Nicole continued to see each other every day. Nicole had been apprehensive about seeing Mark the Monday following their altercation, but he behaved as if nothing had ever happened. The only difference Nicole noticed by the middle of that first week was that although he still treated her with love and respect, he seemed distant. They talked and laughed together. They played with Tiandra, marveling over her growth and constant achievements as any proud parents would. They even had dinner together every night. But he didn't touch her hand anymore as they sat together watching TV. He didn't try to put his arm around her when they walked together. He didn't look at her like he used to. But most of all, when he came and went, he no longer kissed her lips. Instead, he gave her a peck on her cheek.

As he said, not once did he hint about their making love, and this caused her to wonder if he did still want them to be together.

On September 12th, Karen Walter, the real estate broker, called Nicole to set the date for the closing on the house she wanted to buy. She was so excited she called Mark right away at his office. "Mark, guess what?" Nicole said excitedly.

"What?"

"I've got the house. Karen just called to set the date for the closing."

"That's great. Congratulations."

"I'm so excited, Mark. I can't believe it."

"Why not? You deserve it. I'm happy for you, Nicole," he said sincerely.

"Would you come with me?"

"Where?"

"To the closing."

"Sure, if you like."

"I'd really like for you to be there with me."

"When is it?"

"September 25th."

"Denise has my calendar right now, but I'll check it, and if I'm free that day, I'll go with you."

"I hope you are."

"I'll see."

"Are you coming by tonight?" she asked anxiously.

"Yeah, I'll be there."

"I'll get some champagne and we can celebrate, okay?"

"If you want to."

Nicole didn't say anything at the time, but it sounded to her like Mark was not all that enthusiastic about celebrating her good fortune. She hated the way he had been acting lately, as if he was trying to be so perfect and cautious instead of just being himself. *Maybe he had changed his mind,* she thought. *Maybe he doesn't want things to be the way they were before. Maybe all he wants is to be my friend.* Nicole also could not understand why, in two weeks, Mark had not even commented about their marriage.

When he came by that evening, once again he greeted her with a kiss on her cheek. She hated it. She had bought a bottle of Dom Perignon. Before dinner she asked him, "Would you like a glass of champagne to help me celebrate my new house?"

"All right, but just one. I can't stay too late. I've got another stop to make before I go home."

"Oh. All right," she said, clearly disappointed. *He's probably got someone else.*

He drank a glass of champagne with her and stayed for dinner, but for some reason he seemed more distant toward her on this night. Finally, after dinner, she asked, "What's wrong, Mark?"

"Nothing, why?"

"It just seems like your mind is somewhere else."

"Oh, yeah? Well, it's here with me. Don't worry."

"Did I do something wrong?"

"No. Why are you being so paranoid?"

"I'm not being paranoid. You're acting different."

"Different how?"

"I don't know, but you are."

Mark looked at her strangely and shook his head. "Listen, I've got to go. I'm already late."

He rose from his seat and walked over to where Tiandra sat playing with a toy and picked her up. "See ya', baby," he said, kissing and hugging her. He put her back down and grabbed his jacket. "Why don't you relax, Nicole. You're probably tensed up because you're getting the house. Take it easy. Everything'll be all right."

She looked at him without comment. She didn't want him to leave.

Nicole followed him to the door. Once he had opened it, he turned and said, "Oh, yeah, I'm going to come by tomorrow night to get Tiandra. I'm taking her to a birthday party on Saturday."

"Who's birthday party?"

Mark looked away for a moment, then said, "A friend of mine is having a party for their godchild."

"Anyone I know?"

He sighed audibly and said, "Ashlei. Ashlei is giving a party for her goddaughter." Mark noticed that Nicole seemed to wince when he mentioned Ashlei's name.

"I thought you said you weren't seeing her."

"I'm not." She was about to say something else when he turned and walked out, saying, "I'll see you later, Nicole."

She slept poorly that night. She could not figure out what Mark was thinking. Not knowing how he felt about her anymore was driving her mad.

He swore he wasn't seeing Ashlei, but why would he be taking Tiandra to her goddaughter's party? He hadn't even asked her if she wanted to come with them. Ever since the concert, they had been spending time with Tiandra together. This was the first time since then that she was being excluded.

Her heart ached because she was uncertain about their future together. She wondered why he didn't try to come on to her like he used to. He didn't even tease her about their relationship. He just treated her like a 'friend.'

Before she finally fell off to sleep sometime in the middle of the night, Nicole decided she would go to him tomorrow and put her foot down and make him tell her what was going on. There had to be a reason why he was treating her so impersonally.

Nicole walked into Mark's office at two thirty, Friday afternoon. He was on the telephone when she came in, and he gestured to her to have a seat. "I'll be with you in a minute," he said, covering the mouthpiece of the telephone.

He was on the phone for another five minutes before he hung up. Nicole, being impatient for him to get off the telephone, got up from her seat and casually strolled over to the window.

"Sorry I took so long, Nicole," Mark said as he hung up.

"That's all right," she said, turning to face him.

"What brings you up here? Were you in the area?"

"No. I wanted to talk to you."

"About what?"

"Would you mind if I closed the door? It's personal."

"Sure, go ahead."

She walked back across the office and gently closed the door.

Mark could see that whatever it was she wanted to discuss with him was very serious, so he spoke on his intercom, "Denise, hold my calls."

"Thank you," Nicole said of his gesture.

"What's on your mind?"

"I want to know what's wrong with you."

"What's wrong with me? Nothing's wrong with me. Why would you say that?" Mark asked, clearly puzzled.

"Because of the way you've been treating me."

"How have I been treating you?"

"Like . . . like . . . like I'm a stranger or something."

"I haven't been treating you like that, Nicole. What are you talking about?"

"You've changed. Ever since the night you slept over at my apartment, you've changed."

"Oh, really? How so?"

"You're so distant when you're around me. You seem like you're trying so hard to be polite, like we've just met or something. You don't talk to me like you used to," she whined.

"I don't talk to you any differently than I did before. And I don't understand why you'd say I seem like I'm trying to be polite. I've never been out-and-out rude to you, have I?"

"No, but . . ."

"But what?"

"You're acting like we're just friends and nothing else."

"Isn't that what you wanted?"

"I didn't say I wanted us to be just friends. I said I wanted us to be friends as well as husband and wife."

"Well, you don't want me to behave like I'm your husband, so I'm trying to be the friend you asked me to be. I'm doing what you asked of me."

"You don't have to be so distant. You don't even touch me

anymore. All of a sudden, you're kissing me on my cheek like I'm your little sister.''

"What do you want me to do?" he asked, becoming agitated. "You don't want to make love with me, so to make it easier on myself, yes, I'm trying to keep my distance. Do you think I can kiss you and touch you and hold you and not want to make love to you? I'm not a robot. I have feelings, too, Nicole. You know how I feel about you. If you're not ready to sleep with me, fine, I'm willing to wait. But for me to resist you, I have to keep you at arm's length.''

"Don't you love me anymore?"

"Of course I love you. I've never stopped loving you. But I can't give you what you want and have what I want, too. You say you want us to be friends, well, I'm trying to be your friend. That's not what I want. You're my wife and I want you, like a man wants a woman. I'm trying to make you happy by giving you what you asked for, and you're still not satisfied. What do you want from me? You tell me I'm selfish because I keep asking you to sleep with me, so I don't mention sex to you for two weeks, and I'm still wrong. I think you're being selfish now, Nicole. I'm letting you call the shots, so when I give you what you ask for, don't complain.''

"I thought you said you weren't seeing Ashlei."

"I'm not!"

"Then why are you taking Tiandra to her goddaughter's birthday party tomorrow. If there's nothing going on with her, why did she invite you?"

He rose from his desk and came around to stand beside her. "Nicole, we're friends. The only reason I didn't ask you to come was because I didn't think you'd be comfortable around her.''

Nicole moved to the sofa and sat down. She bowed her head and cried softly.

Mark stood where he was and watched her. He felt an over-whelming sorrow for her at that moment. *She doesn't know what she wants,* he thought. He moved over to the sofa and sat beside her.

"Nicole," he said softly as he took her hand. "I love you. I don't want to be with anyone but you. I'm trying to give you the time you said you need to make up your mind. But you have to understand, there's no way I can be with you every day and touch you and kiss you and not want to make love to you. I can't do that. I'm not that strong. If we're going to be friends, like you want, then you've got to understand how I feel and why I have to be the way I am. If I don't keep my distance, you get upset because I'm coming on to you. Now that I'm trying to be cool to keep from upsetting you, you're still getting upset. It seems like I can't win. I don't know what else to do, baby. How can I please you?"

Nicole looked into his eyes and saw tears straining to fall. She looked away quickly, shamefully. "You're right. I am being selfish. I don't mean to be, I'm just so confused. I love you so much, but I don't want to lose you again. I haven't even thought about how you might feel. I'm sorry. Please don't be angry with me."

"Oh, baby, come here," he said as he put his arms around her and pulled her close. The tears in his eyes fell uninhibited. "I'm not angry with you."

His heart was heavy. He didn't know what the outcome of this whole thing would be. He knew she loved him, but he had hurt her so much he wasn't sure if she could trust him again enough to want to live the rest of her life with him. He didn't want to lose her either. "Don't cry, baby. I promise you, everything will be all right."

When she noticed his tears, she immediately reached out to wipe them away. "Oh, Mark, I'm sorry I upset you. I love you so much, but sometimes I get so scared, I don't know what to do. I just want everything to be perfect. I don't want anything to go wrong."

"I know, baby. Me, too."

She tried to compose herself. "I'm sorry for barging in on you," she said as she wiped her nose with a tissue she'd pulled from her pocketbook. "I feel so silly. All this time, I've been telling you how selfish you are when it was really me. Can you forgive me?"

"There's no need, baby. I know how hard it's been for you. I know it'll take time for you to be able to trust me again. I can understand your insecurity about Ashlei and I, but I swear to you, what you saw that night was the extent of my intimacy with Ashlei. I just want to be the husband to you that I should have been from the start. I'll wait until you're ready, Nicole, no matter how long it takes. I owe you at least that," he said humbly.

"And I'll try not to be so self-centered, and will take your feelings into account from now on," she promised.

They sat there for a while, just staring into each other's eyes.

"Why can't love be easier?" Nicole finally asked with a sniffle.

"I guess if it was, it wouldn't be as good."

"Probably."

They sat quietly a few seconds more. "Feel better?" Mark eventually asked her.

"Yes. You must think I'm crazy, huh?"

"No more crazy than I am. Seems like when folks are in love and their hearts are at the controls, their minds tend to take a leave of absence. I know that's the case with me."

She laughed at the phraseology he used. "You know, that sums it up very well."

Once again, they shared silence. Finally, Nicole sighed and said, "It's just that sometimes I get so afraid that things are not going to turn out the way I want them to."

"And how is that?"

"I'd like for it to be . . . I'd like for us to be friends but more than friends, too, like in the beginning. I want to be happy like I was then," she confessed.

"It'll be that way again, baby. Do you know why? Because that's what we both want," Mark emphasized as he gently caressed her face. "We had some good times then, didn't we?"

"Yes. We did," she smiled.

"And they're not so far out of reach now. I guess it just takes time and a conscious effort to make it right."

"And a little less confusion on my part," Nicole added.

"Hey, baby, that's life. Don't worry about it. I'm here. I'm not going anywhere."

She smiled gratefully at him, then leaned over and kissed him softly on the lips. "I'm gonna go now and let you get back to your work. I'm sorry for interrupting you with my silliness," she said, rising from the sofa.

"Don't apologize, Nicole. Any time you need to talk to me, my door is always open to you," he said.

As she walked to the door, she asked him, "Do you think you'll be able to come with me to the closing?"

"Oh, yeah, let me take a look at my calendar," he said as he walked back to his desk and referred to his appointment book. "What day is that?"

"September 25th."

"Yeah, I'm free. I'll be out of town the Monday before, but I should be back that night. Your closing's on a Wednesday."

"Yeah."

"I'll be there."

"Thank you."

He smiled and said, "No problem, baby."

"Well, I'll see you later. What time will you be by tonight to get Tiandra?" she asked.

"I'll come by straight from here. We'll go to dinner tonight and the three of us can do something together tomorrow. Is that all right?"

"I'd like that."

Chapter Thirty-Three

Ten days later, Mark flew to Atlanta, Georgia, to attend a real estate conference. It was a day-long conference and Mark's original plan was to fly back to New York that evening when it was over. On this particular day, Nicole kept intruding on his thoughts. During a couple of the lectures, Mark caught himself daydreaming of her. When the conference was over, Mark returned to his hotel room to get his bags and check out. But first he called Nicole.

She was surprised to hear from him.

"You know, you've been on my mind all day," he told her.

"Really?"

"Yeah. More than usual. Is everything all right there?"

"Yes."

"Is Tiandra all right?"

"She's fine. I was about to wake her up for dinner. She's been napping since about four o'clock."

"I don't know. Maybe I just needed to hear your voice."

"Maybe you miss me," she cooed.

"Of course, I miss you. Don't you miss me?"

"Yes."

"Well, I feel better now that I've talked to you and know that everything's all right."

"I'm glad of that. By the way, have you talked to your sister? She's in Atlanta, isn't she?" Nicole asked.

"No, she's in Columbus and no, I haven't talked to her," Mark admitted.

"Why don't you call her before you leave?"

Mark contemplated this. "Yeah. Maybe I should. I feel sort of guilty though, since I haven't talked to her in so long."

"Well, what are you going to do, wait another few years so the guilt can overwhelm you?"

Mark sighed, "You're right."

"Of course, I'm right," Nicole said with a chuckle.

"Suppose she doesn't want to talk to me?"

"I doubt if that'll be the case. You said it yourself, you're not children anymore. I'm sure any differences you may have had years ago have been forgotten. And anyway, if she doesn't want to talk to you, you can at least rest easy knowing you made an effort to see her," Nicole reasoned.

"I guess so."

"Call her, Mark. You're right there. You might even be able to see her before you leave."

"All right. I'll call. Wish me luck," he said with very little confidence.

"Good luck, sweetheart," she said sweetly.

"I'll see you when I get home."

"All right. Have a safe trip back."

"Thanks. Love you, baby."

"I love you, too."

Mark sat on the bed in his hotel room for a few minutes before he got up and retrieved his sister's number from his phone book. He studied the entry for a few minutes before he finally picked up the receiver. He took a deep breath, then proceeded to dial.

Tina Summers was forty-six years old, the divorced mother of four and the elder sister of Mark Peterson. She was a very pretty woman and looked much younger than her forty-six years despite the plentiful streaks of gray in her hair and a number of trying episodes in her life that would have worn a weaker woman down. Divorced for thirteen years, she had taken on the sole responsibility of raising three sons and a daughter, due to a lack of support from her ex-husband, but she was a strong woman and had never been one to let adversity get the best of her. She wanted a better life for her children than she and her siblings had due to their mother's addiction to drugs and the wrong men.

Although her brothers, with the exception of her favorite, Mark, had all amounted to nothing, she was proud that her baby sister Carol was doing fairly well for herself despite the changes that she, too, went through with the men in her life. And, although, she had not seen or heard from Mark in years, she was glad he was near Carol and that he looked out for her.

She was tremendously proud of Mark. Financially, he had done better than anyone in their family for as far back as she could remember. Much better from what Carol told her. At times she had even considered calling him, but she never followed through. He was probably too busy cavorting with his "high society" friends to talk to her anyway.

Carol kept her up to date on what he was doing, so she was aware that he had finally gotten married, even though it hadn't lasted, and that he had a daughter. She often wished they had not grown so far apart. She would love to see him just to tell him how proud she was of him.

Tina and her two youngest children, Frank and Crystal, were sitting down to dinner when the telephone rang. "I'll get it!" Crystal yelled, jumping up from her seat and running to the phone. She was expecting a call from her boyfriend.

"If you could only move that fast when I ask you to do something for me, maybe I wouldn't be in your case so much," Tina said disgustedly.

"Hello," Crystal said, ignoring her mother's remark.

"Hello. Is this the Summers' residence?"

"Yes."

"Is Tina Summers there?"

"Yes. Hold on," Crystal said into the phone. "It's for you, Mommy."

"Who is it?" She did not like being disturbed during her dinner.

"I don't know. It's a man."

Tina sucked her teeth and slowly got up to answer the phone. *Probably a bill collector,* she thought. Those were the only men that had been calling her lately. "Hello," she said impatiently when she took the phone from her daughter.

"Hello, Tina. This is Mark."

She heard the voice and knew right away that it was indeed her brother, even though she had not heard his voice in years. She was speechless for a moment.

"Tina? Are you there?"

She swallowed deeply and said, "Yes."

"How are you?" he asked haltingly.

"I'm . . . I'm fine. How are you?" she asked, quickly becoming very emotional.

"I'm fine."

There were so many things he wanted to say to her, but he didn't know where to start. He wanted to say he was sorry for not having called sooner. Instead, he said, "How're the kids?"

"They're all fine," she said as a tear fell from her eye.

Frank saw the tear and became agitated that this man on the phone had caused his mother to cry. "Who's that, Ma?" he asked wanting to defend his mother.

She did not answer, but simply waved him off.

"I'm here in Atlanta. I came down for a-uh, for a conference and, well, I was wondering if maybe I could come by and see you."

Tina was crying openly now and Crystal and Frankie were worried. "Yes. I'd love to see you. Where are you?"

"I'm at the Marriott. I can drive out there."

"Do you know how to get here?"

"Give me your address."

She did. She also gave him directions.

"I'll find you. I'm gonna leave now."

"Okay. Be careful."

"See you in a couple of hours."

When Tina hung up the phone, Crystal and Frank went to her immediately to comfort her. "Mommy, who was that?" Crystal asked.

"That was my brother, Mark. I've told you about him. He's coming here tonight."

"Where is he?" Crystal asked.

"He's in Atlanta."

"Is that the rich one?" Frank asked excitedly.

"Yes."

"Maybe he'll give you some money. Maybe he can give all of us some money," Frank said.

"Don't you dare ask him for anything, do you hear me?" She walked back to the table and sat down. "I haven't seen him in over ten years," Tina said reminiscently.

"Maybe he's not rich anymore and he wants to borrow money from you," Frank said nastily.

Tina rolled her eyes at him, but did not answer.

When Mark hung up the phone, he breathed a sigh of relief. He felt as if a twenty-ton weight had been lifted from his shoulders.

It was good to hear Tina's voice. She sounded good. But suddenly, once again, he felt burdened by guilt. She had been divorced now for ... *Damn,* he thought. *It had to be almost thirteen years now. All this time she's been struggling to take care of four kids by herself and I've never even tried to help her. How can I face her?* She was his sister. His flesh and blood. Not a half-sister like Carol, but his true sister. Of the

four men Mark's mother bedded to produce her seven children,
Tina, Mark and a younger brother, William, all shared the same
father.

Damn, what were his nephews' names? His niece was Crystal, he hadn't forgotten that. The last time he saw her she was
about five years old. *She must be seventeen or eighteen by now,*
he thought. He knew her oldest son was Kevin, Jr. and next
there was Harold, but the youngest one he could not remember.

How could he look her in the eye and not expect to see
disapproval? He would not blame her if she lit into him as
soon as he walked in the door. This time, however, he would
let her say what she wanted. He felt he deserved whatever
tongue-lashing he got.

The drive to Columbus took a little more than two hours. It
gave Mark plenty of time to contemplate the forthcoming
reunion with his sister. He found her house easily enough and
was relieved to see it was in good condition. It made it a little
easier knowing that she was probably doing okay.

Tina's heart hit her stomach when she heard the car pull up
in her driveway. *He's here.* She suddenly wondered if he had
changed since he acquired wealth and success, or if he was
still the same sweet, overprotective little brother he had always
been. She laughed to herself when she thought about all the
stupid fights they used to have when Mark tried to tell her what
to do. He'd always told her he knew what was best for her.

Mark got out of the rental car hesitantly. *What will I say to
her? What will she look like?* He wondered if she had changed
much. He could remember how he used to brag that his sister
was the finest girl on the block and that she was off limits to
all the "creeps" in their neighborhood. Not that she ever paid
any heed to Mark's wishes. On the contrary, she seemed to go

out of her way to see guys Mark disapproved of. She had some
temper, too. Worse than his, and his was hot. He was sure he
would feel her wrath tonight.

It seemed to Tina that Mark was taking forever to ring the
bell. Then she realized that she was so nervous, she was actually
holding her breath.

Mark stepped up to the door and hesitated for a split second,
then hurriedly rang the bell.

Tina jumped at the sound. The bell suddenly seemed much
louder than usual.

Crystal and Frank came into the living room. "He's here,
Mommy!" Crystal said excitedly.

"I know," Tina said quietly.

"I'll open the door," Frank said, turning toward the door.

"No! I'll get it," Tina insisted. She straightened her clothes
and strode slowly to the door. She peeked through the curtain,
checking to see that it was Mark. He did not see her. She took
a deep breath and opened the door.

As soon as the door opened and Mark looked into his sister's
eyes, he knew he had done the right thing. A smile crossed her
face and she said, "Hi."

Mark was so choked up he could not speak.

She put out her hand and said, "Come in, Mark."

He took her hand and felt a shiver go through his body. He
grabbed her and held her as tears came to his eyes. He was
unable to tell her how happy he was to see her again. She

embraced him and soon was crying, too. They hugged each other for a few minutes, neither of them speaking.

Crystal and Frankie stood awkwardly to the side, watching their mother and uncle. Crystal was moved by the reunion and her eyes began to water. Frankie's only thought was that his uncle definitely was not broke.

"How are you, Tina?" Mark finally asked as he released her, but still held her at arm's length.

"I'm fine," she said, smiling at him.

"You look great. God, it's so good to see you," said Mark, full of relief.

"It's good to see you, too, Mark. You look good, too."

"It doesn't make sense that I haven't seen you in all these years," he said, choking back a sob. "I'm sorry I haven't called."

She touched his face lightly and said, "I'm as much to blame, Mark. I could have called you just as easily."

They hugged again and Mark said, "Never again will I lose touch with you. That's a promise."

"You always did keep your promises," she said fondly. "Come on in. You're home now."

At the sight of his niece and nephew, Mark knew this was Crystal and Frankie.

"Kids, this is your Uncle Mark. Mark, this is . . ."

"I know. Crystal and Frank," he said. He walked over to them and shook his head in amazement. "I don't believe it. The last time I saw you both was when you were about five, Crystal, and Frankie, you were about two or three. God. You've grown into a very beautiful young lady," to Crystal, "and a very handsome young man, Frank. How are you?"

He kissed Crystal's cheek and shook Frank's hand.

"We're fine, thank you," Crystal said.

"Do you know, Crystal, you look just like your mother did when she was your age. Just like her," Mark said.

"Thank you," said Crystal, blushing.

"How old are you now?"

"Seventeen."

"Damn. So you're what, Frankie, fifteen?"

"Yes, sir."

"Please, don't call me sir. It makes me feel older than I already am," Mark said, with a chuckle.

Tina stood back and watched as her younger brother conversed with her two youngest children. He had changed, she saw, but seemingly for the better. His physical appearance had not changed much. He was still quite handsome, and the flecks of gray in his hair made him look more distinguished, but he seemed more sensitive.

"Tina, where's Kevin and Harold?" Mark asked, turning back to her.

"Kevin's out somewhere. He should be in later. Harold's in college."

"Is he?"

"Yes. He goes to Rutgers University in New Jersey," Tina informed him.

"Really? That's not far from me. What's he majoring in?"

"Engineering," Crystal chimed.

"Really?" Mark said, turning to her. "That's great. You know, I'm always looking for good engineers."

Tina smiled at him. "Mark, have you had dinner?"

"No, but don't worry about it."

"I have some fried chicken and potato salad and collard greens that wouldn't take long to warm up," Tina said.

"And some cornbread. Mommy makes the best cornbread in the world," Frank boasted.

Mark laughed and said, "You're making it difficult for me to say no."

"Then say yes," Tina said.

He looked at her fondly and smiled. "All right. I'll eat. I am kinda hungry."

"Crystal, go put a light under those greens. Mark, give me your jacket. Sit down."

"You've got a nice place," Mark said as he handed her his jacket.

"It's all right," she said as she walked back to the closet near the front door to hang his jacket. "Nothing fancy, but it's comfortable. I should be finished paying for it in another five years."

"How long have you had it?"

"Almost ten years now. Do you want a drink?" she asked as she closed the closet door.

"Some water's fine."

"Would you like some lemonade?"

"Sure."

"I'll get it," Frank volunteered, running to the kitchen.

"You've got nice kids," Mark said as he sat on the couch.

"Thanks. I have my moments with them."

"I'm sure everyone does."

"Carol told me you have a daughter."

He smiled and said, "Yeah. She's sixteen months old. Her name's Tiandra. Would you like to see a picture of her?"

"Of course," she said as she sat next to him on the couch.

Mark reached for his wallet and opened it to a picture of Tiandra. It was facing a picture of Nicole.

Tina said, "She's a doll. She looks like you a little."

"You think so?"

"Oh, yeah. She's beautiful."

"Thank you. That's my baby," he said lovingly.

She noticed the pride when he spoke of Tiandra and smiled. *He's probably a very good father.* "Who's this?" Tina asked of Nicole's picture.

"My wife."

"Oh. Carol told me you were separated."

"Yeah, but we're trying to work things out."

Frank returned with Mark's drink.

"Thank you, Frank."

"You're welcome. Uncle Mark, is it true that you own your own hotel?" Frank asked inquisitively as he sat on the arm of the couch near Mark.

Mark smiled up at him and said, "Yes."

"Is it big?"

"It's decent," Mark said modestly.

"Where is it?"

"In Jamaica. Have you ever been there, Tina?" Mark asked as he turned to her.

"No. I haven't been anywhere outside of the U.S."

"Would you like to go?"

"Can't afford it right now."

"Would you like to go, Frank?" Mark asked as he turned back to him.

"Yeah!" Frank answered enthusiastically.

"When's your next day off from school?"

"Columbus Day. We're off on a Monday."

"Would you like to go down for the weekend?"

"Yeah!"

"Frankie," Tina scolded.

Mark turned back to her. "Tina, how would you like to take the kids down for that weekend?"

"Mark, I told you . . ."

"All expenses paid. You don't have to worry about a thing. I'll take care of everything."

"You don't have to do that."

"I'd like to. I feel like a heel 'cause I haven't been around, that I haven't seen you. I know you haven't had it easy and I should have been here to help you."

"You don't owe me anything."

"Yes, I do."

"No, you don't. Mark, we're both grown. Granted, it's been too long since we've seen each other, but just like you could have called me, I could have called you. I'm very proud that you've done so well for yourself. Very proud. But you don't owe me anything," Tina insisted.

Mark sighed. "When's the last time you had a vacation?"

"I don't know," she said, somewhat exasperated.

"Then let me send you to Jamaica. You'll love it, Tina, I guarantee. The kids'll love it. You can stay in my hotel and whatever you want, you've got it. My people will take good care of you. You won't have to lift a finger for anything. And Jamaica is a beautiful, beautiful island. I have a lot of friends there and all you'd have to do is tell them who you are and they'd give you whatever you want."

"I don't know, Mark," she said with doubt.

"Think about it. Don't say no. Think about it. Frankie, talk to her."

"Come on, Ma."

"We'll see," Tina said firmly, leaving no room for further discussion.

"Uncle Mark, your dinner's ready," Crystal said.

Mark smiled at her and said, "Thank you, beautiful. Tina, where can I wash my hands?"

"I'll show you," volunteered Frank.

When Mark was finished eating, he walked to the sink where Tina stood washing the dishes and gave her his plate. He kissed her cheek and said, "Thank you, sis. That was excellent. I forgot you were such an excellent cook."

"Thank you, Mark. I'm glad you enjoyed it. With my guys, though, I have to be a good cook. Otherwise I'd have a riot on my hands," she laughed.

"They're big guys, huh?"

"Yeah. Kevin is about your height. Harold is taller than him, though. And you see Frank, and he's still got a lot of growing to do."

"Yeah, I see what you mean. Do you want me to dry the dishes?"

She looked at him in shock. "You, dry dishes? I would think you have someone to do all this stuff for you."

"Well, I do, but when Nicole and I were together, I tried to help her out with stuff like this."

"What's she like? Carol seems to think she's the best thing that's ever happened to you."

Mark smiled reflectively and said, "Carol's right."

"Then why'd you separate?"

"It was my fault," he said softly. "She caught me in a very compromising situation, although I was completely innocent. She left me. She didn't believe me when I told her nothing happened."

"How was it a compromising situation if you were innocent?"

He went on to explain.

"So you're trying to work things out?" Tina asked.

"Yeah. We've been hanging out a lot lately. Hopefully, by the end of this month, everything'll be everything. She talked me into calling you, you know. I was really hesitant because I wasn't sure what your reaction would be. But Nicole told me if I didn't call now, while I was here, I'd regret it more later, and I know I would have."

"She sounds like she knows you pretty well."

"She does. She's a beautiful lady," he said reverently.

"I saw the picture."

"Oh, not just on the outside, but inside, where it counts. She's got a really good heart. She's really sweet. I'd like you to meet her."

"I'd like to meet her."

By now, she was finished with the dishes and they moved back into the living room. Crystal and Frank had gone to bed because they had school the next day.

"Mark, what time does your plane leave?" Tina asked as they sat across from each other.

"It left about an hour ago. I'm going to check into a hotel near the airport and leave tomorrow morning."

She looked at him sternly and said, "Don't you even sit there, Mark Peterson, and tell me you're going to leave my house to go sleep in some hotel. Don't you even insult me like that."

"I don't mean to insult you, Tina, but I didn't want to assume anything. I wasn't even sure if you'd want to see me."

"Why wouldn't I want to see you? Don't you think I was curious as hell wondering if the money had changed you?"

"Well, did it?" he asked with a impish grin.

"No, I don't think so. You always thought you were my father," she said, laughing.

He laughed, too. "What can I say? I had to look out for you," he said with a shrug.

"I've always been capable of taking care of myself."

"Now you sound like Nicole. Everybody needs somebody sometime."

"Including you."

"Yeah, including me. Listen, Tina, I'd like to give you something for the kids."

"Mark, I don't want your money."

"I know, but I've never given them anything. Maybe I could help you put them through college or something."

"Mark, you don't have to do that. I don't want you to spend your money on putting my kids through school. You have your own family to think about."

"Tina, believe me, it would be no hardship at all for me to put your kids and you, if you wanted, through school for four years or eight. I've got more than enough money for that. You remember that little apartment we lived in when we were kids?"

"Yeah."

"Well, my bathroom is bigger than that, okay? I don't have any financial worries."

Mark was up at five thirty Wednesday morning. To his surprise and delight, Tina was up also. Considering that neither of them had gone to bed until almost one o'clock that morning, they were both very chipper.

Tina was at the stove when Mark walked into the kitchen. "Good morning, sis. I didn't expect you to be up so early."

"Good morning. I knew you'd be leaving early and I thought you might like some breakfast before you go."

"You didn't have to do that. They'll serve breakfast on the plane."

"But theirs won't taste anywhere near as good as mine will."

Mark smiled and said, "Can't argue with that. Smells good, too."

"Sit down. It'll be ready in a minute. You still like your eggs scrambled, right?"

"Yup."

"Good. Would you like some coffee?"

"I'd love some. Can I help you do anything?"

"No, you just sit down. I've got everything under control."

Mark sat quietly at the table and studied his sister as she went about preparing his breakfast. He was so glad he had listened to Nicole and called her. He never realized before how much he missed her. Spending the day with her yesterday had been pure joy. She took a day off from work, which Mark paid her for despite her persistent protestations, and they spent the whole day reminiscing and updating each other on the happenings in their lives over the past thirteen years.

He thought, and had always thought, she was amazing. She had been through so many changes over the years, and as she told him of some of her not too pleasant moments, or her times of financial hardship, he asked her why she had not called him.

"How was I going to just up and call you one day and ask you for money when I haven't spoken to you in five years?" she asked.

"I'm your brother. You can ask me for anything," Mark answered.

"No, I couldn't."

"Why not?"

"Because . . . because I didn't want you to know I was doing bad. I didn't want you to pity me."

"You're too proud for your own good," was his answer.

"Runs in the family, obviously," was her reply.

That was for sure. Because their mother had been a junkie and had never made an effort to see that her children had basic necessities, they often had to get them on their own. They had often been ridiculed, not only by children, but by adults as well, as if it was their fault their mother was what she was. They learned not to trust others, only to trust themselves and not expect anything from anyone. Pride, maybe too much pride, definitely ran in their family.

As she placed his plate and hers on the table and sat down to join him, Mark said, "It's good seeing you, Tina."

"You, too," she said, smiling.

"You know you've got to come up to New York and spend some time with me and Carol."

"I will."

"Let me know when and a ticket will be at the airport waiting for you."

"I can buy my own ticket, Mark."

"Tina, you're my sister and I love you, but we've been separated far too long. I have millions and millions of dollars, far more than I'll ever spend in this lifetime. I don't want you to be too proud to take from me if I want to give it to you. I'm not going to try to run your life like when we were kids. I know you're capable of making your own decisions. I respect that. But I'd like to make your life a little more comfortable, if you'd let me. I'd like to do something for my niece and nephews. Don't act like I'm offering you charity.''

''I just don't want you to feel like you owe me anything.''

''But I do. Maybe not monetarily, but I think we owe it to each other to look out for one another. There may come a day when I'll need something from you. I won't be too proud to ask you for it. As a matter of fact, that day has already come. I needed you to be happy to hear from me when I called. I needed to see your smile when I walked in that door after not being here for thirteen years,'' Mark said sincerely.

''That's not the same thing.''

''No, it's not. But that smile . . . your smile, Tina, was worth more to me than all the money in the world. See, I've finally realized that what I need to make my life complete isn't money. Yeah, I've got it and it's good having it, but I could live happily without it. As long as I've got my family and friends, people that really care about me and that I care about, by my side, I've got everything I need.''

Her eyes misted over with his words. ''You've changed, Mark.''

He sighed and said, ''I've matured.''

They smiled at each other.

''It's a change for the better,'' she said softly.

''Thanks. You know, Tina, ever since I was a kid, I've always wanted to make you like me,'' he admitted.

She was surprised by his revelation. ''I've always liked you, Mark.''

''But it seemed you were always angry with me for something.''

''Because you always tried to tell me what to do. I couldn't have my little brother bossing me around.''

''I was just looking out for you.''

''I know that now, but when you're a kid, you just don't see it like that.''

''Yeah, I guess.''

They were quiet for a moment.

"I wanted you to be proud of me," Mark said modestly.

"I was always proud of you, Mark. I just never told you. Maybe I should have," she said softly. There was another easy silence between them for a few seconds. "Mark."

"Yeah?"

"I'm very proud of you."

"Thank you, Tina."

"I'm so glad you came."

She got up and walked around to his seat and put her arms around his shoulders and kissed the top of his head. "Would you mind if I came up and brought the kids this weekend?"

"Would I mind? That would be great!" Mark said excitedly.

"I have a little money in the bank. If you pay for the tickets, I'll take care of the hotel bill."

Mark looked at Tina with a frown and said, "What are you talking about, hotel? You'll stay with me."

"But Mark, there'll be four of us."

"I have four bedrooms in my apartment. The boys can share one and you and Crystal can share one."

"You have four bedrooms?"

"Yes."

"How big is your apartment?" she asked incredulously.

"I have a penthouse apartment. It's pretty big."

"How many rooms do you have?"

"Eight, nine?" he started counting to himself. "Yeah, nine not including the bathrooms. No. Ten. I forgot about the maid's room."

"How many bathrooms do you have?"

"Three full bathrooms."

"And you have a maid?"

"Yeah."

Tina shook her head and said, "Smack me, Mark. What am I worrying about? I can't bankrupt you. Would you really send me to Jamaica?"

"Yes."

"God, this is too good to be true. You're really loaded, huh?"

He laughed and said, "So, it's finally sinking in, huh?"

"Well, in that case, can I borrow a cool million?" Tina asked, bursting into laughter.

Mark laughed, too, and said, "Sure. How would you like it, in tens, twentys, fiftys or what?"

Chapter
Thirty-Four

On the morning of September twenty-fifth, Nicole rose at six o'clock. She had set her alarm for seven, but was so excited she could sleep no longer. Today, she would get the deed to her house. Her meeting with Karen Walter and the present owners of the house was scheduled for eleven o'clock. She could have stayed in bed until eight thirty or nine, but she was so exhilarated she could hardly sit still. She had nothing to do but take a shower because she had laid out the clothes she was wearing last night. Since the weather was colder than normal for this time of year, she decided to wear her brown leather and suede skirt suit. She spent almost a half hour the night before trying to decide on the red bow blouse or the cream cotton turtleneck sweater. When she had finally made up her mind, she decided on a pale peach, scoop neck blouse and a brown print ascot.

After her shower, she fixed a light breakfast, one scrambled egg, toast, juice and a cup of tea. At eight o'clock, she called Mark. She got his answering machine. This was the fourth message she had left. He was supposed to have been back from his trip Monday night. He hadn't called and she was worried. She figured he was probably alright though, since she hadn't heard from Carol, but he had promised her he would be at her closing today.

"Mark, where are you?" she said into the receiver. "This is Nicole again. I thought you were going to come with me today. Please call me if you get this message before ten."

At nine o'clock, when she still had not heard from Mark, she called his office. "Good morning, Denise. This is Nicole. How are you?"

"Hi, Nicky. I'm fine. How are you?"

"I'm fine, I guess. Is Mark in?"

"No, he's not. I haven't heard from him yet. Usually, if he's not here by now, he would've called. I guess he's on his way in," said Denise.

"Did you speak to him yesterday?"

"Oh, yeah. He was still in Georgia."

"Damn," Nicole remarked. "Well, if he comes in before ten o'clock, please ask him to call me. It's very important."

"Sure, Nicky, I'll tell him."

"Thank you." She was fuming. It wasn't so much that he hadn't called or that she didn't know where he was. What got to her was that he promised he would be there for her today. If he had not been absolutely sure he could make it, he shouldn't have told her he would.

Mark disembarked from his flight into JFK Airport at five after ten. He was happy to see that Bobby was waiting for him with his car. The first thing he did when he got in the car was call Nicole to tell her he would meet her at Karen's office. When her answering machine clicked on, he hung up. He was sure she'd already left.

"Bobby, do you know if Nicole tried to reach me?"

"I don't know, Mark."

Although he didn't have to wait around the airport trying to find a cab to take him into the city, almost fifteen minutes passed before Bobby was able to clear the airport.

Mark called his office and told Denise he would be in that afternoon. She told him Nicole had called that morning and said it was very important that he get in touch with her. He swore under his breath. *She probably thinks I forgot about her,* he thought.

By the time Bobby pulled up in front of the building that housed Karen's office, it was ten fifty-seven. As he was jumping out of the car, Mark told Bobby, "Take my bags to the apartment. I'll give you a call later if I need you."

Nicole arrived at Karen Walter's office with her attorney, Michael Moore, at ten forty-five. Because their appointment was for eleven o'clock, they were asked to wait in the reception area. They were seated for about five minutes when Nicole approached the receptionist again. "Excuse me, but can you tell me if a gentleman by the name of Mark Peterson has called? He was supposed to be here today, too."

"No, he hasn't called."

"You wouldn't know if he's spoken to Karen Walter, would you?"

"All calls come through here. He hasn't called."

"All right, thank you," Nicole said with a forced smile.

She sat back down next to Mike and said, "I'm going to choke him when I see him."

"Maybe something came up and he couldn't get away," Mike suggested.

"He could have called," Nicole said in a quiet but irritated tone.

At two minutes past eleven, Karen's secretary came to the reception area to take Nicole and Mike back to her office. When

Mark stepped off the elevator and into the reception area, he caught a glimpse of Nicole as she turned the corner going towards Karen's office.

As the receptionist opened her mouth to ask Mark if she could help him, he called out, "Nicole!"

She had already rounded the corner when she heard his call. She stopped in her tracks. "Wait a minute, Mike." She started back to the reception area and they almost collided.

"Hey," he said, a little out of breath, "almost missed you, huh?"

"Hi. I didn't think you were coming," she said truthfully.

"I told you I'd be here, didn't I?"

"Yeah, but . . ."

"I didn't leave my sister's house until six this morning. Hey, I'll tell you about it later. Let's go get your house," he said, taking her arm.

"Hey, Mark," Mike said as he extended his hand. "Glad you could make it."

"How are you, Mike?"

They all proceeded to Karen's office for the business at hand. Nicole was ecstatic. They were with Karen for a little more than an hour. When they stepped out of her office, Nicole held the title and keys to her new home. She was jubilant. As they waited for the elevator to take them down, Nicole had a smile of pure satisfaction plastered on her face. Mark thought it was very funny because he knew she wanted to bust. He could see she was trying very hard to stay cool. He was happy for her, too. She was due for some happiness in her life.

Besides, he had been thinking about buying a house himself. He had always wanted his children to grow up in a house with their own backyard and swings like he'd never had as a child but had always dreamed of. Nicole was making his dreams a reality.

"Hey, listen," Mike said, interrupting Mark and Nicole's reveries, "I'm going to make a stop in the men's room. You go on without me. Nicole, I'll be talking to you, if not later this week, then next week. Mark, take it easy. I'll be in touch.''

''All right, Mike,'' Nicole said with a smile. ''Thank you for everything.''

''Congratulations,'' he told her.

''Thanks.''

''Take it easy, Mike. Thanks a lot,'' Mark said, shaking his hand.

''Anytime. See you later,'' said Mike. He walked away.

The elevator arrived and Mark and Nicole got on. There was no one else in the car, so as soon as the doors closed, Nicole yelled, ''I've got it! I've got it! I've got my house!'' She jumped and put her arms around Mark's neck and kissed him hard on the mouth. ''Oh, Mark, I'm so happy I don't know what to do. I've got my house.''

He laughed. ''Congratulations, baby,'' he said as he held her around her waist. ''You deserve it. I'm happy for you, too.''

''Thank you. I wouldn't have it if it wasn't for you.''

''You don't know that.''

''Yes, I do. Thank you. And thank you for being here for me today. I feel so bad because I didn't think you'd come. Can you forgive me?''

''I'll think about it,'' he said, smiling at her.

She sighed happily. ''I can't wait to take Tiandra to see it. I know she'll love it. There'll be plenty of room for her to run around and play. Oh, God, I'm so happy.''

When they reached the lobby, Nicole took Mark's hand as they stepped from the building.

''So where are you headed now?'' Mark asked.

''I was going to go up and see my new house. Come with me?''

Mark looked at his watch. It was twelve twenty-five. ''Let me call Denise. If there's nothing urgent waiting for me, I'll come with you, okay?''

"Okay."

"How are you going to get there?" Mark asked as he reached into the breast pocket of his jacket and retrieved his cell phone.

"I'm going to drive. My car's in the garage down the street."

"Okay."

Mark called his office and spoke to Denise for about two minutes. When he broke the connection, he told Nicole, "They don't need me."

She laughed. "Good, 'cause I do," she said. "Come on, let's go see my house."

On the drive to Westchester, Nicole remembered that Mark said he had not left his sister's house until that morning. "So, Mark, you saw your sister."

"Oh, yeah."

"So, what happened?"

Mark leaned back in the seat and said, "Ah, it was great! I'm glad I listened to you. That was the best thing I could've done. She looked really good and she was very happy to see me."

"See, I told you. You were worrying for nothing," Nicole said happily.

"You're right. You were definitely right. When I got to her house it was about nine o'clock. We stayed up until the sun came up just talking and laughing and crying. It was nice, though. She has four kids, three boys and a girl, and they're so big. I was amazed. Her daughter is seventeen years old. The last time I saw her she was five. I was going to fly back yesterday, but because we were up so late the other night, she took off from work and we slept just about the whole day. Once we got up, we just hung out again. We had so much to talk about. I was worried that I wouldn't know what to say to her, but once I saw her, it was like we'd never been apart."

"That's good. I'm glad you saw her. I hope you're going to keep in touch with her."

"Oh, definitely. She's going to come up this weekend with

her kids, and I told her I wanted them all to come up for Thanksgiving and Christmas, you know, so we can all be together for the holidays.''

"That would be nice. I'd like to meet her.''

"I told her about you. I told her everything,'' he said and snickered. "She told me I was a fool to let you get away. I had to agree with her. Of course, Carol had already updated her on our situation, so I just had to fill in the details.''

Nicole laughed. "Well, I'm glad you two got together.''

"Yeah, me, too.''

To thank Mark for the part he played in the acquisition of her new home, Nicole treated him to dinner when they left the house that afternoon. When their dinner was over, she invited him to her apartment for some champagne to celebrate her good fortune. The excitement of the day had not yet worn off, and Nicole was a bundle of nerves. When they got to her place, she hurriedly pulled off her jacket and threw it on the couch. She went straight to the kitchen to retrieve the bottle of Dom Perignon she had been chilling since the night before. She took two champagne flutes from her cabinet and returned to the living room with the unopened bottle. "Mark, would you open this? I don't care how many times I try, I can never open a bottle of champagne without it ending up all over everything.''

Mark laughed as he took the bottle from her. "I'm no expert at this myself, Nicole.''

"You're better than me.''

Although he claimed he couldn't, Mark popped the cork on the champagne bottle with expert ability. He poured for both of them, then sat the bottle on the coffee table.

"Here's to you, Mark,'' Nicole said demurely.

"To me?''

"Yes, to you, because without you, I could have never come this far. Thank you for being there when I needed you. Thanks for being you,'' she said softly.

Mark was speechless. He was very honored by her tribute. Humbly, he said, "I don't know what to say."

"Just say, cheers."

He smiled at her and said, "Cheers."

"Cheers," she echoed.

They touched glasses and sipped.

"You know, Nicole, Nick deserves the credit for this," he said as he sat on the couch.

"Nick left me the money, yes, but if it hadn't been for you, if I hadn't been able to call on you, there's no telling what I might have done." Nicole sat beside him. "You were calm and sensible when I was a nervous wreck. You advised me and unselfishly explained how to manage all that money."

"I didn't do anything that spectacular," Mark quipped.

"You came when I called."

"That's nothing I wouldn't have done otherwise."

"You even came after the way I'd treated you when you told me Nick was dead," she emphasized.

"You were upset. I couldn't hold that against you."

"Regardless, you came."

"Nicole, I'm always here for you. Whenever you need me, all you have to do is call me," he said sincerely. "That's all you ever have to do."

She leaned over and kissed him softly on his lips. "Thank you."

"No need. I'd do it all again."

They sat quietly together for the next few minutes, sipping their drinks.

Mark broke the silence. "Do you have any idea when you'd like to move in?"

"By the end of the month. I want to furnish it first, though. I was thinking about driving back up there tomorrow and measuring the floors and windows for carpeting and drapes. I'll probably take Mommy and Daddy up to show them the house. I know they're going to love it."

"Oh, yeah, I'm sure."

"I want to buy a nice bedroom set for Tiandra, too. With a canopy bed," Nicole said dreamily.

"She's not big enough to sleep in a bed by herself yet."

"I know, but when she is, I'll just move her into that room and I'll keep the nursery for my next baby."

Mark smiled slyly and asked, "Are you expecting?"

"No!" she said emphatically.

"Oh, planning for the future?" he asked with a chuckle.

"Yes. I'd like to have another child. Wouldn't you?"

He looked at her quizzically for a moment before he answered, "Yes, I would."

"Well, then ..." Nicole emptied her glass and poured another for herself as she asked Mark, "Want some more?"

"No, thanks. It's getting late. I'm going to get ready to go." He placed his empty flute on the table in front of the couch.

"So soon?" she asked, not wanting him to leave.

"Yeah. I'm tired. You know, I went right to Karen's office this morning from the airport. I haven't even been home yet."

"Where are your bags?"

"Bobby took them to the apartment for me."

"Oh."

As Mark rose from the couch, he stretched his arms up over his head. "Oh, man, I am beat," he puffed. "Let me get out of here." He reached for his jacket that he had placed on the chair and was about to put it on when Nicole spoke.

"Don't go."

He paused and looked over at her. "What did you say?"

Nicole sighed and looked up at the ceiling a moment, then looked him square in the eye. "I don't want you to go."

They stared at each other for a few seconds, neither saying a word but each wondering what the other was thinking.

"I'm really tired, baby. We'll hang out another time. I've got to get some sleep," Mark said as he continued to don his jacket.

"You can sleep here."

Mark smiled and shook his head. "If I stay here, I won't want to sleep. I don't want to get in any more trouble. You remember what happened the last time I spent the night here."

Embarrassed by the memory, she blushed and said, "It was really silly of me to blow up at you like I did. I'm sorry."

He chuckled and said, "Don't worry about it, baby. I'm just teasing. It's just that . . . Well, you know how I feel about you and you know if I spend the night, I'm going to want to make love with you."

"So."

He stared at her for a long moment before he said, "So?"

Nicole took a deep breath and said, "I want to make love with you, Mark. Please stay with me."

Mark swallowed deeply. These were the very words he had longed to hear her say. Why, then, did his stomach suddenly knot up anxiously?

Nicole rose from the couch and stepped up to him. "Take off your jacket and stay with me," she said as she lifted the jacket off of his shoulders.

He did not move; he did not resist. He simply looked at her face wondering if she just wanted him for tonight, or if this was to be a new beginning for them. He prayed it was the latter, although he knew he would stay no matter what the outcome was. Pure and simple, he wanted her.

As he stood there, she took his jacket and hers and hung them in the closet. She walked back to him and stood before him once more, looking up into his eyes. She wrapped her arms around his waist loosely and gently kissed his lips. He responded slightly, although he still did not move. She held him tighter and laid her head against his chest. "I know you're wondering if I'm sure about this. I am." She looked into his eyes and continued, "I love you, Mark. I can't be happy with anyone else. I don't want to be with anyone else. I want you to stay with me and make love to me like you used to."

He moved then, cupping her face in his hands and looking into her eyes, searching for any sign of doubt. "Nicole, are you sure?"

"Yes," she answered without hesitation.

He had to be certain, beyond a shadow of a doubt. "Are you really sure?"

"Yes, Mark. I love you."

Still holding her face, he lowered his head until their lips were touching. He kissed her gently, savoring her sweetness. "I love you," he whispered.

She saw love and joy in his eyes when she looked at him, and she knew it was their time again. He put his arms around her and squeezed her as he kissed her desperately, passionately. With his heart and mind singing joyfully, he held Nicole, the love of his life, the woman whose love he would die for.

As their lips parted, Nicole whispered, "Come to my bed. Let me show you how much I've missed your love." She took his hand and he followed willingly. She switched off the living room light and they walked quietly to her bedroom. She turned on the bedside lamp, not to flood the room with light, but to enable them to see and visually enjoy each other's bodies. Nicole began to remove her clothes and Mark sat on the bed and watched. Although he had a picture of her body etched in his brain, he could not pull his eyes away as it was once again, after more than a year, fully revealed to him.

When she had removed everything but her panties, she looked at him and smiled. "Aren't you going to take your clothes off, or do I have to do it for you," she asked seductively.

"Come here," he commanded.

She immediately went to him. Nicole stood before him and he sat there looking up at her. He did not touch her, but his eyes slowly traveled down the length of her body, drinking in her excellent feminine form. "Take these off," he said of her panties.

She did as he said.

Her body was perfect in his eyes. Even with the birth of
Tiandra, her breasts were still firm and luscious. Her stomach
was flat and although she was self-conscious about them, he
thought the small bit of stretch marks on her belly from her
pregnancy were very sexy. He kissed her there. The triangular
mound of dark hair that led to her female treasure was flattened
against her skin and at the tip was a hint of the jewel hidden
between her legs. He touched her gently, caressing her skin,
running his hands down the length of her sides to her outer
thigh. "You're still beautiful," he said in a reverent whisper.

"Take your clothes off, baby," she urged as she moved
closer and placed her arms around his neck.

"I just want to look at you."

"Stand up."

He stood before her.

She loosened his tie and removed it, then slowly unbuttoned
his shirt, tossing it and the tie on a chair. These items were
soon joined by his slacks, undershirt and socks. His erection
strained against the cloth of his briefs and Nicole slid them off
slowly and let them drop to the floor. As she took in the sight
of him, she was at once reminded of the first time she'd seen
him nearly naked at Peterson & Company's annual picnic. His
body was as lean and as hard as it had been then. The only
difference was the scar from his surgery a year ago. This was
the first time she'd seen it. She gently touched him there before
she pressed her lips to the scar. She immediately felt an involun-
tary tightness in her groin as her lips touch his flesh. She put
her arms around his waist and with her hands, squeezed his
backside. She pulled his body closer so they were touching.
They sighed in unison as the shock of their bodies coming
together ran through them.

Mark embraced her, kissing her hungrily as her breasts, with
their hardened nipples, pressed against his torso. Her body was
warm next to his. She moved her hips, rubbing against him

sensuously, and he felt the fire that burned inside her for him. "Nicole," he sighed. "My Nicole."

The urgency of their kiss slowly rose until the movement of their bodies together sent Nicole to orgasmic heights. She screamed his name over and over as her pulse raced and her loins repeatedly contracted as the orgasm grew stronger.

The feel of her body next to his was intoxicating to him. She was warm and soft to his touch. Her scent filled his head and the sweetness made him dizzy. He had a flashback to the first time he'd made love with her. He'd been obsessed with her then, as he was still. Being with her like this now was like a sweet dream. He looked into her eyes and could see the reflection of his own love and lust. She was his again. This time there would be no mistakes. As tired as he had been minutes ago, holding her, kissing her and knowing soon he would be buried deep inside her, gave him renewed energy and stamina. He would love her slowly, so their magic could last all night. There was no need to rush anything now. They had forever.

He moved his hands slowly down her back until they were resting on the curves of her firm backside. He squeezed gently as he pressed his pulsing shaft to her groin. She cried out yet again. The way she held him, he knew she was climaxing again. Knowing this made his senses reel. He wanted to feel her come while he was inside her, feel her canal tighten around his manhood, squeezing the life out of it, but he would wait. There was no hurry. He moved his hand further down until it was between her legs, and he rubbed her gently, massaging the exterior of her moist cavern as she moaned in ecstasy and moved her pelvis in rhythm to his caresses. He continued to hold her behind in one hand as he parted her opening with the other and slid two fingers into her warm, moist love canal. This time he cried out as the pulse of her core sent a shock from the tips of his fingers to the tip of his manhood as if, somehow, they were connected. She was on fire and her juices poured out in abundance.

"Mark! Mark! Oh!" she screamed breathlessly.

She was driving him insane. *Had she always been this sweet?* He could not remember. *Or maybe she was like fine wine, improving with age?* It had been more than a year since he'd felt her this way. Far too long. In retrospect, he wondered how he could have kept himself away from her for so long. Being this close to her now made the past year seem unreal.

He vowed, as he held her, he would never let her get away from him again.

As her orgasm subsided once more, Mark removed his fingers from her depths. He looked deep into her eyes and she into his, as he slowly brought his hand to his mouth and tasted her sweet flavor. "Sweet," he said softly. "Taste how sweet." He put his fingers in her mouth and she sucked them slowly. This time the feel of her tongue on his fingertips sent a shock to his penis, and he sighed vocally. He removed his fingers from her mouth and replaced them with his tongue so as to penetrate her from all angles. He tightened his hold on her, embracing her so their bodies were as one. She returned his kiss and embrace with an equal passion.

When their lips parted, Mark held her tightly. He could feel her heart beating next to his and he knew then that his was beating for her. "I love you, Nicole," he whispered.

"I love you, too, Mark. I'll always love you."

And somehow he knew she would, just as he knew he would always love her.

"Let's lay down," she said, anxious to feel him inside her.

"Not yet."

"Why not?" she grumbled.

"Because I want to take a shower."

"Do you want me to shower with you?"

"Of course. You have to wash my back."

"I'll wash more than just your back," she said lasciviously.

"Promises, promises," he said, teasing.

"That's right. Do you think you can handle it?" she asked as she took a step away from him and spread her arms out, showing off her nearly perfect feminine form.

"I don't think I have to answer that. You know the answer," he stated as he stood in front of her, his fists at his hips, his erection boldly challenging her.

She stood there and visually examined his body from head to toe. He was in perfect form, his body belying his forty-three years. His chest and stomach were hard, muscles firm. His arms were strong and muscular and his legs were long and lean like those of an athlete. Although it had been more than a year since she had been pleasured by him, she could remember, as if it were yesterday, the things he'd done to her and the way he made her feel. He had taken her to heights she had never before or since reached. He was an expert in the ways of love. He took immense pleasure in pleasing her and truthfully, she had no doubts that he could "handle it." She smiled as she thought about the night ahead of them. It would, no doubt, be explosive.

"Do you know, Mark Peterson, you are the finest man I have ever known."

"Flattery will get you everywhere, baby."

"That's good to know, in case I want to use it later on. I don't think I want to waste too much time talking this evening, though. I have too many other important things I have to do," she said as she grabbed his erect manhood.

"Ooh, baby, you've got such hot hands," he sighed.

"Do you like it when I touch you this way?"

"Oh, yeah," he whispered breathlessly.

She suddenly released him. "Oh, well, let me go start the shower," she said as she strode away from him.

"You're mean, Nicole," he grumbled.

She turned back and smiled mischievously.

He followed her into the bathroom and as she leaned over

to turn on the faucets, he stepped up behind her and pressed his erection to her backside.

"You're so fresh," she said, although she made no attempts to move away from him.

"Better fresh than stale, right?"

"That's corny, Mark," she said, looking back at him, shaking her head.

"Okay, so I have one flaw."

She laughed.

When she had adjusted the temperature to one comfortable for them, she straightened up and faced him. "Ready for me to wash your back?"

"Among other things," he said as his arms encircled her waist.

They kissed.

"I love the way you kiss me," Nicole whispered.

"I love kissing you," he said, kissing her again. "Will you promise me something?"

"Anything."

"Don't ever stop loving me, and please, don't ever leave me again."

Tears came to her eyes as she looked into his and saw the seriousness with which he spoke. "I'll never leave you again, Mark. I'll never doubt your love."

He held her tight, happy she was once again his.

"I've made so many foolish mistakes, Nicole. I love you more than I can even tell you. You're everything to me and my love for you will never end. I know I'm not perfect, baby, but I'll try not to ever make you cry again. I just want to make you happy, Nicky. That's all I want to do. I'm so happy to be with you again," he told her.

"Mark, I'm happy, too. Being with you is all I want. It's all I've ever wanted. My life is so empty without you."

"Never again, baby. We'll never be apart again."

* * *

Mark was happier than he had been in years. Lying next to Nicole, he watched her as she slept. She was the most beautiful woman he had ever known.

The night had been magic. Making love with her again surpassed anything his mind could have imagined. She was warm, wet, wild and wonderful. She loved him hard and soft, slowly then exuberantly. They were perfect together. He dared anyone to dispute this. She had been put on this earth for him to love, and he for her. No one could convince him otherwise.

During their night of ecstasy, they unveiled so many emotions, joy, pain and fear, but most of all, love. They laughed and they cried, together. They were one, inseparable and immovable. Their love for one another was endless. The troubles that had plagued their marriage before were forever buried. They knew their life together was now truly beginning and it would be a long and happy life, filled with good times and laughter, maybe a few tears but nothing that would remove the bond they had sealed this night. He was where he belonged. He had finally found his place in this world.

It was nine thirty the next morning when the telephone rang. Nicole was still sleeping. They had made love on and off all night until six that morning. Mark was tired, too, but he was so exhilarated by being with Nicole again that he could not sleep. He had called Denise about fifteen minutes earlier to tell her he would not be in that day. He leaned over Nicole to answer the call. She groaned a bit but didn't wake up. "Hello," he said. There was no response right away. "Hello," he repeated, a bit impatiently.

The caller asked, "Who is this?"

"Who is this?"

"This is Yvonne. Who is this?"

Mark smiled and said, "This is Mark."

"Mark? Mark!?" Then, "Hi!"

"Hi!" he said, echoing her enthusiasm.

"You know, I must be losing it. I could have sworn I dialed Nicole."

"You did."

"I did?"

He chuckled and said, "Yes, you did."

"Oh." Suddenly it dawned on her. "What are you doing there at this time of the morning? How come you're not at work?"

"I took the day off. Aren't I entitled to a day off every now and then?" he asked cheerfully.

"Yeah, but, what are you doing there so early? Are you guys going out?"

"No. I was trying to go to sleep."

"Are you baby-sitting Tiandra?"

"No. She's not here. She's at Nicky's mom's house."

"Where's Nicky?"

"She's right here. She's asleep, though," Mark told her.

"She's asleep?"

"Yup."

"You spent the night?" Yvonne asked, taking a wild guess.

"Yup," he said simply.

"You did?" she said incredulously.

"Yes, Yvonne, I did." He thought this was all very funny. He knew, before she asked, what the next question would be.

"So, does this mean . . . ?"

"Yes, Yvonne. The war is over," he said, laughing.

"That's great! Oh, that's great, Mark. I'm so happy. Are you happy?"

He smiled and said, "Yes, I am. I'm very happy."

"That's good. It's about time."

"Can't argue with that."

"Is Nicky happy?"

"I think so. She looks happy," he said, kissing her softly on her cheek.

"Is she still asleep?"

"Yeah. She's out of it. You know she closed on the house yesterday," Mark reminded her.

"That's right. Were you able to make it?"

"Yeah, I was there."

"She didn't think you'd be back in time," Yvonne confided.

"It was close. I had to go right to the agent's office from the airport."

"You haven't been home?"

"Not yet."

"Well, listen, I'm not going to hold you. I'll let you go to sleep. I'm sure you're whipped. Especially if you've been there all night. I'm sure you guys had a lot to talk about. Ha-ha," Yvonne said, giggling.

Mark laughed and said, "Yes, we did. We talked well into the night."

Yvonne laughed harder. "You're crazy, Mark."

"So I've been told."

"Listen, tell Nicole I'll call her back or she can call me when she gets up. I'm really happy you guys are back together. Really. I think you were made for each other," Yvonne said.

"I'm inclined to agree with you."

"I know Lucien will be excited when I tell him."

"How is he?"

"He's fine. He's at work."

"Tell him I said hello. Maybe we'll fly down in a couple of weeks."

"That would be nice. It'll be nice to see you together."

"Yeah," Mark said dreamily. "You know, Yvonne, I feel really, really good."

"I'm sure."

"I love this woman. I'd do anything for her."

"I know you would. That's why I love you so much 'cause you take such good care of her."

"She's my heart."

They were silent for a while, both caught up in the moment.

"Well, I'll let you go now. Tell Nicky I'll talk to her later."

"All right, baby. Take care."

"You, too. And good luck."

"Thank you."

"Bye, Mark."

"See ya, Yvonne."

Mark replaced the receiver on the cradle. As he did, Nicole opened her eyes and asked sleepily, "Who was that?"

"Yvonne. She said she'd talk to you later."

"Oh." She rolled over and put her arms around him and laid her head on his chest. "I love you, Mark."

He kissed the top of her head and said, "I love you, too, baby."

"I'm so happy you're here with me."

"Me, too," he said with a smile.

"I think God was testing us."

"I think we passed."

"I think so, too," she said as she lifted her head to look at him. She kissed him softly on his lips, then just stared into his eyes. "You're so handsome."

He grinned and said, "You think so?"

"Yes."

"Thank you."

"Let's make love some more," she suggested.

"You must be a mind reader. I was about to make the same suggestion."

ABOUT THE AUTHOR

Cheryl Faye has been writing as a hobby since her teen years. Writing has always been a form of therapy for her. She is the author of two previously published Arabesque novels, *At First Sight* and *A Time For Us*. She has also published a short story for an Arabesque Mother's Day anthology entitled *Second Chance At Love*. Cheryl currently holds the position of Communications Coordinator and Assistant to the Editor-in-Chief at Essence Communications, Inc. She is the mother of two wonderful sons, Michael and Douglas, II and resides in Wappingers Falls, New York with her fiancé, Bernard Lawley.

Coming in December from Arabesque Books . . .